# LOVE, Theodosia

# LOVE,
# *Theodosia*

## A NOVEL of THEODOSIA BURR
## and PHILIP HAMILTON

# LORI ANNE
# GOLDSTEIN

Arcade Publishing · New York

First Arcade Edition

Arcade Publishing books may be purchased in bulk at special discounts for sales promotion, corporate gifts, fund-raising, or educational purposes. Special editions can also be created to specifications. For details, contact the Special Sales Department, Arcade Publishing, 307 West 36th Street, 11th Floor, New York, NY 10018 or arcade@skyhorsepublishing.com.

Arcade Publishing® is a registered trademark of Skyhorse Publishing, Inc.®, a Delaware corporation.

Visit our website at www.arcadepub.com.

10 9 8 7 6 5 4 3 2 1

Library of Congress Cataloging-in-Publication Data is available on file.

Cover design by Erin Seaward-Hiatt
Jacket images: © IngredientsPhoto/Getty Images (woman);
© Smith Collection/Gado/Getty Images (Richmond Hill)

ISBN: 978-1-950994-09-0
Ebook ISBN: 978-1-951627-98-0

Printed in the United States of America

For all the headstrong women with hearts to match

When any thing amuses me, my first thought is whether it would not also amuse you; and the pleasure is but half enjoyed until it is communicated.

—Aaron Burr to his daughter, Theodosia,
December 9, 1803

We travel in company with the two Alstons. Pray teach me how to write two A's without producing something like an *Ass*.

—Theodosia to her father,
October 29, 1803

Virtue can only flourish among equals.

—Mary Wollstonecraft, *A Vindication of the Rights of Woman*, 1792

---

*Georgetown County, South Carolina*

# November 1801

THE INABILITY TO BREATHE STRIKES HER the most. The function so automatic, without thought or intent, that only in its absence does it make its presence known. Unlike the feeling, just as involuntary, simmering under her skin, whispering in the palm fronds overhead, swirling in the air around her as if one tight grasp at the exact right moment could secure it, bring it in, close to her breast where the ache rages strongest. A feeling living deep in her core whether fingers are entwined or parted—separated by the distance of a gently lit ballroom, a maze of grimy streets, or the length of the Eastern seaboard. A feeling intensified in loss.

Her hand presses the newspaper clipping to her belly and the letter accompanying it flutters to the hardwood floor.

Permanence sharpens every moment. The caressing of a cheek, the sharing of laughter, the merging of hearts and minds for a period so brief it may scarcely warrant a footnote in her time on this earth yet defining who she once was and who she would become.

Such is the power of the human mind. Memory feeds love as much as fertile soil grows the kernels of rice atop the endless rows of green stalks in the fields outside her window. If only life were lived in individual slices, each day with its own beginning, middle, and end. Nothing before. Nothing to come. Starting anew with the first morning breath and concluding each night with a mind

3

that closes along with one's eyes. Joy or sorrow contained within like a book once read and discarded, never to be thought of again.

But memory is as cruel as it is skilled, spinning sorrow and joy into a fiber that cannot be broken even with the strongest of wills. Remembering ravages the heart like the longest of summer droughts, but forgetting turns traitor on the soul. And staying true to that is all she has left.

# Chapter 1

*New York City*

# May 1800

THE CIRCLE MAY AS WELL HAVE been a coop. Theodosia threaded her fingers together, set her hands in her lap, and apologized to her eardrums.

Across from her, Lottie Jewell's trill soprano reverberated off the walls of the parlor. Not even the abundance of velvet cushions tufted in Prussian blue could dampen the sound. The ring of chairs and the women seated in them encroached upon her, and she wished her corset wasn't laced so tight.

A ripple of polite applause followed Lottie's final note, and she gave a small curtsy along with her lopsided smile as she sat back down. The ray of sunlight streaming in through the tall windows behind her shrunk too slowly.

Theodosia should have arranged for their coachman to come for her sooner. She'd forgotten just how insufferable salons could be. Though not even she could turn down an invitation to one hosted by such an important member of New York City society as the commodore's wife.

"A pure delight," Mrs. Frances Nicholson said, rising to her feet and offering a final sharp clap of her hands. She gestured to the red-haired slip of a girl in an apron and cap disappearing into the crimson curtain that hung from the ceiling. "A pause to fill our glasses. Though I do offer my apologies for we appear to be out of burgundy, a hazard for hosting the senator."

Glances cast Theodosia's way, but her smile remained as solid as her spine.

"The commodore fears such imports may continue to be difficult to find despite the revolution in France coming to a close," Mrs. Nicholson said. "He told his guests as they entered this same room not more than a week ago that if some in this town have their way, we'll be a nation of cider drinkers before long."

Theodosia unclogged her ears. Finally a topic worthy of discussion. Even if it were inspired by her family and its affinity for all things French. The senator—former senator—draining the Nicholson stores of burgundy was her father. Though he didn't indulge heavily, she could picture him sipping more than usual in the Nicholson townhome, which had become a meeting place for the anti-Federalist movement. When it wasn't hosting society ladies and their salons, of course.

Salons such as this prided themselves on being sociable places where those in attendance could elevate talk beyond routine reports of weather and travel, yet the reality was banal repartee, off-key singing, and the occasional dull reading, all of it usually devolving into gossip, especially in salons attended solely by women. As this one was.

But purposely or not, had Mrs. Nicholson actually begun to steer the conversation into one that consumed their male counterparts in pubs and on street corners as much as in the grand mansions and elegant townhomes lining the streets of the city?

"My William wouldn't be heartbroken," said Kitty Few, Mrs. Nicholson's daughter. "He's discovered a fondness for cider since our return."

The resettling of Kitty and her family into the city from years spent in Georgia had prompted this gathering. Theodosia fought a shudder, imagining endless days in the blistering heat of the unrefined South, teeming with its swarms of disease-ridden insects as much as languorous ladies.

"More than ale," Kitty continued. "William swears by the brews coming from those orchards along the East River. Believes the breeze infuses a brininess that makes it the perfect match for oysters."

"Ooh, such ugly creatures!" Lottie exclaimed, nearly causing the white plume jutting from the bow atop her head to take flight. "No matter the sale on every street corner, I never imagined I could swallow something that looked like that. And alive! But the other day, I was persuaded—"

"*By a boy!*" The simultaneous singsong tease rang out from Kitty's younger sister, Hannah Gallatin, and Caty Church, a petite young woman with ginger hair and Theodosia's only real friend in the group.

Lottie flushed. She tilted her head in a useless attempt to mask her rosy cheeks with her ringlets of blonde curls.

*Right, then.* Theodosia pressed her hands together and thought of all the things that needed her attention at home. At seventeen, she'd borne responsibility for running her household since her mother died six years ago. Yet she was here. Listening to grown women giggling about boys. Grown women who'd dusted and layered their powders and perfumes with such a heavy hand that the scent of lavender and rose petals adhered to Theodosia's nostrils.

She struggled to take in a full breath as the Nicholsons' servant girl, holding a cut-glass decanter with a strength that belied the Irish girl's pale thin arms, moved in front of her. Theodosia had already consumed her self-allotted, respectable, half glass of wine and thus politely declined. The girl poured a healthy portion for Kitty, and Theodosia resisted the urge to summon her—and the only way to make time move faster—back.

Theodosia distracted herself by assessing the room. Along with the fashionable blue velvet were chairs of mahogany with cushions of red damask and high-backed winged chairs covered in thick beige linen. A portrait of the commodore in his Revolutionary War uniform hung on the opposite wall. Theodosia knew the artist without having to search for the signature, not only because he was a friend of her father's and commissioned by many in her father's circle, but because she knew the strokes and textures in the portrait he had painted of her as well as she knew the actual twists of her dark auburn hair and arch of her eyebrows. She could identify the same brush in the artist's other works. She had come to know the artist, more and more each day.

She pressed her palm above the square neckline of her dress, the small frill lining the edge insufficient to hide the heat spreading across her fair skin. It wasn't so much the topic of boys that bored Theodosia but the giggling women.

Movement in the doorway drew her attention. A young girl of maybe nine or ten hovered in the hall. Her wiry arms held a book Theodosia recognized. Theodosia's involuntary nod of approval must have given the girl the courage she sought, for she crossed the threshold into the room.

"Mary," Mrs. Nicholson said with displeasure. "Is this not the parlor?"

The girl's shoulders rose to her ears, and Mrs. Nicholson's lips thinned.

Kitty tilted her head at the girl. "I would hope you would show your grandmother you've been taught better manners than that."

"Yes, Mother."

"Then what is your response? Were you not told to remain upstairs with your sister?"

"Yes, Mother . . . Grandmother, and I was, but I needed help."

Mrs. Nicholson laughed. "Help that none of our six servants could offer?"

The pride with which she laid out the number ruffled Theodosia. Friend of the family though the commodore may be, all information could be useful information. Theodosia would relay this to her father.

The girl, Mary, shook her head.

"Why not?" Mrs. Nicholson said.

"Because none of them can read."

Theodosia sensed tension though illiteracy was not unusual for servants outside of her own home. Her father had made it a priority that their servants were taught to read and write.

"Oh well, out with it, Mary," her mother said in resignation. "What is it you are trying to do?"

"Read these to Matilda," Mary said, raising in the air the work of the Roman poet Ovid. "Like Father does."

A harmonious laugh rounded the circle of women. Girls did not read Ovid in the original form, because girls did not read Latin. Most girls. Certainly not with full mastery. Theodosia's education was a great source of pride for her father, and he'd never held her back from displaying it.

She addressed Mrs. Nicholson. "I may be able to help."

A conspiratorial look passed between Kitty and Mrs. Nicholson, but the elder said, "How generous of you, Theodosia."

Caty nodded encouragingly, and Theodosia smiled in gratitude. She'd missed Caty, who had only returned from living abroad with her family a few months ago.

Mary scurried across the room and stood before Theodosia. She opened the book and pointed.

A gentle smirk tugged at Theodosia's lips. "A romantic already?"

Yet the girl's face was so earnest that Theodosia took hold of the book with equal resolve and began, "*Amores*. Love. Thus it will be; slender arrows are lodged in my heart and love vexes the chest that it has seized. Shall I surrender or stir up the sudden flame by fighting it?" Theodosia felt a thickening in her throat. "I will surrender—a burden becomes light when it is carried willingly."

All at once came the sight of her mother's brow heavy with sweat, the stench of sick and night soil adhering to Theodosia's skin no matter how hard she scrubbed, the tears that soaked through her skirts as her father wept before her . . . Theodosia breathed through it, though the burden they shared would forever weigh down them both.

The single surge of applause came from Mary. The girl's politeness highlighted its absence in the group of women. Quickly, Caty chimed in and led a soft wave of clapping that soon filled the air.

Mary's big brown eyes shined with wonder. "I want to do that."

Lucinda Wilson, seated beside Theodosia, tsk-tsked. "Why you've no need. Unless your aim is to be a spinster. A needle and thread will do you much more good."

Theodosia clenched the book with her long fingers before passing the poetry volume back to Mary. "You can do anything you wish, so long as you have a fire in your belly. Do you have that?"

The girl nodded.

"Good. Then all you need is a translation dictionary. Keep an eye out for the post. There just might be something in it for you."

Mary hugged the book tight against her chest, and Kitty called upon the servant girl to usher her daughter out of the room. Kitty apologized first to her mother and then to the group, and Theodosia settled back in for more of Lottie's love life.

As the women reengaged in conversation, Theodosia's eyes drifted to the hall. Pride surged at the sight of Mary inching up the stairs, neck bent, escaped tendrils of her simply tied-back blonde hair shielding her face as she buried her head in the book.

Back in the parlor, Lucinda trained her eyes on Theodosia. She wore the same haughty look as always. Be it a dance or a party, no society event would be complete without Lucinda Wilson's judging eyes. If a bow or a buckle were out of place, Lucinda would make sure everyone knew. She'd never get the chance with Theodosia.

Lucinda rotated her head, taking in everyone in the circle. "We owe Mary and Theodosia a thank-you. They've led us to a proper subject for our afternoon. Salons and poems go together like George and Martha Washington, do they not?"

Theodosia forced a nod.

"Splendid," Lucinda said. "Would you care to lead us, Theodosia?"

*No, not at all.*

"Certainly." Theodosia began from memory, "Let me not to the marriage of true minds admit impediments. Love is not love—"

"Oh no," Lucinda said with a throaty laugh. "Not recitation. The game is creation."

Theodosia's spine stiffened. She sat back and gave a deferential nod to Lucinda. "Then by all means."

Lucinda's eyes brightened. She perched herself at the edge of her chair and ensured all the attention was on her. She began:

> *"An imposter in our midst,*
> *Why would destroy our bliss!*
> *Be a smudge,*
> *A blight,*
> *On what we all know is right."*

Lucinda pursed her lips, angled her goose-like neck, and continued.

> *"Man and wife,*
> *Joined against strife,*
> *In their God-given roles,*
> *True to our souls.*
> *The path we are to walk forever clear,*
> *Thus 'tis our duty when the imposter nears,*
> *To set our gaze beyond and offer a sneer!"*

Giggles, applause, stolen glances Theodosia's way. She plastered on a smile and clapped along with everyone else.

Several of the women took a turn, yet Lucinda swooped in after each with another pithy little rhyme. She bested them all. Twice.

Theodosia could quote and recite every poet from Ovid to Shakespeare to Thomas Wyatt. Time spent writing amateur verse like Lucinda's was an indulgence. A trivial pursuit. The studies and duties of Theodosia's life precluded such frivolity.

How many hours must Lucinda have whiled away practicing writing rhymes? With what? This very goal of impromptu salon recitations and excelling at rhyming games like crambo? While Theodosia hosted dinners for everyone from Mohawk Indian chief Colonel Joseph Brant to General Washington himself?

Theodosia's features maintained a calm, pleasant exterior despite the storm swirling beneath her skin, one she feared she'd externalized when a crash in the front hall brought half the ladies in the parlor to their feet.

"Sir, I must insist that you leave," came an exasperated male voice. Presumably the servant—*one of six*—who had earlier escorted the salon guests into the parlor.

"We are of like mind." A younger man's voice, slow and heavy with enunciation, spilled into the room shortly before the young man himself. "For leaving is exactly why I'm arriving." He stumbled into the parlor, clasping the top half of a porcelain vase. The vase had been—and perhaps the bottom half still was—home to a bouquet of orange tulips set on the table in the front hall.

The young man's dark hair was cut short with a somewhat frizzy and windswept mop on top and clipped sideburns winding around his ears. He wore tight black leather boots over his knee breeches, though one leg saw all but a lone button undone. His double-breasted waistcoat fit snug about his chest, all the more visible for he lacked a coat. Undoubtedly his unruly outside reflected the same of his inside.

Though at the moment his insides were soaked in liquor.

"My deepest apologies, Mrs. Nicholson," he said carefully and without a slur. "It seems I'm a tad on the early side, but I couldn't help overhearing. And I am nothing if not a lover of extemporaneous versification."

He over-enunciated the word "lover," and Lottie let out a short squeal.

"Early for what, young Philip?" Mrs. Nicholson said.

"Ah, my reputation precedes me. Incognito though I try to be." He grinned, and half the ladies in the room looked on the verge of needing smelling salts. "I'm merely here to escort a Miss Lottie Jewell home."

With her dark brown eyes growing wide, Lottie shook her head, feigning disapproval at Philip's state, but her crimson cheeks gave away her desire for the young man, as handsome as his father despite the boy's current disheveled state.

"However, since I happen to have arrived at this moment . . ." Philip tipped his chin to Lucinda. "While Miss Wilson most assuredly offers sturdy competition, I've never been one to shy away from a challenge." His eyes roamed those of the ladies in the parlor. When they met Theodosia's, he winked.

An image of a young Philip doing the same in grade school entered her mind. He hadn't lost the showman tendencies he'd exhibited at the French school they'd both attended before Philip was shipped off to boarding school. She'd barely seen him in recent years, though she heard he was attending Columbia College. Majoring in the consumption of ale, it would appear. With high marks.

After receiving a nod from her mother, Kitty slid her chair back to allow Philip to enter the circle. He offered the broken vase to Mrs. Nicholson and sidestepped to the center. He pulled on the hem of his waistcoat and clasped his hands behind his back.

> *"A maiden, a lass,*
> *One with a good measure of sass,*
> *Sought by men, young and old,*
> *And oh, what a sight to behold!*
> *If only one could grab ahold,*
> *What a tale could be told!"*

"Philip!" Mrs. Nicholson cried, though the upward tic of her lips betrayed her.

Philip bowed in apology though spurts of laughter flitted about the room. "My lips are not always as connected to my brain as might be desired. I promise to atone if you indulge me once more." He lowered his chin to his chest, which billowed with his breath before he began:

> "*Devotion from the divine*
> *Must thoughts align*
> *This skin lived in by one*
> *Created by another*
> *Growing ever tougher*
> *A coat, a shield, an armored breast plate*
> *So thick, nothing to penetrate*
> *Not life from without*
> *Not life from within*
> *Why not, then, a life of sin*
> *For we strive*
> *And writhe*
> *Hoping for that feel of being alive*"

His words lingered in the air, settling on Theodosia's exposed skin, slipping beneath. Restrained yet strong, imbued with melancholy, and delivered with a sincerity that Theodosia would wager had never left Philip's lips before. She ran through all she knew, struggling to place the refrain and its author. If Theodosia could not name the poet, not a single woman in attendance would be able to. They'd think it was his. Not a one able to deny that he'd eclipsed Lucinda in her trivial game.

Theodosia sat quietly amused at the indignation on Lucinda's face. And then Philip raised his head and looked directly at her. The room erupted in applause, but it wasn't until the flapping of Lucinda's elbow jarred Theodosia that she brought her hands together the same as everyone else in the room.

"Quite lovely, Philip," Mrs. Nicholson said. "You'd be a welcome addition to a mixed salon."

"Though likely not here." Philip gestured to the painting of the commodore.

"Perhaps not."

"What's that old verse about a name smelling?"

"Sweet. Would smell as sweet."

"Depends on the name, I would think."

"And the perspective." Mrs. Nicholson held his gaze before adding, "But today we are a perspective of women, so I must ask that you excuse yourself."

"Right. Right, you go," Lottie said in an unconvincing plea.

With one more bow that displayed a tear on the side of his breeches, Philip obliged—"assisted" by the footman who plucked the vase from Mrs. Nicholson with one hand and shoved Philip with the other.

"Such sweet sorrow!" Philip's shout from the front hall was followed by the sound of the door closing shut.

A whistling from the street preceded a repeat of his "A maiden, a lass," that took what he had begun much further. When he sang of "entering the temple of Venus," Mrs. Nicholson covered her ears. Hurried steps in the hall led to the door opening and the footman barreling into the street, shooing Philip as if he was a stray tomcat.

An awkward silence descended on the room, and then, all at once, gossip about Philip burst forth from every corner of the parlor.

*Shades of his father . . .*

*Two simultaneously I heard . . .*

*Grades well above . . .*

*No matter, my temple may just have an open door . . .*

Tittering all around, drowning out Philip's singing and the footman's admonishments and Theodosia's ability to think. Or participate. How this lot would love nothing more than for her to layer kindling atop their idle talk pitting father against father. War hero against war hero. Friend against enemy. She could no more engage than she could stay silent. Either action would incite unwanted gossip. All she could do was leave.

"My apologies. The heat." Theodosia placed a hand to her chest and stood as she exaggerated her excuse. "So unusual for the month of May, isn't it?"

Despite Caty's pleading look, Theodosia thanked Mrs. Nicholson and exited into the front hall. She accepted her shawl and lace cap from the sweaty footman as he frantically returned to his post. She passed through the open door, wrapped her hand around the railing, and filled her lungs on the front steps of the three-story townhome.

The air outside may have been laden with the odor of manure and rotting fruit, but Theodosia breathed it in for it smelled of freedom.

Being a sought-after neighborhood toward the lower tip of the city, the Nicholsons' street bustled with men and women, carriages and horses, and the stray pig, its pink snout consuming the detritus of city life. She glanced up and down, but their coachman, Sam, would not arrive with the carriage for some time.

She strode down the stairs and into the street, knowing what the women on the opposite side of the window would think if they set sight upon her. Their judgment lacked subtlety as much as self-respect. Gossip-hungry, dithering fools who refused to see themselves as capable in thought as their husbands and brothers and fathers—many even delighting in their ignorance.

Perhaps it was part rebellion, but Theodosia began the walk herself, relishing the liberation after sitting for so long. Unlike her father, she'd never become accustomed to extended periods seated at her desk; movement in body always fueled her mind. She'd mastered the art of reading while in motion long ago.

Theodosia rounded the corner and nearly stopped short. Philip was leaning against a lamppost whose oil had yet to be lit for the evening.

Surprise wiped away the roguish grin on his face. "I admit I was expecting Lottie, but still, it's a pleasure to see you again, Miss Theodosia."

"Yes, likewise." Theodosia's response was polite but terse. Their fathers had a long history of opposing views that had reached greater and more intense depths in the preceding year.

Her father, a former Federalist, had embraced the Republican party and subsequently won the Senate seat once belonging to Philip's grandfather. Since then, her father and Philip's, a leader of the Federalist party, had been working against one another, vying for party control of the state legislature. Of vital importance as it was this legislature—and those having the majority in it—that would select the state's delegates to the electoral college. Most believed it was New York State that would determine the fate of the upcoming presidential election of 1800. Which they could've been discussing in the salon instead of Lottie Jewell's new fondness for oysters.

*Thanks to some "boy" . . .*

Theodosia clutched the cord of her reticule tighter around her wrist, letting the small bag float against the fabric of her gown as she issued a curt nod to Philip and continued on her way.

Philip fell into staggered step beside her. "Tell me, how were you able to pull yourself away from the salon at the exact moment it was getting good?"

"Unless you have mastered the art of being in two places simultaneously, this is a conclusion you make how?" Theodosia asked without a pause in her stride.

"Because I am confident those dear ladies finally have a topic worth discussing."

"Is that your aim in life, then, to be gossip fodder?"

"I've no aim, Miss Theodosia."

"That much is clear." Her quip had more of an edge than she'd intended, and a silence took over. She expected at each corner he would make his goodbyes, and yet he remained. As the two continued west, the city streets gave way to more rural surroundings with increasingly wider and longer spans of green grass and rolling hills. The stench that came from too many horses and people in too small a space gave way to the delicate scent of apple blossoms and the earthiness of hardy oak trees.

She'd traveled to and from the city on her own before, though her father disliked it. Yet in this she wondered which he would have more of an aversion to: her unescorted walk or her escort being Philip.

"Would you care to offer a critique?" Philip finally said.

"You should wear a coat. And discover a comb."

Philip laughed, a full, round sound that sprang forth with such genuine pleasure that Theodosia felt her own cheeks lift.

"Sound advice," he said. "But in this instance I was speaking of my poem."

"Your poem? You mean your recitation?"

"No, I mean the poem, my poem."

"You're saying you came up with that on the spot?"

Philip cocked his head. "Well, if I am to be entirely truthful—"

"Aha, I knew it wasn't yours."

"And here we've arrived at *your* aim."

"I beg your pardon?"

"Being right. I remember that about you. You always have to be right. Or think you are."

"It's not a matter of opinion, it's a matter of fact." Her lips dropped all vestiges of that smile he'd almost engendered. "The better one is educated, the more they are right."

"A knowledge of books cannot replace a knowledge of life. Not that anyone with their wits about them would want it to."

"And you would know much of the latter and less of the former, is that so?"

Philip shrugged. "If the rumors are to be believed."

"And what are those rumors?"

"Don't you know?"

"I don't participate in gossip."

"A shame. Happens to be a tremendous amount of fun."

Theodosia felt a headache coming on. "Can we return to the poem? Whose is it?"

"I've said. It's mine. The truth part is that I didn't come up with it on the spot. Not all of it, at least. I've been working on it for some time."

"You write poetry? Do you not study at Columbia College?"

"I thought you didn't participate in gossip."

"The attending of an institution is fact, not gossip. And I would think Columbia College would require a work ethic that would preclude writing poetry."

"But you don't know, do you?"

*Because women cannot attend. Yet.*

"If you could attend," Philip continued, "you'd discover college has pursuits both in and outside of the classroom entirely worth pursuing. If your father would allow it, of course."

"And what do you know of my father?"

"As much as you know about mine, I suspect. They're both heroes of war. They understand how important it is to know your enemy."

"They aren't enemies. They just disagree, because your father is wrong."

"Probably."

Theodosia halted. "Probably? Do you not defend your own family?"

"My father is old enough to defend himself. And wipe his own nose and arse. But I do listen to rumors, and it seems the same cannot be said of yours."

"Philip Hamilton, you insult us both and embarrass yourself."

"And you, Miss Theodosia Burr, do not deny it. Your father has always been too dependent on you. How disappointing that the same appears to be true in reverse."

Anger propelled her forward, but she stayed true to the etiquette Philip lacked and managed a "Good day, Mr. Hamilton."

"An escort doesn't abandon his duties before seeing them through to completion."

"I doubt you have the disposition to complete anything but the emptying of a pint of ale. This is far enough. You're not behaving like a gentleman—"

"Thankfully. Gentlemen are so dull. Truly, where's the girl I knew who once on a dare locked a pig in the school outhouse and nearly got Tommy McIntyre's bum bitten off?"

"She grew up." *After a tongue-lashing from Papa that stung worse than any switch could have.* "Something you might try."

"Not if it means being a snobbish bore."

"I should instead be an aimless drunk, seeking pleasure in the skirts of young girls whose only thoughts are the ones they're told to have?"

"Is there an actual contest between those choices?"

"You're a disgrace to your father, Mr. Hamilton."

"Better than being a puppet."

Theodosia's arms flew out and she shoved him. "You are . . . a . . . rapscallion scoundrel!"

That laughter once again, and this time, Theodosia's lips pursed, and she bit her tongue before she let loose the vent boiling up inside.

With thundering footfalls, she marched away from him, toward the plank set over the ditch in the marshes of Lispenard's Meadows that would take her to the footpath and then home.

"If only one could grab ahold, what a tale could be told!" Philip shouted after her.

Theodosia clenched her fists until her nails dug into her skin. Her feet settled into the familiar gravel and she thanked every stone and every pebble that would lead her home. Inexplicably, with her next step, she found herself pausing to look back. He stood, facing her, with an enormous grin on his smug face.

His smug, infuriating face.

His smug, infuriatingly pleasing face.

"This is why I despise salons," she muttered under her breath.

# CHAPTER 2

THE SWAMP THEODOSIA CROSSED HAD A new name: Philip Hamilton. Just as dirty and full of muck and to be avoided at all costs.

She traversed the rising ground, allowing her breath to slow with each step of ascent. To the right, fields variegated with grass and grain extended deep across the land. In front flowed the waters of the Hudson, studded with small vessels carrying the harvests of the neighboring countryside. In the light of day, the Jersey shores could be seen.

Theodosia walked through the iron gates and down the winding road bordered by evenly spaced towering oaks. As the curve came to an end, the aroma of tulips and hollyhocks welcomed her home. The plantings in the flower beds began as seeds her father had brought back from his travels. Each time he returned, they'd work the soil together, as if the beauty outside might help obscure the darkness within.

For Richmond Hill was home. But Richmond Hill was also where Theodosia's mother had died. Theodosia often wondered if her father's travels would have been as frequent had they moved after her mother's death. Their townhome in the city would have been plenty big enough for the two of them and more convenient for her schooling and his work in town. But Aaron Burr desired grandeur in all things.

And Richmond Hill was nothing if not grandeur.

Set high on a hill, amid more than one hundred acres, with English-style gardens, meadows rolling to the Hudson River, and at Burr's request, a man-made pond gracing the entrance, the mansion sat on an elevated site, taking full advantage of views in all directions. Views afforded by the abundance of windows spread across the breadth of the house over its two and a half stories. A large portico supported by Ionic columns enhanced the majestic facade, noted by all who'd ever laid eyes upon the home, including Abigail Adams. She and her husband claimed the mansion as their official residence during his first term as vice president before Theodosia's father purchased the property.

She'd never felt quite so strong a dislike for her home's Federalist ties as she did that day.

She pushed open the heavy front door, nearly colliding with Alexis, her father's personal attendant and the home's jack-of-all-trades.

"Mademoiselle!" Alexis's light brown face puzzled in surprise at seeing her home. "I just came from instructing Sam to ready the horses," he said in his native French.

"No need," Theodosia replied in the same. "I walked."

"Is everything all right?"

She set her sights on the mahogany staircase. "I'm fine, everything's fine."

"Shall I send your supper up?"

"Thank you, but I've no appetite."

*Except for throttling Philip Hamilton.*

A ripple of pleasure traveled through her as she imagined her hands around his neck, her fingertips pressing against his skin, already colored from the sun, unbecoming of a man of his position. But he wasn't a man. He was a boy. A boy with unruly hair that she pictured her fingers getting lost in.

Before she throttled him.

Theodosia tossed her small bag and shawl on her bed. She sat at the edge, untied her outdoor shoe, and wrestled both the clog and slipper off. She tugged her cap free and fell back onto her mattress—her hard mattress, thanks to the thick planks her father had ordered set beneath. Better for her posture.

And what was wrong with that? Ladies should have excellent posture.

She could have had them removed any time she wished. But she respected her father and his teachings just as he respected her. Maybe Philip with his mother and siblings and indulgence in liquor couldn't understand it—maybe he couldn't say the same of his own relationship with his father. Something that she was sure was entirely his fault. And deserved no more of her precious time.

Her teeth began to grind against one another, and she sat up. The bedroom's furnishings had become more Spartan with the recent selling off of her chest of drawers and an armchair, but across from the bed, her desk still sat beneath the window, her quill waiting for her.

Her father had gone north of the city to Pelham for a brief visit with his stepson, her half-brother, Frederick. Despite the short duration of his absence, he'd be expecting a letter. He always did. And today she had plenty to tell him.

She positioned herself in her straight-backed chair, ignored the strain that reignited in her tailbone from an afternoon of sitting, and set a piece of stationery before her. With the contentious nature of this election, her telling of Philip's drunken pursuit of a "genteel" maiden, if Lottie could be called that, might be useful to her father. Each party was guilty of using the press to fling insults, one more wild and inflammatory than the next. But this wasn't wild or inflammatory; it was true and entirely relevant. If Colonel Alexander Hamilton couldn't keep a rein on his firstborn son, how could he be expected to lead his party?

Once Philip's licentiousness and public drunkenness was in print—including his appearance at the home of a well-known anti-Federalist—it would seem a mockery of all his father espoused. The colonel would be furious at Philip. If her behavior caused an equivalent accusation to be raised against her own father, strife would separate them despite the same blood running through their veins.

Theodosia dipped her quill in ink and began:

*Having full knowledge of the scolding that awaits for leaving you bereft of my wisdom and charms for nigh a full week's time, cher père, in these pages lay a treat you will think worth the delay.*

Where to begin? Lottie? Philip's lack of defense of his father? His insulting of her own?

And yet it was his poem that crept into her mind.

*"Devotion from the divine
Must thoughts align"*

She shook her head. *Memorization.* Any fool could do it, and Philip was quite the fool. Even Lucinda employed a measure of intellect with her absurdities, though far below the talents of Theodosia's mother. At parties and salons and private dinners, her mother's mastery of wordplay had never lacked, be it delightfully intricate conversation she'd made appear simple or creativity-based games like Lucinda's. Theodosia's father had lit up upon bearing witness. Despite their shared name, Theodosia had yet to match her mother. Her mother existed on a different plane, one reinforced by her death and the enormity of the grief that came with it. Raw, still.

*"This skin lived in by one
Created by another"*

Theodosia thought back to the tightening of Philip's jaw and the gravity in his voice upon finishing, at odds with his teasing laughter and impish grin. And she knew: the poem was his. That meant the feeling was too. The sadness. And the loneliness.

Theodosia's quill hovered above the paper, its tip laden with ink, waiting for her to transform it into words. Instead, she opened the top drawer of her desk. There, shrouded in white linen, beneath a letter in her mother's hand, lay a tortoiseshell brooch.

Simple upon first glance, yet its color shifted from yellow to green to brown to gold with the change of light, as luminous and surprising as her mother to whom it once belonged.

Her mother who, like Theodosia, found herself judged for things others knew nothing about.

Theodosia pushed her letter aside and reached for the geography book her father had brought home from his previous trip. He wanted her to seek a clearer understanding of the lands beyond those that hugged the coastline. Study should be her pursuit, not gossip. One afternoon surrounded by hens, and she'd almost forgotten who she was and who she aimed to become.

Upon opening to the table of contents, a yawn snuck up on her. She covered her mouth with her hand, continued to scan the list of chapters, and then—

*Snobbish bore.*

It was as if the words were whispered in her ear. She slammed the book closed. Stared at it. Then gently opened it once again, checking that she hadn't damaged the spine.

*A bore?*

She could be as frivolous as Lottie Jewell or Lucinda Wilson if she wanted to be.

*Lucinda Wilson.*

Theodosia would wipe that haughty look off her face at the next salon that etiquette demanded she attend. She snatched a new piece of parchment. She spoke French, Italian, Latin, and Greek. She could do ciphers in her sleep. At the age of ten, her writing was of such high quality that her father—Aaron Burr, war hero, the best attorney in the city, and an elected member of this government—had shown her letters to generals.

She could write a silly rhyme.

Theodosia put quill to parchment and summoned words from the vocabulary she had spent her childhood and teenage years learning. She pressed down with the tip and out came her rounded cursive script.

She awoke the next morning fully dressed atop her quilt. She had worked long into the night, and all she had to show for it was a desk bearing a mound of misshapen wax where her taper candle used to be and nothing but cross-outs, scribbles, and a quartet of incoherent phrases like the babblings of a child.

Unadulterated proof. Simple confirmation of how time could and should be better spent.

She shifted onto her side, her back bellowing at having been confined to a rigid corset all night. She stood and shook out her arms, bringing life back to her body and mind.

She'd wasted the evening, which meant more to do today. With the sun already high in the sky, the morning light made the green hills glow. It would have been the perfect day for exploring the fields and groves surrounding Richmond Hill atop her favorite mare. She hadn't ridden in weeks. Her father had been coming and going with such irregularity that she'd been unable to adhere to a routine—the very thing her younger self fought against with the strength of a mule. She'd been constantly on call, overseeing dinners and greeting overnight guests, ensuring her father always had decanters full and that she stay abreast of all the happenings, ready to assist her father in conversation on even the smallest nuance. Every detail mattered, for what was at stake was nothing less than the future of this young nation her father was integral in building. And she by his side.

"Theo!" Her best friend's joyful voice put a smile on Theodosia's face. She didn't bother to push in her chair or rumple the sheets of her bed. Nathalie had found Theodosia asleep not just atop the quilt but at her desk more times than either of them could count. Though usually it was with her head lain upon something like ciphers or newspapers, not random lines of verse.

Theodosia tucked the parchment under the geography book before Nathalie reached her.

"*Bonjour!*" Nathalie said, flopping onto Theodosia's bed and running her fingers along the quilt. "How kind of you to lessen your chambermaid's tasks for the day. The young Nancy will be delighted. Was there no sleep at all?"

"No. Some."

"Single syllables! Dear sister, tell me you're not still mad?"

"Why should I be mad?"

"You shouldn't. And yet that hasn't stopped you before. I don't find salons as contemptible as you. I would have accompanied you—"

"If Madame de Senat had not so *desperately* needed your help."

"I'm choosing to ignore the mockery in that tone, but my ears do hear it." Nathalie spread out the shawl Theodosia had left balled on her bed. "Now what was wrong with this salon?"

"For me, everything. For you, the lack of hairy chins and large feet."

"I see, so Mrs. Livingston was not in attendance?"

The two girls broke out in laughter, their years of rivalry now firmly rooted in a deep friendship, as close as the sisters they would be had they shared actual blood. The parents they did share had made sure of that. Aaron Burr had been a surrogate father to Nathalie, and Madame de Senat a substitute mother to both Theodosia and Nathalie for the past seven years.

"You're lively this morning," Theodosia said.

"Am I? I would think you would be too, considering who's to visit."

"Visit?" Theodosia's eyes widened. "Visit!" She spun in front of her chair, knocking it to the floor.

Nathalie laughed, somehow infusing a dose of the French accent that had become less prominent in her speech in recent years.

"Why didn't she wake me?" Theodosia rushed to the doorway to look for Nancy. "Why didn't you?"

"How delightful!" Nathalie said.

"What are you still doing sitting there?" Theodosia struggled with her dress. "Do you need a formal invitation to assist?"

"'Tis a glorious day to see the proper Theodosia Burr all a-flutter."

"I'm delighted to be such entertainment for you." Theodosia nearly ripped her sleeve in two. "Where is that girl?"

Nathalie scooped herself off the bed and met Theodosia in front of the trunk at the end. "Stop fussing." She pushed away Theodosia's fumbling fingers. "I'm enjoying this."

"What?" Theodosia impatiently rocked on the balls of her feet.

"You, being excited."

"Because I'm normally so dull? Shall I remind you how even our dear General Washington was charmed by my wit?"

"Oh, yes, yes, your cleverness is legendary. You labor so very hard to make it so."

"I do no—"

"It's required of you as a dutiful daughter. No apologies. But as your friend and sister, I tire of watching you reserve all that good humor for others. It's well past time to see you indulge yourself."

Indulging was a sentiment one might readily expect from the daughter of a French aristocrat. But she was not just that, she was also a refugee. Nathalie de Lage de Volude was the godchild of Louis XVI and Marie Antoinette. Nathalie's mother, terrified of the mobs that had taken such violent reins of justice during the prolonged French Revolution, had fled and dispersed her children, including Nathalie, who had sailed to America with her governess, Madame de Senat.

What must it have been like for young Nathalie—the arduous journey with rolling seas and cold cabins and no arms of her mother to hold her and warm her and let her know what waited at the end. This life here at Richmond Hill had not been planned or intended. But it came to be because of Theodosia's father. Always with an ear to the ground for news of France, when he heard of the plight of these French refugees, he took them in with no expectation of compensation or remuneration. The two had been a part of the Burr household since 1793 when Nathalie was eleven and Theodosia ten.

Though that had been a full year before the death of her mother, her father well understood loss and longing. He'd never known otherwise. As a boy, a babe still, not even three, death wearing the cloak of dysentery and smallpox stole his father, mother, grandfather, grandmother, all in the span of a single year. Burr was made of loss as much as he was blood and bone.

Nathalie slipped Theodosia's dress off her shoulders. As it fell to the floor, leaving her in her shift, Nathalie rested her soft, warm hand against the bare skin of Theodosia's collarbone. "It is past time you released your heart from the locked cage in your chest, Theo."

Theodosia's throat swelled. Nathalie and Theodosia were alike in many ways. They'd both lost a mother. They both cared for her father with the affection of daughters. But only Theodosia bore responsibility for the Burr name. For all her father desired it to be and become. For all those who had not lived to be witness to it.

He spoke little about them, but they were there in his every push to achieve things well beyond his age or assumed capacity and in every letter he wrote to Theodosia. Life was short and unpredictable and demanded all tasks be tackled with urgency and intensity; he insisted she employ "determination and perseverance in every laudable undertaking." That time nor talent be wasted, guided Burr. Leave nothing to chance. Because chance had proved to be the most unkind of foes.

With scurrying steps, Nancy finally entered the room with a pitcher of hot water. At eleven, Nancy was beginning to resemble her mother, Eleonore, all the more. The two slept together in Eleonore's room in the attic, declining Burr's offer to outfit a new space just for the girl.

Nathalie relinquished her role and fluffed her own blonde ringlets. "Let us greet the day. And what—or shall I say, *whom*—the day will bring."

A thrumming of energy reverberated through Theodosia's veins, easing the constriction in her throat. Nathalie's enthusiasm was infectious. And yet Theodosia was Aaron Burr's daughter, first and foremost. Today was no different.

Thanking Nancy for filling the washbasin, Theodosia returned to her desk and the stack of papers in the corner. She grasped a sheet of stationery, laid it flat against the wood, and wet her quill, writing a note back to the vendor who delivered their produce, assuring him that the outstanding bill would be paid once (and she couldn't help but snicker at the utter ridiculousness of the words she wrote) her father "instructed" her on matters of the household accounts. She wrote a duplicate letter to the man who brought them meat and a third to the purveyor of milk. They'd expect no payment for weeks. Sometimes being a woman had its benefits.

After washing and dressing in an informal gown, Theodosia left her room to go downstairs, passing by her own portrait in the front hall, painted by the "who" Nathalie had been referring to earlier: John Vanderlyn, a favorite family friend ever since his stay at Richmond Hill as an "artist in residence" four years ago during the spring and summer of 1796. Such was what inspired her father to turn the window-lined hall beyond the parlor into a gallery to display his art collection. Vanderlyn had been back from his studies in Paris for some time now and had become a frequent visitor to the Burr estate. Initially he and Theodosia had talked of the need to have a new portrait painted, for she was no longer the girl she'd been when he put brush to canvas. A point he had been the one to note.

He'd been calling on Theodosia for the past month, and yet they had not begun her sitting for a new portrait. How could one sit when there was so much to stroll? Richmond Hill's fault, really, with its majestic riverbanks and shady oaks.

Theodosia closed her eyes and trailed the silk bottom of her slipper along the wide planks of the wood floor, pretending they were grass and she were barefoot. And not alone.

"My beloved Miss Priss!"

Her eyes popped open.

The man before her wasn't the one in her mind's eye, yet the juxtaposition of who was ignited a blushing greater than if he had been.

The shadow that lurked in Aaron Burr's eyes faded as he greeted his daughter with the term of endearment he had bestowed on her in infancy. His eyes, a deep hazel and shades darker than his daughter's, swept over Theodosia. His long sideburns shone raven black, the same as his hair, despite the few trespassing strands of gray. Receding from a gentle widow's peak, it was secured in a queue, bound at the nape of his neck with a black silk ribbon.

"Papa? You gave me a start. I had no notice of your arrival today."

"Because it was last night. A gentleman knows better than to disturb a lady during the hours that replenish the suppleness of her skin and the softness of her hair."

"And the energy to deal with the gentlemen in her life."

As always, they each took great delight in competing to outwit the other.

Burr raised an eyebrow. "The use of the plural is intriguing. A fault of my ears or your grammar?"

"Neither has ever failed before."

"Unlike your quill. While I come home to letters from our dear friend Dr. Eustis, Mr. Clinton, and a bright young man from South Carolina, I do not see a letter written in your expert hand on my desk."

"You've arrived home just in time. I'd intended to have it sent to Frederick's. I shall have to retrieve it from Alexis."

"Lucky for us."

"Very much so."

Theodosia's letter writing, a tool he considered integral to her education, had always been too infrequent for her father. With his political career keeping him away from home for extended periods, Burr implored his daughter, from the age of nine, to detail her every action and amusement, even the most trifling. Conceding that accounting for every minute of her day might be an unreasonable expectation, he compromised by asking her to sit for ten minutes each evening and journal her daily activities for him. Though he'd have preferred twenty.

A girl of nine wanted to do more than sit behind a desk and write her father, no matter how much she adored him. So did a woman of seventeen. Though she obliged more than not. Sometimes more quickly than others.

"You were scarcely gone long enough to miss this time," Theodosia said. "But a treat to have you home."

"Bearing gifts."

"Papa! You shouldn't have." Theodosia meant this not to be polite or coy but literally. Their finances couldn't keep up with her father's desire to show affection through material goods. She was formulating further reprimand when, from his inner pocket, he withdrew a piece of folded cloth. He opened it to reveal a dozen tiny brown nuggets.

Theodosia instantly admonished herself. It'd been some time since her father had brought seeds back from a trip. And all at once, that same childhood wonder returned, her imagination awash with what they might become.

"Blue aster," he said, knowing her question before she voiced it. "Shall bring butterflies by summer's end."

Theodosia accepted the package and carefully rewrapped the seeds. "Thank you, Papa." Though he waved her off, his eyes bore a deep satisfaction at having pleased her. And his cheeks seemed rosier than usual. "Good travels this time? No hint of a migraine? Ill humor?"

Ever since the war, her father had been plagued with spells of poor health. Headaches, trouble with his eyes, and even his temperament, despondent for reasons unknown to them both.

"Fit as a stallion," he said, to her relief. "Now, any news worthy of report?"

Theodosia clasped the cloth between her hands as she pictured Philip Hamilton. The story of his appearance at the salon would bring delight to her father and strife to Philip. He deserved it for being so critical of her devotion to her father and having none of his own. Family was family. Didn't he see that?

*"So thick, nothing to penetrate"*

Or maybe he did see, but he didn't feel it.

This wasn't her place. Instead she said, "None of consequence, unless you count Mrs. Nicholson being proud of her number of servants."

"She's as vain as my dear friend the commodore thought," he tsked.

Vanity? Did such imply the ability to offer the servants a wage? Something that couldn't be said of those in her own home, most a result of her father's marriage to her mother. Shortly after her mother's enslaved property had become his, her father had proposed a bill as a member of the state assembly. One that called for the immediate emancipation of all slaves in New York despite their entrenchment in labor and households of families prominent and less throughout the city—in numbers more than double that of their Philadelphia and Boston neighbors. As one who spoke out against the practice of slavery, her father had held his ground, insisting on the bill in full, in opposition to amendments that restricted the right of free Black people to vote, to serve on juries, to testify against whites. The bill did not pass. Instead, nearly ten years later, they had a gradual emancipation law, which did nothing for Eleonore nor Alexis nor all who had once belonged to the Bartow Prevost family.

Aaron Burr stood in the front hall at nearly equal height with his daughter, which was fitting as the two were equals in a multitude of ways. "And yet," he said, "as the commodore understands, appearances must be kept."

One, if not the foremost, of her father's guiding principles. Which could put his actions at odds with what she knew was in his heart, beliefs he'd instilled in her own. Though he had previously granted liberty to those in service in their home—Theodosia had vague memories of a pretty young woman, gone since she was a child—he spoke little of abolition now, now that he had joined the Republican party, the party of the South. And perhaps more than that, now that their finances offered no possible way to employ paid servants.

Something that weighed on Theodosia as she studied her father, his serious eyes, his long nose a replica of hers. As much as she had dominion over household affairs, in this, she had no consultation. Still she said pointedly, referring to the commodore's home as well as her own, "Appearances must be kept, especially when one hosts the party elite."

Such was also why, unlike her bedroom and the rooms on the second floor, the front hall and the parlor had not seen so much as a vase up for sale.

"Precisely, Little Miss Priss." He embraced her warmly but swiftly, a quick peck on the cheek. Burr usually kept his emotions concealed, often behind a layer of sarcasm. Since the death of his wife, his affections for his daughter revealed themselves in words more than action. Their relationship developed on the page due to his absence in her daily life; his career had kept father and daughter apart more days than they were together, both before and after her mother's passing. The distance afforded by parchment had been a blessing for them. They might never have gotten as close without it.

Her father led her into the parlor, well-lit by the abundance of windows lining the front of the house, and waited until Theodosia set the seeds down on a small table and lowered herself onto the settee. He then sat opposite her, adjacent to the large hearth. Above the carved cherry mantel, the gold frame of a rounded looking glass reflected light as well as Aaron Burr's preference for all things French. The gracious surroundings were designed to impress, and like a French salon, to create an atmosphere of taste and learning. He personally supervised the restoration of the estate, ensuring, like many prominent men in the city, that the home was not just a place to lie one's head and entertain family, friends, and foreign travelers, but a statement, a reflection of his rising political and social status.

"Now," he said, "ask me if *I* have news to report."

"No, don't tell me." Theodosia inhaled a deep breath and pressed her palms into the linen cushion. "Fine, tell me."

"The election results are in."

"And your efforts . . ." Theodosia said.

"Yielded what we hoped."

"No."

"Yes."

"Success?"

"Fully."

Theodosia resisted the urge to spring from her seat and simply gave a sharp clap of applause. They'd been waiting three days for the final tally. Her father's trip to Frederick's had been born partially of the need for distraction. "Papa, you amaze. Not me, for I expect nothing less of *the* Lieutenant Colonel Aaron Burr. But the others . . . Mr. Jefferson must be pleased."

Burr jutted his chin. "The only thing that pleases Mr. Jefferson is his beloved Monticello. Set upon that savagely steep hill, as if designed to evoke Olympus."

"So the man set to become our next president considers himself a god too?"

"Indeed. The arrogance I contend with." He leaned forward and rested his elbows on his knees. His lips widened to a devilish grin. "The entire slate, Theo. All thirteen."

With the release of the words, he floated up from his chair. His energy refused to be bound, and he paced in front of the fireplace. Though surely where Theodosia inherited her preference for movement, usually her father was able to contain himself. But this was too big. It meant too much. It meant everything.

The Constitution left the manner of selecting presidential electors to the states. In eleven of the sixteen states, it was the state legislature that chose the electors. New York was one of those eleven.

For the past few months, the Republican and Federalist parties had been engaged in both public and private battle. Each sought to fill the seats representing districts in New York City with assemblymen loyal to its party. Philip's father, Alexander Hamilton, had been pushing the Federalist candidates while her father had been advocating for and conducting closed-door dealings on behalf of the thirteen Republican ones. Their Manhattan townhome had served as a command center with committees in session day and night in the weeks leading up to the election. Committees requiring endless food and drink and the refreshing of bedding and funds, funds that were already scarce.

Yet her father couldn't be dissuaded on the vitalness of this vote. The wards in question had previously been Federalist strongholds. Flipping these districts would help to end the Federalist majority in the state assembly and by extension, the full legislature. On Election Day, Burr had stationed himself—without intermission—outside the critical seventh ward polling place for ten hours. He had barely paused his campaigning to eat what Theodosia had brought him.

But his Republicans had won. All of them.

The Republicans controlled the assembly. With the assembly having more seats than the senate, the Republicans now effectively controlled the entire state legislature. The combined vote of both chambers would determine the makeup of presidential electors, electors favorable to the Republican side. This all but assured that Thomas Jefferson, the Republican favored for the office of the president against Federalist and current President John Adams, would receive the entirety of New York's electoral college votes come December. The Republicans controlled the presidential vote—and not just for the state of New York. Many believed securing New York was the key to pushing Jefferson ahead of Adams. Four years ago, it was the opposite, with New York's Federalist leanings allowing Adams to prevail.

"That will teach them for ousting you," Theodosia said, the bitterness still fresh on her tongue.

Her father had served but one six-year term in the US Senate seat he had won from Philip's grandfather. After losing reelection, he'd moved on to win a seat in this same New York State Legislature he'd been embroiled in, but he lost that reelection as well, less than two years ago. Some cited "unscrupulous behavior" and "compromising with his opponents." They dared not say it now, now that he had delivered precisely what the party needed to seize the presidency.

"If only they had your intellect," he said. "What they have is short memories."

"So you must capitalize on it. Move swiftly. The governorship—"

"Is within my grasp."

"What's been said? By whom?" Theodosia worried for her father; she had seen his hopes raised before and not fulfilled.

"Ma'am?" Eleonore, their cook since before Theodosia's mother died, dipped her chin upon entering the parlor. As she raised her head, the sun shone through the window into her dark eyes and on the dark brown skin of her face, which showed her surprise. "Sir, I wasn't told you were back. Excuse me, Ma'am, I didn't mean to interrupt."

Aaron Burr extracted his pocket watch from his waistcoat. "No matter, Eleonore, I must depart. I'm to be in town for meetings."

"But Papa—"

"As are you, my dear. Nathalie tells me she is to attend Madame de Senat this morning. You should join her. It would not look right if you didn't."

*This morning?*

But Vanderlyn was to arrive that afternoon.

Her father reached for his hat. "We'll continue the discussion this evening. During our celebration. We are due. Eleonore, I'm in the mood for . . . *A. Ham.*" He used the abbreviation Hamilton favored in his correspondence and winked at Theodosia. "My weight in it. I believe it may be a dish I shall never tire of consuming."

Theodosia stood and set her hands on her hips. "You'll make me wait for more on the governorship?"

"Patience is a skill forever in need of practice."

"As is cruelty."

Her father grinned. "Then we both get training today."

And Theodosia's routine had been upended once again.

After her father left, Theodosia turned to Eleonore. "With Mr. Burr having been traveling, he'll want plain boiled potatoes to accompany his ham." *A. Ham.* It wasn't enough to best his rival, Alexander Hamilton, in this game of political strategy; her father aimed to gloat. He was as giddy as a schoolboy released from his lessons.

That the opposite must have been true about Colonel Hamilton occurred to her. The mood in Philip's home would be counter to the one in hers. If her father knew the twinge of sadness pining her at the thought, she might be tossed in the river. And Theodosia couldn't swim.

She rattled off the rest of the courses for the evening's feast, including not a pie but the more elegant tart. "Pear, if we have it." Though her father rarely ate sweets, Mr. Vanderlyn had been in Paris until recently where desserts dazzled beyond the ubiquitous apple.

Her father got along well with John. There was no reason not to include him in her father's celebration. In fact, with her father in such a good mood, Theodosia realized there was every reason to include John.

Tonight would be the night for John Vanderlyn to express his interest in Theodosia and gain her father's consent.

# CHAPTER 3

THEODOSIA GATHERED THE FABRIC ON THE sides of her high-waisted gown and curtsied. An uncoordinated round of applause followed. Beside her, Nathalie flung her arms out as if the tips of her fingers could touch the walls on either side. She dipped her torso and head so low, she might as well have kissed the ground. The applause grew twofold.

"Show-off," Theodosia whispered.

Nathalie righted herself and winked.

"That is all for today, boys and girls," Madame de Senat trilled. "Thank Miss Burr and Miss de Lage de Volude for their magnifique readings."

The scraping of chairs, scuffling of little feet, and excited murmuring of young children filled the schoolhouse. Theodosia watched as Nathalie assisted Madame de Senat in helping the children to gather their belongings. For no one else save her father would Theodosia have made a trip into town on a day as important as this.

After Madame de Senat had escorted Nathalie to New York City as her governess, she'd set up a school whose lessons were taught entirely in French in order to support herself and her charge. Such a school naturally came to the attention of Francophile Burr, and soon enough, the plight of young Nathalie tugged on his heart. In the townhome he owned in the city, Theodosia's father offered Madame a place not just to live but to work, and there she had been running a school ensuring French émigrés and the children of prominent and influential New Yorkers received a French education ever since. Theodosia and Nathalie had attended. Along with Philip Hamilton.

Theodosia wandered around what had once been the town-home's parlor. Surrounded by walls of light green, small desks and chairs lined up in rows like soldiers in formation. On each desk sat a piece of slate and chalk. Madame had artfully declined Burr's offer to outfit the classroom with the more expensive pen and paper, saying that the lack of permanence of the slate forced students to employ their skills of memorization in earnest. Such was a sentiment that Burr would cling to, and Madame knew it. She also knew, as few did, that the Burrs' finances had become strained.

Maybe they always were. Maybe Theodosia's father had simply shielded her from the knowledge. Growing up, Theodosia had never wanted for anything. And still Nathalie was a child born of a privilege Theodosia could scarcely imagine.

At the front of the schoolroom, Nathalie pulled a candy from her apron pocket and dropped it in the hand of an awestruck young girl. Theodosia knew the feeling.

Yet when this slender girl with flowing blonde hair and an accent that delighted her father had arrived, Theodosia's blood ran green. Her father doted on the child. He often held Theodosia up to the standard set by Nathalie, expecting his daughter, weighed down by her studies, to instantaneously display not just the etiquette and charm ingrained in Nathalie by her royal French heritage, but her unabating good sense, levity, and affection. Nathalie's letters to Burr were "perfection" while Theodosia's were "slovenly and illegible."

At the time, Theodosia saw Nathalie as a rival. She was unable to tolerate or understand the attention her father gave the girl, especially after Theodosia's mother died. She was his daughter. She had lost her mother.

But Nathalie had lost everything.

When Nathalie had boarded that ship for America, she had done so with assurances from her mother that the rest of the family would soon follow. Whether the promise had been empty when made, Nathalie would never know, for no one else had ever come.

All she had left of the life she'd once lived was her governess. And still in the wake of such tragedy, Nathalie, not even a full year older than Theodosia, had exuded warmth and positivity and a sense of humor that eventually won over Theodosia the same way it had her father.

Nathalie had needed them, and though Theodosia was slow to realize it, they needed her just as much.

"Hellooooo!" A young boy with a mass of dark hair sticking out in every direction dashed across the room like greased lightning, narrowly missing Theodosia. He leapt into the air and was caught by a man with hair of the same color and grooming. The smile that burst forth upon sight of the boy took the man from attractive to all to pieces irresistible. Theodosia lingered on the delicate heart shape of his lips before lifting to his deep eyes of chestnut and his cheeks of—

She gasped, her id finally allowing her mind to intervene. It was Philip. Philip Hamilton.

Theodosia spun so fast she made herself dizzy. *Philip Hamilton?* The man whose breeches were half falling off the last time she saw him was a father?

The boy couldn't be more than seven or eight. Philip was nearly her age, scarcely more than a year older. But then . . .

"Miss Burr," Philip said, his tone tinged with amusement.

Theodosia steadied herself and turned. "Mr. Hamilton. Has Columbia College sent you for some remedial work?"

"Such thinking is understandable, Miss Burr, for your esteemed education seems to have omitted the practice of 'leisure.'"

"A practice you have perfected."

"Why, thank you for noticing."

"Off to a spree right now? Here looking for a companion?"

"Is that an offer? Let me fill a horn for you. Your father must have something stored away?"

No longer. The committee sessions had drained their purse along with every last drop, allowing Theodosia to counter honestly: "You are mistaken. My father's office upstairs is purely for work."

"Dull work." Philip rubbed his chin, long and angular, the same as his nose. His face was thin but healthy, yet it was his eyes that commanded all attention. A soft brown and full of life, so vibrant that their energy radiated through Theodosia. "Made all the more dull by him being so pure. Tell me, has he fully converted you to the same? Would be a pity . . ." Those eyes wandered to the exposed skin above her collar.

Theodosia laughed. "I applaud your efforts, for I'm sure they're quite taxing for someone with a mind so simple, but I promise you, I'm not easily shocked."

"Ooh, do I love a challenge."

"Of course, that's why you're here. Scoping out young governesses to corrupt? Keep at it, Mr. Hamilton, and one day maybe you'll be lucky enough to be as lecherous and defamed as your father."

Philip's mouth fell open.

"Father?" The young boy beside Philip drew his soft brows together. "What's she saying about Father?"

Theodosia's stomach dropped to a depth she wished she could follow.

His brother. His little brother.

A hand seized Theodosia's forearm, and she jerked around to see Angelica Hamilton, Philip's younger sister, eyes wild with fury.

"Do you have any sense?" Angelica snapped, the skin not covered by the frill of her neck ruff reddening. She dragged Theodosia to the far corner of the room and dropped her arm like a scalding cup of tea. Angelica hastily brushed back the auburn curls she'd inherited from her aunt, her mother's sister and her namesake.

The New York that the Burrs and Hamiltons occupied was small; those at their level of society crossed paths often. Though Theodosia's studies and her father's decisions on who was worthy of their time made it less so for Theodosia.

"Angelica . . ." Theodosia's tongue, so free a moment ago, became stuck. She hadn't seen Angelica in some time. She'd heard she'd been in Albany visiting her grandparents.

When they were younger, before the chasm between their fathers grew too deep to cross, she and Angelica would ride the grounds of Richmond Hill together while their parents and the New York elite drank and dined inside the house. Richmond Hill still hosted guests; its first-floor bedroom was practically a boardinghouse, always open for gentry making the journey north to New England or south to Philadelphia and the lower states. But before her mother died, the home had entertained on a grander scale. The Hamiltons, the Washingtons, the Clintons, the Nicholsons, all were among the once frequent visitors to the estate.

Angelica would accompany her parents, and she and Theodosia would ride to the edge of Richmond Hill, Theodosia always prodding Angelica to go beyond and Angelica always pulling Theodosia back. One day, they picked wildflowers, and Angelica had tried to weave them through her horse's forelock, who would have none of it. She set on Theodosia instead, singing softly as she braided the flowers through Theodosia's hair. She'd had a lovely voice, which she practiced as much as she did her piano with a dedication Theodosia gave to algebra and Latin.

Behind her, Theodosia heard Philip ask his brother about his lessons. The excitement in the boy's response highlighted his young age, and Theodosia cringed in shame for alluding to Colonel Hamilton's extramarital affair, no matter how public it had become.

Gossip had swirled around her own parents for years before they'd married. Her mother's home in New Jersey had been ten times the boardinghouse that Richmond Hill would ever be. Travelers, often young men on respite from the war, stayed for long stretches at a time, Theodosia's father among them.

Her mother's first marriage was to a British officer, with whom she'd borne children, Theodosia's half siblings, including Frederick, all too old to share a home with her or feel like relations the way Nathalie did.

While her mother's first husband was away at war, she'd been forced to employ all of her wit and skill to ensure her lands and home were not taken from her and her family.

At the time, laws had been passed allowing states to seize property of known Loyalists. To save her beloved home of the Hermitage from being confiscated, Theodosia's mother had mastered the skill of neutrality, remaining loyal to her husband and the British military while simultaneously supporting the patriots' cause. A scholar with the skills of a socialite. She cultivated the Hermitage as a neutral haven for military on both sides of the war.

It was during this period that Theodosia's father and mother became close friends. Her father even advocated on behalf of her mother and the Hermitage. Between his frequent stays at the home, her then-husband being stationed in Georgia and then Jamaica, and her being ten years his senior, rumors of improprieties ran rampant through society. An attraction between her parents must have been obvious, for her father was the only guest romantically linked to her married mother. Malevolence was aimed at the couple, what then Governor Livingston had called a "tongue of malice." The reputation was one her mother fought hard against. If she'd heard Theodosia's ill-mannered quip about Philip's father, she'd have been terribly disappointed.

"I'm sorry," Theodosia said with a calm but deferential tone. "I shouldn't have spoken that way."

"He's a boy," Angelica spat. "Impressionable. Vulnerable." She stole a glance at her siblings, but her eyes lingered on the elder. "And you should know better than to speak of those whom you barely know. Do you enjoy when the same is done to your family?"

"Of course not. But Philip did start it—"

"Are you a child?"

Theodosia tightened her lips.

"You hardly were," Angelica said. "You're too old to start now."

Angelica's pale face was flushed with anger though her eyes had the same softness at the edges that Theodosia remembered. And recognized—from Philip.

Theodosia lowered her head. Angelica swept past her, and Theodosia found herself calling out, "Still singing?"

Angelica's back arched. "Some. I'm surprised you'd remember. Or care."

Did she? Care, for her memory was impeccable.

"You seemed to love it, is all," Theodosia said.

Angelica peered at Theodosia over her shoulder. Her face was devoid of expression. "So does Father," she finally said. "He has such a magical voice and especially loves to use it in times of trial. I've become quite adept at the piano at his urging, so mostly, I accompany him."

"As a good daughter would," Theodosia said.

Regardless of the walls they lived within and the pursuits demanded of them, as daughters of powerful men, they had as much in common now as they once did.

Angelica gave a slight tilt of her head and returned to her brothers.

"Full marks?" Philip clapped his hands. "This deserves a star!"

"Full marks? On what?" Angelica said.

"John is a perfect speller. Let's make sure the world knows." Philip bent over a desk and nabbed a stub of chalk. He pressed the end to the young boy's forehead and drew the outline of a star. The boy squirmed and giggled as if it tickled him, but when Philip finished, John beamed and ran to Madame de Senat to show her.

With their brother gone, Philip turned to his sister, gently shaking his head. He embraced her, before whispering in her ear. The intimacy made Theodosia feel like she was intruding. A weight had settled in her chest, and she took in a breath to ease it.

Across the room, a book fell with a *thunk* at the feet of a young girl.

"Too heavy?" Theodosia moved to help, grateful to have something to occupy her. "Here, let me place it in your bag."

"No," the girl said. "I'm taking it out, not in."

"Mastered it already?"

The girl shook her head. "Madame de Senat wants me to move up in my arithmetic lessons."

"How wonderful. Congratulations!"

"I told her no. So I'm returning the book."

"No? Are you worried about the effort required? If Madame believes you're ready, then I'm sure you are. All it takes is concentration and dedication. Same way we became this great nation." A rhyme. Theodosia had always been a fast learner.

"It's not that," the girl said.

"Then what is it?"

"Papa says I've already learned more than enough to prove I can keep the household books in my future marriage. Any more would be beyond my sex."

Theodosia bit her tongue.

"Says I'm to spend the hours on dance instead," the girl said. She popped up on her tiptoes and spun.

Theodosia forced a smile. "Well, that's wonderful too."

The girl twirled her way toward the door, and Theodosia rose to her feet. She realized that though she had apologized to Angelica, she owed the same to her brothers.

But when she turned back around, Philip was gone.

# CHAPTER 4

"THIS WON'T DO, THEO, IT JUST won't." Nathalie circled Theodosia's bed for what must have been the tenth time, clucking her tongue.

"He's seen it before. I wore it on our first outing when he returned."

"*Merci, mon amie*, for you have made my argument for me." Nathalie shoved the gown off the bed. "A special night deserves special attire. Would you wear a burlap sack to a wedding?"

"Depends whose wedding."

"You are impossible."

"I am busy. A difference."

Theodosia pushed aside the new ladies' magazine Nathalie had left for her to read so she could "connect with the lives of her contemporaries," as if Theodosia had time or interest in connecting with pie recipes—or idle gossip, as her blunder with Philip and Angelica illustrated.

She flipped open a page in the geography book. With the unexpected trip to the schoolhouse, she'd had little time to acquaint herself with the contents. Her father had been known to quiz her before. She wouldn't embarrass herself in front of Vanderlyn.

"Luckily I am less so," Nathalie said. "And, luckily, I am here. And generous. Because you're as unskilled in sewing as a cow." She pulled another of Theodosia's dresses from the trunk—one designed to be worn with a large hoop that had since gone out of style.

"Even I know not to wear that," Theodosia said with what she pretended was a cursory glance though her eyes lingered.

"I am an excellent teacher. This will not do either, but I can fix it. Mr. Vanderlyn will be accustomed to Parisian styles. Unlike these American boys."

"A comment borne of someone specific?"

Nathalie gathered the acres of fabric in her lap. "My suitors aren't as plentiful as yours."

"Suitors?"

"*Suitors?* We're nearly attached at the hip, aren't we? Do you forget when the mayor gave you a personal tour of the French warship? I may have been two paces behind with that dreadful secretary of his, yet I heard Mayor Livingston declare that you, Theodosia, '*must bring none of your sparks on board for we shall all be blown up.*'" Nathalie made a gagging sound.

"An afternoon fully wasted. Tattered sails and soot-covered cannons and the mayor's banal and condescending explanations. Three hours? Such a bore, I ached for the shore."

Did that count as rhyming? She was getting good at this.

Nathalie opened her quilted sewing box. "Then how about your escort to Mrs. Clinton's dance?"

Washington Irving had escorted them both.

When Theodosia didn't respond, Nathalie pressed, "He was there for us two, yet his arm remained entwined in yours."

"If we're remembering, I recall your dance card was always full."

"Boys seek flirtation with the danger a French royal represents, but the threat of the guillotine keeps serious inquiry at bay."

"Nathalie! That's your family!"

"The reason I can say such things and know them to be true. Now, what about Dr. Eustis?"

"He's an old man!"

"Who you pined for. Writing him letters about dreaming of his visit—"

"I was a silly girl with an even sillier crush."

"And yet he seemed interested."

"He's a friend of Papa's. I dare not to think of the amusement my love-struck oaf routine brought to him—and to Papa. Humiliating. To be such a . . . a girl."

"Deny all you might, but you, my dear Theo, are one, same as me. And Angelica and Caty and Lottie—"

"Please."

"Despite your father's intentions."

"Is there a point to this?"

"You, Theodosia Burr, are aptly named for you have all the cleverness of the woman lending you your given name and the sharpness in mind of the man responsible for your surname. Why the combination should make most men run for the hills, and yet your suitors are many. But aside from Dr. Eustis, your sights have never been set on anyone until now."

Theodosia sighed.

"Vanderlyn," Nathalie said with a playful smirk.

"Well, what of it? Can you make something flattering of that gown or not?"

John Vanderlyn arrived early.

His sandy brown curls framed his oval face and ruddy cheeks. Long sideburns drew one's eye downward to where they terminated beside his lips. Pink, in perfect contrast to his light-green eyes.

Theodosia arranged herself in the same parlor chair her father had sat in earlier. That her own breaths quickened upon seeing Vanderlyn in his tailored tan waistcoat did not mean she was love-struck. It was merely attraction. A smart girl knew the difference.

And then Vanderlyn smiled.

Theodosia laced her hands together in her lap to conceal their shaking. Vanderlyn stood in the entry to the parlor without saying a word, while she pressed her palms together, waiting.

The dress was overly fussy. She *knew* it. Nathalie had kept the shape but refastened the full skirt to hang in two, open in the front and lain over her linen shift. The soft white peeking through contrasted against the blue silk and matched the sash Nathalie had fashioned out of the edging running along the bottom of the original gown. She'd painstakingly removed the embroidered fabric and sewn it to fit high on Theodosia's waist. But the sleeves puffed too much. The neckline scooped too low, her hair sat too high, and she itched everywhere.

"Accept my deepest apologies," John Vanderlyn said with a tentative step into the room. "I forgot myself for a moment."

Theodosia slid off the chair and clutched the sides of her stupid gown. "Seems we may be in for an early summer. The heat can do that to you."

"Indeed, but not in this particular instance. You, Miss Burr, are ravishing."

Theodosia squeezed the fabric of Nathalie's brilliant dress. The pounding of her heart beneath her ribs unsteadied her. She inhaled deep through her nostrils. "And such flattery makes you the best guest we've had all day."

Vanderlyn's brow wrinkled. "Shall I take that to mean I am merely one of a string of gentlemen arriving at your doorstep? Entirely understandable, of course. Is there perhaps a way to keep the door closed?"

"Walk with me. Stay for dinner. And then . . . we'll see about that door."

He bowed.

"I'm not finished."

"Pardon me, Miss."

"Talk to me more of Paris."

"You are your father's daughter, bargaining with such force."

"I've only just begun, Mr. Vanderlyn."

They strolled the grounds of Richmond Hill for almost two hours. He spoke like the artist he was, painting with words the view from the Pont Neuf and the Parisian buildings made of white limestone and, when pushed, of the fires burning in the streets, the devastation resulting from the French Revolution.

It pained Theodosia to think of the suffering in a country she had never set foot upon yet considered her second home. She breathed in its soil in the wine she drank, warmed herself in its sun as she lay between bedsheets made of French linen, and embraced its passion for life through her best friend, for France was not just a place of art and history and architecture but of Nathalie's birth—and banishment.

Vanderlyn laid a finger on Theodosia's elbow as they neared the sloping grounds that led down from the house toward the river. A blanket had been spread atop the grass, and a straw basket and bouquet of flowers rested in the center. The excited Nancy had followed Theodosia's instructions exactly.

Theodosia and Vanderlyn settled on the grass, facing the Hudson.

"Is this much like the Seine?" Theodosia asked.

"They're both long and wide. And wet."

"Why whatever would I do without your astute observations?" she teased.

"You would be stuck learning all from books, and how boring would that be?"

"I see, so you're my tutor now?"

"There are subjects I could teach you."

"And I you."

It was Vanderlyn whose cheeks reddened. Theodosia didn't hold back, smiling coyly, and he responded with a shy grin of his own. Theodosia's body ignited and relaxed at the same time. The comfort in having known Vanderlyn from a young age laid a foundation for something new, befitting the ages they were now.

"If you're to stay, that is," Theodosia said.

Vanderlyn looked down, rubbing a callus on the inside of his middle finger. "When I first laid eyes on these shores, my return had yet to even begin and Paris was calling me back. It's a city of beauty." His eyes flitted to hers before refocusing on his rough hands. "Though none surpassing what sits before me."

A breath trapped in Theodosia's throat. "The Hudson has its charms."

"It has nothing on you, Theodosia." As he used her given name, he dared to meet her eyes. "Because it is you whom I see in my every stroke."

She blinked, pausing to recapture their casual flirtation. "Careful, your patrons will not be keen on every painting looking the same."

"I confess, Theodosia, I will never match your wit, yet I will also never tire of it." He kneaded the callus. "You know that string of gentlemen callers? I'd very much like to find a pair of scissors and cut that string."

"Fine by me." She was even more pleased than she'd expected to discover that he too felt they'd been tiptoeing around this long enough. "I've no use for string."

He reached his arm across the blanket, and though it was her hand that he took, it was her heart that felt held.

"Father will be at dinner," Theodosia said.

"Will he? I'll be delighted to see him. That will be . . ." Vanderlyn's fingers slid from hers. "A . . . a delight. Delightful."

"Suddenly I understand why you gravitated toward the brush instead of the pen."

Vanderlyn shook his head, and Theodosia worried her jest was not received in the spirit she'd intended. "I'm sorry. I tease too much."

"Not at all. It points to a truth. My skill with the brush is no match for your father's important work."

"He's your biggest patron. He praises your paintings above all other artists. So do I. There's great value in what you do."

"Trivial in comparison."

"Nonsense."

A trivial pursuit was what she thought of Philip and his writing of poetry. Because Philip Hamilton was a drunk and a tomcat. Vanderlyn was a respected artist with a thriving profession. Not the same thing in the least.

Theodosia let her fingers skim Vanderlyn's, feeling the physical evidence of his hard work. She wrapped her hand around his, her hold as firm as her belief in the words she spoke. "What good are our lives without beauty?"

# Chapter 5

I n the entry to the parlor, Theodosia released Vanderlyn's hand a second too late. Her father's eyebrow rose. Assessing a situation in the blink of an eye was a skill so useful that he'd not only mastered it himself but ensured Theodosia do the same.

Thus she merely tilted her head in response to the question posed by her father's bushy brow and in two strides offered her hand toward the unexpected guest before her. "Commodore, what a pleasure. Though I must apologize."

"Miss Burr." Commodore Nicholson jerked his pointy chin and even pointier nose too far forward as he clumsily cut short his bow—the customary greeting between gentry of equal status—to accept her hand instead. "A treat for the eye as always. Never apologize for that, my dear."

"Nor should you," Theodosia said, flattering the graying and rounding man whose naval uniform would fit only the image of him captured in his portrait. "Yet my apology is for not being here when you arrived. If I were, your hand would already be holding a flip."

Burr sighed heavily. "I'm remiss in my hosting duties. I must confess I've no idea what goes in that concoction."

"And why should you, eh?" the commodore said with a laugh. "It's why God gave us women, is it not?"

A polite smile transformed Theodosia's lips. "Not the only reason, Commodore, as your household of beautiful daughters suggests?"

The commodore's sunken eyes popped forth like walnuts cracked from their shell. Behind him, Burr's own eyes danced with amusement. He'd taught his daughter to spar like a man.

"James!" Burr said. "Aren't you a sly one? I saw no one but that gruff footman at our last gathering."

"Good thing," Theodosia said. "Rabble like you aren't suitable for such fine ladies."

Burr feigned shock, bringing his hand to his heart. "A daughter would say such a thing about a father?"

"When that daughter knows that father well, as I do you, Papa."

Though his heart would forever remain entwined with her mother's, his pursuit of sexual adventures was no different from that of most men, and even some women, but especially pervasive among elected politicians, few of whom brought their wives to live with them in Philadelphia. Her father's letters mixed his serious critiques of her grammar and behavior with lighter musings on his romantic mishaps, though he would conceal the females' identities by using code names, like the latest, "Celeste."

"Because," Theodosia continued, "you are one who—and correct me if I'm misquoting your last letter—'has a great love for the finer arts, especially sculpture'?"

While uttering that last word, Theodosia tactfully gestured to her bosom to make clear the meaning behind her father's metaphor. Her eyes shifted first to the commodore and then to Vanderlyn whose face, Theodosia was pleased to see, showed a mixture of bewilderment and enjoyment. "He tends to ramble when his hand finds a pen. Especially when it comes to those who catch his eye."

Burr exaggerated a frown. "And she tends to forget her hand knows how to hold a pen. Two things you can count on my daughter for. Slow correspondence and—"

"*And?*" she mocked.

"Slouching."

Theodosia rounded her shoulders in playful defiance that brought the expected smile to her father's lips. She then smoothly linked her arm through the commodore's. "I trust you'll do me the honor of repaying your wife's hospitality by dining with us?"

✳

The commodore, directly opposite Theodosia, scraped at his empty bowl, eyeing the full one before her father. The first course of corn chowder sat untouched in front of him at the head of the table. He avoided rich foods, believing they wreaked havoc on a person's constitution, and the soup's abundance of cream made it heavy. And delicious.

Theodosia stole another small spoonful while her father tore off a piece of an unbuttered roll.

They'd been discussing Vanderlyn's study in Paris and the techniques he wished he'd known earlier, including when painting the commodore's portrait.

Burr nodded. "It is a smart man who understands the lifelong pursuit of education and growth in one's endeavors. And yet, while I support and applaud your studies, John, I remain unconvinced that you could best the portrait of my dear Miss Priss. I would not pay a dime for you to redo it."

*Because they could scarcely afford it*, Theodosia thought.

Seated beside her, Vanderlyn smiled. "I agree entirely. Thankfully, some subjects allow the artist to transcend their skill; even an unlearned painter would have a hard time not capturing the soul of your daughter, Mr. Burr."

Theodosia nearly winced. This was not a subject to broach in front of Nicholson. She took the reins of the conversation. "I'm certain the same would be true of the commodore's granddaughter, Mary. What a precocious young girl. Her determination and initiative will serve her studies well. Don't leave without reminding me to give you the dictionary I promised her."

The commodore gave a snort. "Don't fuel her, Miss Burr. That child has an imagination that surpasses the reality of her sex."

He lifted his goblet, and Theodosia's nostrils flared. "Her s—" Her father gave an almost imperceptible shake of his head. "*Soft* nature," Theodosia continued, "is a gift."

She watched the commodore bob his head in polite agreement before draining his wine. She picked up her own to do the same. *Half a glass, my ass. A rhyme. How lovely.* The full weight of her father's judgmental stare settled over her. If he wanted her to keep her opinions to herself, then he could follow suit.

Nathalie, who likewise had been instructed to keep to half a glass, to avoid butter and gravies, and to eat sparingly of dessert, polished off her claret. As a surrogate daughter, Nathalie had always been more free to choose which of Burr's commands to follow to the letter. As a French-born girl, those related to food and drink were the ones she ignored most. "It would appear that we need another bottle of wine," Nathalie said. She rang for a servant before Burr could object. Not that he could with the commodore present.

The commodore picked up the thread of his granddaughter. "The word is nuisance not precocious. Mrs. Nicholson reprimanded the girl for interrupting—her mother too. It actually made her almost grateful for the appearance of that Hamilton boy. Distracted everyone's attention from our ill-mannered offspring."

Confusion furrowed Burr's brow before his lips thinned. Such was news he expected to hear from Theodosia. She gripped the stem of her wineglass.

Tom, one of the Burr servants, entered the dining room with a tray carrying a decanter of wine and their next course: oysters, which her father must have requested for Theodosia did not. Impressing the commodore meant Theodosia would have another letter to write.

The commodore snickered. "Philip Hamilton." He lifted an oyster shell and slurped down first the liquid and then the oyster itself. "What to expect though, eh? Son of a conniver and a troublemaker, that boy was doomed the moment they laid him in his father's squirrely arms. A philanderer shaming his wife and family and still having the gall to try to lead his party?" The commodore tossed a fist in the air, landing it hard on the table. "Trounced!"

All the plates hopped and clattered, but the commodore didn't seem to notice. His face reddened and his fist shook. Nathalie widened her eyes and protectively wrapped her hands around her bivalve-filled plate. Beside her, Vanderlyn knitted his brows in diligent attention, but the hint of a smile played on his lips.

"Trounced!" the commodore repeated. "Trounced those Federalists were! A man with actual pride and self-respect would concede, but not our Alexander Hamilton. Calling on the governor for a special session of the legislature—those mangy Federalists think they can institute a new procedure for naming presidential electors? To take away the power that is now ours? That of our newly elected assembly? Printed in today's paper. Lies in the form of facts. Claiming this must be done as a matter of 'public safety'?"

Burr's face remained stoic despite, as Theodosia knew, previously advocating for the same as Hamilton: a change of the state's rules for district elections. Hamilton was but one of many—both Federalist and Republican in places like Massachusetts, New Hampshire, and Virginia—who sought to bend and adapt election standards for his party's gain. But unlike Hamilton, when that Republican effort had failed in New York, her father had found another way.

The commodore's own cheeks continued to redden. "Not to leave out Hamilton's incessant advocating for a less-forgiving policy toward France. Burr, a response!"

"Now, Commodore," her father said, "we must consider our allies, near and far. I believe patience serves us well. In fact, I've been communicating with a gentleman from our South, a Mr. Als—"

"No! Apologies, Burr, but we cannot remain silent. No matter if he calls you a French sympathizer." The commodore insisted that for the good of the Republican party, they must continue to press on how the principles behind the recently ended French Revolution matched those behind the American one. "Do they not forget our own history?"

America's war for independence ended the year Theodosia was born. That it ended in freedom was directly due to aid in the form of guns and ships and men offered by the French. Over the past few years, a reversal of roles had been in play, with the French looking to America to assist in its own crusade against what it believed to be an oppressive monarchy. With the beheading of King Louis XVI, Marie Antoinette, and thousands more, the guillotine had come to symbolize the French war, leaving her countrymen split over America's duty to support or decry the revolution. Conservatives, namely the Federalists, had been horrified by the violence and social leveling and had applauded Great Britain's efforts to stop it, seeking an alliance with London that would restore ties between the two countries. Meanwhile the Republicans, under Jefferson, had claimed this was akin to returning to British colonial rule. With the young general Napoleon Bonaparte's recent coup d'état, the war in France had ended, but the debate in America had not. Both parties saw the public's perception of the war and America's response to it as critical to the tenets of their own nascent country.

The commodore lowered his hand, but shook his head emphatically. "They call the French Revolution chaotic."

"And a bloodbath," Theodosia said, scooting to the edge of her chair. "Thousands slaughtered. So many that some towns had to share guillotines. A shortage. Can you conceive of such a thing?" She glanced at Vanderlyn whose brow was still creased, but his smile was gone. He nodded solemnly at Theodosia, and she wondered how much he'd left out of their earlier discussion.

"It is fascinating though, isn't it?" Theodosia continued. "To think that as our countrymen recently sat with a pint of ale before them, debating whether we should get involved in another country's battle, so the French citizens must have done the same during our own revolution seventeen years earlier."

The clink of the oyster shell the commodore dropped on his plate echoed through the dining room.

But not even the resulting silence could deter Theodosia, finally with an audience willing to engage in such important debate. "What this means for future crises in other countries is a philosophy to be guided by the next president, presumably Mr. Jefferson, a leader Papa—"

"Theodosia," Burr said in a tone deeper than usual.

She nodded to him. *Of course.* "A leader Papa *and* the commodore have been instrumental in putting in such a position."

Commodore Nicholson's lips parted, closed, frowned, and parted again. Like a flopping fish.

Amused, Theodosia sought out Nathalie, and her breath strangled in her throat. Her best friend's thin lips, downcast eyes, and shaking hands spoke to Theodosia's self-indulgence and utter lack of tact. For the preponderance of necks lain upon knife's edge had belonged to clergy and aristocrats, to families like Nathalie's. Perhaps even to Nathalie's own, for they'd received no word of her relations left behind. If Nathalie and Madame de Senat had not fled . . . Theodosia could not even complete the thought. She stared at Nathalie until her chin lifted. Theodosia drew in a breath and exhaled a silent but earnest apology. With all the restraint she'd been taught, Nathalie both accepted and blinked away the moisture in her eyes.

Burr cleared his throat. Theodosia deserved whatever scolding may come her way.

"This is what happens when you leave letters to be sealed and mailed with a girl in need of diversion." Her father chuckled. "Perhaps I should allow her more free access to our library."

*Every scolding but this.* Her father would blindfold her for a week and force her to muck out the stables if she didn't freely access their library daily.

Nicholson laughed. "Take care with that, Burr. Even novels puzzle the weaker sex, for they have difficulty discerning fact from fiction." He wiggled his thick fingers above his plate before choosing the plumpest oyster that most resembled his ample midsection. "No, no, this is entirely my fault. Ladies, I beg your forgiveness. Such talk is not meant for mixed company. I fear my passion gets the better of my manners at times." He guzzled down the oyster. "My word, but these are incredible. Better than any in France, I contend, no matter what our French brothers may say. Do you know, during the war, a French officer once compelled me to try a snail?" He screwed up his face. "Unbelievable, eh? Tell me, Vanderlyn, what oddities did those Frenchmen force upon you? And how much bread did they stuff in your gut? Their incessant bread-making almost gave our position away more times than I can count. Setting up brick ovens at every camp, and the smells! How far they carry. Why once when my ship was . . ."

Theodosia tuned him out as heat rose in her chest. She glared at her father. *Allow?* she mouthed.

Burr drilled his eyes into his daughter's. While Vanderlyn and Nathalie, her countenance giving away nothing, listened to the commodore drone on, Theodosia plastered on a lopsided smile. He wanted her to be a Lottie, so she'd be a Lottie.

Inside, she continued to seethe. With no one other than her father did she have the same intellectual connection that she needed—that he'd caused her to need—as much as the air in her lungs. Still in close company, especially that of influential men like the commodore, her father had always encouraged her to display her intelligence, proud that she was as learned as any man twice her age.

"Speaking of reading," Theodosia said, taking advantage of a pause in the commodore's monologue, "we've been fortunate to acquire a new ladies' magazine, haven't we, Nathalie?" The emptiness of her words nearly made Theodosia cringe.

"Oh," Nathalie said. The devilish grin aimed Theodosia's way assured her forgiveness. "Quite so. Quite fortunate. Why don't you tell us what piqued your interest?"

"You first, dear sister."

Nathalie set her own charms in play, leaning forward, elongating her neck, and letting her eyes travel between all the men seated at the table. "Theodosia doesn't want to admit in such esteemed company how taken she was with the embroidery patterns."

Theodosia flinched and shifted in her chair to cover.

"You say embroidery?" The commodore's tone was as if he were speaking to a toddler. "How marvelous. A skill quite useful, Miss Burr. No need to hide such interest."

The muscles in Theodosia's jaw tightened, but she managed a nod and a smile.

Nathalie began to describe the pattern in detail, adding that it was submitted from a reader, as much of the content in the magazine was. As if advice from the masses was to be celebrated—masses who didn't read scholarly texts, masses who weren't encouraged to read anything because their feeble brains could not "discern" real from imaginary. Masses who—

A hand found hers beneath the table. Vanderlyn's head never shifted from Nathalie's, but the entire time Nathalie spoke, his fingers remained entwined with Theodosia's.

While the gesture couldn't erase her anger at her father, it did ease it. And she barely noticed that the tart served at the end of the meal brimmed with apple, not pear.

# Chapter 6

Vanderlyn sat one floor below with her father and Commodore Nicholson, discussing things "not suitable" for Theodosia and Nathalie.

After dinner, the women excused themselves, and the commodore wished them well as they "got along with their sewing and other womanly pursuits."

"Can you believe him?" Theodosia paced Nathalie's bedroom, her steps heavy in a passive-aggressive protest.

"And so we begin." Nathalie sighed. "Theo, the commodore is old and—"

"Forget Nicholson. His wife and Kitty and Hannah and the rest of his large and docile brood surely fill his ears with much about me—how my reading is 'wholly masculine' and how I 'remain blissfully ignorant of domestic matters.' That if my future husband wants his home kept he'll need a second wife who understands her role. Whispers are as loud as screams to my ears, Nathalie, I assure you."

"*Mon amie*, do not let—"

"It's not him, it's not them, it's Papa. Forcing my tongue to still. Is that my reward for rising at five in the morning? Thirteen hours of study a day, letter writing every night, allowed a mere hour of horseback on Saturdays and Sundays? He humiliated me!"

"Perhaps you're overreacting?"

"I could read and write at the age of three—he *made* me able to read and write at the age of three. A child, and still I did what was asked."

Nathalie smirked.

"Don't look at me like that, I did."

"Hmm . . . I seem to remember an afternoon hiding from your tutor and lacing up our skates for a few turns on Burr's Pond. '*Quels imbéciles!*' he bellowed at us upon his return."

"He wouldn't allow me to ride for a month. Which proves my point. He prized my education. It was everything to him."

"You say, as if it's not also everything to you." Nathalie held out her palm against Theodosia's impending protest. "Maybe not always, but now, you're grateful. Indebted even?"

Theodosia crossed her arms in front of her chest. Nathalie knew her too well.

Nathalie continued, "But to your point, yes, his punishment was for skipping a lesson, but you do know why it was so harsh, don't you?"

"Because he's a tyrant."

"Perhaps. But he was and is and will always be terrified of something happening to you. There is no man in this country who acts with more intent than your father. He has a reason in this as well. Who can you trust if not your own father?"

"Who indeed," Theodosia mumbled. She faced the window. He'd have never done the same to her mother, for she was, as her father oft repeated, "the best and finest lady" he'd ever known.

With her mother gone, she became her father's world, and he hers.

*Forehead to forehead, tears streaming down each of their cheeks, his hands a vise around hers, "For what else do I live?"*

Theodosia's intake of breath stung as if the air were crystallized with ice.

"Theo," Nathalie said. Theodosia turned to face her. "Come." Nathalie patted the bed. "I should not have teased. I see now where this is coming from."

"Oh?" Theodosia tightened the link of her arms across her chest as she moved to sit beside Nathalie. "And where's that?"

*Best and finest lady.*

Nathalie laid a hand on Theodosia's wrist and unlocked her arms. "It's not so much what your father said but who he said it in front of. Mr. Vanderlyn will be smitten with you until the day the Hudson flows backward."

*For what else do I live?*

"No, that's not—"

"Don't worry a bit," Nathalie said.

Theodosia nodded pensively, unable to share the truth about what was darkening her heart. "You're right, you're always right." Maybe she was. Maybe Theodosia was overreacting. And maybe it was because of Vanderlyn. But maybe it was because tonight her father pulled the strings, and she danced.

Just like the puppet Philip said she was.

Her spine stiffened, and Philip's smug grin flashed in her mind. Then her father's. And then, Theodosia slouched.

Nathalie slid herself back on the bed, leaned against the wooden headboard, and reached for the ladies' magazine. Theodosia rested beside her and began to read over her best friend's shoulder. Nathalie flipped one page, then another.

"Wait," Theodosia said. "What was that?"

"The article? I already read it. It's what I wanted you to read." Nathalie peeled back the page. "The magazine is not all cosmetics guides and pudding recipes."

Theodosia leaned closer to read the headline: *"New Jersey Women Debate the Right to Vote"*

"Can I—" Theodosia said.

"Here." Nathalie handed her the magazine. "And next time—"

"I'll listen."

"Probably not, but the spirit behind is appreciated."

The shadow of a candle flame crisscrossed the pages of the *From the Fairer Sex* magazine as Theodosia read at her desk. The article was written by female readers from New Jersey, the only state in America where women—provided they were white—held the right to vote. In the article, the women argued that this right should be extended to women in all states. And they went further, asking why free Black men and women should not also be given this same right.

The notion shocked Theodosia—not the idea of women and free Black men and women voting but that a publisher would dare to put such thoughts in print when written by members of the female sex. She'd heard of no one doing so save for Mary Wollstonecraft.

While Theodosia's mother and father were devotees of the writings of the British woman who advocated for equality of the sexes, few others in the burgeoning United States appeared to be listening. Yet it was precisely this burgeoning status that implored ears and minds to open. What better time for change than now?

Theodosia's mother firmly believed women should be educated the same as men, with roles in business and, especially, in politics. With reverence would her father refer to her mother's "exceptional and luminous intellect" despite a lack of formal education as was consistent with her being female. Theodosia's mother read Plutarch and all six volumes of Gibbon's *History of the Decline and Fall of the Roman Empire*—something Theodosia herself matched by the age of ten—and could debate philosophy and theology better than most men. Her mother's French, her cleverness, her strategizing eclipsed that of her husband. And he loved her for it.

Her father's intelligence was his most prized possession, and in laying out a rigorous course of study for his daughter, mimicking his own eighteen-hour study days at the College of New Jersey, he expected her to not just match but surpass what he loved most about her mother: her mind.

She would be a tribute to his wife. A daughter with exceptional intelligence, one with an inner serenity allowing her to rise above petty insults and develop a mental firmness, a stoic confidence to allow her to overcome life's inevitable difficulties. Traits thought to be exclusive to the male sex.

From this intent came his every criticism of his daughter's diet or posture. Yet he also lavished compliments on everything from

her calligraphy to her fluency in French. Constant was his thinking of and scribbling to her, his style of writing to her at the age
of ten one that would have done honor to a girl of sixteen. When
away, he would respond to her letters first, even when his list of
necessary correspondence included names like Jefferson, Monroe,
and Washington; he encouraged her pursuit of nearly exclusively
male skills like fencing and pistol marksmanship.

But with her mother gone, so was what gave balance to her
father's single-minded tendencies. There was no one to advocate
for the importance of offsetting hours of grammar with piano,
math with horsemanship, language with afternoons spent being
the little girl she was.

A career in politics aside, his primary goal was making his
daughter into a female version of himself, able to exercise her reason as naturally as any man. But one, like her namesake, able to do
so with the grace and dignity of a woman.

Theodosia turned each page, reviewing the entirety of the journal's contents, from the advice on child-rearing, to the sewing patterns and recipes, to the fictionalized short stories, to the poems of
love that brought her mind back to Philip Hamilton. She flipped
aggressively. At the back, on the very last page, was a submissions
request from the printer based in New York City, urging readers to
share what they knew best.

Theodosia returned to the article on women's right to vote,
thought of her mother, and slid a new piece of parchment in front
of her. Her father had always encouraged her writing to be true and
in pursuit of critical thought. She gathered her inkwell and sand
and dipped her quill. And then she began to write.

# Chapter 7

Three days had passed since the dinner with Vanderlyn, and Theodosia still had no word from him. The commodore's presence had delayed any mention of a possible courtship. Though Theodosia held out hope that perhaps Vanderlyn had found a way to speak with her father alone that night after she'd retired upstairs or in the three days since.

On the fourth day, Theodosia marched down to breakfast, determined to address the matter herself. Her father was already seated at the table.

"Nathalie has not come down?" Theodosia took her usual chair to the right of her father.

He looked up from his newspaper. "Madame de Senat required her assistance early this morning, but I made sure Eleonore packed her two boiled eggs."

"I see, good then." Theodosia and her father would be alone. The opportunity was hers for the taking. She sat up straight. And her liver went white, all courage gone. "On the governorship, is Nicholson behind us?"

She returned to the news her father had recently shared. That the position of governor of the state of New York might, with the right support, soon be his.

He held the newspaper tight. "Quite so. But it will be the Clintons and the Livingstons who determine how this all will play out."

"And you will just stand by and wait?"

"Patience—"

"I know, I know." *Enough, either do it or start clucking, Theodosia.* She cleared her throat. "I do have another issue I'd like to discuss with you."

Her father folded the newspaper beside his plate. He wouldn't allow anything but the most singular focus on her during their conversations. "My ears are always open to you, Miss Priss."

Theodosia took a sip of her coffee, black. In her father's absence she'd add a teaspoon of sugar. Maybe two. She gingerly swallowed the offending bitterness. "It's about Mr. Vanderlyn—"

"Ah, yes, John sends his regards."

"You've seen him?"

"No, you know I've been occupied with meetings these past days."

"But when—"

"The evening he departed."

"From here?"

"Ah, yes, well . . . I was fortunate to see him once more. Two nights ago when he departed for France."

A buzzing clouded Theodosia's ears.

"He departed France for here," she said.

"And here for there."

She rubbed her temples. "Papa, I do so love our witticisms—and forgive me if I am misunderstanding—but either you or I may be having an episode for are you telling me John Vanderlyn is gone?"

"My dear Miss Priss, be mindful of your word selection. Gone has far greater depth of meaning than suits this circumstance. Mr. Vanderlyn is merely aboard a ship bound for more of what we all require: introspection. Self-knowledge lays the foundation for all knowledge. Constant vigilance is required so that we remain sharp as a knife."

A surge of heat behind her eyes forced her to lower her gaze. He left without saying goodbye? Had she misconstrued their conversation? Her plate lay empty before her, and the same sense of hollowness filled her stomach.

"Eh, eh, eh, posture, my dear!" her father said.

Reflexively, she pushed back the shoulders she hadn't realized she'd dropped.

Her father stared at her as if in her seat was someone whose acquaintance he'd yet to make. "What is it? Are you ill?"

Theodosia shook her head. "He . . . he didn't give you a note or a letter or—"

"No time." Her father cracked the top of his boiled egg with the edge of a spoon. "Ship had but one spot left, and he had to act with haste. He asked me to wish you well in all your future endeavors."

*Future endeavors?* He was to be a part of those "future endeavors." "But are you sure he didn't say anything else, perhaps about his return?"

"No return date. One cannot put a time limit on introspection, as I told him."

"You told him."

"Quite so."

"You."

Her father set down his spoon. "That's it, I'm calling for the doctor. You are not yourself, Theodosia."

"When did you tell him this, about introspection?"

"We were discussing it after dinner, how important it is to know yourself before you can master your profession, the precursor to all other decisions in life."

Theodosia bobbed her head in agreement as per the custom with her father's lessons, but her mind churned. She looked at him with searching eyes. "Whose idea was setting sail to accomplish this introspection?"

Her father raised his brow. "It was a lively discussion. One cannot claim origin in such circumstances."

She twisted her napkin in her lap. "He's lucky there was a place for him so quickly."

"Luck had nothing to do with it. Favors are key to cultivate. I was able to capitalize on one and book him passage."

Theodosia's face paled.

Her duties were laid in stone the day her mother died with barely time to grieve. She was to become what her mother had been—her father's closest confidant in business, his closest companion in leisure, and mistress of his households, both Richmond Hill and the townhome on Partition Street. She knew it as she mopped her mother's sickness from her chest and sweat from her forehead though Theodosia was not yet eleven years old. Theodosia had nursed her mother alone in her final days, as her father was in attendance at Congress in Philadelphia—a place her mother would not let him abandon even as the stomach pains that had plagued her for years worsened. Among the last words her mother spoke to her was a plea to take care of her father whose *"needs are plenty and insistent but who in return gives a fidelity and devotion many men reserve for God."*

Filling the void left by the woman her father loved set out a difficult enough task, and yet her father was beginning to demand more.

Theodosia fought the heat behind her eyes that longed to manifest into tears. "You sent him away."

"I assisted his desires."

Vanderlyn thought the way to earn her hand lay in pleasing her father, something her father was perceptive enough to turn to his advantage. Thus assisting Vanderlyn's desires easily masked the fact that sending Vanderlyn away assisted his own—perhaps leaving room for a match that might suit not just her, but himself.

Her father leaned forward. "Your countenance makes your displeasure clear. Come now, Theodosia, twas a year we spent ensuring you learned to maintain the appearance of openness, serenity, and intelligence no matter the emotions underneath."

As Aaron Burr's daughter, the commands she were to follow might have been particular, but the notion of children's will being bent by their parents was universal. Many had come to find truth in writings such as those by philosopher John Locke, who supported reason in child-rearing, believing children could be molded with careful parental diligence. Instilling correct behavior early meant it would not be necessary later in life. In this, Theodosia was no different from many, including Angelica Hamilton.

"We eradicated sneers and frowns and discontent," her father said. "I did not believe you still required such observations from me."

"No, Papa." Theodosia's heart, so warm from Vanderlyn mere days ago, grew cold.

"He was a good friend to us both."

*Was* a good friend. And she wasn't supposed to use "gone"?

He dug his spoon back into his egg, lifting the soft yolk to his lips. "Any other good friends who may have escaped mention?"

Theodosia flattened her napkin in her lap. "No one new." Despite the grip on her heart, she transformed her face into one he wished to see.

"Or opponents? Don't think I've forgotten you neglecting to mention the fracas that Hamilton boy caused."

"Sorry, Papa. But he scarcely seemed worthy of your time." Theodosia's lie dripped with flattery.

"Quite considerate. Yet no more oversights. You know every hour of your day interests me. So much more than my own dreary existence." He raised an eyebrow, trying to lighten the mood, but not even his self-deprecating humor could do that today. He rang for Theodosia's breakfast.

She ate sparingly, just as she'd always been instructed.

Upstairs in her room, she closed the geography book she'd spent the past hour reading without absorbing. On the grounds outside her window, her father's horse was being saddled. Soon her father greeted Sam, taking the reins from the coachman's slender, brown-skinned hands.

She trusted her father. He had his reasons. And she'd learned to have the same.

In her desk drawer, she lifted the letter from her mother, fingered the linen cradling her mother's brooch, and retrieved the pages she'd begun writing the previous night. It was a satirical tale of a young girl transported one hundred years into the future. She arrived on Election Day in the year 1900, and through what Theodosia hoped was a humorous series of mishaps, became mistaken for the presidential candidate, for this was a future Theodosia saw as clearly as her mother had: one where women, not solely men, voted, where women held political office, where women not only attended college but ran them.

And, yes, there was a love story.

It was to entertain the masses of ladies, after all, was it not?

# Chapter 8

THE WOODEN PLANK SUNK AS THEODOSIA pressed her foot against it. She would have to remember to tell Alexis before it completely disappeared into the ditch. Nathalie had already dashed across the makeshift bridge in Lispenard's Meadows, heading toward the footpath that led home to Richmond Hill.

They were returning from another visit to Madame de Senat's school. This time at Theodosia's urging. After the last trip, she realized how much she'd missed being out with Nathalie, something that had filled their childhood.

Up ahead, Nathalie's skirts swayed as her eyes met Theodosia's, entreating her to run alongside with that same mixture of joy and mischief and, always, an undercurrent of sadness. It had bonded them over years. During all their walks through the gardens of Richmond Hill, their rides along the river that kissed the shores of the estate, and their nights alone in their room after Theodosia's mother had died.

Nathalie had but a year with her. And though it was a year of pain and foreboding for her mother, still her mother's appreciation for life's pleasures never left her. She and Nathalie were alike in this way. Different from Theodosia, who, instead of picking up the mantle left by her mother, aged twofold, committing to her education and her father's needs at the expense of all else.

At least that was what Nathalie would say. Had said.

Philip Hamilton too.

He was on her mind for he was the second reason she had chosen to visit Madame de Senat. Her first, if she were being honest with herself. But he hadn't appeared to pick up his brother.

75

She focused on the pond in the distance, the same one she'd been scolded for skating on as a child. As summer neared, it took on an entirely new persona, surrounded by trees and flowering shrubs like the tiny orange Jerusalem cherries and clusters of pure white snowball flowers that would darken to purple by fall. Her father had created Burr's Pond by damming the small stream that had once curved its way to the Hudson. Molded to his desires, molded to his will. For her. He knew how much she'd loved to skate and how it had soothed Theodosia's ill mother to sit in the window and watch.

All a reminder of why Theodosia's indiscretion with the Hamiltons plagued her. No matter the gossip or exploits of others, she was taught to keep such thoughts tight to her chest. What might be speculation within the confines of one's mind transformed into truth when landing upon the ears of others. Truth not only regarding the third party but about oneself—and that only limited one's opportunities. Thus Theodosia always remained focused and practical. Humor, wit, most certainly. She *had* charmed George Washington—that was not an exaggeration. But such charms she employed with calculated restraint. Except for that day at the schoolhouse with Philip.

Had he egged her on? Without doubt. But she'd been raised to rise above. She'd been raised to be a Burr.

The door had barely opened when her father yelled, "Theodosia! At last!"

It was as if he were perched with an ear to the road and an eye to the window, waiting to pounce. Theodosia removed her cap and set her reticule on the narrow table by the door. "I guess we should—"

She turned to Nathalie, yet found her already halfway up the stairs.

"Coward," Theodosia said, but Nathalie just keep on climbing.

Theodosia sighed. This stretch of her father remaining at Richmond Hill was turning into one of the longest she could remember. As much as she enjoyed his presence, without the distance afforded by letters, the intensity of him was, at times, exhausting. Another reason she had suggested the outing to Madame de Senat's.

"Papa." Theodosia greeted him in the parlor.

He popped to his feet upon sight of her, brandishing a newspaper above his head. "I've a mind to set every member of our household in a saddle and have them ride about the city, gathering the lot of these, and then we'd treat them with the respect they deserve: the biggest bonfire New York has ever seen!"

"What's it—"

"Federalist rantings and inflammatory lies meant to scare, not to educate. This . . . this . . . ." Rage stole his breath, and he pressed a finger to his temple, a sign of a migraine building. "This essay argues that the Federalist party's defeat in the election means, and I quote 'the happiness, constitution, and laws of our nation face endless and irretrievable ruin.'"

To calm her father and stave off his debilitating headaches, Theodosia waved her hand dismissively. "It's merely trying to make some noise. Be heard among the abundance of opinions being spewed about the election." All the newspapers had been ramping up in intensity, denouncing the opposing party and making extravagant claims. "It's incendiary, but is it that different from the others?"

"The others do not name me as integral in the result."

"Named you?"

"And it's not just this . . ." Burr shook the newspaper. "It's not just contained within. Already, that self-serving, uncivilized Alexander Hamilton has publicly agreed with such comments."

And there lay the true crux of his anger. While her father, who sipped unsweetened tea from porcelain imported from France, had long been seen as a French sympathizer, he'd remained less vocal of late, as he was during dinner with the commodore. He'd always refrained from using the press in the way that Hamilton and the majority of the top political players did. And still it was her father most often labeled "unscrupulous."

She stepped toward him, noticing a slight pull at the corner of the rug. Soft as the highly tufted pile of this Brussels carpet was, it had cost them a fortune. It could not be allowed to unravel any more than her father could. "We know the Federalists are prone to statements of grandeur."

As such, they were doing all they could to turn voters against the Republicans by linking the party with the rioting and death toll in France. The Republicans countered by declaring that France's fight for independence was akin to that of America, thus painting the Federalists, and Adams himself, as denouncing the principles behind democracy. Those behind Jefferson pushed the notion further, claiming Adams anxious, argumentative, and jealous, wishing to be a prince with a monarchy.

In truth, Adams appeared to be splitting his own party, with most having more belief in Alexander Hamilton than in him. But Jefferson was everything Adams wasn't. Supremely intelligent, sophisticated and worldly, calm and cool, so much so that his critics wondered if he'd actually rule if elected. But he supported a freedom for citizens, for the press, and claimed the opposite of Adams. Yet on extending those freedoms to slaves, on supporting emancipation as Theodosia and her father did, Jefferson had remained largely silent, leaving just the legacy of those five words: "all men are created equal." And despite having daughters partially educated in France, he'd also remained silent on the cause of women.

"Facts should prevail," Theodosia added. "Insults aren't fact."

"And yet they are presented as though they were. This election is testing the system we've put in place. The people of this country would have followed Washington to the ends of the earth."

"An absence in need of filling?" she said, only partly in jest.

He laughed softly as he peered into the hall. "Which reminds me, when does the post arrive?"

"Expecting news from Albany?"

"No, this time, from the opposite direction."

"The South?" She visibly recoiled.

He frowned. "Open mind. Especially in these times. Make no mistake, my dear Theo. The victor of this election will set our nation's course for generations to come. Perhaps for the length of our nation's existence. Nothing is more important than this."

Theodosia nodded, agreeing with her father, for the issues involved in this election were important; the differences between the Federalists' and the Republicans' temperaments, perhaps even more than their views, would set the tone for the country. But even so, she found herself thinking less about political agendas and more about the young girl in Madame de Senat's class and the daughter of Commodore Nicholson.

She took her light supper in her room. Her father had sped off to meet with Nicholson and other members of his party to formulate their response. Theodosia now sat in one of the two chairs left in the library. With this being a room rarely shown to guests, the rest of the furnishings had been sold. But not the books—not yet, at least.

Floor-to-ceiling shelves lined each wall of the small room, making it appear as large in scale as it was in importance. She sat surrounded by the knowledge the words in these pages had passed on to her and the knowledge she still had to learn from them.

She set a large dictionary on her lap to serve as a desk and placed a piece of parchment on top. She dipped her quill in the bottle of ink on the floor beside her chair and began to write a letter to Vanderlyn. Though she had no forwarding address and no intention to set it in his hands, she needed to issue the goodbye that had been taken from her.

Then she drew out new parchment and wrote one more letter: an apology to Philip Hamilton. Whatever he was or purported to be, he was a big brother first and foremost. She could see that in the intimacy between him and his sister and in the awe from his little brother. While Nathalie was a sister in many ways, she wasn't a Burr. What would it have been like had the child her mother had given birth to when Theodosia was three lived? Who would Theodosia be, who would her father be, if Theodosia had a sibling who shared her same mix of blood? Someone who carried the Burr name? Would she be jealous? Or relieved?

Upstairs at her desk, she folded each note. The one to Vanderlyn she tucked away in the drawer beside her mother's tortoiseshell brooch. From that same drawer, she retrieved the pages she'd been writing late into the evening. She stacked the sheets, straightened the edges, and folded them. She secured them with a seal of red wax. On the front, she wrote:

To: *From the Fairer Sex magazine*
*From:*

Her quill hovered, then she gripped it tighter, and with a flourish signed: *Miss P.*

## CHAPTER 9

SAM HELPED THEODOSIA OUT OF THE carriage. "Are you sure, Ma'am? The horses aren't too tuckered to take you farther."

She thanked him but declined. "A walk is good. Meet me back here in an hour?"

He nodded and issued another, "Ma'am."

She left the coachman on the corner with their carriage and set off down the shop-lined street alone. She had accompanied him into town under the guise of needing to purchase more ink and quills, an excuse born of truth thanks to the pages she carried. Sam, who had letters to deliver on behalf of her father, had offered to shop for her, but she'd insisted that the choices were too particular and ones she had to make herself. Though now, standing on the streets of the city, she wondered if this was all a mistake.

She was already certain she'd be found out. The pages concealed in the small bag on her forearm raged like a signal fire. She smiled as she passed two women resting beneath the awning of a bakery, shielding themselves from the sun. They nodded politely in response, though one tilted her head quizzically as though she could see the flames and smoke rising from Theodosia's bag. Did she know who Theodosia was? What businesses were housed up ahead? Theodosia's smile faded, and with it, a slight ache in her cheeks. She'd been grinning too broadly. Of course she'd drawn odd looks.

Theodosia clutched the strings of her reticule but slowed her pace, observing the carriages filling the streets, the men in brimmed top hats off to attend to the business of their day, and the women

81

in flowered and frilled caps doing . . . whatever it was normal ladies did in the middle of a sunny day.

At the next corner, she made a left toward a shop she'd been to before, though her true destination was to the right. Inside, she quickly chose a bottle of powder for ink and a handful of quills. She paid, being sure to reserve a coin or two, and tucked her purchases in her small bag.

As her foot hit the cobblestones, she moved with the grace required of a woman of her status despite the pounding of her heart. She reached the same corner and paused as if, on a whim, deciding to turn right.

Three-story buildings of stone and of clapboard painted in light greens and yellows and reds hugged one another with no space in between. She casually glanced through the wavy glass of the windowpanes at street level. Behind each sat a different shop, business, or office.

Toward the end of the street, the offices clustered around the same profession: printing presses. The bag looped around her arm grew heavy. Before her hung the shingle for the same newspaper her father had longed to collect for a bonfire. And then, two doors down, her spine stiffened. She couldn't look but straight ahead as she made her way past the windows of the ladies' magazine.

A streak of light shone out from in between two buildings, and Theodosia aimed for it, concealing herself in the tight alleyway as her heart leapt in her chest. Foolish, terribly, completely, foolhardily foolish. What was she to do? Wedge the pages beneath the door and run? Stroll in as Aaron Burr's daughter?

Foolish, foolish, fool—

*"Thomas Jefferson's fit for farming! Read it here! Only six coppers!"*

A young boy with chestnut hair sticking out of a hat that sat crooked on his head skipped down the middle of the street waving a newspaper. *"Six, just six coppers! Be the first to tell your friends!"*

He zigzagged across the street, offering papers to busy gentle-men, moving hastily from sidewalk to sidewalk as dust swirled about his feet.

"Six copp—" the boy stopped short. His eyes met Theodosia's. "Interested, Miss?" The satchel that lay across his small torso bounced as he sprinted toward her. "For your husband?"

Theodosia grimaced and shooed him off.

He planted himself in front of her. "Then your father? He'll want to read all about it, the boss says."

"No, thank you." Theodosia tucked herself farther back into the alley. She couldn't be seen. This boy was going to ruin—

Theodosia stretched out her arm and nabbed him by his ill-fitting jacket.

"Whatcha . . .?" He shrugged his homespun coat free, returning it to hang loose on his shoulders. "Now you want a paper? How's about two? Just a short bit."

"I thought they were six cents each? That would be a dime and—"

"A short bit and two coppers. I know my monies, Miss, but for you, a sale price of two for ten. Whaddaya say?"

"I say you are an excellent businessman."

The boy beamed and dug into his bag.

Theodosia set her hand on his. "So good, in fact, that I want to offer you a job."

"Already got a job."

"This one's special. A one-time effort, for which you'll be paid twice your hourly rate."

The boy's eyes widened. He then quickly returned them to their normal state and furrowed his brow. "That'd be a dollar, Miss."

She raised her eyebrow. "Fifty cents an hour? Why I must get into the newspaper business, myself."

"All the good jobs are taken, Miss, but I'll put in a word if I hear of an opening."

Theodosia forced back a grin. "Much appreciated . . . What's your name?"

"George. But everyone calls me Georgie. After the general."

"Naturally." The general, not the king the country fought to separate from. But thanks to the two, America has a generation of Georges, a legacy for them both. "How does this sound? I'll give you that short bit if you deliver something for me."

Georgie sucked in his lower lip, trying to hide his excitement. "Gotta be extra for long distance. I'm supposed to sell these papers 'round here."

"Lucky for me. You only need to travel a few feet."

The boy frowned.

"Unless you don't want—"

"No, you betcha. I want." He held out his hand.

"First, a promise."

"To deliver? I'm a man of my word."

"As you look, which is why I chose you. But I also need the delivery to be secret. You have no idea who I am and if asked will say the same."

"Easy enough. I've no idea who you are. Should I?"

"No, not especially." Theodosia opened the drawstring on her reticule. The sealed pages addressed to *From the Fairer Sex* magazine lay at the bottom beneath her ink and quill and above the letter containing her apology to Philip. She lifted the pages by their wax seal, and her throat tightened. With a deep breath, she set them in Georgie's hand. The opposite ends curled toward one another, and she pressed her palm on top to flatten them.

"Can you read?" she asked him.

He nodded. "Some."

"So you know where this is to go?"

He pointed toward the office. "Just down that way."

"*From the Fairer Sex* magazine. Be sure you hand it directly to the publisher, no one else. Understand?"

"I'll understand a mite better once I see that short bit."

Despite the rough seas in her stomach, Theodosia lay the dime in his palm. "Remember, our secret. Now go. I'll be watching."

With a spin that slammed his satchel into his backside, Georgie darted out of the alley.

Theodosia pressed her hand against the brick wall and tried to calm her nerves. She peered around the corner, watching Georgie charge past a man in an expensive coat and stark white breeches. She heard the ding of a bell, and Georgie disappeared into the magazine's office.

A tentative smile spread larger and larger until Theodosia pushed herself off the wall of the alleyway and spun, just once, just like Georgie. An extra spring infused her step as she righted her skirt and rejoined the foot traffic on the main street. She casually strolled past the storefront of the magazine, not risking even a fleeting glance.

Instead she caught a glimpse of the well-dressed man whom Georgie had circumvented. He entered the building housing the Federalist newspaper she was once again approaching. She wasn't yet in front of it when she heard a strong voice shouting through the closed door. *"That vain Adams will destroy the principles this party was founded upon rather than admit any wrongdoing!"*

The voice settled into a rage rivaling that of her father, and she paused to listen, hoping to feed her father something useful.

*"And those unscrupulous Republicans. Dining and drinking their way to pockets full of wealth, getting sponsors for campaigns and refusing to call it what it is: electioneering. A disgrace. Our nation must be saved from them. We must be saved from the fangs of Jefferson. Though the worst among them is not Jefferson, who at least has the good sense to appear above the scheming, but the power-hungry Burr and his cronies, like that arrogant Alston. What this paper published was an understatement. Print my words down to the exclamation point, or you'll see your bank account much lighter."*

The door flung open, and the man Theodosia had gotten but a glimpse of burst through the door. She recognized him though she had not seen him in some time: Alexander Hamilton.

Even Theodosia could tell the green broadcloth of his jacket was fashionably cut, perfectly fitting his slim but strong frame. The peach of his complexion spoke to the natural auburn of his hair lurking beneath its layer of powder. A handsome man, made extraordinary by his deep blue, almost violet eyes.

"There you are!" Alexander Hamilton shouted, and Theodosia turned to stone.

*Foolish, foolish, foolish.*

"What happened, son?" he said. "A pint of ale leap into your path on the way to the market?"

"No, whiskey."

Theodosia turned, and there was Philip, and his arm brushed against hers as he moved beside her. He tipped his chin in greeting, and she bowed back gently. An unexpected blush spread across her cheeks.

Colonel Hamilton laughed not just with his voice but his whole self. Unlike her father's measured movements, Philip's father seemed to possess a kinetic energy constantly on the verge of exploding. "That's my naughty boy." In one swift go around, he whisked the basket of apples and bread from Philip's hand and swung open the newspaper office door.

"Sir," Philip said, causing his father to turn to him impatiently. "Mother said you might be in need of my assistance this afternoon?"

"Assistance? Heavens, no." Alexander looked from Theodosia to Philip. "Go forth. Be a boy, my son. Have your pleasures while you still can and leave the work to the men."

Philip's jaw clenched as his father reentered the building. He then pulled an oval flask from his inside pocket. "My lady?" He held the bottle out to Theodosia.

"No, thank you."

"Right. You've no need, coming from stock with skin tougher than leather. Still, accept my apologies on behalf of my own stock. Thick in head if nowhere else."

"Apologies for what?"

Philip tipped the flask toward the windowpane. Behind it, his father was leaning over a desk.

"Your father?" How long had Philip been behind her? Had he heard what his father had said about her own?

"Thinks he's subtle." Philip took a swig. "Pleasures? He insults all of us."

*Oh.* "Oh, you can't mean he thinks you and I . . . he thinks I am—"

"Like Lottie."

"I am nothing like Lottie Jewell." Theodosia jammed her hands on her hips. "Wait, what is Lottie like?" She shook her head. "Don't tell me. I'm nothing like her."

"Most certainly not. For you are a proper gentlewoman." Philip covered his mischievous smile by tilting the flask back to his lips once again. "Not tempted by a . . . what was it? A rapscallion scoundrel? I was fond of your creativity."

"As well you should be," Theodosia teased, hoping to follow his lead and keep things civil. After what happened at the schoolhouse, he had every right to be curt with her. "But be sure, I'm nothing like Lottie Jewell because an oyster has more brains than Lottie Jewell."

"Oysters don't have brains."

"Precisely." Theodosia plucked the flask from Philip's hand, ignored his raised eyebrow, and drank without a wince though the whiskey burned her throat. She held the flask back out to him.

Impressed, he accepted it and cradled it in the crook of his arm as if it were a delicate newborn.

*"The man sent a peace initiative to France when it was Britain whom we must align with. Adams has less leadership in his entire body than Washington, rest in peace, had in his pinky toe . . ."*

Hamilton's words, which Theodosia imagined she and her father reading in a day or two, rang out from inside the office. Her father would be utterly delighted at the prospect of the rift in the Federalist party widening.

"Does it bother you?" she asked Philip.

"That oysters don't have brains? Not particularly. I find them quite tasty without. More likely."

Theodosia couldn't help a smile, though the look in Philip's eyes did not match the lightness of his joke. He knew she was asking about being left out by his father.

She loosened the strings of her bag, drawing out her letter of apology. "The other day—"

"No need, Miss Burr."

The parchment remained stiff between her fingers as she waited for more words to be said in jest or to incite her to grovel simply for his own amusement. But no more came.

She closed her bag but did what she knew she must. "No, there is. I was wrong. I shouldn't have said that in front of your brother." Theodosia soothed her tone. "I shouldn't have said it at all. Family is family."

"It is, isn't it?" He glanced at his father once more before setting his gaze, unnervingly, on Theodosia.

She cleared her throat. "Good for your brother. Full marks on his spelling test? Brains run in the Hamilton line. Your father. You at Columbia College. Impressive."

"I'm to graduate in July. With high honors, it would seem."

"Most impressive."

"One might think," Philip said, the presence of his father looming through the window.

Theodosia stepped back to examine both father and son, separated by a wall despite their proximity, a metaphor she suspected characterized more than this present moment. "You resemble one another."

"What a wicked tongue you have, Miss Burr."

"In countenance, Mr. Hamilton. Though perhaps it would not be the worst thing to work on disposition as well?"

He wiggled the flask. "How much of this have you had?"

"I simply mean that fathers of our generation—our fathers, especially—have fought since they were our age. An offer to assist is admirable to most, but to men like our fathers . . . well, I suggest they respond to action."

Philip drank—a long, deliberate swallow. "Like you said. Precisely."

"Why do you do that?"

"I have a reputation to uphold."

"Uphold or create?"

"Is that not the old chicken-and-the-egg conundrum? Hear me, Miss Burr, if you become what others believe you to be, then you can never disappoint."

"Them or yourself?"

"Does it matter?"

Theodosia looked at Philip, really looked at him, past the perpetual smirk, past the teasing flirtation, past the air of nonchalance he tried so desperately to exude. His countenance might have been that of a smug, secure young man well-suited to the wide world in which he lived, but his eyes were those of a little boy whose world was small, whose world was his family—his father. She stood before him as a woman whose world was the same. She was quite sure the answers to the questions she and Philip posed did matter, though she was hard-pressed to say in which way.

"*Miss! Miss!*"

Theodosia turned to see Georgie bound down the stairs of the magazine's office. His back to her, he flew down the street toward the alley. His cap leapt into the air, caught by a passerby who rammed it into the boy's sack hanging about his neck.

"*Miss! Miss!*"

A prickle of perspiration tickled Theodosia's forehead, and she nodded to Philip, taking a step around him and in the opposite direction of the boy.

"Do you have to go?" Philip asked.

"Yes, Sam will be waiting."

"Sam?"

She didn't have time for this! "He's delivering letters for my father."

"Sam is one of your slaves?"

Theodosia said brusquely, "Our coachman. A member of our household longer than I have been."

"I see. Though semantics don't change the reality." Philip shook his head. "A shame that this is where our fathers share a commonality: ideals in conflict with truths."

Georgie continued his cry, and Theodosia could not remain to engage in whatever it was Philip was saying. She was barely listening, instead wondering what he would think if she simply sprinted down the street.

She peered around Philip and caught sight of a carriage slowing at a storefront halfway down. The driver in black livery assisted a well-dressed woman to the ground and stood in front of the carriage as she entered a shop.

"Will I see you again?" Philip asked.

Theodosia's eyed fixed on the carriage. "I suspect so. It seems as if our paths keep crossing."

"Fate, if you believe in those things."

"Do you?"

"I didn't used to." Not a drop of nonchalance infused his tone, and something other than nerves fluttered in Theodosia's stomach.

"*Miss!*"

The pounding feet forced Theodosia to utter a quick goodbye to Philip. With fire in her boots, she aimed toward the carriage.

"*Miss! Miss!*"

"What is it, boy?" Theodosia heard Philip say. "Who are you after?"

"No time, no time. Two pennies at stake!" the boy shouted.

Theodosia hurried down the street, risking a single glance over her shoulder. Philip was now facing the offices of the ladies' journal. The door was open, and a man cupped the elbow of Lucinda Wilson as she stepped out.

Theodosia ducked behind the carriage.

"Thank you for coming in, Miss Wilson," the man said. "We are honored to be the publisher of your family's recipes. And thanks again for the pie. Apple's always been my favorite."

*Recipes. Pie.* Apple *pie.* A smirk consumed Theodosia's face. *How provincial.*

"Miss! Miss, Miss, Miss!" Georgie careened past her. He caught himself at the last moment, stumbling as he halted and nearly fell into the path of an oncoming horseman. Theodosia stuck out an arm and returned with a fistful of jacket and the boy attached.

"Persistent, aren't you?" she hissed.

The boy began talking fast, but a "Why, if it isn't Philip Hamilton?" in Lucinda's singsong voice made Theodosia shush him.

"In the flesh," Philip responded.

"Such a tease, Mr. Hamilton. I'll remind you, I am a lady."

"Reminder appreciated. There was a fellow in the sparring pit on Broadway that looked just like you."

"Mr. Hamilton!" Lucinda cried. "Now you owe me an apology."

"Of course, my *lady*. I'm—"

"I'll take it in the form of an escort to the Clinton party this Saturday."

"Sorry?"

"You will be if you wear that. Please do spruce yourself up, Mr. Hamilton. Women of a class higher than you're used to consorting with expect it."

"But I—"

"Come now, a little effort won't do you harm, will it? You did receive an invitation, did you not?"

"Invitation—"

"The Clintons' party. Mr. Hamilton, I swear it's as if your head is elsewhere."

*Is it?*

"Indeed," he said. "I'm due inside. Late in fact. You know my father."

Theodosia again grabbed Georgie's shirt and thrust him to the edge of the carriage. "Tell me what you see."

"But Miss, two pennies just for finding—"

Theodosia shoved a few coins into young Georgie-after-the-general's hand.

"What luck, what luck!"

"Yes, yes. Now. Look." She pressed his head forward. He looked. "And speak," Theodosia said with frustration.

"Well, it's the lady from Mr. Gunther's shop. She smells like lilacs. Sure hope the scruffy man isn't allergic because they're awful close."

"What?" Theodosia dragged Georgie behind her. She shielded her face with one hand and crouched low.

Lucinda *was* close. So close that Philip seemed to be impersonating a worm, wiggling his way out of the space between her and the window to which she'd nearly pinned him.

"Much appreciated, Miss Wilson, certainly," Philip said. "But I'm afraid that won't be possible."

"Colonel Hamilton!" Lucinda pushed her way past Philip, ringlets of brown hair bouncing against her cheek. "My father sends his regards."

"Why, Miss Wilson, a pleasure." Philip's father stood in the open door of the newspaper's office. "Send my best to your father as well." He placed a hand on Philip's shoulder. "Busy boy, aren't you, son?"

"Yes, just as I was telling Miss Wilson."

Lucinda placed one hand on her hip. "You were doing nothing of the kind, Mr. Hamilton. Unless what you are busy doing is declining to escort me to the Clintons' party."

"Philip!" Colonel Hamilton's voice boomed. "Indeed, Angelica was in conversation with your mother just this morning on her attire, but your sister will more than understand if your escort duties are needed elsewhere."

"Why, thank you, Colonel," Lucinda said. "Please send my heartfelt thanks to dear Angelica."

Philip's father replied, "You can tell her yourself on Saturday."

"I look forward to it." Lucinda held a hand out to Philip, who, Theodosia was pleased to note, took it with all the zeal one might reserve for accepting a live snake.

Theodosia tucked herself back behind the carriage, only daring another glimpse after enough time had passed to presume Lucinda had traveled in the opposite direction.

Philip's hand lay clenched against his leg. "Why, Father, one might think you'd be content with the instructions you leave for my every hour of wake and study and let affairs of the heart be mine."

"One might, if you took it upon yourself to follow said instructions." Hamilton noticed a bit of powder on his lapel, fallen from his highly stylized hair, and hastily brushed it off. "Or if your affairs of the heart didn't risk pulverizing mine."

"An overreaction to my lack of interest in courting Miss Wilson, isn't it, Father?"

"And yet an entirely appropriate response to you consorting with Theodosia Burr. Yes, took me a moment, but that is the young lady you were with?"

"I wasn't with her."

Theodosia's stomach lurched.

"Keep it that way." Hamilton turned to reenter the office. "And you *are* going to the Clintons' party, and you will be escorting

Miss Wilson. We need her father's full support now that Burr has destroyed the integrity of our election proceedings."

Philip reached for his flask, and Theodosia wished she had one of her own. She leaned against the side of the carriage. Shame at intruding upon a private family moment mixed with an understanding of being so dictated to by a father. Her mind swirling, she focused on a pig dragging its snout along the ground in front of her.

"Miss?" Georgie said.

The pig found something of particular interest. A corncob?

"Miss, I gotta sell these papers before dark."

"Am I preventing you?"

"Uh, yeah. A bit." Georgie moved into Theodosia's line of sight. "You alright, Miss? Pa's always saying how ladies need more rest and such for their constipation."

"Their . . . You mean constitution?"

"Sure, that too."

Theodosia sighed. "You had something to tell me? Hopefully not more of your father's wisdom."

He told Theodosia that the publisher wanted her to write more of her story. "Well, *now* he does," Georgie corrected himself. "He didn't, not right away, not until his missus dug the papers outta the trash can, read them, and swatted her husband. Right across the back of the head like my ma does when I forget to take my shoes off before getting in bed. She said—she meaning Mr. Gunther's wife, not Ma—she said something about not putting such high art anywhere but as the lead story. Mr. Gunther rubbed his neck and read the pages and shrugged, saying he didn't get it. Then Mrs. Gunther knocked him again, saying, 'course you wouldn't, but your readers will.' So then he asked where I got it because the story was just signed 'Miss P.' Mr. Gunther said it was a penny name."

"Pen name," Theodosia said.

"Right," Georgie said. "Anyway, two coppers if I can find ya. So what'll I tell him, will ya write more, Miss? After your constipation?"

"I-I don't think so."

"Well, sure thing, writing's hard. If you can't, you can't."

"No, it's not that, it's . . ."

*Papa.*

She thought of Vanderlyn. "I need you to make me a promise, Georgie." She tapped his fist, which clenched the coins she'd given him. "There's another of those for you if you go back to Mr. Gunther and tell him you found me and that I said . . ." *What am I saying?* "Yes," she blurted out. "Tell him to hold back the last page of the story from publication this week. Tease that it'll be a serial."

"A what?"

"To be continued." Theodosia pushed herself off the carriage and rose to her full height. "And meet me back here, next week."

"Here at the carriage?"

"The bakery on the corner. You know it?" He nodded and she said, "Good boy, Georgie-after-the-general."

Theodosia's spirits were high as she picked up the ladies' magazine Nathalie had left on the small wooden bench in front of the extravagantly expensive pianoforte. She flipped through, excitement rising at the thought of her writing being within. Alongside Lucinda's recipes.

"Ha!"

"And what is so funny, Miss Priss?" Her father entered the room, the knees of his breeches coated in a layer of dust. "Surely it cannot be that ladies' drivel?"

"Of course not, Father." She bent to swat at the dirt. "It's this. The image of you rolling around in the fields like a boy half your age."

He broadened his chest. "I do not need to be your age to still have such sprightliness."

"Now that's *truly* amusing. Half your age equaling mine."

Her father extracted a handkerchief from his pocket and wiped his hands, which also bore the remnants of soil. "How did I raise a girl of so little gratitude?"

"You prized cleverness above all."

He exaggerated a sigh. "What a mistake."

"Too late now, *mon père*."

He settled himself in his favorite chair by the fireplace. "Perhaps. But shall you guess at something that won't be too late, thanks to *ton père?*"

Theodosia rested the magazine on the glossy inlaid card table and sat across from him. "Ah, and he tries to trick. For a scholar does not guess. I was raised to be sure of my words."

"So you give up?"

She narrowed her eyes at his smirk and took in that dust on his knees, the dirt on his handkerchief, and answered by thanking him. "However, I do hope you mixed some manure into the soil. Those blue asters will grow to three feet if well-fertilized."

Her father chuckled and wagged a finger at her. "I didn't want you to miss out, so I saved the mixing of manure for you."

"How considerate." With the end of their teasing, his eyes drifted toward the magazine, prompting Theodosia to embark on an assured distraction. "Which is an admirable trait in a governor, don't you think?"

As she knew it would, that launched them into yet another strategizing session on how her father could capitalize on his recent political coup and improve his chances of being elected governor. The prospect of a win had become much more likely now that he'd done what many could not: impress the elite who wielded power in state politics.

Alexis appeared in the doorway, and for a moment, Theodosia thought he knew where she'd been. But he simply held the day's mail in his hand. "The post's been delivered," he said.

Theodosia and her father rose from their chairs in unison. Burr held out his hand, and Theodosia retook her seat, though accepting the mail had been her job as head of the household for months—years—in his absence.

Her father sat back down across from her. On top of the pile was a letter with slanted writing that Theodosia recognized. *Vanderlyn*.

Burr thumbed through and stuffed all the letters but one in his jacket pocket.

She peeled her eyes from it. They were having a discussion; waiting was polite, waiting was what she'd been taught to do, waiting was something she despised.

She set her hands in her lap. "Do you have a trip planned soon?"

"Albany. But I expect to be at Richmond Hill for the better part of the spring and well through the summer."

"How wonderful," she said, holding her eyes back from the letter.

"We have much to do together. Starting with this." He handed her the letter he'd kept free of his pocket. "This, my dear, will be a party the Burrs cannot miss."

The air left Theodosia's lungs. It wasn't a letter from Vanderlyn. It was an invitation to the Clintons' party. She must have been mistaken. Her eyes seeing what they wished to see.

Later that evening, Nathalie sewed new trim on the gown Theodosia was to wear to the party in lieu of the purchase of a new dress, which Theodosia had to plead with her father was not necessary despite him being as aware of their finances as she.

Theodosia roamed through the house, her mind refusing to release the image of the handwriting on the letter atop the pile of mail.

She ambled through the first floor, arriving at the door to her father's study. She knocked. No answer. She glanced down the hall, ensuring no one was within sight. Then, she did something she hadn't done since she was a child: she snuck in.

On her father's desk were the letters from earlier. She sorted through, finding nothing from Vanderlyn. Relief washed over her. There had never been secrets between her and her father—

not even of the women he'd entertained in the years since her mother's death.

No secrets until now.

But this was different. Her story in the journal would be anonymous. Besides, it was "ladies' drivel." It wasn't meaningful. It didn't affect their lives. Unlike Colonel Hamilton's pontificating about the "unscrupulous, power-hungry, and arrogant" Republicans, specifically, her father. But relaying Hamilton's words to her father was impossible for it meant explaining how she knew.

She restacked the letters as she had originally found them. She paused, looking more closely at the return address of one: "Oaks Plantation, Georgetown County, South Carolina."

She laughed at yet another "George," this one surely for the king, but the name above the address harkened back to Colonel Hamilton's bellowing and the "South Carolina" to her father's impatience for a letter from the South—the combination sent a chill down the nape of her neck: "Joseph Alston."

# CHAPTER 10

"WHY, JUST THINK, IF I WERE three inches taller, you'd be out of a job," Theodosia said, taking the extended hand of Washington Irving.

"I wouldn't stand for it," he said, helping her to the ground. "I'd demand carriages be made three inches higher."

He grinned, and Theodosia was once again grateful he was escorting her. While she would know many at the Clintons' party, and even like some, she never exactly fit in at dances. She could twirl and step as well as any girl her age, but her mind wandered too easily, and her patience for *only* twirling and stepping ran out before the music. At least with Washington, she'd have someone to talk to. He was one of her few true friends. He had been since childhood; he'd attended the school across the street from Madame de Senat's, and her father had taken a liking to him. He did that—judge quickly and deeply, forming a bond that would stand through time.

Vanderlyn being the exception.

Washington stepped back to allow her to move out of the street. His joyful smile made his dark eyes shine, and the crisp white cravat about his neck contrasted well with his black hair and sideburns. But he was Washington, her friend; their relationship had always been and would always be platonic—no matter what Nathalie thought.

"Ahem," Nathalie said from inside the carriage, fingers spread wide on her hips.

"Yes?" Theodosia's eyebrow lifted. "Why go ahead, enjoy the benefits of being tall."

Washington set Nathalie's hand in his. "At your service. Don't mind her, she's always been jealous."

"And I of her," Nathalie said. "Though for other reasons, I suspect."

"Then we are a perfect match," Theodosia teased. She fluffed the skirt of her high-waisted ball gown, more than a little self-conscious of the heart-shaped décolletage. Nathalie, in her alterations, had taken it lower—surely in an effort to embarrass Theodosia, for Nathalie, true friend that she was, liked to torture Theodosia just a little.

Nathalie claimed Washington's arm and kicked up the train of her skirt. She'd woven feathers along the hem and even had a matching one tucked in the ribbon of her headdress. Unlike Theodosia, Nathalie was born to attend balls. Theodosia watched the sway of Nathalie's hips as she passed through the front door of this mansion that sat along the east bank of the Hudson. How much did her friend think of the life she never got the chance to live in France?

"Well, then," Theodosia's father said, exiting the carriage. "It would appear you are stuck with me."

Theodosia looped her arm through his, stroking the rich fabric of his dark brown coat as they followed Nathalie inside. He looked quite handsome in his matching coat, waistcoat, and breeches. He wore his tricorne cocked hat, one Nathalie had tried to toss from the carriage, for apparently it was going out of fashion faster than hoop skirts. He'd kept a hand on top of his head the entire ride.

He extended his arm and tucked Theodosia's tight to his torso. "Tonight will be—"

"Short, with any luck," Theodosia said.

"Oh, come now, Theo, you know I lived for dances like this when I was your age."

"For the alternative was being fired upon by Red Coats. And even so, for me it would depend on two things."

"What's that?"

"How good a shot they were and how good I was at ducking."

"Ah, Miss Priss, it's not so terrible, is it? Young men dressed in their best, simply looking for a twirl with a pretty maiden."

She snorted.

"You could try to enjoy yourself," he said.

"Since when are you such a proponent of frivolous dancing with young men?"

"Well, not frivolous and not just any young men . . ."

"Hmm, I see, so have you already had my dance card filled with the appropriate young men?"

"Just one. Clinton's son. We can use all the edge we can get. By the end of tonight, I may have news that will forever change the course of our lives."

"That's quite the assertion. It better not be simple embellishment to coerce me to dance with Clinton's son. He smells like sour milk."

Burr laughed.

"He does," she said, "like a newborn in need of a bath."

"There are worse smells."

"But you're not asking me to dance with them." Theodosia turned her head toward his. "The governorship, then?"

"Perhaps."

"And what does that mean?"

"You will know the moment I do."

"Hardly. Unless you plan to make the waltz a threesome with Mr. Sour Milk. You've been less than forthcoming with me?"

"Only with a hunch. I've been—"

"Waiting, I know."

"The wait is almost over." His eyes were bright and hopeful. "If all goes as I suspect, you will have to force my lips shut, Miss Priss, for we will speak of nothing else. I will need you more than ever."

His voice, always as solid as a tree trunk, cracked. All the travel, all the maneuvering and strategizing, all the slandering in the press, all the gossip about town, all the ambition he held to his chest . . . she realized how much weight he carried. How, beneath the mask, vulnerable he was.

*For what else do I live?*

For what else did either of them?

Theodosia slipped her arm from his and squeezed his hand, easing the tremble in it.

Together, they stood at the bottom of a long, arching staircase whose intricately carved balusters and gleaming wood handrails could only have looked more expensive had they been made of actual gold. Her father reclaimed Theodosia's arm, burying it tight against his ribs as they traveled up the stairs and to the second-floor ballroom.

Her mind could sum the cost as well as his—the rich wood, smooth marble, shining gold leaf, well-dressed servants, full plates of pheasant and duck, countless decanters of wine—but she knew that he alone was calculating how to match it at Richmond Hill. For one so practical, he craved extravagance like a moth did the flame. And would be just as dangerous for them all.

Under the arched opening of the grand ballroom, Burr patted her hand and released her. "Better to arrive with one they feel competition with." He slipped her arm through Washington's, who stood waiting.

Washington accepted it readily, flashed a smile at her, and Theodosia caught Nathalie, on his other side, rolling her eyes.

The three of them headed deeper into the room, which brimmed with all of New York society. The Clinton clan was large enough to make the room feel well populated, but they'd invited the full slate of elite with Livingstons, Gallatins, and Nicholsons on one side and Schuylers, Churches, and of course, Hamiltons, on the other.

"Nathalie, Theodosia!" cried a petite young woman with light red hair wearing a long gown the color of springtime grass.

"Caty!" Nathalie extended her arms and enveloped their mutual friend in a hug.

The two giggled, and assessed one another's dresses, stroking fabric, showing off necklines, Caty flicking the feather in Nathalie's hair, Nathalie pulling a tendril out of Caty's elaborate bun.

Theodosia clung to Washington's arm as an excuse for not participating, though Caty and Nathalie knew her well enough not to expect her to. Still beside Washington, Theodosia waited for them to part and wrapped a hand around Caty's forearm, giving a gentle squeeze.

"Glad to see you're free of scratches, Theo," Caty said.

"Scratches, why would I be—"

"Philip told me of your encounter. My cousin's tongue's as sharp as claws."

Theodosia went quiet. "Is Angelica here?"

Caty nodded. "And spitting fire about how she arrived. Which was not with her brother." She gestured across the room, and Theodosia's body tensed.

Her eyes sought him out—a task made simple thanks to his deep blue coat that looked brand-new, his breeches white as snow, his hair softly swept over his forehead. The smile he wore appeared congenial but forced, yet still couldn't detract from how handsome he was. Her skin prickled like stepping into a too-hot bath, that mixture of pain and pleasure jumbling the decision to retreat or to descend deeper. As if he felt her eyes on him, he turned reflexively. Theodosia's arm fell from Washington's. Philip's smile shifted to one entirely genuine, and Theodosia felt her cheeks lifting, her lips rising to send the same back at him. The woman beside him turned to follow Philip's gaze.

Lucinda Wilson.

On his other side was Lottie.

Across from him was his sister, Angelica.

Theodosia reclaimed Washington's arm. "Shall we?" she said, leading them deeper into the ballroom.

# CHAPTER 11

WITH A BEND IN HER KNEE and a dip of her chin, Theodosia bowed her thanks to George Washington Clinton.

Another George. Another Washington. The man's grave must have been heavy with all he'd left behind. Not just the namesakes whose futures the war he'd won had given them, but the office he vacated, some say too early.

Colonel Hamilton did. Her father said if Hamilton had had his way, America would be another England, with a monarch at its helm. Instead, there was a transfer of power every four years and squabbling every day in between.

Across the dance floor, Eliza Hamilton, the colonel's wife, smiled demurely, nodding to Mrs. Livingston and, Theodosia imagined, trying not to stare at the woman's hairy chin. Colonel Hamilton stood apart from her, his hands a blur, gesticulating wildly as he spoke with Gouverneur Morris.

Upon learning that Burr had outmaneuvered his archrival Colonel Hamilton, Mr. Morris, an ardent Federalist, had been overheard saying (and subsequently quoted in the press, to Morris's supposed dismay) that the business with the assembly was a *"bad sign that the Federalists would face serious difficulties in the presidential election."*

What her father had done was truly a feat unmatched in strategy. The Federalists allowed themselves to be defined as the party elite, and the Republicans, despite the wealth and position of Jefferson, depicted themselves as the friend of the workingman. And yet, in order to secure the recent, crucial legislative win, Burr had made the seemingly contrary decision to stack the slate of candidates for these largely working-class wards with Republican elite: former Governor George Clinton, General Horatio Gates, Robert Livingston—men of power whose stature would have ordinarily made such a candidacy beneath them. But her father had convinced them. Her father could talk a chicken into a boiling cauldron.

*Or a painter onto a ship to France.*

Theodosia declined another round with George Washington Clinton, citing the need to quench her thirst. He immediately set off to seek a glass of wine for her. She lingered at the edge of the dance floor, watching Colonel Hamilton, charismatic even at a distance. Yet his charm equaled a stubborn arrogance, which had allowed him to be outwitted by her father, who'd let the Federalists unveil their legislative ticket first, one fielded by an undistinguished roster of assemblymen—two grocers, a baker, and a shoemaker, as her father joked. A strategy to create appeal beyond the elite that had backfired.

Instead, with his well-known candidates, her father had displayed a deep belief in and strength behind Jefferson, which inspired the lesser-known party leaders to work harder on the Republicans' behalf. And yet he also made sure influential and recognizable names were not the only ones on the Republican side; he'd rounded out the ticket with prominent merchants and trusted ex-assemblymen with whom he'd served, thus simultaneously appeasing factional jealousies and traditional rivalries and ensuring his own presence on the ticket through those loyal to him.

But his most strategic move came with regard to the mechanics, both master craftsmen, who worked in building, manufacturing, and maritime trades, and the poorer class, such as those who made their living hauling goods in carts. This powerful urban constituency had, up until her father, largely supported the growth-oriented Federalists. While he was leader of the assembly, Burr wrote bills for bridges, roads, and waterworks, and his support of lower and fairer taxes appealed widely to these groups.

Hamilton might have been a world-class statesman, but her father had proved himself to be an ingenious politician.

Hamilton remained beholden to ideology and principle, popular or not, which translated to a doggedness akin to bullying— forcing his beliefs upon others rather than persuading them to come to such beliefs as if of their own accord. The opposite of her father. Believing that society and politics worked in the same manner, Burr knew how important befriending people and creating personal loyalties and connections were. Be it raising funds or turning out the vote, he did so personally, traversing the city to speak and urge supporters to vote. He sought to patronize as many people as he could, appealing to all, appeasing many, while getting exactly what he needed to bolster the Republican cause and illustrate the party's dominance to its workingman base— even if that meant publicly taking a back seat himself. Knowing his own name was controversial, he'd left it off the ballot. A gamble they both hoped would pay off by Clinton supporting his candidacy for governor.

A crash and the sound of shattering glass brought all eyes to Colonel Hamilton. In his expansive gesturing, he'd knocked into George Washington Clinton, and the wine that was to meet Theodosia's lips splattered the floor amid shards of crystal.

The laugh in her ear, she knew well.

"The Hamiltons are to drama what pollen is to bees," her father whispered. He nodded toward Theodosia's dance partner. "Enjoying yourself?"

She scoffed, "I'll never partake of a sip of milk again."

"Why then no reason you can't continue with another dance or two?"

"You owe me."

"A debt I have every intention of repaying." He tugged down the front hem of his coat. "If you will excuse me, I have a private party to attend. Even if it is with a tower of giraffes." He punctuated his self-deprecating wink by straightening his spine as he ambled toward the taller Commodore Nicholson, Governor Clinton, Robert Livingston, and Albert Gallatin.

Their departure from the ballroom might have gone unnoticed by most, but not by Alexander Hamilton. Theodosia could see his mind whirling as his eyes followed the group out of the room. The backs of their coats had barely vanished when Hamilton abruptly turned and marched toward his wife. A brief word, a kiss of her hand, and then he strode to the door, pulling on the arm of Edwin Wilson, Lucinda's father, and exiting the ballroom.

Mrs. Hamilton looked across the room with a disheartened expression. Philip, who had been waltzing with Lottie, did not wait for the song to end. He brought Lottie to the edge of the dance floor, bowed curtly, and hurried to his mother's side. Angelica was already there. Mrs. Hamilton kissed each on the cheek and made her way to the large arched opening of the ballroom. There, Caty's mother and Mrs. Hamilton's sister, Angelica Schuyler Church, met her, and the two women left the party together.

Theodosia longed to follow when George Washington Clinton appeared before her once more, glass in hand. She tossed back the madeira in one long gulp. "Let's go," she said, holding out her hand.

Three dances and one more glass of madeira later, Theodosia was relaxing into another Washington's arms—Irving's.

"I haven't seen your father," he said. "Did he already depart?"

"No," she said, "which means neither can we."

"Had enough of rotten eggs?"

"I was going with sour milk, but yes."

"I was here. All night."

"Your arms full of Nathalie and Caty and so many others."

"And yet the instant you call for me, where am I to be found?"

Washington's palm pressed deeper into hers, and Theodosia's stomach hollowed. Friends they had always been, with no thought as to becoming more because . . . because why exactly? Vanderlyn was gone, and with each day that passed, so did the intensity of what she'd thought were her feelings for him. Perhaps it had only been an infatuation, a flirtation, like with Dr. Eustis. Or . . . or perhaps she was too practical to allow herself to pine for something that could not be.

She pulled her head back and looked at Washington. She didn't have to pretend with him. He knew who she was; he was handsome and full of good humor. So then—

"Apologies, my lady, but I believe I am next on your list of engagements?" Philip Hamilton, hands clasped behind his back, words free of slurring, a gentleman to match any in the room, stood before her.

"Forgive me, but you are . . . ?" she said.

His brow furrowed.

"I hardly recognized you without a flask to your lips."

The puzzled expression on his face faded, and he patted his front pocket. "That can be remedied."

"Careful, Mr. Hamilton. Surely public inebriation is not the way the son of Colonel Alexander Hamilton is to behave."

"Is that so? Is there a rulebook I don't know about? It seems the very one in need is the only one without this 'son of Hamilton rulebook.'"

She laughed, and her hands released themselves from Washington's at the same time as she remembered he was there. She felt him hold on a second longer than he should before letting her go.

"Thank you, Miss Burr." Washington bowed and set her hand in Philip's, not once looking her in the eye—for which she was ashamed to be grateful.

But the instant he left, she longed to call him back. The ballroom buzzed with gentlemen and ladies in coats with tails and dresses with lace and faces flushed from wine and keeping apace with the music. As a pair, Theodosia Burr and Philip Hamilton were no different from all the others, and yet they were entirely different from all the others.

Children of two prominent men with a long history of transitioning from friend to soldier to colleague to rival, currently at the height of very public opposition. And here she was, her hand in the enemy's. With no movement save for the darting of her eyes, Theodosia surveyed the room, those closest to her on the ballroom floor and those farthest in chairs set against the mirrors inlaid in the satinwood walls. All were watching.

Her hand grew clammy inside her white glove as her mind churned on the two equally flawed options before her: to decline Philip's hand or to accept. Excusing herself now, in front of all these high-society eyes, including the judging Lucinda's, would humiliate Philip and paint her as coldhearted or worse. Yet accepting would be the ultimate insult to her father and everything he believed.

The drumbeat of her heart echoed in her temples as she latched her hand around Philip's and lifted her chin in what she hoped was a mildly patronizing way, reasoning that a rejection would incite more gossip than acceptance. At least in this, she, a Burr, could be seen as rising above the pettiness and fulfilling her societal role, which would be exactly how she would explain it to her father.

Only then did she settle her eyes on Philip and see his relief. Facing one another, their bodies were mirror images despite all else being at odds. She extended her arm, and he curled his hand around hers. He tightened the distance between them to wind his other arm around her, and she almost withdrew for fear of where his fingers might land, for perhaps a humiliation of her was his aim, but she felt them settling in their rightful place in the middle of her back. Her fingertips pressed into the muscles of his shoulder.

Philip wiggled her arm, trying to loosen her tight, perfect formation. "You give new meaning to the word statuesque, Miss Burr."

"My apologies, Mr. Hamilton. Seeing as how you are accustomed to women of a much looser sort." She flopped like a rag doll, but he was quick, pulling his arms taut to keep her upright. He answered her teasing challenge by bringing her in so close that the laces on his breeches grazed the ribbon dangling from the high waist of her gown.

She heard the sharp intake of his breath.

The first note played, and they retreated to a proper distance. She peered up at him to find his cheeks rosy and beads of sweat dotting his upper lip.

Philip Hamilton—nervous.

He glided forward, and she followed. Years of instruction befitting their station meant no words needed to leave their lips to execute each required step, the same as with Washington. Yet with Philip, Theodosia had the sensation of moving effortlessly as if her shoes were skates carving through ice. Her skirt swept across the wood floors, and with each turn, she fixed her eyes not on the elaborate scrolled pediments above the doorway or the carved mantels above the fireplaces or the dentil-molded cornices but squarely on Philip. The arch of his eyebrow was a silent question, asking if he had impressed her. Perhaps the depth of his skill was a surprise, but it took a lot more than that to impress her. On the next whirl, she propelled her body, urging him to spin to the right instead of the left. He did. He let her lead.

Philip Hamilton—unafraid.

"So how is Georgie boy?" he said.

Her heart seized in her chest. "Georgie?"

"Don't know quite how you managed it."

*Georgie.* After all she paid that newsboy . . .

"Why, I was just—" She searched for an explanation. She would wring his little neck for spilling her secret.

"Doing as your father asked by dancing with ripe old George Clinton. Your stomach must be lined with steel."

"I . . . What?"

"No need to pretend otherwise. We are both aware of the games our fathers are playing. Even here, tonight."

*Here. Tonight.* She recovered with an appropriate response. "Games with high stakes."

"Are they?"

"Of course."

"Hmm . . ." Philip said.

"What does that mean?"

"It means . . . 'hmm.' " He grinned, and the frustration he seemed prone to engender drew her brows together. "It means," he reiterated, "sometimes I wonder if the stakes exist simply because those with the loudest voices have planted them. Is everyone truly so far apart ideologically or is it purely ego and posturing?"

Theodosia pulled back.

"Sorry," Philip said. "I thought you were interested . . . no matter, shall we discuss the weather?"

"I am interested. I just didn't think you—"

"Had a brain?"

"Cared."

"I care about many things that may surprise you."

She cocked her head. "You have piqued my interest, Mr. Hamilton."

"At last. Finally you meet me at the place I have been since the day of the Nicholson salon."

Theodosia searched Philip's countenance, certain a jest must live somewhere in his words, in his tone, in the tilt of his head or lift of his eyebrows. She was wrong.

A silence filled the space between them, and they moved with ease about the dance floor. Despite her structured form, Theodosia began to relax.

They swirled past Lucinda Wilson, whose scowl almost made Theodosia laugh. She urged Philip to remain where they were, and after their next spin, Theodosia allowed the front of her body to meet Philip's.

Her purpose was to shock Lucinda, but it was her own skin that was flushed when she pulled back, realizing what she'd just done and how many she'd done it in front of.

"Ah, so she does exist," Philip said.

"Who?" Theodosia forced her voice to remain steady.

"The Theodosia I used to know."

"I'm sorry?"

"The one who challenged all the boys to a race across the pond behind the school. In November. We'd yet to have our first frost, and yet the little daredevil Theodosia insisted on strapping on skates."

"I reached the other side perfectly fine."

"Yes, but Benjamin Keene had to be pulled out with a rope."

"It isn't my fault Benjamin had a penchant for pie and an inability to accurately assess risk."

Philip laughed with the genuineness of someone on constant lookout for a reason to do so.

They settled into a rhythm with their feet, soon followed by the same with their words, reminiscing about Madame de Senat and her insistence on leading them in song each morning despite a voice that would incite howling in stray hounds; about Nathalie and her grimace upon eating "the sawdust you Americans call bread"; and about the day Theodosia's father arrived at the townhome on Partition Street to find Madame had overtaken both of the front rooms for the schoolhouse and moved Burr's papers to a small office on the third floor.

"He found the situation 'most disagreeable,'" Philip said. "I remember thinking I'd never quite seen someone's neck that particular shade of red before. I figured 'disagreeable' must mean something far more egregious than I thought."

"It was a lesson learned," Theodosia said. "Do not touch Papa's papers."

"A travesty!" Philip cried. "My backside still aches from the time I used one of Father's papers to draw a picture of Mother and me at our piano."

"Paper is a precious resource."

"Especially when the front contains a letter meant for General Washington."

"Ooh, tell me you didn't."

"I did. Not even on purpose. Though he never believed me. I was quite the trickster then."

"Only then?"

"Certainly, Miss Burr. I am nearly a graduate of Columbia College. All grown and proper. Just like you."

"Like me?"

"I believe you are more like me than you may yet know."

"Then all is truly lost," Theodosia said in jest despite the heat rising from her neckline.

The conversation ebbed and flowed like the waters outside her bedroom window and made her feel just as at home. With each turn of her heels, Theodosia found herself wanting another. When Philip abruptly pivoted and swept her in a dip so low they both nearly tumbled to the floor. Laughter bubbled up and out in a manner she scarcely allowed even in the confines of her room. The snort that accompanied Philip's deep chortle sent her into a fit. All heads turned their way.

Her chest seized as she sought out her father. He had not yet returned to the party.

Theodosia released Philip's hand, gave a quick curtsy, and casually but urgently strode to the far corner of the room. Philip followed.

"Don't tell me she's gone already?" he asked. "Our bold, young Theodosia."

They stood beside a table with plates of hors d'oeuvres. He rambled through, fingers picking up a slice of salted fish, nudging a rolled ham, sorting through a round of mutton topped with a pickle.

She pressed her gloved hand to her brow. "Like you said, grown and proper. We all must grow up."

He chose the mutton and bit into it. Then spat it out into his handkerchief.

"Or at least some of us do," she said, though her smile betrayed her.

Philip unearthed his flask and took a swig.

Theodosia yearned to partake, but whatever spell had overtaken her on the dance floor had been broken. She was a Burr. And he a Hamilton. This room was full of people watching for precisely that reason. A polite dance might be explained, but dancing in succession as they had and with such visible enjoyment of each other was another matter entirely. She had provided far too much gossip already.

She infused a gravity in her tone. "In truth, are nights of carousing all that your life is to be? Our families' political philosophies may differ, but your father's a great man. Great things are to be expected of his son."

"Most of all by him."

"But do you not want to succeed?"

Philip did not meet her eye.

"I see," she said.

"I see, what?"

"It's simple." Theodosia threaded her fingers together in front of her stomach. "It's the opposite. You don't want to fail, and the surest way to do that is to not try. That's the boy I once knew. The one who would rather tell a silly rhyme than complete an arithmetic problem in front of the entire class."

Philip pointed toward Washington Irving. "Isn't that what he does? Silly rhymes?"

"Jealous, Mr. Hamilton?"

"Yes, Miss Burr, I am."

He tucked his flask back in his pocket and extended his hand. She could not accept. Not again.

And yet, she did.

All eyes remained on them through one more dance and then another, and Theodosia felt an unexpected closeness to her mother, having a small glimpse into the level of scrutiny she and her father must have endured.

On a pause in the music, Philip's arms tugged at Theodosia as he leaned back to whisper to a young man who had been a spectator all evening. Then he tipped his head toward Angelica, who was now dancing with Washington.

"What was that about?" Theodosia asked.

"Watch," Philip said.

The man raked his hand through his wavy hair and stepped onto the dance floor. He interrupted Angelica and Washington, and her face brightened, reminding Theodosia of the girl who had been her childhood friend. As the next song began, Angelica dipped her head in thanks to Washington and allowed the new gentleman to take her hand.

The smile on Angelica's face remained, though as she and the young man passed by Philip and Theodosia, her eyes shot daggers at her brother. Yet her laughter could soon be heard, filing away the sharp edges on their next passing.

Philip shook his head. "My sister doesn't believe in equality when it comes to meddling."

"She fancies this gentleman?" Theodosia asked.

"Does Adams fancy his own arse?" Philip's smirk was quickly wiped away by a look of fear.

"I assure you, on that, your household and mine agree."

"No, it's not that. Just . . . perhaps don't mention anything to my sister? She already believes I can't keep a secret."

"With good reason, it would seem."

Philip looked at her intensely. "Tell me a secret, Miss Burr."

She laughed. "Did you not hear what you just said? I'm to trust you with a secret?"

"How about I go first?"

She shrugged, then imagined the scolding that would come had her father been there to see. To see everything.

Philip reeled her in so that his lips skimmed her cheek. The room narrowed to just the two of them. "I wish the night would not end."

Everything stopped. The din of the music, the chatter of conversation, the clinking of glass, the rhythm of their feet, the thoughts in Theodosia's mind.

Except one.

*Me too.*

A round of applause brought Nathalie to Theodosia's side. The former signaled the end of the party and the latter the reappearance of Theodosia's father.

There was no more music to cover the sound of Theodosia's heart thudding beneath her rib cage. She placed her hand high on her chest, pressing to contain the life bursting inside. Her gaze met Philip's, and she saw her own truth living in his eyes.

"Goodnight, Mr. Hamilton," she said, stepping back and raising her voice for those nearest to hear. "You are every bit the scoundrel my father says you are. As bad as your own."

With a cock of his head and the quickest of winks he replied, "Well, then I have a ways to go because I was aiming for worse."

"Goodnight, Mr. Hamilton," she repeated.

"It was," he whispered.

Nathalie placed her arm on Theodosia's and guided her across the room. Theodosia knew her friend better than anyone, and so she knew that all Nathalie longed to say remained barely contained within her vocal cords.

Burr met them both, his own eyes shining, presumably at seeing such pleasure in his girls. Though that would change if he knew the reason behind it. Thanks were given to Mr. and Mrs. Clinton, and the trio joined up with Washington, who was waiting for them at the bottom of the ornate stairs.

The actions at the start of the evening played in reverse as Washington assisted Nathalie and Theodosia into the carriage. The ride home brimmed with palpable excitement from all with the exception of Washington.

His stop preceded theirs, and as he exited, he tipped his hat toward Theodosia. "A true pleasure to see you enjoying yourself." He meant every word, and once again, Theodosia was grateful for her friend.

The carriage began to move, and Nathalie's fingers twisted through Theodosia's, cutting off circulation. Theodosia knew a long night revisiting all that happened lay ahead.

She wished the horses would pick up speed.

Finally, Theodosia's fingers blue, the carriage entered through the gates of Richmond Hill. Nathalie raced for the stairs ahead of Theodosia, who had barely crossed the threshold when her father drew her aside. Disappointment slackened her posture, yet he didn't notice.

"It is all but done," he said with a hunger in his eyes.

"What is?" she asked, desperate for it to wait till morning.

"The ballot. I'm to be on the ballot."

"For governor? How wonderful, Papa." She patted his arm as if to excuse herself, eyes set on the staircase.

"No, not governor."

"Not the . . ." Theodosia faced him. "Then what?"

"The election."

"You mean—"

Burr clasped a hand around each of Theodosia's forearms. "Vice president. We are on our way, Miss Priss. From this moment forward, there can be no mistakes. Not a single one."

*"I wish the night would not end."*

Her father embraced her, and the door opening inside Theodosia's chest slammed shut.

# CHAPTER 12

$A$ARON BURR, VICE PRESIDENT.

Theodosia rolled the words over in her mind. They had been there once before. She had not expected their return.

Her father commanded the chair behind his mahogany desk, his cheeks rose-red with energy, his eyes bright, his black hair perfectly tucked and secured with a black ribbon at the nape of his neck. He sat tall and straight as always, yet in the days since the Clintons' party, he seemed to fully inhabit his body, making use of space he hadn't in years.

She found herself doing the opposite. Uncomfortable in her own skin, restless, filled with apprehension over her father's plans yet unable to focus. Perhaps that was because her mind kept wandering to places her body could not . . . to the party, the dance, Philip.

"None of your usual speaking like a book, Theo," Nathalie had said that night as she'd dragged Theodosia into her bedroom, full of questions about how she'd come to dance with Philip. How she'd kept dancing with Philip. How she'd smiled, laughed, shined with Philip.

All feelings Theodosia's father had pillaged from her with his news. His warning against making a single mistake had left her numb.

"Theo!" Nathalie had said, her body as full of spring as her voice. "You should have seen Lucinda's face! You and Philip twirling like paramours. What did he say? What did you say? How did his hands feel against—"

"Splendid," Theodosia had said, her mind finally snapping back like a whip. "Then I do have a future as a thespian."

"No." Nathalie had shaken her head. "No, no, no! You cannot ask me to believe that was all pretend."

"Yes," Theodosia had said carefully. "I can. And because you're my sister, fully aware of Papa's temperament, you will believe. Enjoying the company of Philip Hamilton is a much greater defiance than a girlish skate across suspect ice."

"So you *did* enjoy it!"

"Nathalie, please!"

Nathalie's eyes had filled with disappointment. "Fine, as you wish, but I don't agree." She'd hugged Theodosia in understanding and hadn't spoken of it since.

Neither had Theodosia. Thinking, well, that was another thing entirely.

She'd been doing so in the days since and even now as she fanned herself with the newspaper she'd been failing to concentrate on.

At his desk, her father continued to write, head down but seeing everything. "Completed your review of the day's news? I look forward to a full report."

"As do I," she muttered, ignoring his subsequent scolding in the form of a profound throat clearing. Instead, she stood and walked to the window. The air in the study hung heavy. She would have to ask Nancy to open these windows first thing now that the calendar had turned to June, bringing with it the heat of the summer sun and the prolonged light-filled days of her father running for the second-highest position in the country.

It wasn't an honor bestowed on him without merit. He'd achieved what many thought impossible by gaining Republican control of the state assembly. Such political prowess came not through intimidation, bribery, or brawn, but from an awareness of the wants and needs—and egos—of others. He deftly negotiated to secure the ends he sought. He understood his friends as well as his enemies, though he preferred to categorize opponents as fellow contenders, since wants and needs of contenders might align given the right circumstances. As they did here, but with an outcome that was not his original aim.

She raised the window sash, letting in a warm breeze that carried a hint of salt and earthiness from the river estuary.

Her father didn't notice. His pen scratched against parchment, his pursuit of the vice presidential office darkening the page with every stroke. She pictured Philip's father in a similar position, with his pen working to block her father's. Such had become the way in the past few years, and not just between the Burrs and Hamiltons.

New York City brimmed with influential post–Revolutionary War heroes turned politicians. Each the head of his own family. Each determined to capitalize on the benefits of a hard-won war. Each intent on cementing a long and prosperous ancestral line. Landholdings going back generations gave the Livingston family wealth, grounding, and substantial sway. The Clintons, from humbler ranks yet acquiring wealth and a solid reputation thanks to the war, were not the ruling elite but defenders of "the middling class." And then there was Hamilton and the wealthy Schuyler family into which he had married. In ruling New York, these factions were rivals as often as they were allies.

As Theodosia's father regrettably conceded, the Livingstons had numbers, the Clintons had power, and the Schuylers had Hamilton.

Yet now, the Livingstons and Clintons had Burr.

She watched him work. Industrious and determined. This must have been how Nathalie saw her. No wonder she'd been so buoyed at the thought of Theodosia actually enjoying herself.

But this *was* her father's enjoyment. Despite the reputation it gave him. He'd long been seen as—and often criticized for being—a moderate working with both parties, at times refusing to back a political candidate and align himself one way or another. While he'd gained new attention and respect due to his state assembly success, that wasn't the sole reason he'd been asked to accept the second position on the presidential ballot.

The prominent families, feeling rebuffed and insulted by Hamilton since the end of the war, were aligned in their efforts to defeat him and his Federalists—and not just in the office of governor but in the most influential realm possible. This was no easy task as Hamilton's ties to George Washington and the national government had caused his prominence in postwar politics to soar. But George Clinton was motivated.

Hamilton—being enamored of General Washington and the majestic sensibility he brought to the presidency—had sought to embed the expectation of such noble dignity in all political positions, pushing to make social appearances a determining factor for consideration. Thus, Clinton, with his humble beginnings, often came under attack.

Clinton and the others backing Burr—former friend and one-time political ally of Hamilton—would both punish Hamilton and send a message about who would be in control of New York.

Yet it would be her father who would suffer the consequences of failure.

"Papa," Theodosia started, her words dying in her throat.

"Yes," he replied, his pen still scratching.

"It's just . . . what I mean to say . . . inquire . . ."

His pen thudded against the table. "Firmness of mind, Theodosia. No wavering. Only then can you gain the confidence to surmount life's inevitable problems and inspire respect. Who will trust your opinions if you cannot trust them yourself?"

Her lips thinned, and she laid the newspaper on the edge of his desk. "All you've talked about for months is the governorship and what you could accomplish here, in your home state."

Burr's small eyes almost disappeared beneath his furrowing brow. "But this is my home *country*."

The national election was a much grander scale—perhaps the grandest. And grand was always what her father sought.

"We will win, Miss Priss. Everyone believes this to be so. Even Hamilton."

Her skin prickled at the name. She felt herself begin to fidget, and she gave up on being delicate. "That's what you thought last time, Papa."

Four years ago, in the presidential election of 1796, he'd received the fewest votes of all candidates and came in a disappointing fourth behind Adams, Jefferson, and Thomas Pinckney. And with her mother then dead two years, Theodosia had been the one left to console him and ease him through the nearly paralyzing headaches and depression.

Her father grimaced. "This will not be a repeat. The South will not snub me again."

The South?

*Alston.*

Theodosia pictured the letter with the South Carolina return address arriving the same day as the one she'd thought had come from Vanderlyn and waited for him to mention it.

But instead he picked up his pen. "Work to be done. A good reminder not to be late for your engagement this afternoon."

Theodosia sighed.

"The right salons offer opportunities for both advancement *and* merriment," her father said. "Your mother and I did exactly that. People couldn't get enough of her, Miss Priss."

Theodosia knew the stories as well as she knew the same ones would never be told about her.

Burr pressed his pen into the paper. "As I've said, we suspect the Wilsons are Federalist sympathizers. We may have a stronghold in the North, but only a fool assumes the status quo can never change. If the war has taught me anything, Theo, it is that nothing is better than having a spy on the inside."

Later that afternoon, upon entering the home of Lucinda Wilson, Theodosia suspected her father's biggest "contender" uttered similar words that very morning. For Angelica Hamilton was already seated, pouring a cup of tea for Lucinda's grandmother.

"Theo!" The cry came from one who appeared too diminutive to infuse it with such force.

"Caty." Theodosia's tension eased. Her friend's spirits were perpetually as bright as her ginger hair.

"Wicked thing!" Caty exclaimed. "I've a mind to reach for a switch! You've been in hiding since the Clintons' party. Honestly, to dance with Philip Hamilton and not tell me every last detail?"

Upon hearing her brother's name, Angelica's chin lifted. Theodosia's practiced restraint bequeathed no more than a polite smile despite the excitement swirling beneath her skin. "He was adequate. Missed a step or two, but otherwise acceptable."

Caty frowned. "But I thought . . . well, it appeared as though—"

Her father's "make no mistake" echoed in Theodosia's ears, and she downplayed the interaction, loud enough to be heard by the nearly dozen eavesdropping women, whose ages spanned at least three generations. "He had partaken of the drink? I suspect like most men he'd trained his feet to behave under such influence."

Caty issued a disappointed "oh" as confusion brought out a few feathery lines around her mouth.

Across from them, Anjelica nudged a stray curl out of her eyes. Her knowing look managed to simultaneously settle and unsettle Theodosia.

"No Nathalie?" Caty asked.

"Headache, apparently." That had been Nathalie's claim to Burr, though Theodosia had seen her dressing for an afternoon ride.

"My, my, sheep are herded faster than society ladies," came the sudden cry of Lucinda's grandmother. "In, in, sit, sit!"

The elder Mrs. Wilson waved her hand at the clusters of women filling the corners of the room. She tipped forward, perching her round bottom at the edge of her chair. Her bun, grayed and pulled back high on her head, released not a single strand or ringlet to frame her face. Her light skin and pure white embroidered gown appeared carefully orchestrated to create a neutral palette—one that focused all attention on her sapphire eyes.

"With haste! My tongue's like a cobra, waiting to strike." Mrs. Wilson shifted her skirts to reveal a magazine nestled in her lap. The latest version of *From the Fairer Sex*. The one with Theodosia's story inside. She'd yet to see, let alone hold, it. "This has been living on the tip since my granddaughter brought it to me."

"Brought for the recipes, Grandmother." Lucinda took the seat beside her. Her own blue eyes, not nearly as vibrant as her grandmother's, scolded the same as her words. "Our family's own is featured in the—"

"*Pfft!* Banality for someone else's salon. Not a Wilson's."

Theodosia swallowed down her laugh. She and Caty claimed the two satin-covered seats across from Mrs. Wilson, where Theodosia would have the clearest view of the magazine.

Lucinda pursed her lips as her grandmother curled back the cover to present the drawing of a young woman in a high-waisted gown and hat adorned with feathers, hiding behind a paneled folding screen. She held the same balloon-legged pantaloon and stiff, corset-style jacket that the women in the shop on the opposite side of the screen were wearing.

Theodosia silently praised how well the illustrator had interpreted her description of women's fashion in the year 1900. She longed to hear what Nathalie thought. Surely she'd bring a copy home unprompted?

Mrs. Wilson held up the magazine, slipped on her reading glasses, and began: "Claire rubbed her eyes as if a simple good scrubbing could rearrange the image before her. But when she deposited her hands back by her sides, nothing had changed. A man in a square-necked tunic and knickers sat before the pub's hearth, knitting a scarf. Another was perched at the bar, a pint in one hand and a baby not more than six months in the other. And then there were the women. Four of them, Black and white, at a table, drinks of pink and orange and green liquid before them, animatedly discussing the solution to the lackluster choices in the upcoming presidential election: a woman on the ballot."

Mrs. Wilson paused. "Not to ruin it for those of you who have yet to read, but Claire becomes that candidate. Hilariously." She bounced, barely contained within her wingback chair—the visual embodiment of all Theodosia worked to keep hidden. "Yet also importantly. I'm aiming to visit the physician for a tonic because this, my dear friends, this is a future I wish to live long enough to see."

"But Grandmother . . ." Lucinda's lips twisted into a sneer. "It's unnatural. A woman running for the office of president? Who's to care for her children?"

"And instruct the servants?" said an older woman with a paunchy belly.

Caty huffed beside Theodosia and whispered, "From the looks of her, she's not fetched so much as a sewing needle herself. Old versus the young. I'm constantly fighting with Mother and Uncle Alexander about releasing our servants."

This surprised Theodosia, yet she maintained her neutral expression.

Another young woman added, "And organize the household?"

"Not to mention host the parties?" That was from Mrs. Clinton. The success of her recent gathering incited murmurs of assent from several of the women in the salon.

Mrs. Wilson's intense blue eyes scrutinized the room, and Theodosia clasped her hands together as sweat broke out across the nape of her neck.

"I sit here astonished and embarrassed by you. For you," Mrs. Wilson said. "Awareness may be lacking for you girls with skin still as smooth as kid gloves, but those of us with sagging bosoms and popping joints know the truth. I will not allow us to pretend to forget the farms worked, funds raised, sick cared for, accounts kept, and all manner of horror witnessed during this war. *By women.* All *men* are created equal? A credo we should not abide by without amendment. Weaker in physical strength does not, ought not, and cannot dictate weakness in thought or liberty."

She slapped the magazine shut against her lap. The tick of the grandfather clock provided the only sound, which made the silence that much more pronounced.

And then Kitty Few cleared her throat. "My William reads to our children."

"Reading?" Mrs. Clinton said. "Far from scandalous. To be sure he's not knitting them a sweater."

"No, but he's dressed them. Bathed them." Mrs. Nicholson gasped, but Kitty did not quiet. "And why shouldn't a father do so? Why should his role end after siring?"

Caty looped her arm through Theodosia's. "I'd run for president and take this one as my vice."

She winked, and Theodosia feigned shock, overdoing it just enough to align with those in favor of the intent of her story but not so strongly that she couldn't be seen to represent the more conservative views in the room. Inside, she'd never felt more alive.

Her tale was the talk of the salon.

Her tale had the salon talking.

No insufferable games or poems or weather reports. No quibbling about the correct way to tie a bow or groom unruly children. Politics and women, together. All because of her story of a young woman waking up from a nap only to find herself transported one hundred years into a future where women worked professions traditionally belonging to men, where women voted, where women and men were equals. Though she had to hold her tongue, the discussion was exactly the sort she had always wished would occur. And a bit surprisingly, her supporters outnumbered her dissenters.

"Amateurish, if you ask me," Lucinda said.

To which, Angelica sniped, "I'm certain no one did."

"I didn't," Caty said.

"Me neither," Hannah Gallatin added.

"It's disrespectful to her family," Lucinda said. Her puckered face deserved the same scolding Theodosia received for scowling from age eight to twelve.

But it was Mrs. Wilson who interceded. "Something you are dangerously close to being all too familiar with, my dear."

With the reading completed, conversations erupted all over the room. Pockets of women seated on yellow floral box sofas, in high-backed armchairs, in front of the tall windows facing the street, with teacups in hand and tarts to come, all engaging in dialogue sparked by Theodosia's story. Yet for such to occur so quickly and with such fervor meant the idea of women sharing the full breadth of men's privilege was not an obscure notion—it must have already lived in the female mind. In these influential and prominent females' minds.

*If only Papa could see this!*

She must tell him. He must understand that taking a position in favor of the education of the female sex would not deter those from his party but bring ones to it.

Women. It would bring women. Who couldn't vote. But their husbands could.

Theodosia's thoughts circled around this the entire salon, especially when conversation eventually gave way to the best summer fabrics and upcoming celebrations marking the Fourth of July.

So occupied was she that Theodosia found herself one of the last to depart. Caty pecked her cheek. "We must have tea soon—you, me, and Nathalie. I believe for that her headache will disappear." She leaned in and whispered, "Especially if it's less tea and more claret? Tell her I inquired of her and rub it in that she missed the most spirited salon this city has *ever* seen. "

"Do you truly believe? Ever?"

"Lands sake, bests any quilting bee! And we have our little Miss P. to thank!"

Caty twirled into the hall, and a bit of bile flooded Theodosia's throat. While her father's nickname for her rarely left his lips outside their home, his usage was beyond her control. He even addressed her as such the other night in front of the commodore. What a foolish thing she'd done for something as important as this!

She straightened her spine and approached Mrs. Wilson and, unfortunately, Lucinda. She queued behind Angelica, who had just finished expressing her appreciation for the afternoon. As Angelica stepped aside, Theodosia issued her own gratitude.

"Nonsense, it was a delight to have the two of you." Mrs. Wilson spread out her hands as if to encompass both Angelica and Theodosia, reminding Theodosia of why her father had insisted she come. But this equal appreciation offered no hint of the Wilsons' political leanings. "I don't give a bean for what scuttlebutt goes about. We would not be here bickering over anything but the king's penchant for levies and firing arms had it not been for your fathers." She jutted her round chin. "Posturing now? Well, perhaps they earned it. Doesn't excuse it, mind you. They are grown and should know better. But proud to the bone they each must be of you." She interlaced her fingers and rested them against her waist. "Try as we might, our control over who our children become has its limits."

Theodosia politely pretended not to see the insult registering on Lucinda's face.

Apparently feeling none of Theodosia's reticence, Angelica said condescendingly, "Lucinda, wonderful wording of your cake's ingredients."

"Pie." Lucinda's nostrils flared.

"Forgive me." Angelica placed her hand on her breast. She then turned and, surprisingly, settled her arm in the crook of Theodosia's. "Shall we?"

The pressure of Angelica's arm against her own harkened back to the schoolhouse but had none of the ill intent. Still, Theodosia assessed her with skepticism. Yet instead of malice, Theodosia noted amusement in Angelica's eyes and could feel the excitement in her stride.

Out the door and a full-on burst of energy infused Angelica's hold on Theodosia. "Shall we walk? If you're not otherwise expected?"

Being expected was a constant state when Theodosia's father was in residence at Richmond Hill. There seemed to be no newspaper clipping he couldn't wait to quote, no theory regarding Federalist conspiracies he couldn't refrain from espousing, no strategic move that didn't require her opinion with haste.

"I have a bit of time," Theodosia said, curious as to Angelica's intentions.

She followed Angelica's lead down this street near the Nicholson home but several blocks north of the Burr town house on Partition Street. The clearing of once-abundant maple, beech, and oak trees left only intermittent shade, and perspiration gathered at the back of Theodosia's neck. A horse attached to a carriage clomped ahead, becoming the beat to which they traveled, slowly fading as the animal's considerable haunches outpaced their own.

"A fan would be nice," Angelica said. "Still, I much prefer the heat to mounds of snow. You?"

Theodosia wasn't one for small talk, but fortunately, as she remembered, Angelica was. She filled the air between them with topics of the weather and the ripeness of strawberries coming into season, all the while in good humor, softened considerably since the incident at Madame de Senat's despite Theodosia not apologizing directly.

Though they were children the last time they'd been alone together, Angelica's voice began to lull Theodosia, recalling the comfort and trust that once existed between them. But not all. Theodosia remained far too much her father's daughter to completely relax her worries over Angelica's aim.

They turned east, down a narrow street unfamiliar to Theodosia. The pebbled walk gave way to coarsely cut planks of wood laid end to end between the buildings and the road.

Angelica tightened her grip on Theodosia's arm. "Do tell, Theo
. . ." A sharpness supplanted her soothing tone. "How did your
suitors compare?"

*Vanderlyn.*

*Washington.*

*Mr. Sour Milk.*

"I'm sorry?" Theodosia said nonchalantly, her hackles rising.

"Suitors," Angelica repeated, angling them past a brick ware-
house whose windows appeared long boarded up. "At the Clintons'
party?"

*Philip.*

"Suitors?" Theodosia studied the street before them, alarm setting in as she realized she'd not be able to return to where they
began alone.

"No need to worry."

*Despite it feeling to the contrary?*

Angelica patted her arm. "You remained your most agreeable
self. No favoritism in play, an equally charming admirer for all."

Theodosia resisted the urge to extract her arm. "*Partner* to boys
simply moving from one girl to the next, as transitory as the flush
from a good madeira. You know as well as anyone how dance part-
ners come to be. Not all of my choosing."

"Not all, but some?"

Theodosia feigned a stumble on a loose plank, her self-preserva-
tion instincts kicking in. "Hmm . . . perhaps we've made a wrong
turn?" Up ahead, two dogs tussled in the middle of the street, their
growls justifying Theodosia's attempt to turn around. "I fear we've
strayed far enough that our delayed return will leave Papa as mad
as a March hare."

Angelica drew Theodosia even closer. "Lack of trust between
Burr and Hamilton may surpass that of Red Coat and Yankee. But
let's risk it, just this once?"

The mangy white dog pounced, and the other, a scruffy mutt
with matted tan fur, released a high-pitched whine.

Angelica pulled Theodosia down an even narrower street, too slim and winding to answer to the sun. Like draping a blanket over one's head, darkness fell. Buildings of brick became squat frames of splintering wood, which left none for the sidewalk, and Theodosia's foot landed in dirt.

She steeled herself against her thudding heart. "I noticed you had a turn with Thomas Rathbone, friend of your brother's, is he?"

"Then my brother is on your mind?"

"No more than my cheese and toast at breakfast," Theodosia playfully challenged right back.

"Just as forgettable?"

"Inconsequential. No bearing on my normal routine."

"I see. If that's so, then this will have just been a lovely excursion."

All around them were crooked timber-framed homes and buildings in ever-worsening states of deterioration.

"Quite," Theodosia said, unsure of Angelica's meaning. "But we should be heading back."

"Certainly." Anjelica's feet began to move—not to retread their path but to head deeper in. "Though I'm still left wondering."

"Where we are? Because I've been—"

"About the party. You never answered my question about the gentlemen with whom you shared the dance floor. Truly not a one you'd care to see in the light of day? I admit, even the most stubborn among us may find ourselves smitten under candlelight. And a truly deft partner with a handsome grin may keep a beat in our toes and a lightness in our step all the next day . . . perhaps longer?"

"I defer to you. My experience is limited."

"No, Theo, it's not." Angelica grabbed ahold of Theodosia's shoulders and spun her around. "But let us assume for purposes of good-natured debate that it is so."

Before them sat a dilapidated building with a patched roof, slanted chimney, and splintering wood door. Through the smudged front windows, Theodosia could only see the tops of a dozen or so small heads with hair of gold and brown and black and every shade between.

Angelica continued, "How would your definition of suitor change if I were to describe a young man in soaring spirits post an evening he'd initially been dreading?"

Into the window frame came the dark unruly mop that had occupied Theodosia's vision in the Clintons' ballroom. And mind's eye more times than she cared to admit since.

"The hard edges presented to some, one in particular, suddenly malleable," Angelica said. "Even solicited an hour-long oration on a career in the law."

"Philip entreated such of his father?" Theodosia faced Angelica. "I can hardly believe it."

Theodosia searched Angelica's eyes and found no hint of exaggeration. Just Angelica's determination.

"Neither could I until learning the reason." Angelica kept her eyes on Philip, and Theodosia, eagerly, turned to do the same. "Father had just heard what transpired in his absence at the Clintons' party. The censure barely took root before Philip proved himself more adept in understanding Father than I gave him credit for. He asked if Father took him for a fool. For Philip would not play the pawn in a Burr game of chess. When the young Miss Theodosia Burr sought to incite gossip through societal ranks by offering him her hand, he called her bluff and showed how magnanimous the Hamiltons could be. Then he further pacified Father by asking him to recount his opening argument in the Levi Weeks murder trial."

Theodosia smiled, for perhaps some truth lay in Philip's assertion that the two were alike. Knowing how swiftly tales spread, she'd promptly told her own father about dancing with Philip, painting it as an unavoidable circumstance and one that proved the Burrs, unlike the Hamiltons, were above pettiness. Her father had accepted her explanation and even praised her quick assessment of the negative attention and gossip that might have resulted. Maintaining appearances was necessary—vital—she'd said, repeating her father's words back to him.

Philip appeared equally as skilled, placating his own father by claiming interest in the trial that three months earlier had brought a different Hamilton and Burr together—on the same side as defenders. She imagined Colonel Hamilton's criticisms of his co-counsel to be just as harsh and blustering as her father's had been.

Inside the ramshackle schoolhouse, a young girl in a dress patched with more care than the roof finished speaking and beamed at Philip, who began to clap with gusto.

"What's he doing here?" Theodosia asked.

"Delaying the inevitable, I suppose. He comes to this schoolhouse every week, sometimes twice."

"But what could he possibly—"

"*A treat from one so sweet!*" Philip cried. "*But a reminder, Josephine, the one lesson I truly mean, 'tis not even mine, but, oh, what a find! From my father it comes . . .*" He lowered his voice, "*which admitting's no fun, not for this son. But when it comes to speech, e-nun-ci-ate and gleefully share what you create!*"

Theodosia laughed heartily. "He teaches?"

Angelica noted Theodosia's positive response. "Reads to them, writes poems with them."

"Even the girls?"

"Especially the girls. They've taken a liking to him, for some reason." Angelica goaded Theodosia, but when she didn't take the bait, Angelica added, "The story in that magazine is causing quite a stir."

"Is it?" She focused on a loose thread at her waist.

"Theodosia, you were taught to speak your mind! Why is your mouth nailed shut when I know you have much to say on the subject?"

"It's not my place—"

"It's exactly your place. I was there, remember? You weren't raised to play a rendition of 'Row, Row, Row Your Boat' or ensure the larder was stocked. You were raised to converse with men like George Washington and the Marquis de Lafayette."

"And the judgment that accompanies it isn't lost on me," she found herself admitting. "I see the puzzled faces, the disapproving looks."

"They think you're a spoiled brat and high on yourself. And, well, perhaps you are."

Theodosia's lips parted in surprise.

Angelica waved her hand. "With good reason. Your pursuits threaten them. A judgment of the lives they're leading."

"The lives they are told to lead," Theodosia countered, debating how far to go. But the woman before her was more Angelica than she was Hamilton. "Education could change that, but the women have to be open to it. They must demand it. Men won't give it over willingly."

"Your father did. Philip does. If Burr and Hamilton can be in agreement, if one of each can walk together on this fine day despite a recent discord, perhaps anything is possible?"

"Perhaps . . ." Shame filled Theodosia at Angelica being the one to allude to her indiscretion. "I have been remiss, Angelica. I was wrong to say such a thing at Madame de Senat's. And not only because it was in front of young John. Families are complicated worlds. I'm not fit to judge." She inhaled a breath. "Please accept my truest apology."

"Thank you, Theo. It takes a strong restitution to admit wrong. Especially to do so of one's own accord, not because one's hand was forced. Not like my father." Angelica sighed and tilted her head toward Philip. "He saved them, you know."

"The children?"

"Our parents. When the truth came out . . . when my father facilitated the truth coming out . . . I swear I wouldn't have been surprised to see Mother with a strap in hand striking him from cheek to heel. Yet that's not her way. Her disappointment scars deeper than any weapon could. Father still aches from it."

As well he should for having such a torrid affair and inviting all to be a part by publishing every detail in that self-indulgent Reynolds Pamphlet.

Despite knowing her father would be livid at the notion of her befriending a Hamilton, Theodosia nodded in sympathy. This reconnection meant something to her. She hoped the same was true for Angelica. Even if it could only be this once.

Angelica blinked away the moisture in her eyes. "If it weren't for their shared adoration of Philip, I don't know that my family would be intact. He binds us all. My mother's firstborn, my father's hope for a lasting legacy. My very best friend. How he tries to please all however he can . . . like with Thomas. You asked about Thomas?"

Theodosia nodded.

"At least he ensured I got the one dance. As soon as Father heard that bit of gossip from the ball, well, let's just say a Hamilton-Rathbone union will not atop any invitations." Love and pain combined to shape the angular features of Angelica's face, a softer version of Philip's but equally as handsome. "But Philip . . . my brother is a better man than he will let himself believe." She looked deep into Theodosia's eyes. "Do not hurt him."

Theodosia's countenance fought to remain as neutral as the dust beneath her feet. Did Angelica not hear her own words? Philip couldn't be a friend to a Burr, let alone anything more.

The high-pitched shouts and pleas of children inside the school chimed like church bells. Philip held out his palms. When the noise settled down, he said, "Let's start with a passage that speaks to the place we each find ourselves in, here, today."

"*Love goes toward love as schoolboys* . . . and girls . . . *from their books.*

*But love from love, toward school with heavy looks.*"

He grinned. "Not *this* school, though, certainly."

His pleasure at being with these children brought a lightness to Theodosia, but still the recitation reminded her of his very different one at the Nicholson salon, one that spoke to the pain he—perhaps his whole family—held beneath the public facade, another way Burr and Hamilton were aligned. Theodosia had not cried since the night her mother died. Yet a sudden swelling in her chest made her assert, "We should go."

Theodosia didn't wait for Angelica to respond, simply set off down the dirt street.

Angelica hurried after her, gently taking her arm and guiding her in the opposite direction. Theodosia allowed herself to be led away. But not without one last look through the window at Philip.

# Chapter 13

*Spies.* THEODOSIA KNEW THE WAR MIGHT not have been won without them.

Long Island's Culper spy ring passed vital information to General Washington on British troop movements, fortifications, and planned attacks. Men and at least one woman—Anna Smith Strong, who hung pieces of laundry on her clothesline to signal meeting locations—led double lives. Dangerous, full of great risk, and yet . . . exhilarating.

Or so she imagined.

For that was exactly how Theodosia felt with the second install-ment of her story publishing in *From the Fairer Sex* magazine. She remained unknown, a spectator like everyone else.

Theodosia picked at her plate of chipped beef and coleslaw. Nervous energy consumed her appetite.

"Sparingly, Theo," her father said, pointing the edge of his knife at her place setting. "Eat with care but do eat."

Madame de Senat, who joined for supper less often than usual, screwed up her face. "Monsieur Burr, is such necessary still?"

"Madame, you know my beliefs on the danger indulgent parents pose to children. Did not Mary Wollstonecraft herself assert that sentimentalization was a major defect in the education of daugh-ters? Young girls require the self-control that comes from, and I quote, 'the sober, steady eye of reason.'"

Madame nodded in consent. "Reason she now has. Both of them. And they are no longer girls."

Beside Theodosia, Nathalie smiled at her former governess. "But women who attend salons, where the magazine I introduced us all to is the first word off everyone's lips! My good judgment proven true. No other topic gained a foothold in any gathering this week."

Blood rushed to Theodosia's cheeks. She pushed her fork through the chipped beef and set it in her mouth, chewing slowly, to cover.

Burr set down his knife. "So that's why it was familiar. This morning, Mr. Gallatin mentioned an article his Hannah couldn't tear her eyes from. The last salon she'd attended, the women read it aloud, like a play."

Theodosia began to feel light-headed.

"Must be some pumpkins to incite talk in every spot from home to salon to tavern," her father said. "What do you make of it, Miss Priss?"

"Me?" Theodosia shoved another much larger bite into her mouth, and Nathalie turned to her, eyes quizzical, since she'd been the one to hand Theodosia the magazine, open to the story.

Burr shook his head. "I applaud you heeding my advice, but we don't want to turn fleshy."

Theodosia dabbed at her mouth with her napkin, ignoring Nathalie's stare. When no one spoke, Theodosia finally said, "I fear I'm not as well versed as most." The suspicion in Nathalie's gaze made her add, "I hear it's amateurish."

"All nature adores these stories, Theo," Nathalie said. "How you, especially, could not would surprise me as much as awakening to a sky of emerald."

"What is the fuss about, then, Nathalie?" Madame de Senat asked.

Nathalie's eyes lit up. "A mite extraordinary it is, Madame!" She plunked her elbows on the table. Madame clucked her tongue, Burr tapped his knife against his plate, and Nathalie quickly drew back her arms. "The author is quite clever. Her story is set in a future where women are educated same as men, hold office and jobs, and in all manner of life are commensurate with their male

counterparts. A rewriting of Thomas Jefferson's 'all men are created equal' to include women and individuals of all color hangs
framed on the wall of every establishment. The author could not
be bolder."

Burr's face twisted as Nathalie spoke. He pushed himself harder
against the oval back of his dining chair. "Or more reckless. Who
wrote this?"

"No one knows," Nathalie said. "Signed under a pen name of—"

"No consequence to us." Theodosia rushed to cut off Nathalie.
Sweat sprang from her every pore despite using the pseudonym of
"Miss Q" this time. She'd hoped her addendum would offer suffi-
cient misdirection: *"Now, ladies, when you mind those Ps and Qs,
you will be minding me."*

"Indeed," Burr said. "My dears, within the confines of our home
I couldn't be more explicit on the pursuit of education for you both.
Yet this publication is want of respect and foresight of thought to
advocate on behalf of such a position so publicly. I wouldn't con-
done even a veiled call in this critical hour, but one so devoid of
responsibility cannot be endorsed."

"But, sir," Nathalie said. "Is it not your belief and hope for all?"

"My mind and heart lay open to you." He held the gaze of each
woman at the table. "But we must take care with voicing opinions
on such an experimental view. Now is a vital point in our history,
my beloveds, and to emerge on the correct side in the long may
require sacrifice in the short. I trust as members of my household,
you will abide by my wishes on this and all related circumstance."

Her father reclaimed his fork and knife. Nathalie and Madame
de Senat did not break the silence that enveloped the table, but
they too reached for their utensils. Theodosia could not do the
same. Slight her hunger had been, but now she feared it might
never return.

Yet why should her father's declaration trouble her so?
Appearances were prized, she knew. Beliefs, when necessary, might
require restraint. That had all been core to his lectures.

But lately, "when necessary" had become synonymous with "always." Public perception seemed to be eclipsing the ideals her father held. The ones he instilled in her. The ones she now claimed as her own. Writing her story might have begun on a whim, but now she was devoted, invested, hoping to actually sway thoughts, positive that doing so was important. She knew her father would never approve of her name being directly linked as the author, but still, she'd expected him to support the ideals within. Disappointment darkened her heart at seeing this side of him, a side lying in wait until popular opinion emerged, a side that others spoke of, including Colonel Hamilton. Including Philip.

Theodosia slipped off her shoes. With the library facing north, its wood floors offered a refreshing coolness to her bare skin. She lingered in front of the dark cherry shelves, trailing her toe against the floor and a finger along the spines of the books that she'd read and those she longed to.

She made her way to the library after the departure of Madame de Senat. Here, Theodosia could avoid interrogation on the story in the magazine—and speculation about its author.

"My dearest Theo!" Her father waltzed in as if the whole city, the whole country, watched. And perhaps it did, if only in his mind. "So very alive in this room as you have always been. It's here where I'll pine for you when yours is no longer my life to share."

"Papa," she said. "That will never be. I'm not going anywhere."

"You will. We all do."

"Not soon." She pictured Philip at the schoolhouse. "Maybe not ever."

He set a hand on each of her shoulders. "That will not and cannot be if there is any goodness in this world, as it will reward my exceptional daughter with all she could possibly desire."

Theodosia's throat swelled. His affection for her could overwhelm as much as hers did back. Usually when she least expected it—when she was most annoyed by him. As she was now. That the

two things could happen simultaneously might be the true definition of family.

"Sit with me," he said, yet as she lowered herself into one of
the two chairs in the room that had survived the selling off of
furniture, he focused on her bare feet. For once, he refrained from
condemnation. "I'm indebted to you for quelling Nathalie's zeal-
ousness over that preposterous story at supper. Yet I fear my opine
fell harshly upon your ears."

Theodosia pressed the balls of her feet into the floor. "I understand though the summer heat descends, we must remain vigilant
until December."

What made the presidential election such a protracted affair was
that state legislatures were elected throughout the year, from April
to October. As these legislatures more often than not chose the
presidential electors, the state contests to determine them became
part of the national presidential campaign in all but name. When
Burr facilitated the win of his Republican slate in the New York
assembly election in May, he ensured that the legislature would
lean Republican in its party affiliation. The logical assumption was
that, as a state, New York would vote for Jefferson for president
since the legislature would choose the state's delegates to the electoral college.

The majority of states, eleven of the sixteen, followed this
same method for choosing delegates. In the remaining states,
voters chose the electors directly, and campaigns were effectively
fought over electors pledging themselves to one party and its
presidential candidates. With some states having a winner-take-
all system and others splitting electors among districts, powerful
politicians had been carefully watching their state's leanings and
enacting laws to change the voting structure to suit their desired
outcomes. Thus the partisanship of electors and of state legislatures remained a strong predictor of how those states would vote
in the presidential election, which would not conclude until the
final month of the year.

Theodosia nodded along as her father teased out the likely factions and paths to a win, yet her attention drifted. To the schoolhouse. To Philip.

The only sign her father gave that he noticed her inattention was the urgency infused into his words. "My warning to be circumspect in all debate is strong and to be heeded. I will rely on your attention in this regarding Nathalie's dialogue with those outside our home." He smoothed down the side of his hair, which grew more wiry with the addition of interloping grays. "Your counsel and discretion never fail me, and thus brings me to you now."

Like a dog well-trained, at this, Theodosia focused her attention.

"We have time to influence hearts and minds."

She crossed her feet at the ankles, fluffing her skirt to cover. "Influence how? Didn't even Abigail Adams concede that the Republican ballot had all but won with the Manhattan assembly election?"

Her father tented his fingers. "Predictions do lean toward a Republican win. Yet other interesting rumors abound. Of growing complaints and worries among our own party that Jefferson is soft and lazy, preferring his home in Monticello to the hard work of running the country. If such whispers contain truth, they may be a barometer of an election on the verge of taking a turn. The party indeed spread word of a paired ticket with Jefferson as president and yours truly as his second. But that need not be so."

Theodosia tried to reconcile her father's words with what she knew to be true. *Honorable.* "But you agreed to be his vice president."

"I agreed to join him on the ballot."

"Semantics cannot release you from a shared understanding. Even if it were so, the electoral college will not vote until December."

With an expression as pleased as if he'd moved his knight into attack position on a chessboard, he said, "And here we arrive at the opportunity such a lengthy process provides. With more contests to come, I'm thinking a journey through those states may be useful to us. With Jefferson remaining in Virginia until November, this offers a chance to remind the people who is on that ballot in the flesh. If that encourages a selection of electors inclined to be led by a northern Republican, well, then . . ."

"Do you not worry about backlash?" Theodosia stared at the man across from her, the seeds of anger planted at dinner taking root.

"What am I but a surrogate?" Her father acted the pawn. "As the presumptive vice president, I'll simply be advocating on behalf of dear Thomas."

"While actually seizing on your sudden political capital and making a run for president."

"One cannot be held responsible for the conclusions other minds make."

"As a result of backdoor deals."

Impatience flashed in her father's eyes. "No daughter of mine is naive enough to think Jefferson and Adams sit in their homes playing crambo all day. They sequester themselves in their home states to appear not to be personally campaigning, and yet the post has never been more active coming to and fro, enlisting others to campaign on their behalf. They direct all. My name is in letters just as bold on that ticket." Burr pressed his hands into his knees and stood. "Theodosia, what has years of numbers and language and all manner of study taught you?"

"That you do not value sleep as much as I."

A smile curved his lips. "Your jest masks your discomfort. A skill learned from your *petit pére*. Correct me if you must, but your education above all has proven that nothing is out of your grasp. Everything is open to you if you defy conventional thinking and pursue what your heart and mind tell you should be so." He crossed the short distance between them, himself now the chess piece in play. "If we work together toward a common goal, nothing is out of *our* grasp.

In this, Theo, with you by my side, we will prevail over that coward. He doesn't deserve this. You must see it? Hiding in Paris instead of firing a weapon and defending his country? Even Hamilton engaged in battle. Couldn't stop the arrogant little bastard."

Though her spine strained at the Hamilton slight, Theodosia couldn't pretend to disagree with her father regarding Jefferson, whose war years saw him ensconced in Paris after lingering in his majestic Virginian home, fleeing when the British attacked Charlottesville. Her father would have instantly assessed the prudent course and either led the charge or led his men to safety. No matter what may be said of him now, he was a soldier and a leader who adhered to a code of honor that Jefferson never allowed himself to be in a position to learn.

Her father reached for Theodosia's hand, holding it with as much care as if it still belonged to the newly born version of herself. "We will build on the legacy of my parents and grandparents, rest their souls. We will lead this still-fledgling nation." He bowed before her. "We will make your mother proud."

The tears that pooled in his eyes tightened Theodosia's chest.

"The country will be with us, Miss Priss. You will become the closest thing this new nation has to royalty, for, as a widower, who will President Burr have by his side? Only his beloved daughter. A young girl who lost her mother now grown into a remarkable woman who will be admired by all."

It was a speech she'd have said he'd practiced had she not understood the depth of her father's oration skills. He remained as impressive and persuasive as ever, and though her reservations held strong, his fervent conviction forced consideration. For now, all she said was, "Admiration is for statues."

He beamed. "How about 'followed'? And before you can argue, *not* blindly. With eyes wide open to all you represent."

Her. Theodosia Burr. If all came to be, if her father won the presidency, would she gain a true platform to present the ideas they both believed to the country? If the response to her story was an indication of how most would feel, then combined with her father's role as president and her role beside him . . . might it not open the door to real and necessary change?

"Good, Theo, good. Let your mind work the way it was designed to do. You could not remind me more of your mother." He lowered himself before her, entwining her hands in his. From that subservient position did he make his request.

"Successes aside, my popularity in the North is why the party put me on the ticket. The North is secured. But Jefferson is a Virginian, and he'll prove formidable in the states below it. The unfortunate truth is that the South will determine my fate."

Theodosia bristled. "Our future in the hands of codfish aristocracy."

"*Our.*" He kissed the back of her hand. "There's my girl."

She pulled her fingers from his and swatted his chest. "Don't act shocked. Indoctrination began in infancy. Now go on."

He grinned with the joy of someone declaring "checkmate."

"One state in particular holds much sway," he said. "South Carolina."

With South Carolina's legislature election being the final one to be held that fall, it was not yet known which way the state would lean in the presidential election. Both parties believed they had a solid chance of garnering its electoral college votes.

Burr lifted himself from his knees and stood beside Theodosia's chair, looking out the window onto the expansive grounds of Richmond Hill. "And as it happens, I am privileged to know an influential citizen of that state. A man by the name of Joseph Alston."

*Finally a mention.*

"Bright man of twenty and one," her father said. "A plantation owner, with considerable wealth to his name and the influence that comes with it. He's embarked on a summer tour of the northern states that will take him to the door of Richmond Hill next week. We must host him as if he were King George—before the revolution. Extravagant is to be the theme."

Theodosia cocked her head. "But the expense—"

"An investment in *our* future."

A future that the present threatened with so many bills unpaid since April. As a large estate, Richmond Hill required considerable funds to maintain as did ensuring the home—and those living within—appeared in accordance with the vision her father wished the world to hold of them rather than their reality.

An extravagant dinner was a risk. Her father was passionate and spontaneous but not foolish. He did not leap for things he did not believe were within his grasp.

Or put there.

Her father was a master strategist. One able to discern the needs of his opponents as well as his allies. One able to facilitate deals satisfactory to all. To achieve this new, complicated goal, her father needed political support from the South and was willing to send them further into debt to secure it. Which begged the question, what did a plantation owner like Alston need?

Theodosia stood, arms crossed, beside her father. "Alston owns a plantation."

"Rice. Astoundingly large. They say he tops the list of the richest of South Carolina's planter aristocrats."

"Then he must be immensely interested in the current discourse on abolition." As a man who made his fortune by owning slaves, Alston would sleep much more soundly with support in the presidential office.

Her father responded, "We can bring about change, you and I, so long as we use our heads and not our hearts."

Unease spread beneath her skin. "I thought you hoped to change hearts and minds? Especially on this?"

"We can't have it all. At least not at the same time."

The hope building only moments ago faded.

"Engage Nathalie on this," he said. "Her royal sensibility may be just what we need."

But that "we" Theodosia no longer felt.

That night, after completing the menu and instructions for the Alston visit, Theodosia lifted her mother's tortoiseshell brooch to retrieve a new sheet of stationery and wrote until the wick of her candles gave out. And then, she opened the chintz curtains wide and continued by moonlight.

# CHAPTER 14

O N THE DAY ALSTON WAS TO arrive, Theodosia slipped into her white linen chemise and then her morning dress, which fell loosely to the floor from the gathering beneath the breast. As she ate her eggs and toast alongside her father and Nathalie, her mind ran through all the possible excuses for the trip she must make downtown. And then seized on one.

"But why must *you* be the one to go?" Nathalie said, when Theodosia excused herself from the breakfast table, explaining she was heading downtown to acquire a northern delicacy for dinner.

At this, Burr looked up from the letter he'd been reading. "Send Tom or Sam. Richmond Hill will be a place of much liveliness today. Your careful eye is a necessity."

Theodosia ground her teeth together, trying not express her frustration at Nathalie's meddling. She'd been overly inquisitive since the family meal with Madame de Senat. "Eleonore is well under way. We've gone over every detail of the schedule—twice. And I'll return with time to spare." She set her napkin on the table and pushed her chair back. "Can I acquire anything for either of you?"

Nathalie cocked her head and wisps of her blonde hair skimmed her brow. "What delicacy specifically?"

Theodosia bore her eyes into Nathalie's. "I'm open to all options at present. No need to make a hasty decision."

"But you must have an idea of what you seek to purchase, or you'll be traveling the length of the city. Truly, Theo, someone else must be able to go and fetch—"

"Nathalie," Theodosia snapped. "For an evening as important as this, I must oversee even the tiniest detail."

At that, her father nodded approvingly, as she knew he would, and Nathalie quieted. Guilt twisted Theodosia's stomach at lying to her—about everything. She wanted Nathalie to know. She'd be proud. An enthusiastic supporter. But also, a co-conspirator. Nathalie loved her father, and he loved Nathalie. And Theodosia loved them both too much to put their relationship in danger.

Her ruse in play, she'd instructed Sam to take her to the edge of the market stalls and not to wait for her. She'd return home of her own accord.

As she traveled alone on foot through the city streets on this now-familiar route, excitement flooded through her veins. This time with even more vigor. The next installment of her story rested in the reticule suspended from her gloved hand.

These pages moved the underlying theme of equal rights further toward the surface. She'd been inspired by her conversation with Angelica as much as her father's recusal from the debate.

As her quill struck the parchment, it'd released all she'd internalized from the philosophy of Mary Wollstonecraft. But unlike the British writer, unlike Theodosia, unlike all the women alive in 1800 America, in Theodosia's fiction, women being no less capable of intellect, thought, or reason was not a theory or notion to be pondered and debated. It was simply fact.

Presenting it as such, even in fiction, felt brazen. She suspected her readers would feel the same and hoped they would then question why. It wasn't the beliefs of men in need of challenge but those of women. Women who'd been raised to believe they were not equal to men because they lacked the capacity to be so. She wanted them to see this was a system forced upon them, not a biological necessity.

As much as the younger version of herself had yearned for the saddle and rides along the river instead of her father's strict rules and schedule, the older embodiment understood that education was the key for the emancipation and enfranchisement of women and slaves. Before things went so far that no one remembered what revolution meant or stood for, women in this country should want to be more than their counterparts fanning their faces and curtsying in the British courts.

Excitement quickened her step, and Theodosia forced herself to slow so as to not draw attention to herself. She carefully adjusted the sleeves of her dress, recently shortened by Nathalie to better suit the summer heat. Forestalling the purchase of a new gown was always welcome, and on this prolonged sun-filled walk through the city, Theodosia was even more grateful for Nathalie's skill with a needle and thread. A skill that made her no less of an adversary in intellectual debate thanks to the collegiate-level study her father had imposed on them both, despite it leaving him in the minority, if not entirely alone, in his beliefs.

It was true that politicians and wealthy men campaigned on behalf of the candidates, but they used their personal connections and influence as much as their wallets. Funding newspapers and placing stories without regard for the truth had made insults matter more than policy. Adams was senile, Pinckney the definition of mediocrity, Jefferson a howling atheist, and Burr—her father—a man without principles who would do anything to get his hands on power.

Her father being cautious now stemmed from a history of attacks that Theodosia, while young at the time, remembered. Prior to the election of 1796, her father was the object of two vicious satires published in Philadelphia. The writings took on his appearance by calling out his small stature, his passion by claiming him full of overblown pride and "mad" ambition, and his private life, dismissing him as not deserving of the fame afforded by his prominent ancestry. Most hurtful of all was the slander surrounding Theodosia herself. Anonymously written, the satirical poem "Aristocracy," was published, most likely by the Federalists, in an attempt to discredit her father and prevent his ascendency in government. Though her father was unnamed, the poem closely paralleled the intimate details of Burr's life—including his most daring experiment, the "radical" education of his daughter—and practically accused him of treason, in line with the French, painting his ambition as born of a crippling jealousy of his rival, unnamed but clear to be Colonel Hamilton.

And now her father had been deemed a poison that must not be allowed to infect the country. As Theodosia crossed the street and circled around a puddle left over from the previous night's thunderstorm, she realized she'd been insensitive not to internalize the fears that must have been consuming him in this election frenzy and to understand why he—and she as an extension—needed to be seen as more temperate now. Theodosia had let her own passions, flamed by the response to her story, skew her judgment.

Still, if a costly dinner for some southern big bug was an investment in their future, then so was the coin for the newsboy resting beneath the pages in her bag. Her anonymity as the author allowed her to advocate for change in a way that would protect her father.

She arrived at the printing district for the third time full of confidence. On the last visit, she'd instituted a system that lessened her personal risk and gave Georgie clear, easy-to-follow instruction. Every week on this day, at this hour, he was to extend his newspaper sales to the bakery on the corner. If he saw a scrap of ribbon tied to the windowsill, he was to meet her in the same alleyway where they'd first met.

She could have chosen another street, farther from the printing district or another alley closer to the bakery. But in either circumstance she would have had no reason to pass by the newspaper office frequented by Colonel Hamilton. And, perhaps, by his son.

She adjusted the lace trim tied about her waist. The gown's soft lawn cotton hung straight but not stiff, the taupe still neutral for day but not as prone to soiling as white, a necessary consideration with the restriction on the Burr finances—or what should have been the restriction. Her father continued to act as though nothing were amiss despite the disappearance of a pair of Georgian silver candlesticks from the dining room.

After affixing the ribbon, Theodosia browsed inside the bake-house, allowing time between her and Georgie's arrivals in the alley. The intermingling smells of sweet sugar and savory hog's fat made her stomach growl. Washington Irving's favorite: fried dough-nuts. Perhaps on her next visit, she'd bring enough money to purchase a few and call on him as a surprise. Caty too. If the new city of Washington was to become her home, she'd miss them both. And Nathalie. Her heart twisted at the thought.

When the baker trained her eye on Theodosia for the third time, she purchased the least-expensive item in the bakehouse. She drew the folded pages out of her bag and tucked the small loaf of day-old bread inside. Back on the street, almost involuntarily, she peeked through the window of the Hamilton newspaper. Men with wigs of white and long coats filled the view, and disappoint-ment unfurled in her stomach. She dipped her chin as she hurried past and into the alley.

Where she gasped with such force that it made her light-headed. Pages tight against her chest, she spun, but the squat heel of her clog caught in the muddy ground, and she pitched forward, her forehead hurtling toward the brick wall. She scrambled to find her footing, and he latched on to her. She tried to shake him off, but he only gripped her forearm tighter, his hand warm against her already flushed skin.

"Don't be afraid," he whispered.

But the nub of fear hidden in her chest since leaving Richmond Hill took over, schooling her that fear was a concept she'd never previously understood. It commanded her every organ, nauseat-ing her stomach, hammering her heart, clouding her brain. She squeezed her eyes shut as if she were a toddler for whom the absence of sight made reality disappear. All her father fought for and against and all the fear within his breast suddenly became hers.

She would ruin him.

"Miss Burr," he said, his tone as warm as a hearth fire. "I am in awe of you."

Her eyes flew open. Philip's heart-shaped lips lay parted, his deep brown eyes fixed on her. His dark hair was swept this way and that, and he had one hand hooked in the pocket of his short coat and the other secured around her. Beside him, Georgie clung to the satchel across his torso as if it were a rope and he were dangling off the side of a ship.

Philip inched closer, taking care that his black leather boot did not tread on the trail of her skirt.

Theodosia breathed steadily despite the storm ravaging her insides. "Awe?" She gathered her resolve and her thoughts and said breezily, "For embarking on a summer stroll alone? Do you think that little of a woman's ability?"

He grinned, and she knew he was going to toy with her.

She would not let him.

She yanked her arm, and his fingertips skimmed along her skin as they released. She ignored the gooseflesh and twisted her body—and the papers held against it—away from him. "I've errands to attend to, so if you will excuse me."

"But, Miss!" Georgie cried. "The ribbon! I did just like you said. I saw, and I came, and, well, it's not my fault I like sweets so much. But the magazine's right there. I can still do your delivery."

She took a breath, resigned to addressing this—and Philip—head-on despite the foreboding curdling her stomach. "What is it that you want, then, Mr. Hamilton?"

"Want? As I said, I'm in awe." Philip gestured to the pages in her hands. "I wouldn't have the nerve to do the same."

"Come now. This isn't a juvenile dare of a dance or two before gossiping hens. We both know what this is. So, do tell, what will it be? Wine, whiskey? A bit of griping between Republicans for your father's paper?" She couldn't bring herself to offer money they didn't have. "I can get you something. Within reason. Give it a name, and this all can be forgotten."

Philip's brow creased. "But that would mean I wished it to be."

She straightened. "I'm not a mouse, and you're not a cat, and you will not trifle with me. I've patience for now, but it will not last. Use your leverage well, or you will not have it long, I swear it."

He drew back as if wounded. "This is not going as I'd hoped."

"Meaning I'm not as weak as you thought I would be? Not a fawn afraid of her own shadow? We are Burr and Hamilton, and we each know how these games are played. So out with it, or I am to be gone."

"Go then. No words from my lips will rid you of your assumptions. I was naive to think otherwise." Philip dug into his coat pocket and pulled out a hard candy attached to a stick of rolled paper. "A bonus, Georgie."

The boy's eyes widened, and he shot out his hand. But before snatching the lollipop, he glanced up at Theodosia. "I see you're in a pucker, Miss. I offer loads of sorrys. But I know that don't change nothing, nohow. But I is sorry."

"Am," Theodosia and Philip corrected at the same time.

Their eyes met, and Theodosia felt her stern face soften. In response, some of the tension in Philip's jaw eased.

"Theodosia," he said with caution, using her given name. "I mean no harm. It's not in my nature to take advantage of someone I admire and know is a better person than I."

*Better person?*

That a Hamilton would make such a claim of a Burr would hit New York society like a tsunami.

Philip tightened the gap between them. "Hear me, at least?"

Though she'd seen him through the window at the schoolhouse, they hadn't spoken let alone been this close since the night of the Clintons' party. She could hear his heavy breath, smell the lemon balm from his soap, brush against the fabric of his coat. His eyes were as earnest as any she'd known. She nodded consent.

Philip gave an impish grin. "That first day, our dear Georgie's cries piqued my interest."

Georgie remained huddled by Philip's side, eyes darting between Philip, Theodosia, and the lollipop.

"I'd grabbed hold of his satchel as he scurried past and inquired of him right then. Asked who he'd been so desperate to find."

Georgie's lips twitched.

"To the boy's credit," Philip said. "Said he'd a promise to keep. He uttered not a word."

"See, Miss, see?" Georgie piped up.

"That time," Philip added, and Georgie tried to slink behind him. "But when I next sought him out, sweets trumped a promise and a few coins."

"But he had no idea who I was." Theodosia asked of him, "Did you?"

Georgie shook his head. "Still don't."

Philip ruffled the boy's hair such that it stuck up the same as his own. "He happens to excel in description. Georgie—after the general, naturally—simply confirmed a hunch that had begun during a reading by Angelica. For in one particular passage, the author had employed enviable creativity."

"Rapscallion scoundrel," Theodosia whispered.

"Rapscallion scoundrel," Philip said.

All manner of strategy emptied from Theodosia's mind. If Philip told his father, Colonel Hamilton would make it known to all, the same way her father would have shared Philip's drunken intrusion at Mrs. Nicholson's salon had Theodosia relayed it to him.

But the consequences in this were unmatched.

Her father's bid for the presidency would end. The vice presidency gone with it. He would be lucky to receive a single electoral college vote from his home state of New York. She knew it to be so as well as she knew the proper pronunciation of short vowels and long in Classical Latin.

Uncommonly at a loss for words, Theodosia stood still. Silently, she watched Philip bend his knee before Georgie. From deep within his coat pocket came coins and more sweets. Philip dropped them in the boy's satchel.

"That's twice our agreed-upon rate," Philip said. "It's imperative that you keep this exchange to yourself. And if you do so for a whole month, we'll meet again in this same spot and you will have a promotion. Steady work with steady pay."

"What luck, what luck!" Georgie's glee had him about to burst.

"If . . ." Philip tweaked the boy's nose as if he was his little brother. "*If* you remain silent about all this."

"To be honest, Sir, I'm not right sure what all this is. But you can count on me. I'm a man 'o my word. Not a word!" He frowned and kicked at the dirt. "What I mean is—"

Philip grinned. "You will keep our secret."

"I will keep your secret."

"My good man, now off with you." He stood, gently extracted the pages from Theodosia's hand, and tucked them into Georgie's bag. "You've a special delivery to make."

Philip patted the satchel, and the sound of his palm slapping the cloth jolted Theodosia back to reality—this terrible, terrible reality.

"Wait!" she cried. "You can't. Give them back, Georgie, my papers. Give them to me." She rushed to Philip and clutched him by his elbows. "I can't add kindle to this blaze. They can't be published."

"But was that not your intention by coming here today?"

"No. I mean, yes. I had intended . . . but not like this. Anonymous is one thing . . ." She shook her head. "The risk now . . . No one can find out. Philip, please," she said, his given name rushing to her lips, "I'm not one to beg. But I will if I must. This cannot be used against my father. *You* cannot use this against him. I understand the temptation, I do, but this has risk greater than you know."

Philip frowned. "My reputation is worse than I dared imagine if in your heart you think I would not understand the risk. The risk to you, Theo, *to you.*" It was the first time he'd called her by the nickname reserved for use by those closest to her. "I don't care about political feuds and old enemies and new rivals. This election holds no interest for me. Not in the slightest. Not in comparison to that which consumes my curiosity." He lowered his voice. "To whom."

A chill permeated her bones despite the heat trapping them in the alley. His eyes would not let go hers. In them she saw truth, but how could she know it was *the* truth and not the one he wished her to see?

She continued to hold him by his elbows, and he slid his arms back until his hands met with hers.

"I would never put you at risk, Theodosia. The turmoil that comes from the outing of truths not intended for the common ear can lay waste to even the strongest among us."

His mother . . . his family. After his father's affair became public, Angelica had said Philip was the one to keep them all together.

"It is not a hurt I would wish on my greatest enemy, let alone one I am . . . in awe of."

His every word was right, every syllable uttered with care and reassurance. Yet even if Theodosia wished to believe him, the reality of what she'd done was descending upon her like the hoof of a plow horse and clouding her judgment.

He squeezed her hands, his heat penetrating the fine silk of her gloves. "Your story must continue. One can only imagine the influence if more people could be reached. But that will not happen if you confine these pages to your desk drawer. Theodosia, you are practical above all, so let's consider the facts. The author is anonymous. The only two who can trace the story to you are here beside you, your obedient servants. Thus, the question to ask is if you lock them away, who will be hurt? And the answer stands before me. You have a voice that should not be silenced."

As much as she appreciated his words, she shook her head. "I can't, Philip. I'm sorry. I can't take back what I've done, but I can endeavor to limit it. I have more than myself to consider."

Philip studied her, and she knew he wanted her to change her mind, but her decision was made. It was the one she should have made from the beginning.

"Indulge me, Theo. Please." He tugged her hands gently, and she instinctually allowed herself to be led deeper into the alley where the shadows concealed them as if it were dusk and not midday. "Yours is a secret with grave consequences. I'm not so naive that I don't see this. Entrusting it to another, especially another such as myself—devastatingly handsome . . ."

Theodosia's head snapped up.

"Ah, good then. You were listening." Lightening the mood shouldn't have felt as perfect as it did. "Trust must be earned. If you're to trust that I will keep your secret and that I urge you to publish not for some ulterior motive, then I must be willing to do the same."

"Philip, I appreciate the gesture, but we shouldn't. Our fathers—"

"Let this be our decision, not theirs."

With no sun upon them, his eyes should have been dark, but they shone with so much brightness that in them she found comfort—comfort she wanted to accept, even if false, even if fleeting.

Her silence gave him permission, and so he began. "The outcome of this election weighs heavily on my father as it does on yours. But mine, unlike yours, lost in the state legislature. He is an arrogant, stubborn man, and those citing it as a harbinger for what is to come have placed tremendous pressure on him." Philip swallowed, the Adam's apple in his neck protruding. "This you know. What you don't is the effect now, even as we stand here with our feet muddied. My father is on the verge of a breakdown. We know this not because he tells us, but because of what we see. Many nights, he rambles incoherently, and my mother fears the stress from this election will cause him to lose his mental faculties before ballots are even cast."

Theodosia could not picture the dapper and well-spoken colonel stumbling around the rooms of the home that partially inspired her father to buy one just as grand—if not grander.

"We try to reason with him, but the only thing that appears to help is distracting him with positive thoughts for the future. Especially when that future centers on me." He slapped at his coat pockets. "What a day to be without a flask." He pushed forth a smile, but Theodosia had now been around him enough to tell that it lacked authenticity. "You see, this has left me in quite the bind. Helping Father's anxiety, and as such easing my mother and sister's concern, comes at a cost. One I have voluntarily chosen to pay." He flung one arm to the side and bowed. "Meet Philip Hamilton, the son of Alexander, primed and ready to follow his father's wishes and embark upon the study of law."

"Law?" She drew back. "But you have no interest in becoming an attorney."

"Ah, you commit my words to memory, then. How divine." This time, his smile was genuine. "But family is synonymous with the stockade. For whatever crimes I've done, this is my deserved punishment." Beneath his jest lay the pain of his decision.

"If that's so," she said in response, "then what will be mine when my father discovers what I've done?"

"None, because your secret is safe with me, the same as the secret I have shared is safe with you. Keep writing. No one will find out. I promise."

"Don't make promises you can't keep, Philip."

"I don't. If I'm like my father in any way it's in this. My word is sacred."

Somewhere inside, Theodosia feared that the same might not be true of her own father. With conflict in her heart, she walked back to Georgie, Philip close behind.

"I don't make friends easily, Georgie," she said.

He shrugged. "Me neither. Not much time for playing."

"Then perhaps we can help each other. Be friends."

He shrugged again. "Don't see why not."

"But there's one thing I ask of my friends."

"What's that?"

"Trust." She glanced at Philip. She was practical, that was true, and the exchange of secrets did aid in her decision. But she was also a good judge of character. She trusted others, but she trusted herself more. Returning her focus to the boy, Theodosia pulled out the loaf of bread. She tore it into three pieces, giving him the largest one. "This is our secret. The three of us." She handed Philip one of the two remaining chunks.

Georgie sniffed it, and his stomach growled. "Well, alright then!"

"You swear?" Theodosia said.

"I swear," Philip said.

"Me too!" Georgie shoved the whole hunk of bread into his mouth. Chewing and spitting crumbs, he mumbled, "Oh, and I swear." He swallowed. "Next time, let's swear on pie."

"Done," Philip said.

"Just not apple." Theodosia touched the papers in Georgie's hand. "Now go and deliver before I come to my senses."

Like a horse free of its rider, Georgie galloped off.

Her pulse beating even faster than Georgie's feet, Theodosia faced Philip—and his rakish grin.

"Come to your senses?" he said. "So long as I'm around, such will never come to pass."

*That's what I'm afraid of.*

# CHAPTER 15

THEODOSIA COULDN'T BEAR TO RETURN HOME. Not yet. Not to a place where she'd have to hide the fireworks exploding in her chest.

She shifted from foot to foot, absentmindedly nibbling a corner of the bread while Philip kept watch at the end of the alley, ensuring Georgie delivered her pages without incident.

Alone with only her thoughts and the stale loaf, she marveled at what had just transpired. She should be devastated—and she was. She should be embarrassed—and she was. She should be afraid—and she was. She should not be giddy.

But she was.

She hadn't realized how very much she wished to share her secret with someone until she had someone to share it with.

She would have never imagined that someone to be Philip Hamilton.

"There's our good lad!" Philip clapped his hands. "Georgie after the general has successfully completed his task and is now rewarding himself."

"How can you tell?" Theodosia lifted her hem off the ground and hurried toward Philip.

"The cheeks."

"Are they flushed?"

"Full."

"Fully flushed?"

"Perhaps come see for yourself."

Theodosia met Philip at the end of the alley, and he angled his body to allow her to slip in front of him. Concealed by the edge

161

of the building, she placed one hand on the brick wall and gently poked her head into the street. "Oh, *full*. Like a squirrel in autumn. He's going to have quite the stomachache."

"Later," Philip said from behind her.

His breath warmed her earlobe. She pretended not to notice.

"Not much later if he adds that lollipop. And . . . there he goes!" Imbued with excitement, she whirled around, and hip, arm, bosom, one after the other grazed Philip's torso. She sucked in a breath. The noses on their equally crimson faces were close enough to touch.

He drew back—but not by much.

Theodosia wound the cord of her reticule around her wrist a second time. "He'll be lucky if the sugar doesn't rot his every tooth."

"But he's happy now."

"That's besides the point."

"Is it? I happen to think that's entirely the point."

Philip finally permitted space to come between them. He clicked the heels of his boots together and offered his arm. "Shall I demonstrate?"

"Being happy?" She looked around. "Here?"

"A challenge I would rise to, though it's not my preference. A better place awaits, if, that is . . . you trust me?"

Theodosia hesitated. Not because she was unaware of her answer but because of what that answer was. "Yes, I do." Her pulse beat like a battlefield drum as she wound her arm through his.

Though she'd linked arms with many a boy and just as many a man in parlors and ballrooms grand and small, none had ever felt as intimate as this.

Still, the moment their feet landed on the sidewalk, she extracted her hand and coiled the cord of her reticule around both wrists as if to restrain herself. Philip dipped his head in understanding as he led her out of the printing district and even deeper into the outskirts of downtown.

She kept a pace behind him, preventing conversation but upholding the guise of not traveling with him. His movements were purposeful as they wound through a series of winding, dusty streets. Around them, the brick and clapboard buildings began to decrease in height and increase in scarcity, bringing about an end to the welcome shadows that afforded shelter from the sun. Summer in the congested city was an entirely different season from the same at Richmond Hill, where even on the hottest day one could find a crisp pocket of air rising off the river.

Carriages with drivers tugging on reins became few, then none, and those on foot too became scarce. Soon they passed more bristly haired pigs scouring for scraps than people.

Despite their difference in stature, their gait matched without Theodosia needing to race to keep up like she often did with Nathalie, who liked to gloat over the length of her legs and resulting stride.

She observed Philip from behind. The slight arch in his back. His coat stretching across his upper arms. The fabric outlining his shoulder blades. He was not tall like John Vanderlyn, had not the brawn of Washington Irving, nor the rawboned slenderness of his father. Philip was lean but muscular, understated, a strength hidden beneath fabric and skin that would take one by surprise. He carried himself lightly and with an energy Theodosia welcomed as it became her own.

They turned left onto a street barely wider than the alley from which they'd departed more than a quarter hour ago. Philip slowed, and Theodosia came up beside him. At the end of the street, between the structures on either side, sat a narrow two-story tavern. The single building linked the two sides of the street like the bottom of a "u." With no egress before them, the only way out lay the path behind.

At the tavern door, Philip said, "After you?"

She gave a polite nod despite the nerves buzzing like bees in the pit of her stomach, and he escorted her through the thick oak door, down the uneven steps, and into a rectangular room, dimly lit by candlelight even in the daytime for it lacked a single window to the outside world.

Crude wooden tables of unequal height and girth lay scattered about the room like a flung deck of cards. Surrounding them sat men on short, rectangular benches and women in spindle-backed chairs. The shrieks of a few children filled the room as they played hide-and-seek behind staved barrels, stacks of crates, and the skirts of their mothers. Bulbous bottles of brandy and round jugs of wine lined the walls, and pewter tankards hung above an unlit fireplace that was as tall as Theodosia and as wide as three men.

Like a swift-moving fog, her unease lifted. Here no one knew them, and they only knew each other.

They claimed a table in the deepest corner, and Philip ordered ciders and oysters while she removed her gloves. His eyes lingered on the bare skin of her fingers, and a different sort of unease took hold.

The ciders arrived first, the tapster quick with the item whose repeat would rack up a higher bill. Theodosia threaded her fingers through the slim handle of her mug. She had never been in such an establishment before, what her father would call a "groggery" followed by the phrase woven into her skin since she waddled her first steps: "not suitable for a girl of your position."

She lifted the cider and took her first sip. The sourness puckered her cheeks.

Philip gave a slight smile. "Not quite the city's finest, but at least we know it's not watered down. It's true to its core."

She groaned at his pun. "And here I thought you a poet of renown. I trust the budding attorney will fare better?"

"No chance. Of that, now and forever, I am sure." He claimed his cider. "Grab your bumper, Miss P."

He tipped his mug toward hers, but she didn't meet it. "I will not toast to such a defeatist notion."

He spread his hands flat on the table, feigning shock. "Bewitched by optimism? What happened to the practical Miss Burr?"

"She remains here, fully aware that one can do anything they set their mind to. Papa didn't discriminate when it came to my studies, and now I have an education that rivals that of any man."

"More than, in the case of the one before you, I don't doubt." Philip drank from his cider. "I wonder though . . . about the mind that was set. Was it the girl whose skates cut across thin ice and lured pigs to outhouses or—"

"I assure you it was my backside bellowing from hours in a hard chair."

"Yes, but hours your father commanded."

"*Encouraged.*"

"You did as he wished."

She tapped her mug. "As daughters *and* sons are taught."

"Must you keep reminding me?"

A wisp of disappointment surprised her. "Then you will truly study the law?"

"Yes. Or at least that's how it will appear."

"I'm serious, Philip."

"I know, and that's the problem I aim to solve, Theo."

So smug was his grin that she should have tossed her cider in his face. Instead she sipped to hide the effect that the self-pleased upturn of his lips was having on her. She set down her mug and aimed to steer the conversation toward a less intimate one. "This nation owes its future to the things our fathers did when they were our age. It seems natural that we should trust in their wisdom."

Wisdom that would demand she and Philip be as far from each other as England was from France—physically and ideologically. She glanced around the room, confirming that they were among none who might recognize them. Still, she shifted her chair closer to the wall and its protective shadows.

Philip drank heavily of his cider. "They picked up arms and pen. Does that relegate them to the status of gods?"

"Other than in their own minds, you mean?" Theodosia could not stop her tongue.

Philip knocked the empty mug against the table and issued a hearty laugh. "For the sake of debate, let's say that this nation and those in it do owe their destinies to our fathers; do our fathers then have a say in what those destinies are to be?"

"For everyone?"

He paused as the oysters arrived. "Let's start with us—me and you." He leaned across the table. "What do you want most in life?"

"To help my father succeed." Her answer was instant.

"But what do *you* want?"

"I've just said."

"You must live life for yourself, Theodosia."

"My father and I have always been a team."

"But one led by him."

Philip signaled for another round, and Theodosia placed her finger along the side of her mug, measuring. She still had half a glass before her. Even unintentionally she'd held to her father's instructions. She lifted her mug and drank.

She wiped the corners of her mouth, feeling her cheeks grow hot. "Living life for yourself . . . is that why you've chosen the law?"

He shook his head. "It's why I've chosen to be here in this place now."

"This isn't life, merely play."

"Life should be play. It's too short and full of disease and pain for it not to be." The tapster swapped empty mugs for full, and Philip barely let the bottom strike the table before taking a drink. "My degree won't officially rest in my hands for another month, and still Father's set my course for me." His tone was quieter, without a hint of his usual jest and bravado. "When I pledged myself to the study of law, Father immediately stripped our library of all volumes of poetry."

She drew back. Did their fathers realize it? How similar they actually were?

Philip continued, "I asked him to leave just one—a favorite of mine in French."

"That seems a reasonable request."

"Only to reasonable ears. Not even Mother knows where he hid them. The books will be returned when I show my focus. So . . . those are lost to me forever." The edges of his lips tugged upward, but he could not bring about a full smile.

Theodosia hesitated, then said, "But don't you want more, Philip?"

"Don't *you*? Clearly you wouldn't be writing these stories if you didn't."

"But is it so awful to want to please those closest to us?"

"It is when what will please them has no resemblance to what will please us."

"Legacy is what makes us who we are."

"But if we are only legacy, do we exist in the now?"

Philip awaited her response. All she could do was take another swig of cider. With this second mug, she barely noticed the sourness.

"I shouldn't," Philip said suddenly. "Not with the fever that nearly consumed me. The doctor doesn't know how I survived."

"When was this?" Concern tightened Theodosia's voice.

"Three years ago. Shortly after Father's indiscretion came to light. What's that about sins of the father?"

"You paid."

"Not as much as him. I can only recall bits and pieces, but Angelica remembers it all. She saw him. Distraught, beaten. A man on the verge of losing it all—or what he believes to be all. His 'brightest hope.' He said it then as he administered my every dose of medicine, night and day, barely leaving my side, and he still says it now."

The difference could not be missed—Philip's father at his son's side and her father absent from her mother's. Though that had been her mother's desire, Theodosia was sure of it.

Philip went on, "Father's convinced that I was spared for a reason: I am to cement the Hamilton legacy."

"A heavy burden for one man to carry."

"Especially one like me."

"Especially." He cocked his head, and she added with affection, "Because you are destined for so much more than just being the son of Alexander Hamilton."

"And you are already so much more than the daughter of Aaron Burr."

The treachery of their words even more than this place made her head spin. Or maybe it was the cider.

Philip proved himself an adept storyteller, relaying escapades from Columbia College, of stealing plump hens from nearby homes, employing telescopes to ogle ladies from afar, and engaging in verbal sparring of the most licentious sort, where he learned the skill he showed off at the Nicholson salon. She indulged in self-mockery, speaking of the "friends" she had before Nathalie— Virgil, Terence, and Plautus, as Frederick would tease—and of her first and only foray into baking where she transposed the amounts of flour and sugar and served a cake as dense as stone able to rot one's tooth on contact.

Their talk was punctuated by toasts and laughter, and Theodosia had the unexpected desire to remain here, doing so at the exclusion of all else. As they set the last two oyster shells on the plate beside their empty mugs, each laid a hand on the table. Their skin as bare to one another as the cider had helped their words to become.

Though only their fingers touched, Theodosia felt as though she lived within Philip's skin and he hers. A kinship she could never fully share with Nathalie. She and Philip were bonded as two children born of the American Revolution. But more than that, of children born of fathers with expectations that set the weight of this new world on their shoulders. Philip afraid that his identity was inseparable from his father's, and Theodosia, the opposite, scared of what it would mean if her identity truly separated from her own father's.

"Don't let this end like the dance, Theo." Philip withdrew his fingers from where they lingered against hers to clasp her hand, fully, gently coaxing her across the table so the wisps of hair along their foreheads touched. The desire to remain here talking and laughing burned with something much less innocent. "Allow me to take you on an outing. Sunday afternoon. Choose a spot at Richmond Hill, by the river, one you know well, but others do not. Meet me there. Let me show you the value of the now."

Her heart beat so loudly that she could not hear her own thoughts.

A scrape behind them, and a large man with a scruffy white beard called to the tapster. "Ya have the hour?"

The tapster pulled out a pocket watch. "S'quarter past five and right about the time to rustle up coin for your bill."

A quarter past five. *A quarter past five!* Theodosia leapt from her seat. *Alston!* Due at six o'clock. She'd barely make it! "I have to go!"

She spun around, grasping for her gloves and bag, but the cider and her quick movements made her dizzy.

Philip rose to his feet. "Theodosia, what is it? What's the matter?"

"I'm late. I will be late. I cannot be late!" She took off for the door, but the cord of her bag snagged on a splinter of wood on the table and yanked her back. Heat rose in her chest, coloring her neck and cheeks, and her hands grew clammy. "Philip . . ." Her words were consumed by the lump in her throat. She couldn't let her father down.

Philip must have seen the depth of her despair for he freed her bag, flung money onto the table, and seized her wrists. "I'll get you a carriage."

They skirted around a young boy hiding behind a whiskey barrel and raced up the stairs of the tavern. With Theodosia in the lead, they sped down the alley and back into the street. There,

Theodosia allowed Philip to guide them to a more densely traveled street. The acidity of the cider burned her stomach, and her mind ran through all the preparations for the evening that she hadn't been there to oversee. How long had it taken Nathalie to realize the need to take over? How long before Alexis and Eleonore sought her out, going to her father when she couldn't be found?

Philip released her hand, and she bent at the waist, about to be sick.

Before her, Philip bolted into the street, arms waving above his head. A massive chestnut horse reared, and the carriage to which the animal was attached careened to a halt. The driver yelled an obscenity Philip rightly deserved under any other circumstance.

More money exited Philip's pocket, then a bit more, and the rider inside the carriage stepped out.

Philip turned, his face collapsing at the sight of her. He started toward her, but she righted herself and met him halfway. "Are you—"

"I'm fine, let's just . . . I have to—" Her lungs cramped, and she couldn't catch her breath.

"Inside, quick now." With a boost of his hand, Philip guided her into the carriage. "All will be well, I promise. Richmond Hill is in our sights."

She sunk deep in the seat and found herself reaching for Philip, her breath finally regulating when their fingers found each other's.

The clomp of the horse's hooves further soothed her, and she let herself relax. She had hosted far more important guests than this in far greater numbers. She wasn't the daughter of Theodosia Bartow Prevost Burr if she couldn't handle a southern—

*All blazes, she almost forgot!*

The "northern delicacy" she had used as her excuse. She couldn't arrive home without it.

"We need to stop," she said.

"Is the pace too brisk? I can ask him to slow . . ." He placed a hand on his stomach. "The oysters?"

Theodosia shook her head and explained she needed an item that someone from the South would have never tasted. Instantly, Philip ordered the driver to divert his route. He peered through the open window until something caught his eye.

"Here!" he cried. To Theodosia he said, "Wait for me."

Before she could offer the small amount of money she'd reserved, he hopped out of the carriage and sprinted down the street. She clasped her hands in her lap, restraining herself from asking the driver for the time. Gratitude flooded her as, sooner than she expected, Philip returned with an enormous parcel secured with twine. It landed at her feet, and the iron-rich smell of blood infiltrated her nostrils.

He swung himself into the carriage and ordered the driver on.

"It's your lucky day, Miss Burr, and not just because the preponderance has been spent with me."

Theodosia nudged the package with her toe. "What is it?"

"Bear. A northern delicacy if there ever is one."

Bear meat. Pounds of it. More than they could eat. More than she could afford.

"I'm grateful to you, Philip. And I promise to repay you as soon as—"

"No need."

"But if my father thought your father was putting food on our table, it'd be the last to touch my lips."

Philip's eyes reflexively flicked to her mouth before returning to meet her gaze. "Not a circumstance we will find ourselves in. Especially since it isn't my father's money but my own. You see, Theo, there are benefits to being a rapscallion scoundrel, especially when one is good at cards."

She smiled despite the guilt and shame and the increasing anger at her father for putting them in this position. As if understanding her frame of mind, Philip remained silent as the carriage continued to Richmond Hill.

When the iron gates were behind them, she called for the driver to stop.

"I must go alone from here," she said.

A brief flash of disappointment preceded Philip's nod. "Certainly. I'll return on foot."

"No, you must take the carriage. I cannot be seen arriving in one."

*Because all know we cannot afford the fare.*

She reached for the package of meat, but the abundance made it too heavy for her to carry.

"Theodosia, is this really necessary? We can just explain you were in need of assistance, and we happened upon one another . . ."

"No!" She couldn't be seen arriving with Philip.

The sudden heavy tread of hooves smacking the gravel announced an approaching carriage.

*Alston!*

Her eyes darted everywhere at once. The carriage. The meat. The driver. The towering oaks. The windy road. Philip.

The thunderous footfalls from behind got closer.

The evening would be ruined.

Hers with her father.

And hers with Philip.

"Better the devil you know . . ." she muttered, climbing back inside the carriage.

"Especially this one." Philip had a grin on his face as wide and as smug as the first time he'd escorted her home.

"We'll see about that," she said.

But part of her knew, as she looked upon that smug, infuriating, and even more pleasing face, that she already had.

She was smitten.

And just like that, she had a new affinity for salons.

# CHAPTER 16

THEODOSIA INSTRUCTED THE DRIVER TO VEER off the main road that led to the columned portico at the front of the house. He uttered profanity after profanity as they bounced down a rarely used path cutting through the wild and uncultivated lands that stretched for acres across the property. The route might have been circuitous, but it was also hidden, leaving them just shy of the rear of Richmond Hill.

Where every window held discovery, every door a threat.

Sight of her home had not caused this much dread since returning to it after her mother had been buried. That day too, she'd wished to remain ensconced in a carriage, warmed by Madame de Senat on one side and Nathalie on the other. Today that warmth came from Philip Hamilton.

How unpredictable life could be.

The carriage jounced along, tossing them about like potatoes in a wheelbarrow. They neared the end of the path, at which they'd be forced to exit the clump of soaring oak trees whose plentiful limbs and leaves shielded them from view. Theodosia ordered the driver to stop. She filled her lungs with air, seeking out the murky salt scent of the river to steel her nerves, and stepped down from the carriage. Philip followed, the juxtaposition of him and her childhood home surreal. In all those times Angelica had come, Philip never had.

"Breathtaking," he said.

Though the back side, the height of the manor high on the hill—with its chimneys reaching toward the sky and interlocking diagonal Chinese Chippendale railings adorning the balconies and roof—still impressed even the most worldly.

"It's home," she said. It was in her bones the way it was in her father's. She once thought it synonymous with peace, an Eden, heaven on earth. That was before her mother died. Before her father lost a piece of himself Theodosia had been tirelessly trying to restore. "We should hurry." She imagined her father's worried brow as he paced the floors, waiting for her.

"Not yet." Philip stepped back to see all of Theodosia at once.

She self-consciously lifted her hand to her hair, tucking in the pieces gone astray in their rush from the tavern.

"No," he said. "Leave it be. This is exactly how I will always picture you. Before this grand, imposing structure surrounded by the wilds of nature. A contrast striking in its perfection. A true reflection of its owner." He returned to her side, allowing his head to tilt toward hers such that his lips nearly brushed her ear. "Breathtaking."

For the first time in her life she was more aware of her body than her mind. Alive in ways and places it had never been.

"I . . ." The air was charged. She fought through. "We . . . the house. Must not see . . . we must not be seen." She gathered up her skirts and her resolve. "Tread lightly but swiftly."

"To arrive in a jiffy!" He smirked.

She shouldn't have smiled, but the impulse lay outside her control. Still, she said, "With utter silence."

"As you command."

"Philip, I'm serious!"

"And maddeningly ravishing when you are."

With no notion of the significance of this evening, he was free to jest, and, in truth, his lightness was helping to calm her. More than that, it made her want to climb back into the carriage, back to the tavern, back to anywhere that wasn't here.

She stared longingly at the coach, despite it being much more utilitarian than the one that had taken them home the day they'd buried her mother. She could still picture her father inside, back straight as a rod, eyes unfocused, appearing smaller than he was on that cushioned bench. Theodosia had been the last to enter, unable to leave the grave site, unable to understand that this was where—*how*—they were leaving her kind, clever, beautiful mother. When she'd finally been helped into the carriage by Alexis, her father had looked upon her with a new sense of expectation.

A look that had never left.

Theodosia placed a hand on Philip's arm. The muscles beneath his coat tensed before melting into her. She infused urgency into her tone, "Please, Philip, this is important."

Instantly, his expression shifted to one of concern. He lugged the parcel of meat off the floor of the carriage and nodded his obedience.

"This way." Her eye on the entrance to the cellar, she left the protection of the trees and hastened across the open field leading to the house.

"*Par ici.*"

Her spine stiffened. Her neck swiveled. Her heart leapt to her throat.

"*Viens vite!*"

*Alexis!* She searched the immediate grounds and then looked deeper, toward the house. There, beyond the patch of blue asters whose stalks were already well over a foot, she caught sight of him crouched before a small, nearly hidden door at its rear.

"Follow me," she whispered to Philip, not waiting to ensure he did.

She kept her sights on Alexis and that open door, her legs at a gallop, until she landed before him, breathless. With flustered murmurs in French, Alexis secreted Theodosia and Philip into the house via the servants' entrance, a place through which she hadn't traveled since she was a child.

The darkness struck her at once. Like a cloud obscuring the sun at the height of day. The walls dripped with humidity, trapping the dank odor of mold. A bang and scraping of metal turned her around. Alexis had latched the door to the outside and was now snatching the meat from Philip's hands, heaving it over his shoulder and almost dropping it in surprise. Not because of its weight but because of whom he'd taken it from.

"Monsieur Hamilton?" Alexis said.

Theodosia locked eyes with Philip, entreating him to stay silent.

Drifting in were the smells of freshly cut strawberries and boiled potatoes, her menu being brought to life and rattling her from the spell she'd been under beside the carriage. Beside Philip.

"Alexis," she said in his native tongue, knowing she had no time to waste. "You mustn't draw attention, nor speak of this. To anyone, but especially my father."

"As you say, Mademoiselle," Alexis replied in French.

Theodosia's stomach clenched. She had known Alexis all her life. Though this was not the first time he had covered for her, it was the first time she'd demanded it so acutely. She was no longer a child with a missed lesson, muddied dress, or tussle with Nathalie. She was no longer that young girl, writing letters on Alexis's behalf to the object of his affection, for at that time, Alexis, while quite eloquent in French, had only begun to learn to read and write in English, the language of the woman he admired.

This nation of contradictions had never felt as close to home as it did now.

She remained still, awkwardly so, but then Philip cleared his throat. "A lady and a scoundrel before you, eh?" he said to Alexis. "Shock is understandable, for my body stands here, but my mind tells me that it cannot be so."

He surprised her, both in his attempt to ease the situation and with his fluency in French. He'd never been very good when they were children.

"*Alexis! Where'd you go for those matches?*" a hushed cry from inside the house highlighted the urgency.

"Eleonore," Theodosia said softly.

Alexis hiked the meat higher over his shoulder. "Go." He nodded toward the back staircase used by the servants. "Mademoiselle Nathalie is with your father in the parlor."

"As will I be straight away." Theodosia paused, discomfort mixing with guilt mixing with gratitude mixing with words she could not yet name. She nodded her thanks to Alexis, who left to carry the meat to the kitchen.

"To the carriage," she said to Philip. "You must leave at once." As she hurried to trade places with him, pushing him toward the door and angling herself to the stairs, their bodies grazed one another's. His cheeks flushed, matching the burning she felt in her own. "But thank you for . . . thank you."

Philip bowed his head, reaching for her hand, when a booming voice caused a chill to scutter up her spine.

*"Alexis! Our guest's carriage is swirling dust. The door at once! Still Theodosia has not returned, and I cannot have another thing out of place!"*

Her father. Who would be positioning himself at the front windows, eager to see the expression on "their guest's" face as he took in the grandeur of Richmond Hill. If another carriage left—and not an empty one she could later explain away as having arrived in but one with a man, with Philip, inside—he would see it.

She had no choice. "Hurry," she said, leading him up the stairs, balancing the need for a hasty escape with the soft footfalls it required.

At the top of the stairs, she fled the wrong way, unaccustomed to arriving on the floor with their bedrooms from this direction. She spun about, colliding with Philip. The force nearly toppled her, but his arms wound around, steadying them both, and his warm breath and racing heart set her own insides ablaze. She scrambled out of his arms and rushed down the hall, commanding Philip to follow so as not to be seen.

Her fingers clawed at her dress even before she'd fully entered her bedroom. She caught Philip looking, and he reddened like a boiled lobster. But the sound of hooves shoved aside any notion of impropriety. "No time for that," she said despite the gooseflesh alive on her skin. "Help. Now."

Philip didn't move.

"The laces." She stationed herself in front of him beside her trunk. Her only choice as this garment was secured at the back. Nancy was occupied with her duties, and with any luck, Nathalie with Theodosia's. The dress Theodosia currently wore was not the one her father had chosen. That gown lay across her bed, freshly altered, cleaned, and pressed. "My arm won't grow in the time we have."

"But me? Here?"

"Better in the parlor? Come now, Philip, if I can stand it, so can you." She grabbed his hand, plunked it on her shoulder, swiveled herself around. The fabric slipped, and his fingers grazed her skin. Cold with fear. They trembled as he unwound the first tie. "Faster," she insisted.

She felt the fabric tug as he said, "Must be someone special to have you in this much of a state."

"I said, faster." Another lace, and the dress loosened across her shoulders.

Philip's swallow was audible. "Perhaps I've made his—or her—acquaintance. Is it a couple? From the city or—"

"Philip, please, the laces?"

"Right, yes." His fingers dug in, but the dress didn't budge any farther. "Well, whoever it is, it must be someone truly special."

His statement probed harder than any question, begging a reply, yet even if her father was mistaken regarding Alston's influence, he believed in it now. It was too critical to him for her to risk it.

She said instead, "Less the someone than what he represents."

"Ah." Philip pulled on the fabric, drawing her to him. "So it is a *he*."

"Half the world is. Not so lucky odds."

"Is that it, then, Theo? Have I lost your trust already?"

She spun so their eyes could meet, and the strings he'd been working on twisted with her. "This is less about me trusting you and more about keeping the trust of someone else."

Those deep brown eyes bore into her, holding not only her own, but scanning her whole body, her entire mind, sinking into places she kept hidden, even from herself.

"He doesn't deserve you," Philip said, his voice barely a whisper. "If roles were reversed, would your father act the same, Theodosia? It's the question I always ask of my own father."

She hesitated. "And?"

"Sometimes yes, sometimes no. I'm beginning to believe the key to growing beyond is understanding the difference."

She felt the air leave her lungs, her legs unstable, her memory bringing the past to the present. Her father in the carriage that day they'd buried her mother, calling to her as Theodosia stood beside the pile of dirt that would be her last image of her mother. She'd reached for some, letting the dark grains coat her skin, and then obeyed her father. Inside the coach, her mother's dirt balled in her fist, she'd aimed to sit beside him. Madame de Senat and Nathalie were huddled together on the opposite bench. Tears trailed down Theodosia's round cheeks, and moisture from the dirt began to seep out her clamped hand. She stepped toward him, extending her clean fingers. But instead of taking them—and her—his eyes landed on the brooch that had been her mother's. He shook his head. Once. But firmly. Her dirty hand seized it, trying to unfasten the jewel from her neckline, willing to fling it out the carriage, bury it in her mother's grave if it made him happy, but Madame de Senat was already gathering her up, nestling her between herself and Nathalie.

Later that night, when her father had sealed them off from everyone, leaving just the two of them alone in Theodosia's bedroom, she had offered the brooch to him, returning her mother's gift, desperate for her action to make him accept her again. Instead, he had gingerly pinned it back through the lace of her dress where he stared at it, lost in another time, another place, another's skin whose softness gleamed against it. He clutched Theodosia to him with such pressure that her torso ached. His larger frame should have enveloped her, but he was the one who grew small, curling into her slight body. She fell back, sitting on the edge of the bed, and he collapsed before her, knees on the floor, his head in her lap. The mountain of pain he'd forestalled by not allowing their physical connection in the carriage caved in on him. He wept a river, and she brushed her fingers through his hair, rocking him back and forth and humming softly, as her mother had done to her when she'd been sick, as she had done for her mother in reverse.

Theodosia knew the difference that day and every day since. Their connection had been forged and laid in stone. Her father would give her his last breath, she'd known it before. What she'd learned that day was he might just take hers too.

"I will never do anything to harm you," Philip whispered.

His head bending toward hers. His lips flushing pink. Calling to her own. An impulse she could not summon nor control lifted her on her toes, and she pressed her torso against him, her mouth parting, her neck extending and—

"Theodosia!" A hiss from the hall.

*Nathalie.*

"Hide," Theodosia whispered.

He nodded, and with great reluctance, they parted, then snapped back together. For his finger was caught in the strings of her half-unlaced dress.

Theodosia twisted like a dog after its own tail, groping for the laces. "Is this helping?"

"To turn my finger blue? You're coiling it tighter!"

"Philip!"

"Theo!"

Like clumsy dancers, the two pivoted and pulled, fumbling to free Philip. With one last vigorous yank, the lace broke in two. One half remained tied around Philip's index finger and the other still attached to the dress, which was now crumpled at Theodosia's feet.

Clad only in her thin, linen chemise, she stood as his eyes traveled the length of her. She should have minded. She didn't.

Nathalie entered. Her eyes sprang open, but no words came out.

Theodosia's exposed skin flamed pink. She snatched her dress off the floor and held it against her. "He's leaving." She jabbed her finger at him. "You're leaving."

"But . . . *Philip Hamilton?*" Nathalie spat out.

"It's not what you think," Theodosia said.

"It could be," Philip whispered.

A smile tugged the edges of Theodosia's lips, though her insides burned as brightly as her reddening skin.

"You," Theodosia said to Philip. "Not another word." To Nathalie, "And you, help me get into this dastardly thing." She hurried to the bed and scooped up the gown her father had asked her to wear. It had been her mother's, altered by Nathalie.

She shoved it in Nathalie's hands and instructed Philip. "Once we're gone, travel back the way we came with stealth. Wait there."

"For my invite to dinner?" He grinned, entirely pleased with himself.

"For five minutes. By which time I'll have them all in the sitting room."

Philip appeared to contemplate. "I'll agree to this deal you broker." He stroked his unshaven chin. "So long as you give me an answer."

"Answer, to what question?" Theodosia lifted her arms above her head as Nathalie held up the new dress.

"Sunday, of course," Philip replied. "Considering the level of intimacy we've just shared, I realize it will be a step backward, but still . . ."

Nathalie gasped.

"No!" Theodosia cried, her voice muffled by the fabric enveloping her. She struggled to poke her head through the neckline.

"No?" Philip said. "But everyone loves dining out of doors."

"No, not you." She grasped Nathalie's arms and said, "He's speaking in jest, I assure you. Nothing transpired here."

Nathalie's eyebrow arched. "To the French, perhaps this is nothing but to an American . . . to a Burr . . ."

"Just fasten the sash." Theodosia put her back to Nathalie.

Philip stood across from her, rocking back and forth on his heels. "And me . . ."

"You," Theodosia said with a racing heart, perspiring hands, and more joy than she'd felt in years. "You, you rapscallion scoundrel, yes."

# CHAPTER 17

NATHALIE'S WORDS COULDN'T KEEP UP WITH her brain as she fired off hushed questions at Theodosia.

"In your bedroom?"

"In your shift?"

"How can this be?"

"*Trés* handsome he is, no?"

"Theodosia!"

Nathalie's astonished thoughts accompanied their every pace from the bedroom to the main staircase and down the first few steps leading them to the front hall. Theodosia shushed Nathalie's every utterance, until finally she issued a desperate plea, "Later all, to come, later, I promise. Now leave it be!"

A thrumming ruled her every organ, and yet as the first floor came into view, Theodosia straightened her spine, clasped her hands before her waist, and became the scholar with the skills of a socialite her father had raised her to be.

With an extra bounce in her step, thanks to Philip Hamilton.

The sweet perfume from the vase of roses, clipped that morning, wafted through the gleaming foyer, an entry at odds with the one she'd come through a short time ago. Except it made her feel exactly the same way. Dark and foreboding.

There he was. Joseph Alston. The "influential" citizen of South Carolina upon whom her father had set his hopes and dreams. No matter that he might be the only one ever to do so. Alston was altogether unimpressive. Slender, bordering on sickly, his skin lily white, his thin nose and almost imperceptible chin as effeminate as they were out of proportion with his bugging eyes, too big and round for his face. His dark brown hair appeared just as fragile as his frame, giving the appearance, despite the abundance of curls, that it was thinning.

"Quite the contrast, no?" Nathalie whispered from beside Theodosia.

Theodosia linked their arms. "I hope you decanted enough claret, sister."

Well-trained, they stifled their giggles and tread side by side toward Alston. Shorter than her father, he stood before Vanderlyn's life-sized portrait of the young Theodosia.

"Mr. Alston," she said, plastering on a smile. "Why settle for a facsimile when the real thing lies before you?"

Alston's beady gray-blue eyes fixed on Theodosia. "Miss Burr at last! We were just about to pluck this little portrait off the wall, set it on the sofa, and offer it a whiskey."

*Little portrait?* His very first words to her confirmed everything she thought about the uncultured South.

"We're quite fond of it where it is," she said with a forced playfulness. "Besides, its rehanging would require Papa to pick up a hammer and nail."

Burr laughed heartily while simultaneously imploring Theodosia to come closer and greet them.

She did, reluctantly, wishing she were still back upstairs or better yet . . . heading to the servants' entrance. "Please accept my apologies. I was preparing something special for your visit, Mr. Alston."

"I'm flattered," he said. "Makes the interminable ride worthwhile."

"Only a mile or so outside the city proper," Theodosia said. "I expect your farm is farther from any civilization?"

"My plantation."

She placed a hand to her chest. "Again, my apologies."

Behind him, her father narrowed his eyes, indicating that perhaps Theodosia had veered too far over the line between charm and mockery she was straddling. She dipped her chin and extended her arm before Alston. "Shall we sit?"

She'd meant to simply show him the way, and yet he clamped onto her like a trap on a hare. "Place is small enough for me to find my way, but I happen to like when a lady leads."

Her smile was tight as she released Nathalie and escorted Alston into the sitting room. Through the window immediately beside them, she glimpsed Philip, strolling down the grass in front of the house.

*Does the boy need a switch at his derrière to travel with urgency?*

She swiftly aimed Alston toward a chair, which would put his back to the window. His own rear had nearly brushed the seat when he popped back up, shaking his head. "Where are my manners?"

His dirty boots clicked on the floor as he returned to the front hall, and Theodosia's heart lodged in her throat. She held her breath as Alston passed by the window, silently urging speed into Philip's retreat. She exchanged a worried glance with Nathalie, who, whether by educated guess or instinct, set herself in front of the window.

Through the doorway, Theodosia watched Alston bend to retrieve a satchel, pause to tousle his cobweb-like hair, and turn to face the Burrs and Nathalie.

With a leisurely gait, he returned to the parlor and presented the satchel to Theodosia. "My deepest apologies for the wrapping, but such an item poses a bit of a challenge."

He held the bag while Theodosia reached inside.

"A plant?" she said.

"Not a plant, my child, but a palmetto. A tree as tall as three men. That's *pal-met-toe.* If you happen to have a quill I shall spell it for you."

It was only Theodosia's well-honed willpower that prevented the words she actually wished to say in favor of, "How thoughtful of you."

"No real thought required. They litter the grounds in my home state. Let me guess, our dirt has yet to find its way between your pretty little toes?"

Theodosia's skin crawled with revulsion. "My travels have not taken me so far south, *je suis désolé.*

Alston wrapped his hands around the back of a chair, leaning his full weight on it. She feared he'd break it. "I hope that last part was 'but I'd sell my own mother to go.'"

At this, not even her father could maintain his smile.

Nathalie sped to Theodosia's side. "You do not speak French, Monsieur Alston?"

"I understand something of it," he said. "With a little practice, I am sure I could be fluent in short order."

"Is that so?" Theodosia said. "You must be especially proficient in languages."

"You be the judge. How am I doing so far?"

"My ears catch all you say and even some you don't," she said.

"Watch out, Mr. Alston," Nathalie said. "Theodosia knows all."

"Does she?" he said.

"Tell me," Nathalie said, "have you visited my home country?"

He grimaced. "Fortunately my pursuits keep me closer to home."

"Certainly." Theodosia pressed her crown to the ceiling. If his boots didn't have such a heel, she'd have at least an inch, maybe two, of height over him. She turned to place the *pal-met-toe* beside the fireplace. "I only hope we have enough light to sustain it during the winter months."

"That window right there's your spot." Alston pointed at the glass, beyond which Philip had been only moments ago.

Her pulse echoed in her ears. She fiddled with the fronds on the small tree, commanding herself to quell her fears. They stemmed from guilt, not from reason. Alston was from the South, newly arrived in New York City. A Republican. Surely he'd have never met Colonel Hamilton let alone his son. Even if Alston had somehow seen Philip through that window, he'd have no reason to suspect he was a man of any importance.

Certainly not of the importance he was becoming to Theodosia. Her heart warmed, and a genuine smile consumed her. Alston's eyebrows lifted upon sight of it, and a knot tied in her stomach at the thought of this man believing her affection was for him.

He moved to the window and rapped his knuckles against the glass. "Even at this hour, one can see clear to the river. Must shed light on so much . . . of this fine home."

Her smile vanished.

"Estate," Burr said quickly, his own frustration infused in the one word. Yet he added with deference, "Though surely not as grand as Oaks Plantation. Still, Richmond Hill commands a size-able portion of the countryside." He gestured to the side of the house. "Out this way, you can see clear across to New Jersey."

"Is that so?" Alston said.

"Indeed. It was the land as much as the portico out front that first attracted us."

"Though took a hefty bit of time to rid the place of the stench left by the Adamses I bet."

Of Alston's many insults—to Vanderlyn, their home, and even each of them—this was one Burr could get behind, and her father looked at Theodosia with renewed spirit. Alston's latest crude comment confirmed whose side he would be on in the upcoming election.

The reminder of why he was here this evening didn't lessen the tension in the room. Fortunately, they had Nathalie.

"History is what makes a place, is it not, Monsieur Alston?" Her ties to French nobility and her being raised in the Burr household made her almost as adept as Theodosia in charming guests. "The former occupation of President and Mrs. Adams adds to the patina of these walls. It is what I remember thinking about Versailles—a place is a place because of who has lived and breathed in it. Who else have we had here, Theo? Jerome Bonaparte and Maurice de Talleyrand—"

"Always with the French, Nathalie," Burr said with a laugh. She eyed him quizzically for she didn't know the intricate details of Alston's visit, the ones that made Burr wish to appear as agnostic as possible in all things so as not to offend. "What about Andrew Jackson and Colonel Brant and why General Washington, of course. If he had not used the mansion as headquarters during the war, I might have never laid eyes on the estate."

"And Hamilton?" Alston asked.

Like a reflex, Theodosia intervened. "The colonel has dined on occasion."

"Ah, yes, *the colonel*," Alston said in a way that could be a challenge to Theodosia's words or a denigration of Hamilton—or both. "Why if these walls could talk, what tales would they tell?" His tone was light, but his eyes, somehow pallid and piercing at the same time, unnerved her.

"Ones of love as well as intrigue," Burr said. "Did you know, when this was his camp, Washington was nearly poisoned by a bodyguard seduced by the British? The tales indeed! All fueled by fine wine, I am sure. Of which we are overdue. Come, Joseph. Let's see what awaits us at the table."

Before following Burr into the dining room, Alston smiled at Theodosia in a way that made her wish for her shawl despite the slow-to-fade heat of the day. Proving their sisterly connection, Nathalie wrapped an arm around Theodosia's shoulders. "*Mon amie*, you must set free the distaste in your eyes."

"And here I thought my best friend could read me. I was going for loathing."

"He is arrogant, but what man of his wealth is not?"

"Arrogance I can handle. We're all a bit arrogant, aren't we? But he is . . . that man . . . *pal-met-toe*, did you hear him? What a pompous, presumptuous . . ."

If her father were not embroiled so deep in this election, she'd have finished that statement with words a woman was not supposed to know let alone say, and she'd spell each one out with a quill for Mr. Joseph Alston. But her father was deep in this election.

And she, somehow, was deep in . . . in something with Philip.

Appearances must be upheld now more than ever.

And so with her best friend by her side, Theodosia entered the dining room, all smiles, all opinions tucked to her bosom, all flattery and charm, the female Aaron Burr she was raised to be.

Theodosia's cheeks ached from having to sustain her fake smile throughout the eight-course meal, during which Alston continued to insult the North, the French, Richmond Hill, and everything in between. All the while, her father doted on the conceited man like a smitten schoolboy.

Alston spoke of having the finest tutors as a child, attending Burr's alma mater of the College of New Jersey, and studying law under Edward Rutledge, who had signed the Declaration of Independence and survived being held as a British prisoner of war. Yet these boasts seemed equal to others of abandoning that same college after a single year, never graduating, and having no intention or financial need to ever work as an attorney. A stark contrast to her intellectual father who, after fighting in the revolution, dedicated himself to his own education and legal training and as an attorney weighed himself down in cases but was still forced to sell property and possessions to cover his debts.

When finally they arrived at dessert—a pepper cake whose recipe was copied from *A Booke of Cookery* and hand-delivered to Theodosia's mother by Martha Washington—Theodosia was ready to eat her slice in one bite and leave the men to their talk.

Along with the cake, Tom brought strong black coffee and tea. Coffee after noon was unheard of in the Burr home. And

Theodosia poured herself a full cup. Eleonore followed with a tray of honey and milk.

She'd barely set them on the table when Alston said, "No sugar? Is this not an estate, Burr?"

Her father issued what Theodosia knew was a feigned chuckle. "Eleonore, the sugar bowl, if you will."

Though he'd never admit it, even subconsciously, Theodosia suspected Alston's boorish behavior was partly born of the same underlying fear of inadequacy many men felt around her father. Still, she couldn't help herself. "We thought you'd enjoy some of our honey. From bees on our own grounds."

Alston shook his head. "My dear child, while I'm no man to talk ill of others' traditions, I have to say, the farther North I tread, the more my appreciation grows for our southern cuisine." He dismissively prodded the pieces of ginger and orange peel in his pepper cake. "What did you say that meat was again?"

"Bear," Theodosia said instantly.

"That's exactly what we did, right, Burr? *Bear it?*"

She gritted her teeth. Yes, the meat had been tough. Yes, it was impossible to cook such meat tender in the miniscule amount of time they had. Eleonore had done her best. But the woman's drawn face showed her distress at having heard Alston's every word. Still, she gently laid the sugar bowl beside their guest's cup.

Alston gave no sign of acknowledgment and instead leaned toward her father. "Traditions or not, I must speak a truth." He swooped up the delicate sugar bowl. "Burr, you simply cannot allow this. Sugar's a treasure to be kept under lock and key. Servants pilfer double what they bring you if you indulge them with unrestricted access. Our dining rooms are fitted with locked cabinets. The mistress of the house holds the key, and she's the only one to unlock it. She personally measures each and every portion the servants need for their recipes. Temptation's too great otherwise."

"That seems to speak more of the mistress than of the servants," Theodosia said. "Our servants at Richmond Hill are trusted because we do not treat them as servants."

"Oh, I expect to see you cleaning your own chamber pot, then?"

A *ting* was the only sound as Nathalie's fork struck her plate.

Theodosia concealed her hands beneath the table before they fully balled into fists. "How clever, Mr. Alston. Such quick wit. We must be sure to include you should we ever schedule a game of crambo."

He snickered. "For girls and simpletons."

*Right, then.*

"Yes, well, we shall hold on any and all invitations."

"I didn't say that. Truth is, Theodosia." His informal address unsettled her. "I'm always up for a game."

# Chapter 18

"Splendid, just splendid, my Little Miss Priss," her father greeted her with the next morning.

Theodosia had sat for breakfast an hour earlier than usual. Sleep had not come easily, barely at all. Her mind had refused to settle, instead churning on the day's events. On Philip. On Alston. On how very much she'd come to find the first intriguing. On how very much she'd come to hope to simply never find the other again.

Her father spread his napkin across his dark breeches. "Dinner couldn't have proceeded better."

"A pleasure to hear if not to have endured."

"Grant you, he's a bit peculiar—"

"Peculiar? Is that a new word for 'rude'?"

"When you're as traveled as I am, you will see how customs differ from place to place. That's what makes this a great nation. It's what we fought for."

"Hmm, yes, well, in that case, I shall call myself lucky for this glimpse of South Carolina. For I can cross it off any and all future itineraries."

"We mustn't judge with haste. Sometimes first impressions don't speak to the full breadth of character."

"Since when?"

Her father had always said to trust her instincts.

He avoided her eye. He was making poor excuses. And knew it.

As Eleonore delivered his breakfast of a soft-boiled egg and toast, he pressed his hand to his stomach. "No, no, much too much after the gluttony of last night."

He picked up the egg to return it to Eleonore, but out of spite and not hunger, Theodosia thanked Eleonore and claimed it for herself.

She cracked off the top and slid her spoon in.

He watched but said nothing. Instead, he countered by spreading the tiniest pat of butter on his toast. "In any case, we will soon get another opinion from a trusted source."

"Nathalie will say the same." Theodosia lifted her spoon. Indulging in this second egg felt decadent.

"To think there was a time when I longed for the two of you to join together."

"'Tis a reason they say 'be careful what you wish for' . . ." Another bite. This time, he eyed her sternly, making it feel dangerous.

"Joseph continues his leisurely trip north," her father said. "I have given him a letter of introduction to Dr. Eustis. A Providence stop on his journey suits both his horses in need of respite and our purposes."

"Dr. Eustis? And I thought we liked him." What was her father up to? Tolerating an evening with Alston for political gain was, though not enjoyable, understandable. Possible. *Barely.* Yet sending the crude little man to a dear friend?

He ignored her jest. "I've already drafted a letter for William. Good and loyal friends as we've been these many years, I trust no one more to analyze and anatomize Alston in soul, heart, and body. Thus the good doctor will be prepared to answer all the questions I put to him when we are next together and to offer his firmest opinion of Alston's character. I'm off to New England myself quite soon, garnering support."

"For the party or for yourself?" Theodosia asked.

"They are one and the same," he said.

"With any luck."

"No, with precision, planning, and purpose." He pushed his plate and his hardly touched toast aside. "We make our luck,

Theodosia. Which is why I implore you to give Mr. Alston the benefit of the doubt. He was quite taken with you."

Her eyebrow lifted. "I'd have thought he liked that *pal-met-toe* more. I wasn't entirely encouraging."

"With no one the wiser thanks to your always proper form."

She attempted another bite of the egg, but her stomach roiled at the thought of Alston "being taken" with her.

Alston had done little to change her opinion of the uncultured, boorish, and disease-ridden South—in fact, he'd bolstered it.

She set down her spoon.

Her father whisked away the egg. "Agreed. Quite enough." He scraped his chair back from the table, wiped his mouth with his napkin, and checked his pocket watch. He was almost out the door when he faced her. "I wonder . . . yes, yes, I do recall the inn where Joseph is to stay in Boston. Why, it might be nice for him to have a letter from a friend waiting. Homesick as he must be."

So casual her father was, slipping in this "request," as if an after-thought, them both knowing he'd been calculating to do so since he awoke that morning.

"And your penmanship must be in need of flexing, what with me home so much and no writing to occupy you." He stood framed by the doorway, all puffed up and pleased with himself. Perhaps it was this, this knowing she'd been getting away with something under his nose that made her acquiesce. But first, she reclaimed the egg, plunged her spoon in, and stuffed the remainder in her mouth at once. Her final bite tasted of defiance. Then, she begrudgingly nodded assent. A letter. One. What harm could it do?

But something about the relief in her father's eyes that seemed contrary to the smugness of his demeanor gave her pause.

A very extended pause. As that seemed all she could do as she later sat at her desk trying to write a letter to Alston.

She didn't like the man. His flippant attitude toward the slaves toiling in his mosquito-riddled rice swamps made her blood boil. As did his intimation that the servants in her own home should be treated with mistrust. Her father supported abolition. New York City had a considerable population of free Black people, and as an attorney, her father had defended freed slaves suing for their rightful portion of an estate bequeathed to them by their white slaveholder father. At home, he ensured their servants were taught to read and write. He even declared those who questioned the ability of one of their servants, due to the darkness of his skin, to play the violin with great skill "insensitive" and "unenlightened." As much as she disagreed with her father's decision to not grant full liberty to all their servants, the Burr home was not the Alstons'.

She twirled her quill, her mind unable to write quips and flirtations to that hubris with sideburns when her mind was weighed down by all the things at stake in the election her father was so desperate to win. The provisional army and the heavy taxes to pay for it, the authority of the government, trade with Great Britain, and ever present and ruling it all, the revolution in France.

Politics—the thing she so wanted to be a part of—now enveloped Theodosia. It was suffocating her. She needed to breathe.

And what better place than in the countryside?

She set her parchment aside, replacing it with a blank sheet. On which she wrote the clandestine plans for Sunday's date with Philip. She folded the letter and addressed it not to him but to his sister, Angelica.

"Sam readies the carriage, Theo," Burr said from the doorway of her bedroom. No knock, no greeting. This was business, and he approached it as such. He frowned upon finding Theodosia in bed, quilt drawn to her chin. "A Sunday invitation means the Livingstons are fully embracing us. Gather your things and dress in the coach if you must, but we will not respond by being even a second late."

Theodosia fluttered her eyes open, immediately shielding them against the light with her palm. "I'm sorry, Papa, I must have drifted off again." She winced as she tried to sit up. "I'll be down shortly."

Her father tentatively stepped into her room. "Are you not well?"

"Well? I'm perfectly well." She unearthed a hand from beneath the covers, attempting to pull them back. Was the tremor too much?

"If you are sure . . ."

Not too much then.

She let her eyelids fall shut, pretending to nod off. How easily she seemed to have fallen into a pattern of deceit.

"Miss Priss?" Worry permeated his tone, and Theodosia felt the heavy weight of guilt. "I-I'll send Sam with our apologies and go for the doctor myself."

The soles of his shoes clicked against the wood as he pivoted toward the door. Theodosia bolted upright. *A doctor will ruin everything!* She grabbed the quilt in one hand, preparing to toss it aside when Nathalie appeared in the doorway. Mind as astute as her eyes, she assessed the situation.

"Sir, no need," Nathalie said to Burr. "I'll stay with Theo."

Theodosia gave a grateful nod and swiftly buried herself back beneath the bed linens. The panicked sweat on her forehead might sell her story too well, and she swiped at it with the back of her hand. The death of her mother had left her father in perpetual fear of something dire befalling any of them. His restrictive diet and subsequent rules for both Theodosia and Nathalie were born of such constant trepidation. She was an awful, selfish child.

Nathalie continued to strengthen Theodosia's heartless excuse. "She needs rest and bone broth. Eleonore's already readying the latter, and I'll mind the former. For the duration of the afternoon, I will ensure she's not alone."

This was not a lie.

Her father drew Nathalie to him in a brief one-armed embrace before turning to Theodosia with a pained expression that almost made her leap from the bed.

"Miss Priss, are you sure . . ." He rubbed the skin on the back of his hands. "It's not your abdomen?"

Her mother's illness began in her stomach.

"Not at all," Theodosia said. "A headache."

"Pollen coats the floors," Nathalie added. Then, just as quickly, "Even with Nancy's daily attention. 'Tis just the time of year."

"That must be it," Theodosia said. "Perhaps I should try—"

"Do not think of it. Stay and rest. Let Nathalie care for you. But dispense with the broth. First, chamomile tea. No sugar. If that fails, ginseng. That's what they use in the East Indies and China. Surely, you're in need of stimulus." Though his eyes still showed strain, when Theodosia nodded agreement, his shoulders relaxed their hunch some. "Now," he continued, "I had considered an overnight at Partition Street, but perhaps it's better if I return."

"No." Theodosia rushed to respond, and his brow furrowed. "How worse I would feel to know I'm the source of your changed plans." No worse than shoving her own father out the door to clear the path for a man.

"If it were solely me . . ." he began, a spark in his eye in conflict with the worry. "But a friend from Philadelphia is in need of lodging."

"A friend?" Theodosia teased, sounding too like her normal, healthy self. She put her hand on her forehead. "Give Celeste our best."

Nathalie pecked Burr on the cheek. "Leave her to me. I suspect this may simply be a womanly matter."

As free as he was on matters of flirtation and seduction in his own life, as their many letters featuring the inimitable Celeste, his latest love interest, proved, the notion of menstruation sent Burr on his way. As, of course, Nathalie would have assumed it would.

She knew the meaning of today. And with Burr gone to the city, it could proceed without impediment—except for Theodosia's guilt.

After he bid them goodbye, Nathalie ripped back the quilt to reveal Theodosia not in her bedclothes but in a sheer white muslin dress. One of her most simple but elegant. No elaborate embroidery or strong dyes, no long train, no fussy underskirts. Just a neckline gathered by drawstring, a high waist, and a burgundy silk tie. Her auburn hair, previously covered by a nightcap, was gathered in a casual, flirtatious twist.

"Such risk you take, Theo," Nathalie said.

"I'd expected Papa would be on his way North by now," she said, testing a pair of teardrop earrings in the mirror. "And didn't you tell me to go through with this? To live life for myself for once?"

"Which I still heartily endorse. But feigning sickness? You could have at least prepared me."

"Next time." Theodosia decided against the earrings.

"Next time?"

The words had simply slipped out. Theodosia was acting entirely unlike her methodical, practical self. Was this how her mother had felt upon meeting her father? The need so in conflict with her own duties and expectations? The thought made her cross the room and ease open the top drawer.

She trailed a fingertip along her mother's letter, words written to her father, long ago memorized by Theodosia: "*'Tis impossible for me to disguise a single thought or feeling when writing or conversing with the friend of my heart.*"

Was seeking the same what propelled Theodosia now?

She unwrapped her mother's tortoiseshell brooch. Unworn since the day they'd buried her. Its swirling colors gleamed in the midday light, a physical manifestation of all Theodosia felt. She held the jewel against the red silk tied beneath her chest.

"No, no, no," Nathalie said.

Startled, Theodosia almost dropped it. "Right, of course. It's not appropriate." She snatched the linen, and her quivering fingers struggled to fold the fabric around the brooch.

Nathalie moved beside her. "I only meant, not with the silk. The burgundy dulls the rainbow of that precious tortoiseshell. The hues shine best on their own. Same as the one to wear it." Nathalie untied the red silk. She took possession of the brooch, opened the hinge, and pinned it at the center of the high waistline of Theodosia's dress.

Nathalie stepped back to assess. "Reminds me of a time not too long ago when we stood in this same position before the arrival of another gentleman caller."

Theodosia's face paled.

"No, dear sister, that is not to say . . . I only wished . . ." Nathalie collected her thoughts. "I don't believe you are capricious. I believe your feelings for Vanderlyn were born of more than a schoolgirl's crush. And yet Philip . . . I've had just the one glimpse of you together, but *you* I have been witness to every day since. With Vanderlyn you would have been happy. With Philip, you are alive. Fully Theodosia Burr."

Appreciation for the gift of Nathalie nearly overwhelmed Theodosia. Without her mother to guide her, to listen to her, to conspire with her, she would have only had her father if it were not for Nathalie. While she loved her father and couldn't imagine life without him, she was also beginning to imagine life with more than just him. Theodosia reached for Nathalie's hands, clinging to them and to the lifeline she represented. Theodosia whispered, "I have no idea what I'm doing."

Nathalie squeezed her hands. "I do. When we drop the coy manipulation, when we refrain from the lacquered-on charm, what's left is our truest selves. Our most real feelings."

Each word struck a truth inside Theodosia's heart. But they felt too precise to come from the perspective of mere observer. "Nathalie, is there someone you've neglected to mention?"

Nathalie shook her head. "But I know how it will feel when there is. My parents and yours have been the best of teachers." She released Theodosia's hands and fiddled with the strands of hair around her sister's face. "Oh, how much joy I have to see you this way. And I do wish you to live your life for yourself. And yet . . ."

"What is it, Nathalie?" A pulse of fear skipped Theodosia's heart, and she knew how very much she wanted—needed—to see Philip.

"And yet it should not mean ignoring all else . . . *everyone* else."

Nathalie was barely a step removed from the political and personal enmity between her father and Alexander Hamilton. Though it was far from the same scale, Nathalie's current exile and the fate of her family proved how quickly disagreements could lead to upheaval.

"I understand the concern. And I appreciate it." Theodosia closed the desk drawer, where her letter to Alston sat with nothing more than the salutation written. "But if there's one thing I can assure you of, dear sister, it's that Papa is ever present in all I do."

# Chapter 19

Theodosia rode to the far edge of Richmond Hill's property, that feeling of living for herself in great conflict with her feelings of betrayal. For her flimsy excuse, for her lies by omission, for the stark reality that she'd do it all again if it meant this awaited.

*Philip*.

Standing beneath an oak tree in a crisp black coat, slender white breeches, and black riding boots. A bouquet of orange, red, and yellow wildflowers in hand. His dark hair appeared brushed with an actual instrument, parted heavily to one side. A single curl trailed down his forehead. Lips of pink, cheeks of the same, and eyes bright and intent, awash in affection.

For her.

She pulled her mare to a halt beside him. The struggle to maintain her composure was like putting out a fire with cooking oil.

He transformed upon seeing her, his smile broadening, his shoulders relaxing, his eyes brimming with relief. As if he hadn't expected her to come. She gathered the reins in one hand, and he became a flurry of movement, setting the flowers on the scraggily grass, striding forward, raising his arms toward her. She hadn't required assistance dismounting since she was a child and barely even then. Her instinct was to swat him away.

But then his hand, bare of any glove, rested on the skin above her ankle. He looked into her eyes, his own reflecting the cornucopia of emotions brought by this moment: fear and hope and yearning and surprise and respect—mutual respect. Her instinct born of a need to prove herself equal, to prove herself above, was misplaced here. For Philip already saw her that way. His offer to ·

help free her of her horse came not to point out her need of it, but his own desire to be near her, to look upon her, to touch skin to skin. Her heart pounded with the same urgency. He spread his fingers wide against her calf in a caress that came equally with craving and tenderness. She pinched the leather tips at the end of each fingered glove and pulled, allowing the tan riding gloves to fall to the ground. Only then did she accept his hand and let their fingers connect.

His skin was soft like hers. Children of privilege. Children of a new nation. Children of rivals. Of enemies.

"Miss Burr," Philip said. "What a coincidence."

"A fortunate one, I hope?"

He laid a hand on her waist, pressing into her as he lowered her to the ground. Showing full respect and gentlemanly behavior, he released his hold on her. She couldn't have been more disappointed. "Very. Because it seems I've overpacked my book bag with provisions for the afternoon."

"*You* overpacked it?"

"*It* has been overpacked. By a sister as kind as she is meddlesome."

"Is that the only reason for this fortune? An overabundance of cheese and smoked meats?"

His brow wrinkled, indicating the seriousness of the matter. "And pie."

"Pie, well, then. Would be a crime for a good pie to go uneaten."

"Worse for it to be eaten alone."

He grinned, and she felt her body respond—not just her own upturning lips or the seeds of pleasure that often accompanied flirtation, but something deeper, something cardinal, primal. She felt herself blushing and shifted her gaze. On the grass beside them stretched two long, dark shadows, the angle of the late afternoon sun melding their bodies into one.

Philip again reached for her hand, and she gave it willingly, the sparks upon their first touch yielding to something more nuanced.

With one hand nestled inside Philip's and the other holding the reins of her mare, she walked to the shady spot under the tree where his own horse was hitched. They continued on, approaching the rise in the grounds overlooking the river that she'd described in her message to him.

She loved it here. Her father was enamored of the house that was Richmond Hill, the portico, the sweeping staircase, the library stocked by his favorite London bookseller, the structure's commanding height, standing high above all else. But this here before her, around her, was what made Richmond Hill a home. Unparalleled natural beauty with bountiful gardens, expansive farms and groves, and the noble Hudson, its waters ferrying small vessels laden with fruit and grain of the lands that surrounded them.

Views unsurpassed in all directions with glimpses of the city framed by the great limbs of ancient oaks. The Jersey shores with their rich, well-cultivated soil. Richmond Hill's flower gardens ringed with hedges. Copses of venerable oaks and wild shrubs and birds that serenaded morning and night.

She listened, scanning the horizon, admiring all around them, grateful for Philip to experience this with her, hoping he'd fall in love with it the way she had. "How does it seem to you?"

"Impressive," Philip said. "And quiet. I envy you, the quiet."

"But the city has activity, signs of prosperity and sounds of leisure, all intermingled."

"All overrated. I've often suggested a move uptown, but now that I've been here, seen this, I've a new aim." He faced her directly as he said the last part.

"So you admire it?"

"I admire everything I see before me."

Her breath hitched. "As do I."

"Fond of rapscallion scoundrels, then?"

"I meant the Hudson." She dipped her chin, flitted her lashes, and . . . stopped. *Truest self.* Nathalie's words rang in her ears. Theodosia looked Philip straight on. This was not a boy to trifle with, not a young man to charm, not an older one to entertain on her father's behalf. This was someone she wished to treat as she wanted to be treated herself. "I am fond of it all. If I could remain at Richmond Hill for the rest of my days, happiness would not elude me. And yet . . . all the better if I had someone to share it with."

"A worthy goal."

"One you aspire to?"

"I do now."

They stood amid such natural splendor, the river humming as it flowed, the gentle breeze rustling her dress, threatening to undo the careful part of his hair, yet they remained transfixed on each other. The air felt alive, like the precursor to an afternoon storm, but the sky was cloudless, intensely blue and serene. The only storms lay within Theodosia. A hunger wanting not of sustenance but of him. A yearning she knew existed but had never felt. Her own desire powered her every movement, her every thought, her entire sense of self.

She followed him to the dark wool blanket upon which he'd set the aforementioned meats, cheese, and pie, along with bread and a squat glass bottle of red wine.

"It's lovely, Philip," she said.

"I wish it were more."

"Abundance does not equal happiness."

He lifted her hand and pressed his lips to her skin. "I agree." He cast his gaze upward. "With the exception of wine." He winked, set down her hand, and spread his arm toward the blanket. "Would be rude to keep it waiting."

She rubbed the gooseflesh budding on her forearms nervously. "We cannot have such a stain on our reputation."

"How well-trained are we? Truly, what good little soldiers."

"To that, all this would seem to disagree." Yet still she lowered herself to the blanket, sitting with her knees bent and legs tucked to one side.

"And to that, *I* disagree." Philip placed himself across from her and reached for the wine. "We operate with the utmost discretion."

"Does that make it all right? That we are behind the backs of our—"

"Eh, eh, eh," Philip interrupted. He poured from the bottle and placed one mug in front of Theodosia and another before himself.

She stared at the full cup, and her thoughts betrayed her, unable to refrain from trying to reconcile this growing conflict between what she wanted and what she had been taught. Her father remained ever present in her mind. Alston too. And John Vanderlyn and her mother.

Her mother to whom Theodosia had made promises, to care for her father, to do as he required. What would she think if she could see Theodosia now? Here? A deceit that could only be surpassed if it were Philip's father pouring her wine. But then again, even her mother hadn't been free of deceit.

With the tip of her finger, Theodosia circled the outline of the brooch pinned to her dress. "My mother had to do the same. Omissions, perhaps, truths manipulated, certainly, probably even outright lies. She played two sides, made each believe in her loyalty for years. To ensure her lands would not be taken, her first husband not tainted, the man she loved . . . my father . . . not incriminated or worse."

"Those seem causes worthy," Philip said tentatively.

"Are they? Or are they simply selfish? Are we not beholden to some measure of right and wrong?"

"Whose measure? Not God or some preacher."

The claims of atheism swirled around Jefferson, but neither of their families had ever been particularly guided by religion.

Theodosia responded, "Then perhaps by the measure of those who will be hurt. Those we love being hurt."

"When it comes to love, hurt is inevitable, Theo. The very fact of caring so deeply invites it. Love lays us bare and vulnerable. It makes us easy prey."

"And such a risk is worth it?"

"Always."

"Love should not be so complicated," she said.

"I don't know if I agree. For something to possess one's heart, one's body, one's soul, to make us crave and need and want, to make us do things as extraordinary as twisting truths before British soldiers and taking—on Broadway in full light of day and under the eyes of all—the hand of the man whose betrayal publicly shamed you, it must be complicated. Nothing simple can do all of that."

He spoke of her mother and his own.

Philip lifted his mug. "A toast. To the complicated."

"To the complicated," Theodosia repeated. Because it was already. With more to come. She tilted back her mug and drank it in full.

They imbibed quickly and greedily as if a substitute for what each truly wanted. Each sip eased Theodosia's guilt and further loosened her tongue. Her spine softened, relaxing with a curve that brought her closer to Philip.

There was no more talk of their fathers, none of their families. Nor of the past at Madame de Senat's or the future ruled by the election to come. They talked of that day, of that moment, of the now.

"A swim across?" He gestured to the river. "Possible?"

"For a duck."

"Is that a challenge?"

"No—"

He stood. "Just let me free myself of this waistcoat and these breeches—"

"Philip!"

He flopped back down beside her, the twinkle in his eyes and the consumption of wine challenging Theodosia's ability to keep her wits.

"You're a bad influence, Philip."

"Such kind words . . . yet you hold firm?"

"I have no power but that of will."

"Falsehood if there ever was."

"You claim to know of my power?"

"I claim to experience it. Be under it. Willingly."

"Is this literal or figurative?"

"One can hope both."

As their mugs emptied and the afternoon sun lowered on the horizon, Theodosia asked Philip to recite another of his poems.

His eyes sought out the earth, and he transformed into a shy boy before her eyes.

"That fearsome, am I?" she teased. "Don't let my intellect intimidate, Philip. I promise not to judge any more harshly than I would a young Shakespeare."

He clung to his mug, rotating it in his hands as if invoking a spell whose magic would see it restored to full.

"I'm joking, Philip. I wouldn't judge. Not when your words so transparently come from your heart."

He jerked back with a derisive laugh. "'A maiden, a lass,' why, yes, straight from the heart." He lifted an eyebrow. "Straight from some organ, all right."

He couldn't shock his way out of this.

"Don't," she said. "Don't trivialize what you hold dear." The wine acted like a buoy, her emotions bobbing at the surface. "We can't let them guide us in all we do. Isn't that what you told me? Why I should continue to write my story for the magazine?"

Philip spun the mug with such force it flew from his hands, landing on the grass beyond the blanket. He shook his head and popped up onto his heels. "I need to show you something." He reached into his pocket and extracted a letter.

She unfolded it and read the title: "'Rules for Mr. Philip Hamilton'?" She looked up, confused. "What is this?"

"Just keep reading."

She squinted to better make out the elaborate handwriting with its lavish tails at the ends of letters like "t" and "y" and nearly any word that the author deemed worthy of concluding with a flourish. She read aloud:

*"Rules for Mr. Philip Hamilton from the first of April to the first of October he is to rise not later than Six Oclock—The rest of the year not later than Seven. If Earlier, he will deserve commendation. Ten will be his hour of going to bed throughout the year.*

*From the time he is dressed in the morning till nine o clock (the time for breakfast Excepted) he is to read Law.*

*At nine he goes to the office & continues there till dinner time—he will be occupied partly in the writing and partly in reading law.*

*After Dinner he reads law at home till five O clock. From this hour till Seven . . ."*

She lowered the page. "What is this?"

"Plain and forthright, isn't it?"

"This is from your father?" But it could have been written by her own.

Philip tapped the page. "Do not miss the last line."

Theodosia gave a sympathetic smile, though Philip's eyes were fixed on the blanket between them. She returned to the letter: *" 'He must not Depart from any of these rules without my permission.' "*

*Permission?* Philip was an adult, a graduate of Columbia College. And here his father was dictating his every waking moment. Nearly the same condemnation ran through her mind as had left Madame de Senat's lips not long ago. "You're not a child."

"True. But I'm *his* child."

"That doesn't give him the right . . ." Her voice trailed off, for she knew it did, same as it did for her own. So long as she wished to please her father and be the daughter he wanted her to be. Even at the expense of herself and of what was right in front of her. "Perhaps they've done this to us—muddled the notion of right and wrong. Perhaps, then, a facade matching what's in one's heart is a luxury we don't have."

"Nor my sister."

"Nor Nathalie. She never had any choice . . ." Thinking of Nathalie brought every member of their household to mind, and Theodosia's breath caught in her throat. "Alexis," she said, barely a whisper. Her quick words and tone the night they'd hosted Alston had continued to gnaw at her. Reprehensible as he was, Alston was making her question herself, if her virtues were indeed false when it came to Richmond Hill's servants. She wondered if her father felt the same. She grew increasingly unsettled by his refusal to give voice to what he claimed to believe. The same as Philip's father. And the Nicholsons and all the families whose words about abolition did not match their actions.

Philip set his hand on her knee, an understanding conveyed in his simple touch. The warmth in his deep chestnut eyes came from so much more than their color. "Because life, like love, is complicated."

So intimate it was, to see beneath the mask of Philip Hamilton. It made her wish to offer the same. Not the Theodosia Burr she presented to the world but someone else. Someone she was on the path to becoming.

She brought her legs beneath her, propping herself up on her knees so their heads, eyes, lips were aligned. They couldn't. They shouldn't. Her reputation . . . Her father's by extension . . . So much lay in opposition. So much at risk. So much to lose.

Philip's eyes swallowed hers.

*But, oh, what to gain!*

Her lips were on his, supple and sun-drenched and magnificent. Nothing had ever been so simple. Nothing would ever be as complicated. Perhaps that was how the best love stories began.

"Next week," Philip whispered, his fingers twining in the strands hanging loose beside her cheek. "Same place, same time."

"Must we wait an entire week?"

Philip gave a wry smile. "Didn't you see? The rules give me Sunday afternoon for 'innocent recreations.' "

"Oh? Am I so innocent?"

"I sincerely hope not."

He kissed her again, this time with a hunger a proper society lady would put a stop to. But fortunately, she was not a proper society lady.

"In secret, Philip." Theodosia finally placed her hand on his chest and nudged him back. Her lips burned, engorged and swollen, and she relished the discomfort. "Complete secrecy."

As he helped her mount her horse, she took in every piece of him. His own raw lips, his decidedly disheveled hair, his chest still heaving in a rapid rhythm that matched her own. Side by side, they trotted through the grounds that concealed them. Never had she been more grateful for all of Richmond Hill.

At the fork that required them to separate, she let him kick his horse into a canter first, watching as he rode until he blended with the trees, and she could no longer make out his form. Still, she remained, holding on to the illusion that the world was just the two of them.

# Chapter 20

THAT ILLUSION SHATTERED AS SOON AS Theodosia returned home, Philip's scent still making her dizzy. She floated into the parlor, and her heart stopped.

There, by the palmetto, her father stood, holding a copy of the *From the Fairer Sex* magazine. Each piece of the puzzle struck her like lightning as it formed a whole. The pages of the journal were folded back, open to her story. Her father had read her writings since she was a child. If anyone would recognize the words as hers, it would be him.

Yet her father's dark eyes held no hints. A trick of the fading light perhaps, but they had never appeared quite so black and opaque.

"The taverns can talk of nothing but this," he said. "Have you read it?"

It took all her might to shake her head.

"Seeing as how you are miraculously recovered, would you care for the highlights?"

"I-I can read it later if you think it worthy." A lasso tightened around her lungs.

"Oh, it is worthy, Miss Priss, for the sheer quality of the writing alone if not for the ideals held within."

*He knew.*

"Is it not fiction?" she asked, hoping to continue the charade as long as she was able.

He hooked a thumb in the pocket of his fine navy waistcoat. It looked new, but their finances could not have permitted it.

211

"A clever disguise," he said, "though it appears to have grown bolder in each subsequent installment. Espousing education in arithmetic, language, philosophy, history, one day even law for girls. And being clear that such education should have not the purpose of females being better companions for their husbands but to be fully immersed members of society with all rights including that of the vote."

Always her intellectual ally like no other, he'd summarized her message succinctly and accurately. Which perhaps opened a door . . . she tread lightly, in step and in word. "All of which you believe."

"For you."

"But I'm not the only female in the world."

"You are the only one in mine." Burr slapped the journal against his palm and strode toward her. "For now, an anomaly, not a policy to run for office on. Hamilton has never uttered a word about the rights of women. Jefferson declares the ascension of women is something for which, and I quote, *'the public is not prepared nor am I.'* Should I be different?"

As accustomed as she was to it, his sharpness made her recoil. If only she had the ability of the girl in her story: to lie down for a nap and awake in another time, another place. Philip at her side.

But that was fiction. If she were ever to change her father's mind about Philip, about anything, she must deal in fact.

She held her father's gaze with a strength she did not fully possess. Yet appearing as the situation demanded was as ingrained as knowing her way around these hills. "Yes, you should be different. You want to lead this nation. And you claimed to want to do so with me, your daughter—your *scholarly* daughter—by your side. Were you not the one convincing me that we can make a difference on the beliefs we hold dear? Abolition and the rights of women and education and so much more. Real change. Together."

"Only if I win."

They stood close, the two at near equal height. But in every other way, the distance between them was cavernous. His face was stone. It sliced Theodosia's heart.

Her father rested a hand on her shoulder. "I'm proud of you. You're exactly what I knew you could be. If nothing else, these stories prove that. But it must end. Or it will end us." He released his hand, but the weight remained.

Her tongue lay limp. So much unsaid, so many secrets bricking a wall between them.

On his way to the door, he dropped the journal into the fireplace, and a mist coated her eyes. Before leaving he turned to face her. "Do they pay?"

"No."

"Shame, we could use the money."

He was gone the next morning, off to Philadelphia for more in-person political maneuvering. He didn't wait for her to wake. He didn't wait to say goodbye. He'd left but the most cursory of notes. An expected itinerary, an allusion to a migraine that would make the journey arduous, and a single line "reminding" her of the letter to Alston.

Despite her embarrassment at being discovered and her shame for having continued to engage in an act contrary to all she'd been taught—one of which she knew her father would disapprove—for the first time in memory, Theodosia was not sorry to see him gone.

In fact, she was elated. Free of the reproach in his eyes. Free of the scolding in his frown. Free of him, the constant presence that made difficult the one thing she wished to do: meeting with Philip.

The success of how they had communicated the details of their first clandestine visit prompted repetition. And over the next three days, Theodosia wrote veiled notes of flirtation to him via Angelica, and he reciprocated in kind, writing letters that Angelica's fine script would address to Theodosia. Fortunately, even while traveling, her father never lacked a message she must write and have hand-delivered to this person or that "with haste." Sam's journeys in and of the city allowed the Hamilton home to become a part of his route. If Sam or the Hamilton messenger thought it peculiar, certainly neither would mention this sudden close friendship between Theodosia and Angelica.

Philip's letters were not the heat of his lips against hers or the lightness of his caress on her cheek or the pounding of his heart in time with her own, but they filled the hours trickling by slower than honey from a beehive until Sunday.

As did her quill and the words she set down to conclude her story for the magazine. The writing of it—the publishing of it—had been foolish. Reckless. Dangerous. And the most fun she had ever had.

The most fun alone.

Perhaps it was the introduction of Philip in her life that eased her farewell to her story. Though still she found her stomach knotting as she dipped her pen in ink. She wrote two versions—the first solely for herself, ending with a triumphant call to action, the way she would have written it had her father not discovered her as the author. She poured sand on the ink, allowing it to dry, before shuttering it away in her desk drawer.

Then, with new parchment, she penned the conclusion for the magazine, one toning down—*ruining*—all that had come before. With a heavy heart, she signed "Miss P" for the last time. She would venture downtown that afternoon.

She had written each of the narratives with her father's hasty note resting in the corner of her desk. Her own little mutiny, putting so many words to paper, save for the ones he had expressly asked of her. Alston could wait.

Wearing a white summer dress with short sleeves and the high waist she'd come to favor thanks to Nathalie, Theodosia neared the printing district. Now as familiar as any of her favorite spots in the city.

Early to meet Georgie, she wandered inside a bookshop she had passed on every visit, welcoming the respite from the sun. The sweet, musky aroma mixed with fresh paper and ink, and she breathed it in, feeling at home. Almanacs sat beside bibles that sat amid dictionaries that led to books on theology. The shopkeeper also maintained an expansive selection of chapbooks, small in size, saddle-stitched, and illustrated with woodcuts, the tales inside were those of heroes and legends, crimes and ballads, folklore and fairy tales. Inexpensive, usually crude, and most often anonymous. Theodosia smiled, thinking that she had essentially written one herself.

She puttered about, finding herself before the cramped section of foreign language books, where she was struck with an idea. She scanned the spines, searching for ones in French. None appeared, not even a vacant space indicating they'd all been sold.

"Pardon," she said, addressing the shopkeeper. He wore a dark coat and vest and white linen breeches, everything well-loved but fresh and clean. "Would you be able to direct me to what you may have in the language of French?"

The man went rigid, then proceeded to continue dusting the shelf in front of him, his back to Theodosia. She approached, standing beside him, and repeated her request. Again, he ignored her.

She opened her mouth to repeat for a third time, when he bent his neck and whispered, "We've none, we've never had, and I dare say scarcely will."

She knitted her brows together. "But that's odd, isn't it? A bookshop without so much as a French dictionary or a French—"

"Land sakes, quiet Miss!" he hissed. He tossed his duster onto the shelf and with a grousing under his breath said, "Be here until candle-lighting if I don't tend to you, won't I?" Without waiting for a reply, he hastened to the back of the shop, where he crooked a finger at her.

Peculiar, both the man and the situation, but her curiosity invited her to follow. "Now, Sir, I do not mean to contradict, but I—"

He put his finger to his lips, drew back a heavy curtain, and again beckoned. The small room held crates and tables with books in need of and in varying states of repair.

"Fine, fine, fine," he grumbled. "Yes, I carried books in French, but I had to remove every last one of them. All nature was in here complaining."

"Complaining? You mean your customers?" She shook her head. "I don't understand."

"Of course a lass like you wouldn't, being ignorant of such matters." She felt her nostrils flare. "But my dear, many believe it is the French and the legacy of their revolution that will lead to our own country being torn in two."

"Is that so?" She itched to say who she was and what she knew but didn't want to scare him off.

"I'll allow my own feelings are somewhat indifferent on the matter, but even without, my shop's my livelihood. Customers speak, I listen."

"A pleasure to hear," Theodosia said. "For I'm a customer, and I've need of a book in French."

"Shh!" That finger to his lips. "The death of me, you will be!"

Theodosia lowered her voice. "I simply wish for a volume of poems. Hardly the first shot of war, is it?"

He scrunched his face, doubling his already prominent collection of wrinkles. "Fine, fine, fine, back here." He shoved aside a second curtain cordoning off a selection of haphazardly stacked crates. "That's the entirety of my collection. Look if you must, but you ought not leave without a purchase with all this fuss. And . . ." He once again brought his finger to his lips.

"Not a soul will know. I am excellent at secrets, Sir."

Keeping them and making them.

He grumbled something short of assent and left her alone. Theodosia pulled off her gloves, dismayed by the notion of her fellow New Yorkers insisting on the removal of books solely due to the language they were written in. She could not escape politics and this election and her father anywhere.

She turned her attention to the crates and books, sorting through, allowing her fingers to trail across the bindings and pages, slowing as they traced the letters of a title whose tale she knew almost by heart. Her surprise quickly gave way to the affection she still held for the book after all these years.

Her father had written from Westchester, recounting his seemingly endless search for "proper and amusing" French books to purchase for her and his dismay at finding only fairy tales and nonsense fit for the usual child of nine or ten. Those would not do for Theodosia, despite that exact age of nine being her own. "Flattered" as he was with her skill in French, he'd persevered until he encountered this fantastical story, handsomely bound in two volumes octavo that he deemed worthy of his "intelligent and well-informed girl." She'd loved it. Mostly because she'd loved her father and his extraordinary belief in her. Something that had never waned.

She trailed her finger along the letters on the cover, some of her anger at him lifting.

It wasn't that he was never wrong. But perhaps, in this, in her writing of this story, he was right. First and foremost must be winning this election. They would take each step together, making sacrifices and celebrating successes as they had always done.

She retrieved a handkerchief from her reticule and dusted off the volumes, placing them prominently on top of the highest crate. And there, lurking underneath, was exactly the thing she sought: a book of poems in French. She cleaned it carefully and lovingly before calling over the shopkeeper. She paid him behind the curtain using the money she had intended for a ham. She and Nathalie preferred oysters anyway.

Too large to fit into her small bag, she cradled the book of poetry in her arms while waiting for Georgie in the alleyway. She'd affixed the ribbon to the bakery's windowsill with plenty of time for him to do his check at the appointed hour. He had never been late before.

Her foot tapped unconsciously as she made her way through nearly a quarter of the volume's poems before she heard the call:

"*Aaron Burr's cold-blooded, corrupt, Hamilton says! Exclusive! For your eyes! Just six coppers!*"

Theodosia hurried to the end of the alley, but the boy hawking the newspapers disparaging her father was not Georgie. Tall and tanned with a disinterested gait, this newsboy shuffled along, uttering his sales cry only half as well—or often—as Georgie. Pride swelled at Georgie's skill, less so for his punctuality.

The languid boy plodded past the alley, and Theodosia whispered to him. "*Psst.*"

He barely swiveled his neck.

"*Psst!*" She tried again. "Newsboy. Behind you!"

He turned slower than molasses dripping from a spoon. "What of it?"

She waved him forward, but he stood his ground. "Here, please."

"Ma'am, I reckon I'm selling papers. Not your cup o' tea."

"I've got coin as well as the next."

"Not all the next. I'm supposed to sell these to well-dressed gentlemen."

She grimaced at his slight. "By all means, don't let me stand in your way."

He shrugged and started off.

"All tarnation!" she muttered to herself. She needed him. "Wait! Please!"

The boy caught himself mid-step, lingered for longer than seemed prudent as he was in the middle of the street, before finally dragging himself back. He clutched the strap of the satchel she'd seen looped over Georgie's chest. "Ma'am, I told you—"

"It's fine. I don't need a paper. I'm actually looking for someone you must know. Georgie? Is he here?"

"If he's here, I wouldn't be."

"Is he . . ." She couldn't say "fired" for that would be disastrous for her and Georgie both.

"Not dead yet, 'sfar as I know."

She fell back. "Is he that gravely ill?"

"How the blazes would I know? I'm just selling papers because he ain't."

"So he'll be returning soon? Tomorrow?"

"Not if either he's a goner or I outsell 'em."

Hardly likely from what she'd seen. "Now that's unkind. What if the roles were reversed?"

"He'd do the same. That boy's got gumption."

Exactly what she liked about him.

"But him nor me got this job no more if you don't let me leave."

Two men on the sidewalk slowed, and Theodosia slunk back. "Go on now," she said in a high-pitched trill. "Let me be. I do not require any papers."

"You . . . what?" The boy knocked his knuckles against his head. "So I can go?"

"Yes, off with you." She dipped her chin as the men lingered, watching from under her lashes until they continued on, and the newsboy left.

*Of all the times to get sick!*

Immediately, Theodosia chastised herself. If Georgie were truly ill, how horrid she would feel for only thinking of herself. She would have Philip inquire of him, and she'd surely help in any way she could, but now . . . now . . . *now what?*

She gripped the book to her chest and paced the alley. No way could she ask that fool selling Georgie's papers to delivery her story to the magazine. He'd just as likely drop them in the mud as eat them for all she could discern.

Her father's trip would last the week. She could wait a day, maybe two, then return, hoping Georgie was well and back to work. But what if he wasn't? How long could she wait? Long enough to mail the pages? Perhaps, but with each hour of delay, her father's anger built. As did the threat to him.

She halted. She was already here. Not even a block away. Mr. Gunther did not know her, nor she him. She could be in and out faster than her father's glower at a large slice of cake. She'd casually stroll past the magazine's office and slip the pages under the door. No one would be the wiser.

She smoothed down the front of her dress, ran her hand along the sides of her hair, assuring no strays, and set off.

Purposeful, confident, with nary a wisp of fear, that was how she aimed to appear. The book in her arms served as armor as much for its density as for the person it represented. For this act was for her father but also for Philip. Remaining in good stead with the former might help to bring him around to the latter. A smile widened across her face. She had fallen for Philip Hamilton. Why, anything was possible.

She strode toward the building home to the ladies' magazine, her mind elsewhere.

"My goodness!" a woman cried. "Is it . . . Theodosia? You nearly trampled me like a herd of wild horses!"

Lucinda Wilson, fresh off the steps leading down from the magazine.

Theodosia's neck flushed, and she lifted the book of poems to cover. "Lucinda, what a surprise." She couldn't bring herself to include a "lovely." Her acting was good but not that good.

"Indeed it is." Lucinda narrowed her icy blue eyes despite Theodosia being the one directly facing the sun. "What are you doing in this part of town?"

"Oh, I'm sure same as you."

"Really? Do tell. I didn't take you as one whipping up dessert recipes for prominent publication."

"Another?" Theodosia blurted. "Why, you must have much time to spare." She shouldn't have said that.

Lucinda stiffened. "Hardly. I'm strained at the effort to represent my family name in the manner required. A burden you're fortunate not to face."

Theodosia's teeth ground against one another, and still she managed a polite, closed-mouth smile. "Well, then, by all means, don't let me be the cause of your delay." She aimed to circle around Lucinda when a gloved hand fell on the book in Theodosia's arms.

"Studying?" Lucinda asked. "If you need tutoring, I'm sure Madame de Senat would allow you to attend class again."

"An opportunity I would welcome. One is never too old to gain knowledge, don't you think?"

Lucinda assessed the length of Theodosia, her eyebrow arching. "Ooh, yes, I feel as though I learn something new every day."

# CHAPTER 21

*L*UCINDA *W*ILSON.

What a gossiping, patronizing, uppity flirt. *Who would not leave first.*

Theodosia would have sworn that Lucinda knew exactly where Theodosia was headed with the way she had settled in, like she laid her head at the offices of the magazine.

Theodosia wished she had the power to vanquish her. If only Nathalie's childhood obsession had borne fruit! As a young girl, Nathalie was enthralled by tales of the Salem witch trials. She'd begged Papa to fill her schooldays with texts about them, convinced she had magic running through her veins. She harassed Theodosia so thoroughly that she had finally given in. Theodosia helped Nathalie write a "spell" to make Madame de Senat dispense chocolates with lunch.

Her father had heard, through Alexis, Theodosia later discovered, of their frivolity and had played along. The first day, a perfect round chocolate sweet sat beside their boiled potatoes. Nathalie had clapped and nearly leapt from her seat. But the next day, the perfect little round had been the color of chocolate but the taste of mud. Rotten trick. But it had cured Nathalie of witchcraft. If only it hadn't.

Theodosia's fingers grew numb from her grip on the book of French poems. She bid Lucinda a good day and marched through the streets, heading to the underground tavern that Philip had taken her to. She would sit, have a cider, maybe some oysters, and wait out Lucinda. Theodosia would prove what endurance meant.

Her chest heaving with her brisk pace, she paused at the end of the street. She looked left and right, assessing which direction to go, trying to remember the route Philip had followed. She crinkled her brow. All these streets wound this way and that, and she hadn't really been paying close attention the first time. She twiddled her fingers against the book.

*Oh, just choose!*

She pivoted and set out to the right. With her next step, she lurched forward, stumbling on a loose cobblestone. She dropped the book and planted her hands just in time to prevent her cheek from landing in a pool of mud.

But not her dress. Her formerly white dress.

And all of a sudden, Theodosia was sure that if anyone were a witch capable of spells, it was Lucinda.

She pushed herself up, stretching for the volume of poems, and her boot caught the hem of her dress. The sound upon righting herself was the fabric splitting in two.

"Perfect," she grumbled. "Just perfect."

"Of that I am unsure," a male voice said.

She lifted her head to look directly into a handsome face reminiscent of the one occupying her thoughts night and day.

Alexander Hamilton.

His breeches matched his waistcoat and top coat, all the color of sand, save for a pop of bright blue inside the upturned collar—the better to bring out the azure of his eyes.

He extended a gloved hand and helped Theodosia to her feet. "Hastening toward one's next endeavor is wholly commendable, but we must take care with our footing."

Theodosia nodded, embarrassment and nerves preventing her brain from forming a verbal response. She had scarcely any interaction with him as a child, and the encounter outside the newspaper office had not added anything of substance. Her only knowledge of him came filtered through newspapers, her father, and now, Philip.

"Is there any damage?" he asked, a rakish grin reminding her disconcertingly of his son. "Other than the dress?"

Theodosia brushed her hand against the front, only marring it with more mud. She slid her palms over her hips and wiped them against the back of her skirt.

"No need to fuss," Alexander said. "Without mishaps, how would we measure success?" He placed a hand over his heart, moving with grace and polish. "Ah, yes, forgive my manners, how is Mr. Burr?"

The connection in his train of thought lacked subtlety. "My father is well, thank you for asking." She interlaced her fingers at her waist. "He's currently in Philadelphia."

"Daring man! If summer makes New York City hotter than a kitchen fire, Philadelphia's the devil's lair."

"Cities are quite the furnace. Which is why we are so fortunate to have the breezes at Richmond Hill." She would not refrain from sparring right back.

"In addition to the space, I would posit." His rosy cheeks brightened his otherwise pale countenance, topped by hair of faded auburn. "Our household bursts with young ones underfoot, all charging forward with passions igniting, but I would be remiss to represent wanting it any other way."

No matter what anyone else desired. "And your children?"

"Pardon?"

"They are agreeable?" She tread close to a subject she should not. "To those passions?"

He inclined his highly powdered head as if he hadn't quite heard her.

"To those passions all colliding underfoot, I mean," Theodosia corrected herself, but Hamilton was savvy enough not to miss her implication—and to continue on as if he had.

"Siblings squabble, but they are also the best of friends. Mrs. Hamilton and I are pleased as pigeons. There is nothing as satisfying as seeing one's children grow and prosper. I have had a life that permits the comparison, Miss Burr." His smile was bittersweet.

All the while, Theodosia had been expecting the arrogant Hamilton her father claimed him to be; the demanding one Philip did. Instead, she saw a man. One whose power was shifting, one reconciling who he once was and who he wanted to be. Something she was quite familiar with as she saw the same in her father. Yet without the air of content.

Theodosia gently nodded to the colonel. "One finds the life that suits them."

"One pursues the life they require." Hamilton clicked his heels together and offered her his arm. "Allow me to escort you somewhere you can freshen?"

"How kind. But I'm near to my destination. I can manage."

"Very well, Miss Burr." He placed his index finger on his bottom lip, assessing the mud that had befouled her dress. "Tell your father I inquired of him, but take care with the wording. For without doubt, a learned man as he will be quite familiar with the *Barber of Seville*."

"Throw dirt enough, and some of it is sure to stick," Theodosia said, paraphrasing Beaumarchais's line from the French play, meaning that if one persisted in slander, it would eventually become truth.

His eyes danced with delight. "It is not so easy to impress me, Miss Burr."

"Nor me, Colonel Hamilton."

Her bluntness surprised him, yet his thin lips widened to an energetic smile. "To this, let one always aspire."

He walked away, every footfall resounding with determination.

Theodosia could not deny his charisma. His reputation as a tomcat in his youth was surely well deserved. The notion that his son would travel the same path with respect to his effect on women was entirely understandable. Likely even. She smiled to herself. Never before had she been so pleased to thwart someone's intended path.

She did her best to clean her hands on the torn fabric of her hem. She then wound it into a knot to prevent further tripping. She pushed back the stray hairs fallen loose from her twist, scooped up the poetry book, and retraced her steps, looking for anything familiar.

She ignored the stares from passersby and studied every street and building. Finally, she recognized a narrow opening and hurried toward it. There, at the end, was the same skinny structure with that same sturdy oak door. Her throat itched with the need for a drink.

And her body with another need. For instantly she recognized the dark wavy hair, the strong, lean build, and those perfect lips of Philip Hamilton. Perhaps he and his father had been dining together. Such a shift in their family dynamics must have been what put the colonel in his jocular mood. She wished to know if Philip felt the same.

He hopped up the steps from the tavern, his arm outstretched to hold open the door. Theodosia raised her hand to call to him when Lottie Jewell's beaming face appeared. Her blonde ringlets bounced as she accepted Philip's hand. He bent his head toward her, close enough to whisper in her ear. She tucked her chin, shyly, and he trailed his finger across her cheek. She giggled. He laughed.

And a small noise escaped Theodosia's throat. She whirled around so quickly she made herself dizzy.

*So naive!*

Her heart beat in her ears.

To think she had diverted Philip from his womanizing path!

She charged down the small street.

Diverted after one outing and a spin or two on a dance floor? Embarrassment consumed her as she thought of the letters sent, the flirtation filling the days before they were to meet again. Never before had she been so gullible.

She felt her cheeks flush, her mouth tightening, tears budding in her eyes and fought it all. But the fury building beneath her breast . . . that she let in . . . that she welcomed . . . that she allowed to guide her. Back to what was important. Back to her purpose.

Her feet moved double time as she stormed toward the printing district. Her father would win this election. She would help him. Whatever it took.

She yanked the clips from her hair and coaxed it out of its twist. Her auburn waves fell past her shoulders. She found a still wet spot of mud on her dress and gathered it in her fist. The dirt seeped into her skin, spilled through the cracks around her knuckles, just as it did on the day of her mother's funeral. She squeezed until her nails left marks. She ran her filthy hand through her hair and across her cheek. Covered in mud, no one would think her to be Theodosia Burr.

With a gait as determined as Alexander Hamilton's, she marched up the stairs to the printer's office and shoved the letter under the door.

*What was she thinking?*

*About everything?*

She would not be a fool.

Not for anyone.

# CHAPTER 22

HER MIND SPINNING, THEODOSIA RETURNED TO Richmond Hill. She could not see anyone, not Nathalie nor Alexis nor Eleonore. She would not let them see her like this. Not the mud nor the dress but with her heart so bare.

She sped past the portico and the front door and circled around to the servants' entrance. With a silent plea to find it unlocked, she nudged the door open. She listened for voices and footsteps before slipping through and bounding up the stairs. In her room, she dropped the poetry book she never should have purchased and peeled off the ruined dress. She held its frayed hem in her hands, and a gale swept through her. Her shoulders hunched, and her lungs seized as if she'd been struck in the belly. She wrung the fabric in her hands, twisting, pulling, until a new piece tore, the surprise halting her, but then her hands moved without thought, tearing another and another. She couldn't stop. She ripped the dress from hem to hem until there was nothing but a pile of rags.

They surrounded her, and she hung her head in shame. Nathalie would have been able to repair the initial tear. Nancy clean the mud. Now all Theodosia had done was find herself with one less garment to carry her through the summer months. And a mess for Nancy to clear. Like her mother, the girl was up before Theodosia and asleep well after. More chores she did not need.

Theodosia gathered the fabric into a neat bundle for Nancy, leaving all but one piece beside the door. The girl had thankfully filled the basin with fresh water, and Theodosia used the reserved cloth to wash her cheeks, hands, and neck. Dirt floated in the bowl. She swirled a clump to the side and splashed her entire head—face, ears, hair. She raked her hands through her muddied hair, freeing it from all that weighed it down.

After, dressed in a clean shift, her light supper of bread and cheese on a tray on the edge of her desk, untouched, she picked up the letter that had arrived from her father that afternoon.

*My dear Miss Priss,*

*The harshness with which I departed leaves me with a bitter taste in my mouth that no amount of burgundy will wash away. Please accept my deepest apologies. I mistakenly allowed my emotions to overtake the moment. I cannot sleep, eat, nor engage in business affairs with the knowledge that we are at odds. This life has a singular purpose and that is our continual devotion and relentless trust. It is the reason for all of this.*

A lump swelled in her throat.

*For what else do I live?*

She continued reading, through his accounts of bickering senators and a stilted exchange with Jefferson, and the ease with which they'd corresponded her entire life filled her with a sense of calm and purpose. What else could come of her hours and years of study but this, listening to, debating with, and offering counsel to her father. She liked being needed—liked her *mind* being needed. It reinforced her desire to assist however she could. And then she came to his final paragraph.

*I would be remiss if I did not mention the pleasing letter I received from Joseph. Why Mr. Alston consumed more than a page of expensive parchment to detail how taken he was with my little Miss Priss and how he would endeavor to accept my invitation to once again visit Richmond Hill as he passed through New York on his return to Georgetown.*

*Adieu, adieu, chère fille.*

*A. Burr*

She smiled to herself as she folded the letter. This was the man she knew and loved, faults and all. And he knew her just as well. He did not repeat his request for her to write to Alston, but instead found a new way to remind her.

Her nose crinkled at the thought of enduring another meal across from that toad. Seeing Alston again would be just as bad as seeing the scoundrel formerly known as Philip Hamilton. Her lips tightened, picturing him. She was too smart to let herself be blinded by good looks and strong shoulders. But Philip was more than that. He understood her, and she him.

She shook her head. *Enough nonsense.* She had duties greater than thinking of Philip Hamilton. She must write her letter to Alston and fulfill her promise to her father.

Only a few sheets of her most expensive parchment remained. She chose one and dipped her quill in ink.

*"Dear Mr. Alston,"* she began.

Her quill floated over the page. She pursed her lips in thought. Submerged the point of the feather again. Sat. Thought. Dipped.

But no other words came. All that came was nonsense.

*Nonsense* sitting beside her.

*Nonsense* laughing at her jokes.

*Nonsense* holding her hand . . . entwined in the strings of her dress . . . *nonsense, nonsense, nonsense.*

Writing to Philip came as easily as breathing. But what could she possibly say to the man whose presence she suffered only for the sake of her father? She had expected she'd come across as unremarkable to Alston as he had to her. The notion of penning a single witticism with romantic undertones made her skin crawl. But she need not tease or be coy, she could simply be cordial, inquiring as to how his trip proceeded. Of how he found the New England cuisine. And the homes' stocks of sugar.

She gritted her teeth. She committed herself to her task. But the words only came when she pretended she was writing to Philip.

Theodosia busied herself with a complete reorganization of the library. Home to more than two thousand books, the task would consume her attention all day. She would have no time to even think of . . . *nonsense.*

Nonsense waiting for her by the river for their planned date—if he even showed. Though he had sent letters in the days preceding. *Two*.

She owed her father for his unrelenting teachings on restraint. She'd shut both letters away in her desk drawer unopened. She'd sent no response, no canceling of their plans. Let him ride all the way here. Let him wait for her, wonder where she was, why she wasn't coming. Let him feel the confusion and embarrassment haunting her since she saw him with Lottie. *Whispering in her ear. Stroking her cheek.*

Theodosia slammed down a book of fables improperly shelved beside ones on religion. She reached to dust off a book on theology, realizing this one had belonged to the Reverend Aaron Burr Senior, the grandfather she'd never met, the father her own scarcely knew.

A hardworking and frugal man, her grandfather had died of exhaustion when her own father was but a year. He'd left behind a substantial estate that had passed to his son, one they were now struggling to retain. What would her grandfather—whose will directed his funeral to be held with minimal expense and any monies saved given to the poor—think of this library and these books being among the few possessions his son would not sell? At least thus far.

The election would consume the next five months, and if her father used each day to entertain and travel and campaign, she shuddered to imagine what would be left of the legacy bequeathed to him. So little remained, and not just financially. By the time her father had turned three, he'd experienced more loss than Theodosia had at the age of seventeen. His need for devotion now came from his yearning for it then.

The hole gaped too wide and deep that not even the love of his daughter could fill it. He needed more. He needed people, public opinion, power. He needed the whole country. She aimed to help him get it.

She gingerly placed her grandfather's book on the most prominent shelf across from the door and dove into a stack of biographies.

"So much clattering, Nancy!" Nathalie said as she strode through the door to the library. "All the way to the sitting room, can I hear the racket." Theodosia turned. "Theo?" Nathalie's brow wrinkled. "I thought . . ." She rotated her head, searching the room. "This is you? The commotion? Here?"

"Astute, sister," Theodosia said.

"Wearing that?" Nathalie frowned at the out-of-style dress Theodosia grew beyond two seasons ago and the apron she wore over it. "With your hair such a sight? Am I like the girl in that story? Have I slept too long and awoken on a new day? Is it not the hour of your tête-à-tête with Philip?"

Theodosia shrugged and continued to dust.

"What is that? That is not a response." Nathalie swished her hand in the air, mimicking Theodosia's dusting. "I'm due a verbal issuance, and it best be complete."

Theodosia put her back to Nathalie to avoid her scrutinizing eye. "I have too much to do to go riding. Our guests will only increase in number these coming months. We must be prepared, and that means this house needs attention. Everywhere."

"Since when is this your occupation?"

"I'm as fit as anyone."

"Or perhaps you're having a fit. What's the meaning of this, Theo?"

Theodosia heaved a full shelf of books onto the floor. The notion of telling Nathalie made her feel even more foolish than she already did. A schoolgirl's crush, ill-placed once again.

Nathalie moved beside her. "Has something happened? Your father, is he—"

"Fine, he's fine, Nathalie, please, do not worry."

"But I do, *mon amie*, for this is not the girl I helped dress a week ago."

Theodosia sighed. "No, it's the same girl, just one with the wool no longer covering her eyes."

Reluctantly, Theodosia shared what she'd seen outside the tavern. Try as she might to act as though it didn't affect her, Nathalie knew her too well.

She wrapped both of her long arms around Theodosia's waist and hugged her with force. "Scoundrel," she hissed into Theodosia's ear, the word tugging at Theodosia's heart.

*Rapscallion scoundrel.*

She should have seen it coming.

Nathalie pushed Theodosia back. "I will help you in . . ." Nathalie waved her hand at the library. "In this distraction. But only with copious amounts of claret." She kissed Theodosia on the cheek and scurried out of the room.

Nearly a full hour later, finally footfalls resounded. Cobwebs decorated Theodosia's hair, grit wound its way under her fingernails, and a smudge of something sticky kept attracting the duster to her cheek.

With her back to the door, Theodosia peeled free the duster for the thousandth time. "My heavens, Nathalie, did you go all the way to France to retrieve a bottle?"

"No, but I would if you asked."

The voice that answered was much deeper than Nathalie's. Theodosia closed her eyes, a scolding of Nathalie on the tip of her tongue. She turned to deliver it, but Nathalie knew better than to linger. Theodosia barely caught a glimpse of Nathalie's skirts as she picked up the nearest book and heaved it across the room—intended for Nathalie or Philip or both, she didn't even know.

She missed.

Nathalie shut the door.

And Philip made the dire mistake of attempting to speak. "Theodosia, please, you must hear me—"

"I must do nothing but this." Another book. Another toss.

Philip's eyes widened.

Theodosia seized a third book, and Philip ducked. But the weight of it in her hand and the delicateness of the spine and the lack of its culpability wouldn't let her release it.

Philip righted himself. "Yes, well, good. Now as I explained to Nathalie—"

Theodosia crouched behind a tower of books, and when she rose to her feet, it was with a potted palmetto in hand.

It met its mark, and an astounded Philip yelped. He fell to the floor. At the sight of the gash on his forehead and the blood that sprang from it, Theodosia cried out.

Alexis and Nathalie burst into the room.

"Cloth and water!" Theodosia said, rushing to Philip's side.

"But Mademoiselle—" Alexis started, his eyes darting about the room.

"I'm fine, but he . . ." She placed a hand on Philip's brow. "I'm so sorry. I don't know what I was thinking. I wasn't thinking. I—" She looked up. "Alexis, please!"

Alexis sped out of the room. Nathalie hurried forward, untucking the lace collar from her neckline. Theodosia accepted and pressed it to Philip's head. She dabbed at the blood while dust swirled around them both. He attempted to sit up.

"No, no, don't. You mustn't—"

"I must," he said. "I can't bear to have you think . . ." He shook his head and winced.

"Philip, please, it's all right."

Nathalie placed a hand on Theodosia's shoulder. "Let him talk, Theo."

Yet before he could, Alexis returned with a clean cloth and water and began to tend to the wound. Theodosia thanked Alexis, sent him from the room, and insisted on doing it herself. Philip relented, allowing her to minister to him before again trying to sit or speak.

After he drank a full glass of water, she helped him up and crouched before him on the barren wood floor of the library.

He seemed to want to reach for her hand but refrained. "At the tavern, I wish you would have announced your presence. I would have explained at once. Lottie would have understood. One sight of me looking at you, and she'd have to, because she resides in the exact same spot. You see, I was with Lottie that day . . . I have only ever been with Lottie . . . to help her be closer to the true object of her heart. The son of the tavern owner."

Theodosia looked at him quizzically. "But her parents would never hear of it."

"Someone of such a class with their daughter? Never. In some ways, her situation is not so different from the one we find ourselves in."

"She's courting in secret," Theodosia said, her eyes drifting to the door Nathalie was pulling shut behind her, ensuring their privacy.

"I've been playing the role of courier," Philip said. "But the day you had the misfortune of seeing us together, I'd served as companion, allowing her to see the boy in person. Without context, it's all understandably misconstrued. But believe me, those whispers you saw me delivering were his words, not mine. Her beloved brought out the laughter and joy you witnessed. Not a thing due to me."

Relief flushed through Theodosia's veins. "Far from the truth, as nothing could have occurred without you." She trailed her fingers through his curls, brushing his hair back from the wound. "A hopeless romantic." His soft grin ignited a fluttering in her chest. "I'm starting to fear what I've gotten myself into."

"No, no fear, not with me." He pulled himself up to his knees to be equal to her. "And no more secrets. I should've told you, and if it were my secret I would have but—"

"I understand." She was the one to join his hand with hers. "It's all right." It had to be, for that was the only way she could justify not telling him about Alston. The letter was a favor to her father. Nothing more. "Wait here," she said.

"I'd rather come with you," Philip said but released Theodosia, watching as she crossed the room and unearthed the book of French poems from a scattered pile.

"To distract you," she said, referring to his father's explanation of why he'd removed all of Philip's books from their home library.

Philip caressed the cover with a tenderness that made Theodosia jealous. For once, he did not joke. He remained still before her, the glistening in his eyes baring all that lay in his heart. The heat between them was enough to create sparks greater than any flint.

Despite being in the home of her father, in full defiance of all he held dear, she was the first to tilt her head. Who was responsible for the initial brush of lip against lip did not matter because before long there were too many to count.

# CHAPTER 23

THE SUMMER PASSED IN A PATTERN of anticipation and gratification. Theodosia's yearning to see Philip was distracted, though not sufficiently, by her duties at home.

These weeks of fine weather saw a continuous stream of travelers in need of lodging, and as always Richmond Hill welcomed them. Politically important friends of her father's were cared for with as much pampering as the extension of debts to merchants would allow. Theodosia's days were filled with transitioning from one round of visitors to the next. Often alone, for her father used these same weeks to travel himself, mostly through New England.

Though a Federalist stronghold, Burr believed the region held promise for being swayed to the Republican side, and he aimed to spend most of the summer and fall electioneering in the states of Connecticut, Massachusetts, Rhode Island, and Vermont.

He'd scarcely left on his first summer trip when a paranoia took hold. He began to fear that his efforts to champion himself would be discovered and blocked. Convinced he and Theodosia must proceed with the utmost of caution, he demanded their correspondence be circumspect, making use of a shared code, especially when referring to named parties. His need of Theodosia as confidant had reached such proportions that she was answering his letters every day, sometimes twice.

With each pen stroke, her guilt over Philip deepened. And yet, the long, summer days of caring for others, of tending to her father, meant nothing without the other days. The days when she'd ride to the farthest grounds of Richmond Hill and beyond in her most simple of shifts, hair loose and free, mind and body both in need of one thing.

The pleasure that spread through her upon sight of him, the heat upon nearing, the elation upon his touch, all yielded such a euphoria that it almost made the days waiting, craving, worth it. The longer the stretch of being apart, the greater the rapture of being together.

They continued to pass letters through his sister. Despite Theodosia's niggling worry that Angelica might be tempted to indulge her curiosity and break one of the seals, Theodosia held nothing back.

She was in love.

She was also a liar.

Her father had asked her to keep up her correspondence with Alston, and she had obliged. It'd become easier once she'd found her voice, much like when writing for the magazine. She'd been cordial initially, but Alston's arrogance dripped from his every word, and she couldn't help but respond in kind. She'd channeled Lucinda Wilson, haughty and stiff and more than a measure condescending. He'd been delighted. His return letter expressed even more of an infatuation with her. Though entirely unexpected and unwanted, his interest in her might make him more predisposed to help her father. And thus she'd adopted a flirtatiously aloof tone and continued to correspond.

Another few weeks. That was all that was required now that the end of August grew near. The South Carolina state legislature was to be elected on October 24. Her father hoped to persuade Alston to use whatever influence he had on Burr's behalf. To push and prod his prominent social circle and ensure the makeup of the legislature would yield a favorable vote for Burr for president. The wrongness of it all tainted her reflection, like a slow-releasing poison. Yet she carried on.

Alone in her bedroom, she hugged her arms to her chest, pretending they were Philip's. They would be soon enough. She was to meet him that afternoon. She moved to her desk to retrieve her mother's brooch. She secured it to her neckline, the jewel now a standard part of her attire when meeting Philip. Like a good-luck charm. But also an assurance that her mother would approve of all the wrong being done for the right reasons.

On the desk before her lay the letter from her father that had arrived the previous day. She reread the end:

*Many are surprised that I could repose in you so great a trust as that of yourself; but I knew that you were equal to it, and I am not deceived.*

*I perceive that I am not very explicit; but you will reflect and discern my meaning. Montesquieu said he wrote to make people think, and not to make them read.*

All she did was think. In only one place did her mind find rest. She smiled and left to give her mind that much-needed respite.

Theodosia wedged a hand between her and Philip, pressing against his chest, whose weight she had desired on hers from the moment she'd climbed off her horse.

Lying flat on the blanket, she drank in the puffy white clouds and fought for breath. His hair flopped toward her forehead, and he bent to let it tickle her skin.

She giggled—a sound she would have sworn lay beyond her capabilities before Philip. But that, along with excelling at deceit, now came without effort.

He lay down beside her, his shoulders tight to hers, their hands entwined. They seemed unable to be within reach of each other and not touch. Hands, lips, thigh, breast. Over her dress. And once, once, under. Briefly, gloriously. Anything more was beyond the scope of even this version of who Theodosia had become. Not that she didn't desire it. Desire him.

So accustomed to talk of intimate relations was she that she had never internalized what the act actually meant, how it would feel, how strong its pull.

Those lessons in restraint continued to find new purpose.

"Are you deep in the writing of something new?" he asked.

After her final installment published, to Philip's understanding but still disappointment, they'd talked of her taking this passion further. Writing another story for the magazine or perhaps a full novel. Yet with all there was to do at home, her pen had been relegated to her father—and Alston.

"Not yet. Letter writing takes so much of my time."

"Perhaps your father can wait an extra day? Or receive a shorter letter?"

"It's not just him . . ." Theodosia wished to tell him about Alston. But telling him meant telling him why she was writing to the arrogant toad. Telling Philip the truth meant betraying her father's trust.

*I knew that you were equal to it, and I am not deceived.*

She cleared her throat. "I've so many responses to write to our guests. How polite they are, sending thank-you notes upon returning home."

Philip sat up, her hand still encased in his. "But you must put yourself first sometime, Theo. How long can you live in his shadow?" He shook his head. "No, not live in, *be*. Be his shadow."

Shadow she would have welcomed. Instead she stood on near equal ground with her father in these political schemes, a step or two ahead when it came to Alston. Yet she couldn't counter Philip's claim without admitting her deceit—and thus her betrayal of him as well. She righted herself and instead gave in to the frustration that mounted each time they were together. "Oh, Philip. Look at us. Sneaking around like Lottie and her tavern boy. Where are they now? I heard she's betrothed to one of the Livingston brood." Her nose wrinkled. "I hope it's not Mr. Sour Milk."

Philip sighed. "No, but it might as well be with how devastated she is. And you should see her tavern boy."

"She had to know it would end. How could it not? From two different worlds. It could never be."

He appeared as wounded as if she'd drawn back a bow and landed an arrow in his chest. "I try not to think in 'never's. I think in possibilities."

He retook her hands, and his skin on hers made her want to forget everything but being here, just as it always did. He held her gaze intently, searching her eyes for something she was not sure she could give.

He then lifted her hand and placed her palm against his chest. "My whole life, my heart didn't function properly. But I didn't know. I lived, I breathed, I ran and studied and played piano along-side my mother and defied my father and through it all, my heart beat." He tapped his hand against hers. "Here. It pumped blood in and out, beating, night and day. But without purpose. The after-noon of the Nicholson salon, suddenly my heart gained a reason to beat. *You* gave it purpose, and you give it every second of every day. I breathe because of you. I am alive only because of you. So don't speak of never and different worlds. If that's your true belief, then my dearest, Theo, I will die here on this hill overlooking the shores of New Jersey."

"Don't say such things, Philip."

"Don't give me reason to."

"Philip, I . . ." The betrayal—of him, of her father, of two men both claiming too-great a need of her—consumed her. "I don't know where this will go, but I fear where it will end."

He squeezed her hand against his breast. "I told you. Don't be afraid. Together we can do anything. Just believe it."

How much easier life would have been had she been more like Philip. But wanting something to be true didn't make it so.

She smiled weakly. "Nathalie always says I'm too practical. A mind full of ciphers and accounts and language and politics. Reasoning through it all with precision. That's who I've been ever since my mother died." *And liked being.* She wriggled her hand free and touched her mother's brooch. She pulled his finger to it, letting him feel it, absorb all the promise and pain held within the tortoiseshell. "Maybe if she'd lived, maybe if my father hadn't commanded me so . . ." *Needed me so.* "But the truth is, I'm not sure

I *can* believe that." His frown deepened. "And yet, I do believe something as fiercely as I believe the earth to be made of dirt and the sun a star. I believe in you."

The relief and desire in the upturn of Philip's lips left her breathless. He brought his hand to her cheek and traced a circle as he'd come to do before each kiss. This time, he stopped midway around. "I love you, Theodosia Burr."

Just like that, her heart had purpose too. "And I you, Philip Hamilton."

And Theodosia's beliefs added something more: that she would never in all her days tire of kissing this rapscallion scoundrel.

# CHAPTER 24

THE END OF THE SUMMER SAW Theodosia's body at Richmond Hill but her mind in Boston.

Letters with the city's postmark arrived every day. From her father, from Alston, from Philip. He'd been sent by his father. He'd passed through Providence. He'd pass through again on his return trip. Just like her father. Just like Alston.

Theodosia's imagination crafted fantastical tales of chance meetings in taverns and inns. Of deliberate rendezvous between her father and Alston. Of them secretly trailing Philip. Of Philip doing the same to them.

In truth, it was not a coincidence that Colonel Hamilton had packed off Philip, prescribing his son's every move, which so closely matched those of her own father. Hamilton was nervous. Suspicious. Of course, rightfully so on both counts. And Philip was a reluctant spy. As was Theodosia. The only difference was Philip had told her as much.

He'd written to her of the message the colonel wished his son to convey to all he encountered in New England:

*"Burr's election would bring an attempt to reform the government à la Bonaparte. He is as unprincipled and dangerous a man as any country can boast—as true a Catiline as ever met in midnight conclave."*

A Catiline, a true conspirator . . . Alexander Hamilton was veering close to unearthing her father's covert mission of positioning himself atop the Republican ballot.

It had fallen to Theodosia to warn him. Telling her father made her a traitor as much as not—only in telling, it was Philip whom she betrayed.

243

Anew. For she continued to write to Alston.

His letters no longer disguised it—they professed his affection for her. Her stomach soured upon reading his words, picturing his wispy hair, those beady eyes, that tongue of spite. He spoke of perhaps returning to the profession of law, which he had abandoned without ever practicing despite passing the bar the previous year. All the better to appeal to her father, for in every other way, Alston embodied a "Palmetto Plutocrat," the name given to him by those in the North not as taken with him as her father.

Only the very rich could travel so slowly and elegantly, making it clear that the law could never hold Alston's attention for long. It was the thread of hope to which Theodosia clung, that the same would be true of his infatuation with her. Once she no longer fed it like a cow's teat to a calf, he'd drift along to something else with more luster.

Until then, she did as her father implored, sustaining Alston's interest with the sarcastic, almost caustic tone that seemed to hold him in her sway.

She knew what was at stake and why. Still, these underhanded political dealings—now that she was integral in them—gave her insight into why some viewed her father negatively. It felt wrong. And yet was Alexander Hamilton not as conspiring? That he was less skilled in it didn't make her father's prowess any more unethical. At least, it shouldn't have . . .

She sealed the last letter she'd write to her father before he returned home and went in search of Nathalie.

"Say it in French." Nathalie cocked her head to the side in the entry to the parlor. "Perhaps it is a lapse in my English vocabulary that's to blame."

Theodosia rose from the settee. "Yes, yes, have your fun. But get on with it, because I need your help."

In that letter to her father, Theodosia had confirmed that she would begin preparations for the seed she'd planted previously. One that she hoped would sprout with enough vigor to secure herself back in her father's good graces and lead to freeing herself of this dalliance with Alston. She'd suggested they host a mixed salon to cultivate support among the influential families of the New York City elite. He'd been delighted. The same as Nathalie was. Though hers came more from seeing Theodosia squirm.

"The Hamiltons?" Nathalie hopped her way into the room. Up and down. *Hopped.* "He specifically said to include the Hamiltons? All of them?"

Theodosia watched Nathalie bounce and shook her head. "This isn't as much fun as you think it is."

"Oh, but it is!"

"It's not."

It wasn't. Not in the least. Theodosia had scarcely seen Philip in public. Hiding her true feelings would be the ultimate test of all of her father's teachings. And yet, it was less herself that she worried about. Philip's heart waved like a flag. It was part of what she loved about him. But the same as after the Clintons' party when she'd first danced with Philip, her father had said: "Let the Burrs be above the fray." No excuse she could muster would change her having to invite the Hamiltons to the salon.

Nathalie's blonde hair skimmed her shoulders as she gave one final hop toward Theodosia. Joy and mischief mixed in her warm brown eyes. "It occurs to me that this might present the perfect opportunity for the truth to be out."

"No," Theodosia said with force. Her father could not know about Philip. Not yet. "It's too soon."

"*Pfft!*" Nathalie wagged a finger at her. "You're in love. He's in love. It's not too soon, it's overdue."

"After the election. That will be the time. It's only another month or so."

"A month?" Nathalie's head gave an emphatic shake. "Has so much kissing affected your ability to count? It's three!"

Theodosia's lips parted. She'd been referring to the October legislature election in South Carolina, not the full presidential one in December. She shrugged for Nathalie's benefit. "Days melt into one another when one is in love. Now *that* is something well overdue. My Nathalie needs a full and proper suitor of her own."

Nathalie brightened. "An excellent reason for going over that invitation list."

He was not on the list.

Joseph Alston showed up unannounced.

Theodosia's heart lodged in her throat as she heard her father introduce him to Mr. and Mrs. Livingston.

His waxen face was the definition of smug as he stood amid her salon guests. His last letter had said nothing of arriving in New York this soon.

Seeing him here before her was like a mirage. Ink and parchment brought to life in the most unwelcome package. Words on a page she could pretend were just that, nothing more. But faced with his physical form and those words being given volume and voice . . . her palms began to sweat. What would he say to her? What must she say back? In front of everyone . . . in front of Philip.

Her father laughed at something Alston said that she'd missed. He then spoke of the array of influential New Englanders he'd ensured Alston would meet on his travels, his tone infused with almost fervent respect. And she knew, he did this. He invited Alston. Some shiny toy to show off. Show off to the Hamiltons. The colonel would intuit the purpose of Burr's friendship with Alston as fast as her father would had the situation been reversed.

Alston accepted a drink from Tom without a nod or a glance as if the glass merely fell from the sky. Theodosia put her back to his arrogant, slight form and slunk out of the parlor. Straight through the dining room, nodding to Mr. Sour Milk, into the hall, forcing a smile at Lucinda, past the empty kitchen, as Eleonore had moved outside to the summer kitchen to help keep the house cool.

Out the back door, Theodosia crossed the grass, past the blue asters nearly in bloom, hoping to catch her breath and formulate a plan. How to keep Alston away from Philip. How to stay away from Alston herself. Maybe she could ride off, just hop on her mare and leave all this to her father who was determined to make her fake courting with Alston even more unbearable.

She paced, her shoes tearing at the grass, her mind whirling, her deception circling her neck like a noose.

"Ma'am?" Eleonore was nearly upon Theodosia before she'd noticed her. "Is something wrong?"

Theodosia's chest tightened upon sight of this woman who had been in her life longer than her own mother. *Because she is not free to do otherwise.*

Whether it had been his intention or not, Alston brought into focus her own complicity in her father's contradiction of being an abolitionist while employing servants.

*No.*

Slaves. *Owning* slaves.

A word whose definition she'd turned a blind eye to. A condition she'd justified. No matter that countless northern families did the same, convincing themselves that the practice in their own homes was unlike that of the South. That such somehow made it all right. Theodosia prided herself on being different, which made the very fact that, in this, she was anything but, far worse.

Her heart heavy with shame, Theodosia assured Eleonore all was well even though it wasn't. Even though this country of freedom and liberty remained at odds with itself, in need of reconciliation that—she herself was unwittingly evidence of—wouldn't come swiftly or easily. And yet if those in power changed, if Alston helped those in power to change, if her father indeed held the highest position in the land, would such reform eventually come? Was she *that* sure of what was in her father's heart?

She clasped her hands against her squeezing stomach. The only thing she could be sure of was that she would no longer set aside what was in her own. She might have no authority to grant liberty, but she did hold favor with the one who did. She must find a way to use it to make things right, starting in her own home.

From the doorway, her father called to her. Alston stood beside him. She donned a perfect smile, inhaled a breath, and walked toward them.

# Chapter 25

Her feet were like lead, but she trudged on. The hostess of Richmond Hill. The daughter of Aaron Burr. The woman this man was courting.

"Mr. Alston," she said with a swift bow.

He returned it twofold. "Finally, Miss Burr. I was beginning to think I'd have only this version of you as my companion." He opened his garish blue jacket to reveal the tops of folded letters sticking out from an inside pocket.

She refrained from the sneer that pulled at her, but their relationship thus far had allowed for the equivalent in words. "Serve you right, I would think, for such abominable behavior as arriving without notice."

He grinned, all teeth and no grace. "Some call that a surprise."

"And some call it rude."

He laughed, taking delight in her being so ill-mannered, which said all there was to say about him.

Her father cleared his throat. "I call it fortunate for us to be in one another's presence again. On this fine, fine day. I was just about to show Joseph the grounds now that so much is in bloom compared to his previous visit. But perhaps—"

"A most excellent idea," Theodosia blurted out. There was no way *she* was sharing these grasses and groves she loved with Alston. "But alas, I must check in with our other guests."

Alston studied her, then smirked. "Let them have you by day. I'll be here all night."

249

Theodosia drew back in revulsion, which Alston took for shock. He slapped her father on the back. "There you go, Burr, raising a good and proper society lady!"

Not even an apology for his lack of social etiquette. She'd embarked on this charade because she owed her father, but she suspected by the time Alston left, her father would be the one owing her.

Before either of them could protest, Theodosia hurried back to the house. She attempted a casual mingling, but her heart pounded with the thought of half the influential families of the city witnessing her unraveling. With furtive glances, she scanned every chair, every table, every corner, looking for Philip. Maybe she could entice him to leave early with a promise to meet him in their secret spot. Her father's tour would never take Alston that far.

Perspiration gathered on her neck as she circled through the house. She arrived at the front hall where Angelica was being kissed on the cheek by her mother. Beside them, Colonel Hamilton tipped his hat at Theodosia.

That Philip would be leaving before Theodosia even had the chance to see him left her stomach in knots, but not having to juggle both Philip and Alston . . . what relief!

And then Colonel and Mrs. Hamilton walked down the porch steps without Angelica. She turned to Theodosia. "There you are! We've *all* been breathless with anticipation!" She winked.

A drop of sweat trickled between Theodosia's breasts.

From just inside the entry to the parlor, Lottie gave a sad smile.

Appearing behind Lottie was Nathalie with a tense, "Theodosia, you've been missed. By so many."

Beyond the doorway, Lucinda's shrill voice rang loudest: "Mr. Hamilton, how prepared! Bringing your own book for recitation? May I see it?"

"Of course." Philip's voice ignited Theodosia's skin, and she nearly leapt into the parlor.

"French?" Lucinda clucked her tongue. "Where did you happen on something so exquisite?"

"It was a gift," Philip said.

A river now flowed beneath Theodosia's bosom.

"Is that so?" Lucinda smirked, a gesture that deepened as Theodosia appeared beside her.

Dizzy with all the deception, Theodosia almost reached to steady herself by grabbing hold of Philip's arm. Nathalie caught her just in time.

Lucinda handed the volume of poetry back to Philip. "How educational."

There was little doubt that Lucinda recognized the book as the same one Theodosia had held outside the offices of the magazine.

Sensing something off, Nathalie came quick with an excuse. "Theodosia, I'm sorry to interrupt, but Eleonore requires your direction."

"Certainly," Theodosia managed, her voice tight. She couldn't let herself meet Philip's gaze and only hoped the fact that she didn't would lead him to her.

It did.

Nathalie swiveled her head, assuring no one was within sight, before waving Philip toward them. Theodosia stole a glance out the door of the summer kitchen.

It was the perfect place. No one from the salon would ever venture to it. If the guests left the house at all, the heat would keep them closer to the river and other shaded parts of the grounds.

Eleonore had done as Theodosia had asked and was replenishing summer fruits inside the house. But she would be back soon.

Nathalie traded places with Philip, saying, "I'll provide cover, but don't be gone long, Theo. I'm certain your absence has already been noted. Especially by some who've traveled a great distance to be here."

She clearly meant Alston, having no knowledge of just how tenuous this was.

Nathalie had scarcely taken a single step out the door when Philip rushed forward. He lifted Theodosia off the ground at the same time as he pressed his lips to hers. Every thought but one vanished from her mind: "Let's run away."

"All right," he said, nuzzling her neck.

"No, I mean it. Philip this is . . ." *A mess. A disaster. All her fault.* "We're going to lose everything."

She meant her and her father. She meant her and Philip. She meant her and Nathalie. So many secrets, she could barely keep track.

Philip held her face between his soft hands. "My love, we don't need everything, we only need each other."

"I'm not teasing, Philip." Anxious of being discovered, Theodosia hurriedly explained about Lucinda.

Philip laughed, not in a patronizing way but in a way that wished to ease her worries. "Lucinda Wilson will not be the cause of us losing a wink of sleep, let alone everything."

"But she must know we are connected."

"By a book. A book is not scandalous." He wrapped his arms around her. "Don't think of her. Don't use our time alone thinking of anyone but us."

She leaned into him, surprising him with her weight, but he simply held on tighter. She closed her eyes and tried to summon the courage to tell him everything. She stepped back, opened her lids, and through the side window, she saw him. Joseph Alston.

He looked her way. And headed toward her.

Theodosia shoved a tray of smoked fish into Philip's hands. He cocked his head. "If this is your way of saying you love—"

"Having strong, helpful men around. Yes, indeed." She batted her lashes, and he eyed her quizzically, having no idea that Alston was behind him. "Well, if it isn't our distinguished guest, all the way from South Carolina!"

Facing only her, Philip winked in understanding. He then turned and lifted the tray. "Smoked oyster? I, for one, couldn't wait and followed our hostess who so kindly came to retrieve them for me."

Alston screwed up his lips. "Not a fish man, myself. I prefer things I can take down with a bullet."

"That's one philosophy," Philip said.

Theodosia forced a chuckle, a sound foreign to her and Philip both.

"You Yanks sure love your fish," Alston added. "From Providence to Boston, I couldn't sit for a meal without some nauseating, beady-eyed thing being offered to me."

Theodosia knew the feeling.

Philip said, "Providence and Boston? I am just back from both myself. It's a wonder we didn't cross paths."

Alston hooked his thumbs in his coat pocket. "That it is, Mr. . . . ."

"Hamilton. Philip Hamilton."

Alston's eyes narrowed. "Son of *the* Alexander Hamilton?"

"That honor is mine," Philip said with such conviction, Theodosia believed he believed it.

"He's going to lose this election," Alston said.

"He's not running, at least as far as I know."

"He's destroying his own party out of spite. In the South, men don't have to see eye to eye to help each other out."

"The South has many . . . traditions, we do not."

"I've come to see that," Alston said.

"And you prefer your own?"

"Sure as our lockboxes of sugar. To think, they eat bear here."

Philip stiffened, unquestionably putting together the meat he acquired for her and her refusal to tell him who it was for. Now that "who" stood before them, and everything was about to explode.

And it did, but simply with Philip's laughter. He covered well. "But it can be taken down by a bullet."

"So can men, and I don't care to have them plopped before me on a plate." Alston held his belly and laughed.

As did Theodosia.

Philip turned toward her, so many questions alive in his eyes. She had to ignore them all. And give him one more.

"Allow me to escort the woman hosting the salon of the summer back inside?" Alston offered her his arm.

"How kind." Theodosia's skin crawled as her arm nestled inside Alston's. Just before her foot set on the grass, she glanced over her shoulder at Philip. "Thank you, Mr. Hamilton."

She begged for her eyes to speak louder than all of Alston's words. She needed Philip to remember that he was the one she loved, at least until she could explain herself. Yet as Theodosia reentered the parlor with Alston clutching her arm like a snake wound around a tree, it was Angelica who needed the explanation. Fury colored her cheeks at what appeared to be Theodosia's betrayal of her brother.

Only with Nathalie's assistance did Theodosia make it to the end of the salon without being impaled by something other than the daggers in Angelica's eyes.

As Theodosia accepted the endless stream of thanks and good-byes from her guests, all she could think was *Society is too damn polite*. She tapped her foot with impatience. Alston was nowhere in sight, despite having otherwise remained at her side since leaving the summer kitchen—through Lottie's singing and Lucinda's crambo and Philip's confused stares. Now Alston was missing. As was Philip.

When the line finally dwindled, Theodosia hastened to find Philip. She saw him marching out of the back hall near the library, arm in arm with Angelica. Theodosia's smile came straight from her heart.

"Philip, I—"

Angelica wedged her elbow in Theodosia's side as she passed. Skin pallid, Philip refused to lift his gaze from the floor. Theodosia began to rush after them when she noticed Lucinda preening like a peacock, a pleased-as-pumpkin smirk on her face.

Torn every which way, Theodosia hung back as Philip and Angelica accepted their things. Then, they were gone. Without a glance. Without a word.

Lucinda offered an oh-so-polite thank-you and allowed Tom to escort her to her carriage.

With a heavy weight descending on her chest, Theodosia watched them exit. She then retraced Philip's steps. To the library with its thousands of books but barely any furniture—what must Philip and Angelica have thought! But their suspicion would mean nothing compared to that of Joseph Alston. She found him, just inside the library, holding a stack of letters in his hand.

*Her letters.*

Her mouth went dry. She swallowed, calling forth enough saliva to ask if Alston was in need of anything.

He held up one of her letters. "I've got all I need right here."

Theodosia reluctantly infused a playfulness into her words. "Once again, the real thing is before you, but like with my portrait, you are content with something inanimate. Curious you are, Mr. Alston."

"I often find 'real' to be a suspect concept, in many cases at odds with what we project."

Theodosia felt as though he'd bared his teeth.

"Look at that Hamilton boy," he continued. "From all outward appearances, he'd seem to be a strapping, confident man familiar with the inner workings—and outer workings . . ." He laughed. ". . . of little ladies, and yet a single glimpse at one of your hardly what I'd call salacious letters, and he turned as red as a boiled beet. I think you embarrassed the boy, Theo."

Her spine prickled. He'd never before called her by that nickname. She didn't like it.

And then what he had said fully registered. "Philip . . . he read my letters? To you? Why, how could—"

"Just the one. By complete and unintended accident—don't think I'd share our intimacy, my dear. The boy happened to come in as I was taking a break from the persistent chatter. Northern ladies like to prattle on, don't they?"

Philip read her letters to Alston. Salacious, no. But encouraging? Receptive? Yes, a yes that made her nauseous, but a yes.

She had to explain!

Every muscle in her body screamed at her to charge after Philip. She couldn't let him think . . . she couldn't let him imagine her letters to Alston were *real.*

But before her was a man she was coming to see projected something much more calculating than the truth.

Just like her.

Her stomach twisted. There would be no dashing after Philip, not now. She couldn't give Alston a reason to question her loyalty. She couldn't even hint that what she projected in those letters was utter fiction.

Her lungs squeezed with every breath, and she tried to cover, tried to read him, see into his eyes, see who he really was. For was this all an innocent happenstance or did Alston orchestrate it? Have his suspicions confirmed? Ones that might have begun that day he gave her the palmetto and been reinforced by something witnessed in the summer kitchen? Was Alston as skilled in manipulation as her father? And if he was, who was playing whom? And for what?

She commanded her legs to hold her up, to keep her here, to lead Alston into the parlor for a drink with her father, to show him to his room for the night, all the while the hole in her chest where her heart used to be growing wider. She laid her head on her pillow, hoping that Philip would not just understand but forgive.

# CHAPTER 26

HER LETTERS TO ANGELICA RETURNED TO Richmond Hill unopened.

Alston stayed the week and into the next. She couldn't go to see Philip. But he came to her.

She'd been in one of the apple orchards beyond the house. She'd been about to dismount when she saw him atop his own horse, the same one whose hooves had indented the grounds of Richmond Hill over the past few precious months.

She'd felt herself flush, blood once again flowing through her veins as if a dam had broken. Philip gripped the reins, aiming to spur his horse into a gallop toward her. She wanted it. She wanted to see his eyes up close, feel his breath on her cheek, his hands anywhere, everywhere. She wanted to explain this charade she'd been forced to continue and how what he saw and what he read that day at the salon wasn't real, and she wanted him to marvel along with her at how her heart had been somehow miraculously continuing to function despite being ripped from her chest at the thought of hurting him.

She breathed in, long and deep, her mind tricking her by tickling her nostrils with the lemon scent of the soap Philip kept using once she said she loved it. And then the scent was replaced by fear. Alston was due to meet her at any moment.

She faced Philip fully and shook her head. He pitched back as if struck by a weapon, which was what Theodosia had become.

*Philip. Her poor Philip.*

When she'd heard the pounding of Alston's approaching horse, she propelled her own animal on to head him off.

"Miss Burr!" Alston had bellowed in that grating drawl. She had no way of knowing if Philip had heard.

He had not come again. Stuck in the cage that was her houseguest of Alston, Theodosia had been unable to escape to the city to explain. Her father had ended his nomadic travels, remaining at Richmond Hill, pushing Theodosia toward Alston, and falling over himself with flattery for the toad. The two men stroking each other's ego and making her their audience. She no longer had to do anything to lead Alston on. The disinterest she could not fully hide seemed to be all the fuel he needed to fan his infatuation. There was nothing she could do but hold out a little longer and get through the South Carolina legislature election. If Alston discovered her true feelings before then, all she'd done would have been for nothing. She only hoped that Philip would be there for her when she was able to tell him the truth.

Which, thanks to Nathalie, who was now crouched on the floor with her sewing basket open, would happen soon.

Just days ago, Alston had finally ordered his belongings packed and departed Richmond Hill. His carriage horses had dug their hooves into the dust beyond the portico, and there her father had been: giving the arrogant man the high honor of delivering Burr's personal messages, sending Alston off with letters of introduction to the most important members of his party, including James Madison and Thomas Jefferson, who was to receive Alston at his grand home of Monticello.

Theodosia had almost gagged when her father had recited the words he'd written to Madison, describing Alston as "intelligent, sound in his principles, and polished in his manners."

*Compared to what? A hog?*

"Theodosia!" Nathalie cried. "Suddenly you are part worm, *mon amie*! Still, please!" Nathalie tightened her hold around the sewing needle she'd been trying to wriggle through the fabric at the hem of Theodosia's dress.

Theodosia shifted before the mirror. "I feel as though I've been still my entire life, Nathalie."

"*Pfft!* And they say the French are dramatic!"

To keep her eyes off the mirror, Theodosia focused on the vase of blue asters on her desk. Nathalie had been the one to pick them. As much as they brightened the room, they were hard for Theodosia to think beautiful. The one who'd brought her the seeds, the one who'd laid them in the ground, was the same as the one asking so much of her now. She'd felt she'd owed something to her father for writing her story for the magazine, and she did want to help him ascend to the presidency. And yet, the longer Alston had stayed and the greater her distance from Philip, the more she'd come to see his request as too much—and wrong. The same as his refusal to reason with her regarding the release of their servants. She feared her father wasn't the man he once was. Or maybe he was. She wasn't sure which was worse.

She flinched involuntarily and Nathalie pricked her ankle.

"Be still," Nathalie said. "We cannot have your first encounter with Philip be in that pink thing with the hoop."

"I would have never worn it."

"Except to guilt me into making this for you. Which was as necessary as a horn on a kitten for I would rather move to the wilds of the west than see you matched with that southern weasel."

Burr forging a match between the wealthy Alston and those in need of wealth—themselves—did not require a leap in logic. Nathalie didn't know the true reason, the political wrangling, and Theodosia didn't want her to know. Not because of the picture it would paint of her father, but because of what it would reveal of herself.

Theodosia covered her discomfort. "That weasel would never appreciate this dress, Nathalie. It's as close to our goal of perfection as could be."

"*Mon amie*, the goal is Philip. The dress is a means to such." Nathalie straightened the train. "And it *is* perfection. It will accomplish what we wish."

This was their shared goal. After Alston had finally put Richmond Hill behind him, Theodosia had rushed into the city to the dilapidated schoolhouse and Madame de Senat's and even the tavern. No Philip. She'd been prepared to go straight to the Hamilton home when Nathalie had intervened. Her best friend had become determined to help repair the damage caused by Alston, which Theodosia now believed to have been deliberately inflicted. Though Alston had never again even mentioned "that Hamilton boy," his constant air of gloat had convinced Theodosia that he must have seen something, enough to suspect that Philip would be a threat to any potential romantic engagement.

Eventually, Nathalie had come up with a plan. And true to her French royal self, at its heart was a ball.

Theodosia's eyes traveled the length of herself in the mirror.

Perfection this dress was, and a splurge for the Burrs now in the way it never would have been in her mother's day. The fabric was a rich silk, the hue a red with undertones of silver and black and hints of white, making it appear in movement even when still. Sophisticated and delicate but not overly feminine with a high waist, low neckline, and short, slightly gathered sleeves. A band of embroidered rosebud garlands in pink, red, and green chenille lined the band around the neck, sleeves, and V-shaped insertion in the bodice in front, designed especially by Nathalie to frame the tortoiseshell brooch. The embroidery repeated at the hem with a wider trail of roses and rosebuds that vined onto the rounded train.

Nathalie remained hunched over the fabric for hours at a time, embroidering with the care of a mother giving a newborn her first bath.

It was the first time Theodosia had regretted her own lack of skill. Nathalie had created a masterpiece as impressive as any other form of art. She could spend a lifetime trying to repay the debt owed to her beloved friend for all she'd done to help in this quest for Philip's heart. That was what this was and had been since the day of the Nicholson salon, even if Theodosia had refused to let herself see it then. Philip had gotten under her skin and opened her heart.

Her heart would be laid bare before him at the Blackwell ball, which was to be held after the legislature election in South Carolina. Theodosia would no longer have any need to correspond with Alston, no need to protect this secret. She would present herself and all she'd done before Philip and ask for forgiveness. Everything depended on this event, hosted by the eccentric William Drayton Blackwell.

Taking his cue from a new trend in London, Blackwell was on the cusp of investing in downtown real estate that he would turn into a private club—invitation only—for the most elite members of New York society. Provided they were male, of course. Ironic, that the club members would consist solely of men, and yet this upcoming ball to determine those members saw the inclusion of wives and daughters. It was their charm and skill on the dance floor that would reflect favorably on the men in their families and engender those private invitations.

Not a single prominent man and his family would miss the ball, which meant the Hamiltons would be in attendance. Philip would be in attendance. Nathalie had already confirmed it through his cousin Caty.

Theodosia carefully hung the finished dress on a hook on the wall across from her bed. Each night she laid her head on her pillow, counting down the days until she'd wear it in front of the man she loved, the one she hoped still loved her back.

Theodosia held in her hands a letter from the man claiming to love her, though he'd not used those exact words. She was a "sweet friend" and "amiable companion." And he was either exceedingly lucky or quite skilled in strategic timing. His letter arrived the morning of the Blackwell ball. The same day that news of the South Carolina election reached them.

"A tie?" Theodosia said as her father stood with his hand on the back of a chair in the parlor for support. "But how can it be a tie?"

He yanked a handkerchief from his pocket to wipe the beads of sweat on his brow.

"Papa, I asked you a question." Seeds of anger sprouted as Theodosia clutched the letter. Alston had tricked them. "How can the seats be evenly divided between Federalists and Republicans?"

Her father's fingertips pressed into the linen backing on the chair. "A matter of counting and finding equality, I suspect. Ciphers are no match for you, Miss Priss, but this escapes you?"

"Do not be flip with me."

"Do not ask me questions I cannot answer."

Theodosia ground her teeth. This was what happened when one engaged in underhanded dealings. By their very definition, those willing to enter could not be trusted.

"He lied," she said. "Alston lied straight to your face. Making promises he could not possibly keep. Ones he likely didn't even try to keep! Please tell me you see that, Papa?"

Her father patted down the back of his neck and moved to the open window. Underneath, leaning crooked in a new pot, was the palmetto from Alston. Alexis had it repotted despite Theodosia's insistence that such was not necessary. Or wanted.

He trailed a finger along one of the fronds and faced Theodosia. "What I see is entirely the contrary. The election was a tie. How do you think such a closeness was achieved? Certainly not a coincidence."

"Don't defend him."

"Merely a truth. Joseph worked hard on our behalf—yes, don't look at me like that, *our*. He is entirely under your spell, Theo."

Theodosia twisted the letter.

"He would do nothing to risk losing your affection. He got us a tie. A *tie!*" Her father strode back to the chair in front of the fireplace and sat, pushing forth a calmness that grated against Theodosia's entire sense of being. "Now the choice will be made by those not beholden to one party. Those people can be moved. Yes, yes, this is a good thing."

Her father extracted a letter written in the same devious hand as the one Theodosia had to refrain from tearing into pieces. "Right here, Joseph says he is quite friendly with those unaffiliated gentlemen. This is where he will prove his connections. This is where he will come through."

Theodosia looked upon her father, this passionate man of exceptional intelligence and unyielding loyalty whose desperate need for power and acceptance was making him delusional. A feeling washed over her, one she had never felt before when it came to him: pity.

She couldn't let him be taken advantage of; she had to prove that Alston was manipulating them both.

"Papa, I need to show you something." She kept her tone flat, non-accusatory, as she approached. She drew forward a chair and sat in front of him, so close their knees touched. "It arrived today, which is proof itself of his plan."

She laid the letter from Alston across his lap. He stared down at the writing he surely recognized, for Alston's correspondence to the Burr home had never been relegated solely to her.

"Open it," she said. "Read it."

Like a child being instructed, he did as she asked. She clasped her hands, waiting, studying his every movement, the shifting of his eyes, the creasing of his brow, the upturning of his lips.

No. *No, no, no, no, no.*

"Ah, Theo, he is captivated! I am in your debt, *chére fille.* You've ensured he will work hard for us." He popped up from his chair, knocking his knees into hers before scooping her up with him. He aimed to reach his arms around her when she pushed him back.

"Papa, no, do you not see what this is? He couldn't be more transparent."

Burr looked down at the letter. "Well, I dare say he could have . . ." He read, "'*Ever could there be so perfect a heaven from our uniting in every study, improving our minds together, and informing each other by our mutual assistance and observations'* . . . not exactly a direct proposal, but the rest of this . . . add it up, and indeed a marriage he seeks."

"I meant transparent in his bribery."

Her father shook his head. "I confess to a quick perusal rather than an extracted study, but I see nothing of the sort."

Theodosia dug her hand into his pocket and tore out his letter. She held it in the air, grabbed the one sent to her, and joined them as one. "Here. Now do you see? In one letter he speaks of ensuring you victory, and in the next, he names his price for doing so."

"You?" Burr stepped back. "But that would not be . . ."

"Right? Fair? Decent? The secret to a happy marriage? This is the type of man you're putting so much trust in, Papa." She released the letters, and they floated to the floor, one landing in the unlit fireplace. She picked up the second, tossed it in after, and reached for a match. "Let go of this. Of him. You don't need a man such as Alston to win this election. And if you do, then perhaps it's time to see that you don't need this election as much as you think."

It was like she'd slapped him. The reality of his need showed in the hurt and fear in his eyes. He recovered quickly, befitting a Burr.

"It's not me who needs this election, Theodosia, it's the country. Another Adams presidency will ruin us."

He stooped to retrieve the letters from the fireplace, and she heard the creak in his back. This was aging him, the work, the travel, the stress. It was obvious that he didn't want to delve deeper into Alston, but this was no longer just about him.

Theodosia ensured her tone was calm. "And if that was all you were truly after, then perhaps things might be different. For then someone like Alston would not have such leverage over you. But you want more than to stop Adams. You want this for yourself."

Burr's lips tightened. "I don't want this. I deserve this. I have waited for this moment, and here it is before me. I'm so close, Theo, so very close. My destiny lies before me."

When Aaron Burr was just eight months old, he'd fallen so ill that his own mother was resigned to his coming funeral. And yet, he recovered. He'd survived. And Theodosia's grandmother was convinced it was a miracle. Her son was saved—"given to me from the dead," as she wrote to her sister—because he would achieve greatness.

Theodosia shook her head. "Papa, you can't know that."

"But I can, Miss Priss. My fate has been paved by prices paid. Illness and loss—so much loss. I endured years of war and peace time being underestimated by Washington, belittled by Hamilton, pitied by the Livingstons and Clintons, and now, look at where I am. Where we are. So much is in our grasp, all that's asked of us is one simple thing."

She stumbled back. "Simple? A marriage to this southern fool? And in case you need reminding it's not asked of you, it's asked of me."

Burr hesitated, seemed to consider reaching for her hand, but restrained himself. "Would it be so bad?"

"Yes, it would. It cannot be, Papa."

He sighed in reluctant understanding.

"Good, we are in agreement," she said. "I will write to him at once and prevent an actual proposal—"

"Perhaps not so promptly." Burr held up his hands before she could lash out. "Decline, eventually, if he endeavors to ask directly. Truly, is there a rush?"

*Yes, and his name is Philip.*

He added, "A month until the presidential election."

"More."

"Not much."

"I cannot."

"Not literally true."

"I will not."

Burr stepped forward and placed his hands on her shoulders. "What's the harm, Miss Priss? You've done so much fiction writing already this year, what's a little more?"

Her eyes fluttered shut. It didn't surprise her that he would bring up her story any more than him orchestrating this as perfectly as a symphony. Beginning by floating the ridiculous notion of saying yes to Alston before retreating into merely asking her to placate Alston, his skill in strategy had been employed brilliantly.

"Play along," he said. "It's flattering! And who knows, perhaps with a little more back and forth, getting to know each other—"

"No, Papa. I promise you, no."

He sketched a smile on his face, perfectly pleased. "Fine, then a delay in your response. That settled . . ." He clapped his hands together. "We must prepare for the ball."

The ball? It was as if a sudden gust from the river tossed her off balance. The start of the Blackwell ball was mere hours away.

The very night when she'd hoped to convince Philip that court-ing with Alston was a charade, well behind her. Which would now be a lie.

She could instead tell him the truth and ask him to stand by while she pretended she was interested in marriage with someone else. A challenge to any man's ego and requiring a level of trust in her she was not sure he still had.

Theodosia looked at her father. "I won't be attending." Guilt and sadness mixed at the thought of her beautiful dress, painstak-ingly crafted by Nathalie, going unworn. And her heart grieved at the notion of not seeing, not being close to Philip after all this time. She'd set all her hopes on this night. She needed it like she needed air in her lungs and the grounds of Richmond Hill beneath her feet. But neither the lie nor the truth would do. She would wait. When this endless election was over, she would be free. "It appears I have a letter to write."

Burr laughed. "Delay, I said. Men need to pine."

Theodosia stood her ground. "My mood is not favorable to being charming, Papa. Besides, if you're president, they have to invite you to be a member of the club."

She aimed to leave the parlor, but he cast a mournful glance her way. "So much have I asked of you . . . I should not ask this."

She closed her eyes against years of responding yes, yes to all he asked.

"It's a party," he said. "We all deserve a little fun, don't we? Especially Nathalie."

"Nathalie doesn't require me for fun. If anything, at social events, I hold her back."

Burr's lips parted, then pursed together.

"What?" Theodosia asked.

"Not a thing, my dear. If you're not up to this, I shall not force it."

Concern lined her face. "Papa, if something is amiss with Nathalie—"

"Oh no, don't fret, nothing of the sort. The opposite in fact." He spread his hands. "Our dear girl is smitten."

Theodosia drew back. "Nathalie has not said a thing."

"To me neither. Frederick told me. She met a young man while visiting him last month. Seems they were quite taken with one another."

Last month? At her half-brother's in Pelham? Why would Nathalie have kept this from her?

"Sumter. Thomas, like his father. Strong Republican allies too."

"The name's not familiar."

"But the place is," he said. "The South Carolina Sumters. His father was a general."

A knot tied in Theodosia's stomach. A general and a Republican meant he was well known to her father. And useful.

She marched to him and seized his hand. "I will go to this wretched party. I will continue this perversion of all that is right with Alston. I will do whatever you ask."

Relief filled her father's eyes.

"But," she continued. "I ask one thing of you: leave Nathalie out of it."

"A chance meeting, that's all. I had nothing to do with it, on my honor."

She held his gaze, her eyes saying all that she could not: for that phrase, coming from him, no longer held any truth.

# CHAPTER 27

THEODOSIA CLUTCHED THE ARM OF WASHINGTON Irving as if it were a rail on a sinking ship. She'd scarcely let go since finding him soon after she'd arrived in the red dress that indeed was perfection. She imagined it as dejected as she at not being used for its intended purpose.

The truth or a lie, neither would do when it came to Philip. Distance was her only option, remaining at it, yearning for him from it . . . feeling his toward her.

When she'd crested the staircase, whose landing opened into the already well-populated ballroom on the second floor, he'd been passing right in front of her. Crossing from one side of the room to the other. Eyes fixed straight ahead. She'd had no chance to catch them. Which was just as well as she had no idea what she would have done if she had.

All she knew was her heart beating so hard she could feel it in her stomach. Her hands dampening and staining her gloves. Her life not what she wished it to be.

He appeared to have escorted Lucinda Wilson to the party. And though his eyes would not meet hers, Lucinda's would and did and made Theodosia loathe the color blue.

"Claret?" Washington asked as they finished an introductory circle of the most prominent guests and settled near an open window at the back of the ballroom. Already the crowd and plethora of lit candles had made the heat oppressive.

Theodosia cocked her head. "Something stronger?"

"Madeira?"

"Brandy."

269

Washington bowed and set off for what would be her second glass. She hoped her father was counting.

She slunk deeper against the wall, almost disappearing into the long brocade curtain framing the window. The home laid claim to land beside the East River, and the breeze carried hints of the algae and brine with which she was intimately familiar. As welcome as it was, it now also brought reminders of Philip.

He glided around the dance floor, his hand on Lucinda's back. He'd still not looked Theodosia's way. Not at this stunning dress, not at her hair in its elaborate twist woven with green ribbon matching the rosebud embroidery, not at her eyes to see them weighed down by melancholy.

The whole time she'd been circling with Washington, she'd tried to meet Philip's gaze, but either he turned away or Angelica turned him away. Lucinda was ever present. Using every opportunity to direct a superior glance toward Theodosia.

The volume of poetry connected Theodosia to Philip and to the lie Theodosia had told regarding it. A secret fueling suspicions—a secret Lucinda would use.

Theodosia clasped her arms to her chest and pressed herself against the wall beside the window. The fall brought with it shorter days, and as darkness overtook the outside, the more the candelabras cast shadows inside. From them, Theodosia watched. Not just Philip, but Nathalie, placing a flirtatious hand on the arm of an attractive man with sandy brown hair and a height that exceeded hers. He laughed at her jokes, ferried to her petite pastries, and expertly spun her about in reels and waltzes. The man remained entirely focused on her. Theodosia had been introduced to him, the charming Thomas Sumter, Jr. He had been pleasant and polite, and she had no reason to dislike him but one: Joseph Alston.

Make that two: Aaron Burr.

She studied her father, moving from Clinton to Livingston to Nicholson to Gallatin like deciding which to allow on his dance card. Power had transferred to him. They could see it; the room could feel it. An energy charged the air around her father, buzzing over everyone, including Alexander Hamilton. Hamilton rested his delicate fingers on the curve of the white piano in the far corner of the room, leaving his wife without a dance partner, yet she looked neither perturbed nor surprised. Probably not the life she wished it to be either. But she'd stayed. With all he'd done, she'd stayed.

Brow arched, Washington returned with two brandies and a plate of ratafia cakes balanced on his forearm. Theodosia reached for the glass, and he pulled it back.

"First, eat." His peachy complexion gave him a playful appearance. "Your father will never forgive me if he finds you deep in the cups."

She sighed and chose one of the small white cakes. "The only reason I give in." She bit into it, the aromatic almond and overwhelming sweetness more satisfying than she wanted to admit.

Washington leaned against one of the vine-carved inlays that lined the walls of the ballroom. "It is lovely being near the river." He smiled at her. "Not that I have to remind you of that. I do believe it is Richmond Hill that's been inspiring all my trips up the Hudson of late."

"The Kaatskills . . ." She accepted the brandy and washed down her cake. "That remains your favorite spot?"

"I swear it has a witching effect on my imagination. I think of it constantly. In fact . . . I'm sorry, I'm boring you. A dance?" He offered her his arm. "That's what we're here to do."

Beyond them, Philip and Lucinda whirled about.

"Me, that's what I'm here to do—all of us women. Dance and make the men in our lives look worthy."

"Difficult?"

"Depends on the man." She sipped her brandy. "Certainly not the one in front of me. You're never boring, dear friend. I adore your imagination."

"Well, then . . ." His eyes shone with appreciation. "I'd like to set a story there, in the Kaatskills. I've a notion of an idea already . . . " He gestured to the room full of smartly dressed men and women engaged in conversation, frivolity, and consumption. "All of this may not have been. I think of it often. These families who owe much to the war. And the ones out there." He tipped his head toward the window. "The ones who lost nearly everything, the families not lucky enough to turn a profit. The war defines us. Every one. So what if . . . what if we . . . someone, a man, say, missed it? Slept for ten, perhaps twenty, years straight through it. Awoke to find all the portraits of King George replaced with my namesake George Washington's. What would this sleepy man think? What would he have missed?"

Theodosia brought her glass to her lips to hide her surprise. The foundation of his story reminded her very much of her own. Yet she couldn't fathom how he'd have come across it, let alone connected her to it, if that was indeed what he was implying. "That sounds so . . . creative. Have you begun writing?"

His peachy cheeks tinged darker. "Not yet. And I have to admit, I was inspired partly by the lush landscape of the mountains but also by something Mother read to me. Perhaps you've heard of it? It was a story in a ladies'—"

Theodosia coughed, nearly spilling her drink. Only Washington's swift movements to take hold of the glass saved it.

"What skill, Mr. Irving!" came a pretentious trill that almost caused Washington to drop the glass he'd just caught. He spun to face what Theodosia had seen coming.

*Lucinda Wilson.*

"Washington *and* Theodosia," she said. "All hidden away like a pair of lovebirds!"

Washington flushed again, turning altogether crimson.

Theodosia smiled as thinly as she could. Taunting her was one thing, but she wouldn't let Lucinda use Washington for her own perverse fun. "Or friends skilled in intelligent conversation," she said. "Which is not your forte . . . *forgive me* . . . I mean, interest."

Lucinda smiled back with the same measure of veiled disdain. She wore a deep blue gown made of patterned silk velvet that cost more than three of the Burrs' outstanding bills combined. "What is of immense interest is that brandy." She looked up at Washington expectantly.

"Yes, of course." He turned to Theodosia. "Another?"

"Why not?" Theodosia said. "It is a party, after all."

Washington was scarcely out of earshot when Lucinda began, "You two are well suited. I've always thought so. A much better match than you might be for . . . others."

Theodosia's hackles rose. "Mr. Irving and I are the best of friends."

"I'm sure, with all that you have in common."

"We have known each other since we were children."

"Perhaps why you've come to share the same pursuit." The words hung heavy. Lucinda gave a wry smile but said no more, leaving Theodosia to conceal her growing dismay. Finally, Lucinda leaned in, her breath hot on Theodosia's cheek, and whispered, "Miss P."

Theodosia shrunk back, her hand flat against her belly. Her inability to express even the barest of sounds confirmed Lucinda's suspicions. Lucinda postured before Theodosia like a predator trapping its prey.

Theodosia's mind whirred trying to make sense of what was happening. She'd not given Lucinda enough credit, never imagined she'd be clever enough to put the clues together, of seeing Theodosia outside the offices of the magazine, perhaps watching her intently as the story was read in the salons they'd both attended. Had she ever heard Theodosia's nickname? Perhaps at the summer salon, perhaps her father had called out a "Miss Priss" when Lucinda was in earshot?

Of the secret Theodosia expected Lucinda to have and use, this was not the one.

"Amateurish, the writing. It seems, I was quite correct," Lucinda said, full of conceit. "Never fear, my friend, I promise not to humiliate you by allowing your name to be linked to such drivel. Your secret will live right here." She patted her bosom. "Or it will if you do one simple thing." Theodosia locked her jaw, and Lucinda laughed. "Stubborn as always. But all I require is a nod. A tiny tilt of your pretty little bookish head. Ready, Theo, dear?"

Theodosia debated between running away and throttling her. "Whatever you wish to say, just say it."

"Very Burr. Not a confirmation nor a denial. Here it is, Miss P. No one will know . . . your father and his desperate party will not know as long as you stay away from Philip Hamilton."

Having steeled herself for whatever was to come, Theodosia managed a derisive laugh. "Philip Hamilton? How much farther away could I be? There's no love lost between us."

"I suspect only half that phrase contains truth." Lucinda clasped her hands together. "No matter, whatever was, is no more." Her garishly red lips widened into a sickening smile. "I've made sure of that. Intimately sure."

Theodosia's gut twisted.

"In fact, I've recently become intimately familiar with many parts of Philip, including his rather loose tongue. So do as I request, Theodosia, stay away from Philip Hamilton, and your secrets will remain as such."

Theodosia's weight seemed too much for her legs to support. "You've quite the imagination, Lucinda."

"Nice of you to acknowledge my prowess in poetry, but this is pure fact. Confirmed fact."

Fact? Not suspicion? With Georgie unaware of her true name, only two people could speak of Theodosia's involvement with certainty. And her father never would. That meant Theodosia was right not to give Lucinda any credit for connecting clues but also that she was wrong—so very wrong—about Philip.

*Loose tongue.*

Her every breath became a battle. Still she maintained her stoic exterior save for her eyes, which darted around the room from her father to Nathalie to Sumter to Eliza Hamilton and Angelica and Philip. Her Philip. Who wasn't anymore.

Stomach churning, she elbowed past Lucinda, keeping her head focused straight ahead. She rushed toward the grand staircase, descending with haste to the front hall, not pausing to receive her shawl or the arm of the footman, flustered at not accompanying her, as she raced down the front steps of the mansion.

She gulped the night air, nearly choking on the memories carried with it. All she held in her heart refused to believe that Philip would reveal her secret to anyone, least of all Lucinda Wilson. Yet the mind she had worked so hard to sharpen like a knife on a stone knew something else.

If Philip believed she and Alston had been courting at the same time as she and Philip had been, then he'd see her as a liar. Perhaps one with an ulterior motive, which she actually had— only it applied to Alston. But Philip had no way of knowing that. The feud between their fathers would naturally cause him to think he was the one being duped. Used for some political purpose that would surely be detrimental to his family, to his father. If his thoughts spiraled as such, then might he have let the truth about Theodosia slip? Might he have released it willingly, purposely? Out of anger and spite and humiliation?

Yes, yes, and yes. *Oh, Philip!*

Her feet moved her everywhere and nowhere, pacing up and down the line of carriages, searching for hers. Fury built beneath her breast, stung her eyes, balled her hands into fists that she pounded against the sides of this heartbreakingly beautiful dress that she actually thought might make Philip forgive her.

He'd betrayed her. Because of Alston.

*Alston.* That arrogant, pompous, beady-eyed, balding, manipulative toad. This was all his fault. This was all her father's fault. This was—

A splayed hand wrapped around the back of her arm, and she whirled around in surprise. Her heart thundered in her chest, and she shook Philip off. She could not bear to see him.

Her lungs squeezed as hurt mixed with anger mixed with confusion mixed with brandy, and she stumbled. A fleeting look of concern dimmed the rage in Philip's eyes. His arms outstretched as if to catch her. She righted herself, but still he seized her hand. His soft skin against hers stopped everything but the incessant pull of her heart toward his, and she followed willingly as he led her down a gravel path toward a copse of maple trees. Shrouded within, he unceremoniously released her hand, and her blood simmered once again.

Theodosia straightened her skirt. "They say a Burr is fickle, but seems a Hamilton can move on just as swiftly."

"At least it is a move on and not concurrent," he quipped.

"A betrayal is a betrayal."

"Quite so. Though your current state of distress makes me shocked that you would admit it."

"You stand there all big-headed trying to be the definition of virtuous when you told *Lucinda Wilson* my biggest secret."

Philip's brow furrowed.

Hadn't he followed her because he knew what Lucinda had said inside the ballroom?

His brow flattened and he laughed derisively. "And here I thought *I* was your biggest secret."

Chests heaving, breaths quick, eyes searching, they stood in silence. The flames of anger swirling between them could have lit every lamppost in the city.

Theodosia couldn't bear it another second and stormed straight past him, pressing on despite the scent of his lemon soap threatening to stop her. She reached the edge of the thicket of trees when Philip cried, "A maiden, a lass!"

She halted, the train of her dress nearly caught under foot in the abruptness.

> "*A maiden, a lass,*
> *One with a good measure of sass,*
> *Sought by men, young and old,*
> *And oh, what a sight to behold!*
> *If only one could grab ahold,*
> *What a tale could be told!*"

That he had chosen this, the bawdy poem he recited at the Nicholson salon, not the more serious one that had tugged on her heartstrings, was absurd and presumptuous and so entirely Philip.

Her Philip.

She clutched the sides of her dress, bunched up the fabric, and ran. His arms lay open, waiting for her, enfolding around her, bringing lips to lips and body to body, the world just the two of them.

*Why can't the world be just the two of them?*

*Can the world be just the two of them?*

Theodosia felt like a bottle of champagne, uncorked and bubbling over. "Philip, you must understand, I never meant to hurt you, it was never to go this far, not that it's gone anywhere, but first my chest of drawers and favorite reading chair and not the books, not yet, but how long before because the bill's overdue for the milk and the election is a tie—a *tie!*—and Alston is a disgusting toad with his . . ."

Theodosia's words tripped over themselves to tell Philip the truth about her family's finances and her father's desperate need for support in the South and Alston. She told him the truth about Alston. That she had allowed the man to believe they had a future together. That he had asked her, that very day in his last letter, to have a future with her.

Saying it all out loud drowned her in shame. "I've acted like a woman who belongs in a brothel."

Philip's eyes widened.

"No, no, Philip, oh, devil come for me, no, not in act, in name only." She clutched the lapels of his coat. "I would never, I could never . . . I mean . . . never with anyone . . . only with you. It's only you. Only ever been you."

Pools of moisture filled his eyes as he kissed her, his lips soft and warm and strong and relenting, and she knew she would forgive him anything for the chance to remain like this for eternity.

But Philip set his hand between their chests and forced them apart. "I must explain." He swallowed hard. "About Lucinda."

The image of the two of them side by side atop a quilt, Philip's hands going all the places Theodosia wished to ask them to go on her own body, made her shudder.

"I was upset, drinking . . . drunk, I was drunk, and Lucinda . . ."

Theodosia bit her bottom lip, preparing to hear the "intimate" details Lucinda had taunted her with earlier.

"She was there, and I was hurt. Theo, you must know I was only so angry because I thought you and that man . . ." He squeezed his eyes shut. "How could I let that arrogant excuse for a gentleman make me doubt you? I was such a pigheaded fool for letting my pride stop me from coming to you."

"But you did," Theodosia said. "That day, you came, and I sent you away. I had to. I couldn't risk Alston seeing you and thinking I was disloyal. Of course, that meant I was disloyal to you instead."

"That day . . ." His hands clenched into fists, and she reached to unwind them.

"I wish I'd done it differently. I wish I had thought of another way . . ."

He pursed his lips as if picturing her dismissal anew. But then he shook his head. "You wrote. But I instructed Angelica not to read your letters or even tell me of their arrival. Think of it: Me? Pride? This was the time I chose to find some? I drank whiskey and whined like a child. Lucinda knowing you're the author of those stories is entirely my fault."

"I . . . If I were you, if I'd thought you were in love with someone else—"

"You'd have asked me. You are of superior intellect and patience and restraint. I act impulsively. It's what it will say on my gravestone."

"Do not." Theodosia pulled him against her. "Not even in jest. I forgive you, Philip. We will sort this out, so long as we are together, we will sort it out."

His eyes clouded over. "But it already is. Lucinda will not disclose the information."

"But how can you be so sure?"

He tried to draw back, but Theodosia wouldn't let him. "If you're not, if you were speaking simply of hope—"

"No, I'm sure. I've already given in to her demand." He brought their enfolded hands to his heart. "What a pair we make. You leveraged to Alston, and now me to her. Her price for silence is me."

Lucinda's "request" of Theodosia had been simply added assurance.

"Well, then," Theodosia said. A pair they made, indeed. Each backed into a corner by their own shortcomings. "Here we are. Each pretending to be enamored of another—"

"While entirely in love with each other."

"Entirely." She buried her head in his chest. He stroked her forehead, and she stayed with him, feeling entirely at peace. It was as if all the while they were apart she'd been sitting atop her mare in boots and gloves waiting, and now she was off, wind in her hair, muscles taut, riding free. But they weren't free.

She pressed her lips to his chest and nuzzled a kiss. Then, she stepped back and inhaled a steadying breath. "This is all for show, Philip. Keep that in your head and don't doubt it. No matter what you may see or hear. Know that after the election, whatever the outcome, I will end things with Alston. You and I will be together.

Not in secret, but out for all to see. I will stand before my father and tell him I love you. What he thinks will not matter and will not stop me."

Philip's cheeks sunk. "You're going through with this?"

"Playing along. It's only a few more weeks. What's a few weeks compared to the lifetime we will have together?" As she said the words, she felt such relief, for now she could help her father without the pain and guilt of lying to Philip. "And there's also Lucinda. If you break things off with her, she will retaliate. It's entirely within her nature. But if she does so after the presidential election, she can't hurt me. Can't hurt us."

Philip held her, his head shaking. "No, no, Theo. The way is clear. That future must be now. No more looking back. Look forward. Look to me. We can start over, anywhere we want. We can free ourselves from these looming shadows we've lived under. We can be whoever we were meant to be—together."

Her chest tightened, and she reached a hand to his cheek, trailing her finger along his flushed skin the way he would do with her. "Forever my poet who thinks in possibilities."

"Don't dismiss me. Theodosia. This is our moment. I feel it in my soul. If you do this, if you keep up this pretense with Alston, if I must continue my own with Lucinda, it will be the end of us."

She shook her head. "Just a pause. I have promises to keep."

"He asks too much of you."

"Yes, he does. But I will do this for him. I will keep my word." Not just the promise to her father, but the one to her mother. Completing this charade would release her of that vow to care for him; if her father were elected, he wouldn't need her quite so much. If Alston could place her father in office, he would have the power of influence he desired. Why, a win would even mean her father had bested his rival in the ultimate of games . . . so much so that he could even claim his rival's firstborn as son-in-law!

Her chest fluttered at the thought, one that transformed into not just a hope but a plan. She'd always thought she would have to find a way to lessen the tension between the colonel and her father. But if her father became president, that tension might mean the opposite. His need to lord all over Hamilton might make him more inclined to accept Philip. Either way, she would use this time to prepare him.

Theodosia spoke with certainty. "In keeping my word to my father, we will benefit. I'm sure of it, Philip."

His face tightened, his eyes nearly squinting as if in pain.

Theodosia added, "You must trust me."

"You have to trust *me*, Theo. Run away with me. Tonight," he said, his words a desperate plea.

It took all the strength she had—the strength returned to her by being in his arms again—to resist. "Papa and I are off to Albany soon. He wants to wait out the election results from there, away from the gossip and speculation of the city."

"Then let him go and wait. It makes it the perfect time for us to get away."

"Oh, Philip, I would love nothing more. But I must finish what I've started, ill-conceived as it may be. If I left with you, and he were to lose, the blame would consume me. And eventually us. But when the election is done, we'll be together."

"You can't be sure."

"I can, and I am. These past weeks have taught me that living without you is not living. I won't do it again." She gave him what she hoped was a reassuring smile. "Patience is required of us both. Wait for me. I promise it will be worth it."

"*Theodosia!*" a faint but concerned cry reached them.

"There he is," Philip said, recognizing her father's voice.

"Trust me, Philip, the way I trust you. With my whole heart."

She brushed her lips against his and turned to leave, putting her faith entirely in the hope that he would.

# Chapter 28

THAT FAITH FED HER EVERY THOUGHT and action. Theodosia
had little need for roasted squash or boiled potatoes or smoked
venison. She ate sparingly, pleasing her father, because she sub-
sisted on a diet of unbridled hope. And as of today, on a diet free
of Joseph Alston.

She lifted her fork and its small bite of eel pie. Across from her,
Nathalie ate greedily. Her appetite had only increased after the
evening spent twirling with Thomas Sumter, as if filling herself
another way would lessen the hole left behind. Theodosia knew it
would not.

Shortly after the Blackwell ball, Sumter had returned to
South Carolina, inciting a deluge of letters arriving for Nathalie.
Richmond Hill had become a beacon for letters with the South
Carolina postmark, with ones also appearing regularly for
Theodosia and her father.

Nathalie was not so absorbed with her own heart not to notice.
Disappointment filled her at having seen Philip and Lucinda at
the ball, at the idea of Theodosia being stuck with the toad. As
much as Theodosia wished to tell Nathalie the truth, it was easier,
both in practice and in thought, to keep the deception simple.
When all was done, then Nathalie would delight in the truth the
same as Theodosia.

She had delayed almost two weeks in responding to Alston's
letter with its equivocal proposal, and when she did write, it was
of the weather and the stores of beets and potatoes for the coming
winter and a simple coy line or two to encourage his interest yet

not address his cloudy words of a shared future. He'd not brought it up again, much to her relief.

Her father had decided to postpone their trip to Albany and remain in the city in the days leading up to the electoral college vote, so entirely reassured by Alston that South Carolina would be on his side come Election Day.

This day. The third of December.

A long, fretful month had passed since she'd last seen Philip. Though the start of winter had brought a newfound chill in the air, anticipation had kept Theodosia warm, on edge, counting down to this moment.

Her pen no longer belonged to Alston. Her energies would soon be spent the way she desired: with Philip.

Her father had barely touched his plate, which was not necessarily unusual for him. What was out of character was the slowly emptying carafe of wine on the table.

Perhaps even at that very instant, representatives from all sixteen states were casting their ballots for president. The culmination of nearly a year's work. The electors, whether chosen by popular vote or by their state's legislature, were finally serving their purpose.

And yet the authors of the Constitution, James Madison and Philip's father among them, had envisioned something far different from what had occurred in this election. They designed and named the "electoral college" to represent an idyllic "collegial" setting where gentlemen would come together to cast one vote for each of the two men they believed best-suited for the presidency. A vote in which electors exercised their independent judgment, regardless of their own party affiliations.

It was a system that had put Federalist John Adams in as president and Republican Thomas Jefferson as vice president four years ago. But that election had been held in less-divisive times. Debate over the strength of the central government and over the revolution in France had led to extremes between the two parties being heightened. The rivalry between her father and Philip's, as well as her father's unprecedented electioneering over the past few months, had fueled the contention.

With such strong partisanship, even before this day, the tally among Jefferson, Burr, Adams, and Pinckney could be made with reasonable assurance. The electors were mere proxies for their affiliated party—*party*, which said nothing of the man in particular: Jefferson or Burr. And therein lay the hope for her father.

The hope from South Carolina. All resting on Alston's influence with electors who could be swayed.

Her father had made whatever promises he could make. To back a banker's need for more liberal practices, a farmer's for debtor relief, a merchant's requirements for easier expansion, and a trader's for better commission. One man's need for one thing would always be at another's expense, but none would be the wiser until it was too late.

There was nothing more he could do—nothing more anyone could do. Including Theodosia.

She smiled reassuringly at her father. His eyes beneath his now perpetually furrowed brow lingered on her tortoiseshell brooch. She'd come to wear it every day. It made her feel closer not only to Philip but to completing the request her mother had made of her all those years ago.

*For what else do I live?*

A lot, it turns out. For them both.

"Theodosia!" her father called up the stairs, an unrefined bellowing that demanded her immediate presence. One he'd come to take advantage of as time stretched awaiting news of the election.

Theodosia set down her quill. Washington had written a first draft of the story they'd discussed and had asked for her opinion. She spread sand to set her first comment: "something more memorable, perhaps?" The title and the character's name irked her: Ron

Winkle. It was in need of something with more verve . . . she began to run through names in her head when a second "Theodosia!" rattled the walls.

She sighed and pushed back her chair. Traveling through the empty parlor, she found her father behind the desk he'd had moved into the library.

"The door, please, Theo," he said.

She did as he asked, noting the piles of papers that seemed to multiply each day, threatening to undo all her work cleaning and organizing the space. "Is something—"

He jabbed his finger at the newspaper spread out before him. "The results."

"Finally!" It had been a full two weeks since Election Day. She'd hardly been able to bear it. Winter's fallen leaves and coating of snow made clandestine meetings on blankets difficult, though the impossibility of seeing Philip came more from a second set of watchful eyes joining her father's: those of Lucinda Wilson.

They'd been as sharp as a hawk's last week at Hannah Gallatin's salon, for once a gathering Theodosia would not miss. She'd hoped to see Angelica, to have her pass a message to her brother, perhaps even a letter. But Theodosia couldn't even offer Angelica a polite greeting without Lucinda inserting herself. Though in the end, Theodosia had gotten something even better: a glimpse of Philip. The terrible reality that he'd come to escort Lucinda home eased when their eyes met. The trust she'd asked him to place in her was still there. As was his desire for her, as intense as hers for him.

Her father's constant presence and obsession with the post and messengers made communicating as she and Philip had in the past impossible. The discord between Burr and Colonel Hamilton burned like a lit cannon. If discovered, a letter written in her hand to any member of the Hamilton family, even Angelica, would demand explanation if not his immediate reading. She couldn't take the risk any more than she could ask others to do so for her. Asking Sam or Tom or any of the servants to secretly ferry letters to Philip would put them in defiance of the man who held their lives in his hands.

Behind his desk, her father laid those same hands flat against the newspaper. "The whispers must have finally become loud enough to be considered fact."

"But still unconfirmed?" Theodosia said, desperate for the opposite despite knowing the election wouldn't be officially resolved until the new year. Legally the ballots had to remain sealed until February. Yet an official count wasn't needed for the Burrs to know their fate. Electors talked, outing their vote—usually much faster than this, which had added to the frustrated mood in the Burr household.

"See for yourself," he said.

Theodosia circled the desk. Standing beside her father, she read the article, her pulse quickening with every line. "But that would mean . . ." She pulled the paper closer. The *National Inquirer* was reporting that the presidential election was a tie between her father and Jefferson. *Her father and Jefferson.* Locked. Not a top vote getter winning the office of president and the one in second place becoming vice president, but equals. "How can that be?"

He gave a wry smile. "Smart electors, but not quite smart enough."

The Republican electors had cast their ballots with such unity that they neglected to account for the fact that with every elector casting the required two ballots and not deviating from the party line, they would engender a perfect tie. The ballots made no distinction between the offices of president and vice president.

The animation in her father's eyes showed his pleasure. "Thomas and I each appear to have seventy-three votes. Best estimates have us at least eight votes ahead of Adams and nine in front of Pinckney."

"So you've actually won?" All this time, all this waiting, all these machinations for the past year had led them here. A surge of pride rushed through her. "Papa, you've won!"

"The White House will be ours." Despite his reserved tone, his smile was wide and true. "If these whispers are indeed fact, when the ballots are officially opened, the Republicans will have made a clean sweep." That furrowed brow returned. "But that does not mean I've won, Miss Priss. That is for the House of Representatives to decide."

"Federalists." They held the current majority in the House, which would be the one to vote and break the tie, choosing solely between the two men receiving the top votes. For Adams and Pinckney, the contest was over. A sense of foreboding descended upon her for what this meant for her father—for her.

"Most of whom have deep ties to Hamilton." Concern clouded his eyes. "An impossible choice it would seem given the colonel's distaste for us both."

She didn't want to linger on Philip's father and instead refocused her own on his win. "But you have as equal a chance as Jefferson."

"Because of you. You've done more than I had a right to ask. You have ensured this would be our path. Look here, if you continue reading, you will see that neither Adams nor Pinckney received a single vote from one particular state."

She froze. "South Carolina. Despite being Pinckney's home state."

"Perhaps thanks to this." He handed her a recent clipping from the *Charleston City Gazette*.

She scanned the article, which appeared to be an exceptionally strong endorsement of her father, praising his qualifications for office:

*"Endowed with a mind vast, liberal and comprehensive, America owns not a citizen more fitted than Col. Burr, to be placed at the head of her government. With an energy and decision of character peculiar to himself, while other men are debating, he resolves; and while they resolve, he acts."*

It was signed: "A Rice Planter."

She drew in a breath. "This is . . ."

"Proof that Joseph has been on our side and will continue to be. The race is far from over, Theo." He rubbed his hands together. "We're just getting started."

His words struck like a blade. This was to have been settled in all but name already. Electors would spill their votes as they always had, the winner would be known, and the opening of ballots in February was to be no more than a formality. With this, a tie to be decided by Federalists, what she'd assumed—what she and Philip had assumed—would be a separation of merely a few weeks had turned into months.

All because of that "rice planter."

The carriage bounced all the way to Albany. As did her father. The final week of December had arrived, and still the rumors persisted, becoming fact in all but name. He and the current vice president were tied.

Burr flapped a sheet of parchment and read aloud in the cramped carriage: "*It was badly managed not to have arranged with certainty what seems to have been left to hazard. Decency required that I should be so entirely passive during the late contest that I never once asked whether arrangements had been made . . .*" He scowled before continuing to read, "*Nor did I doubt till lately that such had been made.*"

He shook the letter from Thomas Jefferson in the air. "Not even veiled! Accusing me of impropriety."

She cocked her head but said nothing, which encouraged him to mutter, half to himself.

"That I should have made these 'arrangements' . . . I am not the leader of our party, which was made clear to me on all the occasions for which it suited him. And now, I was to 'arrange' this?" He folded, then unfolded the letter. "Oh, he congratulates me, assuredly, in case this were to fall in hands other than my own. But already he fears the Federalists blocking us and the government devolving into a president of the Senate."

Her father had spoken to her at length about the possibilities if the official results indeed revealed no clear winner. The matter first would go to the House of Representatives, where each state would be given one vote to break the tie. The candidate supported by the majority of congressmen in that state's delegation would receive the vote. If the congressmen happened to split evenly, the state would abstain. A majority of nine garnered the win. Confusion clouded what would happen if a majority were not able to be achieved by Inauguration Day on the fourth of March when Adams and Jefferson's current terms expired.

In the absence of a president and vice president, the Constitution authorized Congress to make laws designating who would lead the nation—perhaps a Cabinet member or judicial officer but likely a Federalist. Some even said Adams should be left at the helm. Others that a new election be held.

It kept Jefferson up at night. But not her father, because he believed the situation would never progress that far.

He leaned toward her. "Do you know what else Thomas says, Miss Priss?"

As he went on, she felt ill. It was still, or again, all dependent upon one state: South Carolina. Jefferson had been informed—apparently misinformed—that during the electoral college vote, one elector from that state would withdraw a vote from Burr, abstaining or casting it for another, in which case there would have been no tie.

But there was. A direct cause and effect in her father's mind.

Which was how Theodosia came to find herself attempting to reply to an actual proposal while lurching along in a carriage on the way to Albany.

After receiving her banal letter about beets and potatoes, Alston had replied in kind. She'd barely skimmed his subsequent letter on the state of the rice fields. His words had been so perfunctory that she'd assumed she'd been wrong about his interest in her. Or that perhaps her detached letter had changed his mind. But then, this new letter had arrived. One that was undeniably a real, if entirely dispassionate, proposal.

"*A man should not marry until he is six and thirty,*" she wrote in the carriage, quoting Aristotle as part of the tack she'd taken. Her father had implored her not to reject the proposal and risk Alston losing his motivation at this tenuous moment. Still, a yes was a preposterous notion. Instead of saying no, Theodosia would hold Alston off by pretending this was simply an academic discussion, and within this context, she would relay the disadvantages of marrying young.

And yet the way her father fixed on Alston as savior sat uneasily. She found herself including in her letter to Alston a detailed list of the problems of South Carolina, from the dull routine of country life to the abundant disease to the uneducated and uninformed women to the deplorable treatment of the enslaved. She couldn't help a line that criticized Alston directly. With as much whimsy as her words allowed, she cited the need for her intended to have command of the civilized language of French. For her intended did. Philip was fluent.

She acknowledged their "sincere friendship" and concluded the letter with details of her travel schedule, noting any correspondence to be directed to Albany, where they would remain until the second week of February. Such a long time for this deceit to continue, not just hers but Philip's. His might have even been worse. At least she had hundreds of miles between her and Alston. Philip had Lucinda and her talons to resist in person, all without drawing suspicion.

She needed him to hold out, to know he was foremost in her thoughts. With Nathalie still in the dark, the only one Theodosia trusted was Washington Irving. She'd written to him before they'd left, not without guilt, to beseech him to pass along a single phrase to Philip: "*Friend of my heart, wait.*"

February could not arrive soon enough.

In the coach, as her father carried on about Jefferson and allies and enemies, she grew tired of writing to the man who stood between the life she had and the one she wanted. Her final lines to Alston were a specific taunt:

*My movements will after that depend on my father and you. I had intended not to marry this twelvemonth, and in that case, thought it wrong to divert you from your present engagements in Carolina; but to your solicitations I yield my judgment. Adieu. I wish you many returns of the century.*

She envisioned this as calling his bluff. For a man intent on truly wooing a woman would respond not with words and parchment but with himself. This long-distance courting would come to an end, one way or another.

And it did—after the year turned to 1801 in the snow-covered valley of Albany and Mr. Joseph Alston of South Carolina arrived on the doorstep of the home the Burrs temporarily claimed as their own.

# CHAPTER 29

THEODOSIA CRUMPLED UPON SIGHT OF HIM. That skin nearly as blinding as the snow whitening the ground. Those snakish eyes alive with twisted amusement upon seeing her shock. Those fragile strands of hair curling and beckoning like the scythe of the devil.

She found him revolting. Unlike her father, who strode forth and embraced Alston as if they were already joined as family.

"Joseph! That ship must have a sail under some sort of witch-craft to dock so swiftly. Your letter only just arrived a day ago with your intended schedule."

Behind Alston, Theodosia glared at her father. The frequency of his correspondence with Alston surpassed her own, therefore him knowing of these plans was not surprising—unlike his deci-sion to keep the information from her.

He angled out of her harsh gaze, resting an arm on Alston's shoulders and ushering him into the small home they were occu-pying in town. "No matter, our door is always open to friends in need of lodging. Theodosia, have Tom and Nancy get to prepara-tions."

She gritted her teeth but let forth a polite affirmation. They'd only brought two of their servants with them as this visit was not to be one of hosting dinners or parties but of respite. Waiting out the news to come and giving the appearance of having no role to play within. Throughout the first third of January, the *Inquirer* had continued to report the election as a tie, and it'd come to be taken as fact by all. By now, all electors had spoken up, and the split between Burr and Jefferson assured.

292

Her father had been running through various scenarios since they'd arrived in Albany. Letters were sent, and letters were received, half wishing he'd vie for the position publicly, the other demanding he resign from the ticket altogether. Rumors swirled regarding negotiations and deals with both Federalists and Republicans, on his side as well as Jefferson's. And yet Burr's years of remaining neutral, understanding not only what each side stood for but what individuals within each side needed—craved—allowed him to do what he did best: wait. What a future president could offer tempted many. But to act too quickly, to offer, to negotiate before the time was right, could backfire.

Burr was close. He knew it.

The Federalists, seeing their chance to bar Jefferson from becoming president, were coming to Burr's side despite Alexander Hamilton's well-known dislike of his rival. Prevailing over Jefferson occupied every waking moment between Theodosia and her father. They sorted through the possible means to his desired outcome again and again, she always seeking a route that did not involve South Carolina. A single Republican defection in Vermont or New Jersey or Georgia or Maryland could turn the state's vote against Jefferson. Two defections in New York would swing Burr's home state. If every Federalist congressman voted for him, Burr would only need three or four strategically placed Republican votes to carry the needed nine states. On and on. And unfortunately, always in the mix, Alston.

Theodosia reluctantly sat in the small sitting room across from the southern mosquito she couldn't seem to swat away. He'd claimed the seat nearest the fire without even a tilt of his head to offer it to her first.

His costume shone in its gaudy light coral velvet, as if he were playing the role of someone from the North in a farce. He rubbed his hands together, warming them by the flames. "I believe I'd just as soon work a day in the fields than come this far North in winter again."

Alston had never worked, let alone labored a day in his plantation, enduring the arduous work forced upon his slaves.

He clapped the chill from his hands and laid his searching eyes upon Theodosia. "Only the biggest toad in the puddle could call me here."

Theodosia offered a strained smile as it occurred to her that perhaps it was not her father but the challenge she'd laid out in her letter that had brought him here. She thought she'd been calling his bluff, but he had called hers.

"Let us apologize in advance," Theodosia said. "For other than a ride in a sleigh, little exists to pass the time. And the climate with which you are acquainted would make even that most difficult."

"Eh, lots of ways to stay warm, little Theo." He faced her father. "Isn't that right, Burr? Speaking of . . ."

"Brandy," her father said before Theodosia's tongue unfurled itself.

"I'll check on Nancy." Theodosia stood, grateful to take her leave. That was until Alston spoke.

"And perhaps find some other pursuit after," he said with that drawl that haunted her. "We'll be deep in political ruminating, I suspect. No sense letting it spin your head."

She clasped her hands in front of her, digging her fingernails into her palms.

"But don't say I leave a girl bored." He lumbered to his feet, stomping them either to make his command of the situation known, increase his circulation, or both. "For you." He withdrew a letter from his breast pocket. "Delivered by hand, written with heart."

He smiled in a way she'd never seen before, almost . . . genuine, without his usual blustery arrogance. Somehow it unnerved her even more.

She accepted the letter as if the parchment dripped with poison. The only man's words she wished to read belonged to Philip. But the small quarters in Albany made correspondence not just a risk but impossible. Her father was on high alert for anything out of the ordinary. The only word she'd received came from Nathalie, who'd been seeking every shred of gossip, the latest being Philip's long hours of study making him a poor and scarce companion at Lucinda's side.

Theodosia departed from the room, but before seeing to the requested brandy, she lingered just out of sight.

"Any news from the new capital?" Alston asked.

Her father's eagerness infused his words. "Gallatin wrote that it being so recently settled sets this in our favor."

*Our.*

He continued, "The City of Washington is too new to have any of the cosmopolitan nature of Philadelphia. Gallatin said that some do drink and gamble, but by and large, the majority drink naught but politics. With little opportunity to mix socially, politics is all they have, so they can't help but inflame one another and remain locked in partisan combat."

"And who is more partisan than old Thomas," Alston said. "Any whining from the vice president—now *and* future?"

Her father laughed—heartily. "After writing him that my personal friends are perfectly informed of my wishes and can never think of diverting a single vote from him? So I would be his vice president? No whining yet. But what could he say, as each word is perfectly true."

"Since 'think' be not the same as 'act,'" Alston said.

Her father's bluntness worried her. Him holding Alston in such confidence would only make Theodosia's rejection of the man more difficult for him. Alston being here, in the flesh, did that already.

Theodosia needed a brandy herself, and she didn't stop at one. As her father and Alston plotted and tallied, her stomach tied itself into knots reading the tome Alston had written to her. Pages upon pages, twenty in all, such that she knew his every curve of an "s" and dot of "i" as well as her own. He'd countered each of her claims, presenting an opus on why she must concede to marriage.

His dissertation challenged her case against marrying too young, implying she was misguided in "adopting the opinion of anyone, however respectable his authority," even Aristotle. He went on to say:

*Suppose (for instance, merely) a young man nearly twenty-two, already of the greatest discretion, with an ample fortune, were to be passionately in love with a young lady almost eighteen, equally discreet with himself, and who had a "sincere friendship" for him, do you think it would be necessary to make him wait till thirty? Particularly where friends on both sides were pleased by the match. Were I to consider the question personally, since you allow that "individual character" ought to be consulted, no objection certainly could be made to my marrying early.*

Friends on both sides? What friends? The only one who even knew of this was her father.

Alston went on to defend South Carolina's use of slaves and praised his home state, assuring her that, despite the distance from the ocean, the *"seabreeze"* afforded cool, crisp air over the rice swamps, which were not *"at all unhealthful."* He flattered her by writing that the *"ladies of the Lowcountry were not generally as handsome as those in the northern states"* but still refuted her claim about them by saying, *"their education is perhaps more attended to than anywhere else in the United States. Many of them are well informed, all of them accomplished."*

That he'd put forth such a notion proved one of two things: either he didn't know Theodosia at all or he was even more arrogant than she'd imagined. In truth, it proved both. Especially the latter. He even boasted, despite a lackluster experience at school and never actually practicing the law, that he had great confidence in his ability to learn languages rapidly.

*You wish me to acquire French. I already understand something of it, and, with a little practice, would soon speak it. I promise you, therefore, if you become my instructress, in less than two months after our marriage to converse with you entirely in that language. I fix the period after our marriage, for I cannot think of being corrected in the mistakes I may make by any other person than my wife. Suppose, till then, you return to your Latin, and prepare to use that tongue with me, since you are adverse to one understood by all the canaille.*

Canaille? He thought himself one of the "common people"? Common people didn't have stores of sugar they locked away and hundreds of acres of land they had worked by slaves.

She flipped page after page, incredulous. This was no love letter, not even a poor attempt at one. It was as if he were pleading a case to a jury.

Not one she was on though. He was using this to prove to her father that if Theodosia rejected his hand in marriage, she did so without cause.

She might doubt his assurance of learning languages with ease, but he was even more skilled in manipulation than she thought. These twenty pages demonstrated a clear goal of receiving her hand in marriage. But why? He didn't actually care about her, of that she was sure. She was not so fetching or beguiling—there were others with far more beauty and more amenable to life as the traditional wife he surely sought. Not in a single letter had she given him cause to think that of her—in fact, she'd emphasized the opposite.

Here he was, body present, and he'd tried to convince her in writing. Could he not maintain the illusion in front of her? She'd make him and uncover his motives that very night.

# Chapter 30

"Plumb tuckered out," he said with a grand, impolite yawn. Alston shook her father's hand and bowed to Theodosia. "Ice and carriage wheels are an exhausting combination. Just a light supper in my room, my dear?"

Theodosia held her tongue as she gave an abrupt bow in return. Supper would be solely with her father, who appeared rattled after his long afternoon with Alston. She'd had her own prolonged day with him via his now infuriating self-professed "folio volume."

"You should have warned me," Theodosia said over her cup of broth at the dining room table.

Her father reached for his wineglass, filling it to the rim. "Don't make too much of this, Theo. You're the one who invited him."

"That was hardly an invitation. And even if interpreted as one, I never expected him to come."

"One must expect everything. If I've taught you anything, I've taught you that." He gulped down his wine, his fingertips tapping the table, his eyes resisting meeting hers.

She'd scarcely seen him in such a perplexed state. "What is it, Papa? Did you receive another letter? Is it Sedgwick again?"

The Federalist Speaker of the House, Theodore Sedgwick, had reportedly *"spoken for all"* Federalists when he said they regarded her father as grasping, selfish, and unprincipled. Sedgwick had claimed Burr *"without character and without property—bankrupt in both."*

Her father righted himself against the spindles of the rigid chair. "Joseph had another view on the matter."

298

Because somehow "Joseph" was as entrenched—if not more—in her father's inner circle as she was.

He continued, "He's spoken with some in the South who believe that as egregious as such insults are, they may serve us in the end. For those very traits might be seen as affording my willingness to cooperate with the opposing party." He drank deeply of his wine. "They believe I would be indebted to them. Easily turned into their creature."

His voice broke at the end. She set down her spoon and looked into his eyes. For the first time since sitting at the table, she saw how strained they were. Lined with red, the skin beneath drooping, his cheeks below sallow. She tried to remember the last time she'd seen him eat something of substance. Despite spending their days together, she'd lapsed in her role as caretaker.

"Papa, don't think that way. What of all the others? How many have confirmed you're more vigorous and pragmatic than Jefferson? He's a coward, they proclaim it still. What did the senator from Maryland say of you? '*A soldier and a man of energy and decision.*' They know you to be a lawyer, more keen to support their business interests than Jefferson, the farmer."

"Yet also a balloon."

"Not again, Papa. Adams is bitter and jealous and seeing his power gone."

"But there's power in words, Theodosia."

Adams had accused Burr of subjecting "*all the old patriots, all the splendid talents*" of both Federalists and anti-Federalists alike to the humiliation of seeing him "*rise like a balloon filled with inflammable air over their ears. What an encouragement to party intrigue and corruption.*"

Theodosia tried to dismiss it as usual. "Posturing in the press. That's the game. You're also the one to instruct me on that."

He abruptly stood, knocking over both his soup and his glass. He brought his hands to his face, and Theodosia looked on, unnerved.

"Insults never affect you this much. What has you in such a state? Did Alston . . ." She wasn't sure what to ask. If Alston had delivered positive news. Or the opposite. Perhaps neither, and Alston had instead told him of his letter to her, of its contents, of his expectations. Yet if this wasn't about the two of them, she didn't want to make it so.

He pursed his lips, his head rotating toward the direction of Alston's room, but he said, "Hamilton. Always Hamilton."

She stiffened, her heart in her throat.

"Despotism," her father grumbled. "That's his most recent claim. Said directly to a friend of Joseph's who happens to be the former governor of South Carolina." He began to pace. "Too far. He has never known a line he would not cross."

Theodosia swallowed. "But you must expect him not be pleased with the situation."

"Pleased he'd be if they support Jefferson over me. His letter-writing campaign to Federalists in Congress is nothing short of extraordinary. Portraying me as a cunning, diabolical intriguer willing to do or say anything to gain political power and private wealth. You know what he wrote: that I love nothing but myself, that I think of nothing but my own aggrandizement. Permanent power, that's the only thing to make me content."

The words stung the same as when she'd first learned of them. That Philip's father would condemn her own so strongly. That he was ignorant of the deep affection between her father and his family. But also . . . that he might have been correct about power being the thing her father craved most. A betrayal for her to even think it.

She reached for her father's hand. "Hamilton has lost credibility in his own party. When he wrote that screed against Adams, which all who knew him pleaded with him not to write, it backfired. He looks vindictive now. Fearful that his own party elevating you to president will mean a loss of his position as party leader. Congress sees that, which is why so many are behind you."

Her father's back was to her, his head hung low, chin to chest. "Are they? Truly?" He spun, and Theodosia could not contain her gasp. His face was as transparent as a ghost.

"Papa . . . I . . ." Her words left at the sight of him, old and young at the same time, those deep lines etched around eyes as scared as a lost child's.

"We need them, Theodosia."

"You will have them." She could not allow a bout of ill humor to disable him. "And if not—"

"No!" He raised his voice along with his fist. Then his head whipped toward the hall and Alston's bedroom, eyes dilated in fear. "It must be this way. It must be now." He started toward the door, pausing under the wooden frame, his head shaking, his hands ricocheting against his sides. Just as Theodosia began to lift herself out of her dining chair, he pivoted and rushed to her. "I haven't shielded you as well as I should have. So young you were . . . and I was in such despair . . . you took on a role meant for someone more than twice your age."

He was rambling. He was shaking. He was scaring her.

"Papa, perhaps it's time for rest. We can talk more in the morning."

"No, it will be too late. Time is already running out, Theo."

"This isn't good for your health. Your headaches, you mustn't get in such a state that they return. I'm starting to worry if the election has you this upset, what will the pressures of presidency do?"

He squeezed his eyes shut, opening them and releasing the moisture built within. "Pressures I would welcome, Theo, for they would be less than these."

"I don't understand."

"Joseph can help us." He dropped to his knees in front of her. "He's the key. I've gone over it a thousand different ways, but if we don't have South Carolina, we will have no chance in any of the other southern states. He's the link."

"And he's said he will help. He has been helping, hasn't he? Because if he hasn't . . ." If she'd hurt Philip, been apart from him all this time, and Alston wasn't fulfilling his promise, then she'd toss him right out into the snow that very night.

"He has," her father said, "but the game continues to change."

"You mean he changes it."

"He needs things. Wants things."

"Things that you have?"

"That I can deliver. That a connection to a strong name can facilitate. Especially one high in government."

She knew it. She knew Alston was using her father.

Just as her father was using him.

Just as they were both using her.

She pushed her chair back. "I've played along against all that lives in my heart and mind, and I promised you that I would continue to do so, but I will not voice the word. I will not formally agree to marry him. Not even as a lie."

"Good." He swallowed back moisture, his voice now nasal. "Because it cannot be a lie. He would see right through it. He has more intellect than you allow for."

"Then let it be done. He's close enough to you now. Once he delivers, you'll be in a position to assist him in whatever laws or appointments his disreputable business requires. It's time for him to show us something."

He sighed. "He has. This tie would not have been were it not for him. He confirmed it—what Jefferson had been told. Joseph prevented the South Carolina delegate from taking a vote away from me."

"You have no proof."

"His word is proof enough."

"A man you barely know and yet trust implicitly, going against everything you are."

"And that's proof too, Daughter. For I have no other choice. He will deliver the presidency, but he's no fool. He senses your hesitation, and in truth, you don't make it particularly obscure. He wants the marriage before the House vote. For what other reason do you think he came all this way?"

Ice flooded her veins. *Marriage before the House vote?*

Her father clawed for her hands. "Hear me, Theo, if you don't agree to marry him, here and now, he's done."

*Good!* The notion that he—that her father—would expect a marriage here, instantly—how entirely absurd! She almost laughed. Instead, she softened the tenseness in her shoulders, eased the tightness of her jaw, looked at her father with understanding and care. "We'll do it without him. You've made immeasurable progress on your own. And we still have time, another week. We can write to Bayard and Gallatin, and in truth, you are so close. Perhaps in another four years—"

"No. I may not have four years. Already I'm older than my parents when they passed. And your mother . . ." He shook his head and gripped her hands. "It's not just the election. A marriage to Joseph does more than bring the South to our cause. It also . . . it . . . it preserves Richmond Hill."

Theodosia drew back. "By preserve, you mean . . ."

"Our debts are greater than you realize."

*Save, he means save.*

"I didn't want you to worry. I had things under control. I was sure of it. We would be flush once again. But then an investment didn't yield the return I was promised, and Frederick had to sell his house and farm to cover the bond he signed for me, and now . . . we've nowhere to turn. We will lose it, Theodosia. All of it. Joseph has agreed to invest in the Burrs completely. He knows you adore the estate. He wouldn't allow it to be taken from us."

*But he will take away everything else.*

Her blood boiled with rage that this single man had so much power over their lives. Leaving them ensnared like hares in a trap. She and her father had thought they had the upper hand, and now they were being brought to task for their deception and lies.

Their home, *her* home . . . Richmond Hill, the place that had become her comfort after the true source had been taken from her . . . losing it would be like losing her mother all over again.

And yes, her father coming in second, to the office of vice president instead of president, might break him. The way he was latched on to her now with sweaty palms and trembling lips, she knew he would need her desperately. Excruciating it would all be. But bearable.

But the alternative was not. Marrying Alston might save her home and deliver her father all he desired, but it would erase Philip from her life. She would not. She could not.

"I'm sorry," she whispered.

An audible sob ripped free from his throat, and her own eyes burned.

He laid his head in her lap, just as he had done the night they'd buried her mother. She brushed back the more abundant strands of gray in his hair. She must end this. For good.

"Papa, I want to do this for you. I want to give you the life you need, but I cannot. I know you will understand because you were once where I am: in love with someone in circumstances that made it complicated. But you found a way. I must do the same."

He slowly lifted his head, dragging it from her lap, revealing cheeks glistening with tears. She wiped them with the back of her hand before reaching across the table for a napkin. She held it out for him, and he accepted with gratitude.

He patted his eyes and cheeks and squeezed the linen in one hand. "Don't attempt to ease this with falsehoods."

"I'm not. I swear it." Theodosia caressed the brooch on her dress, giving a mournful smile. "I'm in love. For quite some time now."

Her father struggled to comprehend, and then, a light dawned in his eyes. "Irving? Naturally you've known him since you were children. A family of merchants—rising, it's true, and another time, perhaps a match could have been considered but—"

"No, Papa. It's not Washington." She tried to pull her father to his feet, but he resisted, as if that could prevent whatever was coming. "Please, sit beside me. Let us be joined in this as we have always been."

Reluctantly but with no shame, he rose and took root in the chair Theodosia had brought directly in line with her own.

She connected them, holding both of his hands in hers, grounding him in the depth of the affection between them, assuring him that nothing, not even this, could wash it away. She breathed in, her lungs quivering, but the words released with as much relief as fear. "I have found someone who makes me feel the way Mother made you. And I'm sorry, Papa. So very sorry, for I have a new understanding of the suffering of such a loss . . . one I couldn't have conjured prior. I'm immensely proud of you." Expectation brimmed, and she knew she couldn't delay further. She cleared her throat. "The object of my affection is one who will surprise you the way it did me. But believe me, it's true and as real as my love for you and Nathalie—"

"Theodosia, please!"

"Philip Hamilton," the words burst forth into silence.

Not a sound. Not a movement. Not a twitch in the muscles of his jaw, not a flicker in his eye. He stared straight ahead as if lost in time.

"Papa?" She pressed her skin to his. "Did you hear me?"

He continued looking at a spot on the wall beyond her, but he wrenched his hands free. Moments passed. One or a thousand. He processed it alone. "Go," he finally whispered. No scolding or lecture or rage or even appearance of shock. "Go home, Theo."

She tried to make him look at her. "That's not what I want, not yet, I want to remain here with you, see this through together, as we have always done, with everything."

"But that's not true. This you have done all on your own, so perhaps it's time for us to follow suit. To be on our own." He stood and dried his hands on the napkin before casting it onto the table.

She felt as it was, tossed aside.

"There's no need to give Joseph a response." Her father's tone was full of authority. "I will relay the unfortunate news. You do not have to marry him. Things will fall where they will, but you will be happy. What more can a father ask? So go, prepare your things, leave us, if this is truly what you desire. Come first light, I'll make the arrangements for you to return." His voice was clear and even and sparked a foreboding in her blood. "But know, Miss Priss, if you do, you will destroy me."

She couldn't help her response. "Your career, perhaps, but even that, I don't—"

"My career, yes. But also me. My heart. My life. Us." He stepped back and spread his arms wide across the dining room. "Because I can no more sit at a Hamilton table than I can bring life to your mother."

She shook her head, felt the pleading in her words. "It's an old feud. It must end."

"And it will one day. One way or another. Of that I am sure. But for now the world is not big enough for Hamilton and me, so how can his table be?"

She leapt to her feet, fighting the childish whine at his stubbornness. "You don't have to accept the father to accept the child."

"Ah, Miss Priss. If only that were so. But father and child are inseparable. So go, be with . . . with Mr. Hamilton. You can make a life. But if you choose him, you lose me. And then I am lost to us both."

His eyes were big and round and tugged at her despite this measured response. Anger she could battle. Tears she could mend. But this, this simple resignation . . . she couldn't bear to look at him any longer.

*Selfish. So selfish.*

He knew exactly what he was doing, and she knew that he knew exactly what he was doing. Yet still the guilt ravaged her like a predator. Her heart twisted at the image of him on his knees before her at the same time as her mind raged at his manipulation. The thought of going to Philip brought her light, the reality of Alston under this same roof, nothing but darkness.

Her father was attuned to the shifts in her and shaved the edges off his reserved tone. "Do this for us," he begged once more.

"But this isn't for us." Her hands balled into fists at her sides. "It's for you. You know this, and still you ask."

Shame in his eyes, but he answered, "Yes. It is for me. I am weak; it is for me."

*For what else do I live?*

*His needs are plenty and insistent.*

*He gives a fidelity and devotion many men reserve for God.*

But her mother was wrong. He does not give fidelity and devotion. He demands it. She had stood by him her whole life, unlacing her skates, eating half of what was set upon her plate, burying her head in books, hosting his guests, answering his letters, living her life the way he instructed. Becoming the female version of himself. With all of his abilities. A scholar with the skills of a socialite. An excellent student who would now surpass her teacher.

"February the second," she said.

Her father's brow crinkled. "And what is February the second?"

"Apparently, it's my wedding day."

# CHAPTER 31

THEODOSIA STOKED THE FIRE IN HER bedroom from dusk till dawn. By the time the sun painted over the darkness with trailing strokes of red that gave way to orange that faded to yellow, the walls were sweating like an August day, and she had a plan.

The notion had struck her last night as her father's true self lay exposed before them both, asking her to sacrifice more than he had a right to with no compassion, no understanding, just need. His own.

She knew then that she would do what she was asked to win him the office he desired more than anything—more than a relationship with her. That was the price of what he thought he wanted—or maybe not thought, maybe it *was* all he desired. She could not see into his heart. Difficult enough had it become to see inside her own. Now she made the only choice she could make.

Her plan would not save Richmond Hill. She grieved for it, the towering oaks with their welcoming branches, the flowers grown from seeds she'd planted by her father's side, the bedrooms she and Nathalie shared then separated into, the long rides to the farthest groves, the fires warming the hearth and brightening the rooms on short winter days, the cold of the endless nights her mother lay with the life draining from her. Like her father with his tallies of states and votes and representatives leaning this way and that, she explored every possibility. None did all that was required. Won her father the presidency. Paid their debts. Saved her home. Led her back to Philip.

She had little more than a week to make arrangements. It would be enough. Sometimes the more simple the plan, the more chance of success.

With a gentle knock, Nancy entered the bedroom with a pitcher of warm water.

"Thank you," Theodosia said, setting her eyes upon the smooth, dark skin of the girl's cheeks. A contrast to that of her hands, already growing callused. "I hope it hasn't been too much, being here?"

"S'fine, Ma'am. Maybe too quiet, but we'll be home to Richmond Hill soon, won't we?" Nancy poured the water into the waiting basin, and Theodosia nodded despite her chest squeezing.

Richmond Hill was her home—but not only home to her.

The notion threatened a retreat back into her brain, to start all over again, searching for a way, but then . . . she watched Nancy, this young girl with so many years before her—years of the same. The gradual emancipation bill not setting her free until her twenty-fifth year. Unless her father did first.

Perhaps this could actually be fortuitous. Her father would soon have a new household in the nation's capital. She would be with Philip. With no Richmond Hill to maintain, their servants would no longer be needed. Nancy, Eleonore, Alexis, Tom, Sam, all a part of her life for as long as her father had been. By way of a marriage from a Prevost to a Burr, by way of a man unable to lead with a truth in his heart and mind, out of status or appearance or all manner of which Theodosia could never really know. But with this, she would finally have the strength and command over her father to force him to act upon the ideals he spouted.

"Ma'am?" Nancy hovered in the doorway. "Is all well?"

"Not yet, Nancy. But it will be."

Something about the way they moved unnerved her—smooth but unnatural. Peering into the river, she'd rub her hands over the gooseflesh flaring along her arms, imagining them circling, coiling around her, slippery and wet and compressing until her breath left her body.

Embracing Joseph Alston turned out to be exactly as she'd imagined an encounter with an eel.

"Splendid!" Her father clapped his hands. "A toast. No matter the time, a celebration we must have!"

Alston released her and thumped her father on the back. "Let me introduce you to Elijah Craig. Preacher in Kentucky distilling bourbon that makes that French wine you're so enamored of taste like swamp water." He gave a voracious laugh. "That would be, even *more* like swamp water."

Alston then smiled at Theodosia, all puffed up with conceit. He reminded her of Lucinda. Both believing they'd steered their way into situations advantageous to them. Both soon to be proven wrong.

He plopped into a chair by the fire. "Get that twig of a girl to fetch it from my room, would you, fiancée?"

That one word stung with the strength of a thousand bees, yet Theodosia simply said, "Allow me." Demure was not in her vocabulary let alone her behaviors, but the art of pretending in the near term for reward in the far was well ingrained in her.

She walked with purpose, slipping inside his room with a mix of revulsion and curiosity. An opportunity handed to her to see what lie beyond the facade of the toad. Her eyes scanned from bed to dresser to mirror to chair. A bottle of amber liquid sat open on the small dresser. His hat on the end of the bed, already straightened and tucked by Nancy. A leather bag lay on the wooden chair to the side. Fully closed. She slunk near to open it when more laughter drifted toward her. The risk was unnecessary. Her plan relied not on who Alston pretended to be but who he was. An arrogant simpleton expecting others to do all for him.

In this, Theodosia would happily oblige.


She hurried toward Elm Tree Corner in the center of town, named for the giant elm planted in front of the home of Philip Livingston, tied to the family of the same name in New York City and a signer of the Declaration of Independence. With more land and space, the prominent families of Albany had homes as grand as Richmond Hill, many within the confines of down-town. Livingstons and Schuylers mixed with Bleeckers and Van Rensselaers. The Dutch heritage of the city lived in the brick, tiles, wood, and iron imported from Holland. Even the bell of the church had traveled across the ocean before being installed in the structure on North Pearl Street.

With the ribbon of her bonnet tied securely under her chin to combat the biting wind, Theodosia passed the homes of merchants, offices like those of the *Albany Gazette*, and the magnificent Vanderheyden Palace, whose architecture was steeped in the Dutch style. High above the double gables whirred a horse at full speed, the weathervane spinning and urging her on.

As she neared the river, she arrived on Market Street. Farther out, a mile beyond the city, she'd find the home of General Philip Schuyler, Philip's namesake and grandfather. But closer in lay the old church in which she was christened. The stone structure still stood though it had been replaced with a new meeting place on North Pearl Street, a circumstance that while a benefit for the growing community was unfortunate for one man—the wife of whom she aimed to see.

She moved past the church and the ghosts of her parents, young and in love, holding her infant body, no way of knowing how short their time together would be. It saddened her to think that her father might not have done anything differently—not spent more time at home—had he known. She liked to think he would have, would have prized their family above all, but she was no longer sure. She didn't need to be sure of him to be sure of what she would do, the lengths to which she would go to ensure her own future was the one she wanted. She pressed on, reassured of her mission.

Smells of apples and pears mixed with brine and the metallic scent of blood as she came upon the Old Market House, a single-story structure with open walls. Beneath the roof supported by brick columns were vendors selling vegetables, fruit, meat, and fish. Yet this was the transition period, when men loaded their wagons with the unsold goods and departed, leaving the space free for the leisurely drinking and gossiping that would occupy it in the late afternoon and evening. It had been then, near where the potatoes and turnips were being carried off, that Theodosia, on a brief respite from her father, had met Ms. Anna Hun Bassett.

And there, up ahead, past the Albany Bank, Abraham Ten Eyck's bookstore, and the leather merchant making gloves and breeches, sat the home the woman shared with her husband, John Bassett.

Theodosia adjusted the front of her long outer pelisse, tucked the basket with its freshly baked pie to her waist, and knocked on the door.

"You have more patience than I, Miss Bartow." Mrs. Bassett laughed. The soft curls hanging free of her dark brown plait skimmed her forehead. "I'd have married my John the day we met had he been smart enough to ask."

In the chair across from her in the home's small front sitting room, Theodosia attempted to sound forlorn. "It's difficult, but necessary nonetheless."

"Which makes you a better daughter than I was too." Mrs. Bassett leaned forward and whispered, "I suspect better than my brood combined."

Theodosia gave a shy giggle, unsure if she should agree or disagree but desperate not to offend this woman whose help she needed for her plan to work.

Twenty years her senior and the mother of two with a third ballooning her belly, Mrs. Bassett had invited Theodosia into her home and listened, enraptured, to the tale she'd spun. Of a wedding planned far from here, with friends and family and a pastor revered by her fiancé. Of a bride's father distraught over obligations preventing him from attending this impending marriage of his only daughter. Of a daughter willing to go to any lengths to please him. Even if it meant a ruse. A small lie for the good of all.

Theodosia joined her clammy hands in her lap. "Your husband would perform the ceremony same as any. Though the shorter the better."

Mrs. Bassett cocked her head.

"My father's leg," Theodosia said quickly to cover. "An old injury. The war makes itself known even still." When Mrs. Bassett nodded somberly, Theodosia continued. "On the day of the wedding, your husband wouldn't have to do a thing out of the ordinary."

Mrs. Bassett rested her teacup atop the rise of her stomach. "But after . . ."

"Yes, well, after, that's where his care would be most appreciated. It should require no effort on the part of your husband. In this, I daresay it'll be easier than usual!" Theodosia laughed, but Mrs. Bassett's face remained stolid. "Such things should not matter so much as the end result, I know. But it's the best I can think to please all involved. Your husband simply would forgo any official recording of the marriage."

"I see." Mrs. Bassett slowly began nodding her head. "No certificate, no register, no legal marriage." She clicked her nails against her teacup. "The Reverend is a good man. Not normally accustomed to such chicanery."

Theodosia steadied her hand as she reached for her own tea. "Entirely as I would expect."

"And yet . . ." *Tap, tap, tap.* "These *are* extenuating circumstances." *Tap, tap, tap.*

Theodosia gave a conspiratorial nod. "I appreciate you being so understanding. Such is a trait my dearest friends value most. Writing to them is among my most favorite pastimes. Second only to bringing new friends together."

Mrs. Bassett held Theodosia's gaze. "How fortunate we happened upon one another."

"Quite so." Theodosia smiled. "You are very kind, Mrs. Bassett."

"And you are very generous, Miss Bartow." Mrs. Bassett's eyes flickered to the wall shared with the home of her parents next door and said no more.

She had said all that was required during that chance meeting at the Old Market House when Theodosia had first arrived. And quite a bit more, so upset she'd been, having just stormed off from an argument with her husband, who after thirteen years as associate pastor at the Dutch Reformed Church, had been passed over for the senior role of minister. The Consistory had chosen another man—a younger man—adding further insult. Mrs. Bassett thought her husband weak for remaining in his subordinate position. She insisted he leave. Having spoken with the many clergy from New York City who would come to Albany to visit family and friends, Mrs. Bassett had decided upon Long Island, far enough from the church for him to seed a new reputation but not so far from her parents.

What the Bassetts needed were letters of introduction. Theodosia "Bartow," using her mother's maiden name for discretion, happened to be both well-connected and nimble with a quill.

Thus a ceremony would take place, her father would become president, and she would be on her way back to Philip before Alston discovered the truth. A circumstance that would make him ill inclined to invest in Richmond Hill. But her mother's death had shown her that physical presence did not determine how deeply something remained a part of one's heart and soul.

Theodosia relished her final sip of sugary tea. It'd been weeks since she'd had more than a pinch thanks to being under her father's watchful eye. Mrs. Bassett had insisted on three cubes. Theodosia set down her cup and rose from her chair. "Thank you for the tea, Mrs. Bassett."

Mrs. Bassett heaved herself up, waving away Theodosia's offer of help. "And thank you for the pie."

With heavy steps and her hand resting on the shelf of her belly, Mrs. Bassett led Theodosia to the door. As Theodosia buttoned her wool pelisse, she turned to the older woman. "I'm without doubt that your children would do most anything to please you."

Mrs. Basset nodded appreciatively. "Now they'll have the chance."

"February the second." Theodosia tipped her head toward Mrs. Bassett and returned to the icy streets of Albany.

# CHAPTER 32

A CHILL PERMEATED THE SMALL PARLOR, BUT still Reverend Bassett perspired as if a dozen hearth fires were lit within. Mrs. Bassett handed him a white handkerchief, and he mopped his brow beneath his receding hairline. She gave Theodosia a reassuring smile, which did little to suppress the winding knots in her stomach.

*Soon it will be done.*

Not the thought she would've expected to have on her wedding day. But fitting for the person she was about to marry.

He wore a skirted coat she hadn't seen even once during the preceding week, and it made her skin crawl to think he'd saved it for this—*brought* it for this, so confident he had been. Her father so transparent.

A deep purple velvet, the front of the double-breasted coat sloped to form two squared-off tails that hung above matching pantaloons tucked into shiny black boots. He looked like an eggplant.

Nerves and fear and the absurdity of him in that ridiculous outfit and her in her plainest muslin dress and simple short cape and her father crimson-faced with hands twisting in front of his coat buttons—it all collided in a tense, almost hysterical giggle that she had to work hard to not let come forth.

The reverend welcomed them despite the ceremony taking place in the home occupied by the Burrs. Grateful to have another place to focus her attention, she turned from Alston to him. Beside her husband, Mrs. Bassett looked on, proudly. Before this sham began, Theodosia had privately explained who her father was, believing he'd be recognized. Rather than dissuade Mrs. Bassett, the knowledge appeared to bolster her resolve to help. Her father certainly was popular in the North.

The reverend began to speak of the union of marriage, of the joining of man and wife, and Theodosia fought every instinct to flee. Cobwebs spun in her mind, blanketing every corner with dread. She pleaded with herself to remain still, to remain here, to remember that this was not real.

It would be, one day soon, and on that day, she would be staring not into the light-green eyes of Reverend Bassett but the warm brown of Philip's. She let her eyelids flutter shut, picturing him, feeling the tingle on her skin, the devotion in her heart, calling on it to carry her through the wretchedness of this moment.

The words the reverend chose were short, delivered hastily, without pomp or ceremony, as she'd requested. A wave of gratitude washed over her, for as they approached the only words either she or Alston had to say, her legs grew weak.

She compelled herself to face him. That thin nose and those disappearing lips and his entire smugness of being. He met her gaze, so full of vanity and ego that Theodosia actually smiled at the pretense. With her heart pounding in her ears and the image of Philip in her mind, she said what she must to commit to this in full.

Reverend Bassett stammered the last line to pronounce them wed.

Something flickered in Alston's eyes—so swiftly that had Theodosia not been hesitant to take the hand he was offering her, she would have already turned away and missed it.

Victory.

Mrs. Bassett placed a pepper cake on the table, and Theodosia's new fake husband grimaced.

Decorum dictated they hold a small reception, but the invitation list consisted solely of the reverend and his wife. Theodosia wished nothing more than to keep the masquerade secret until after the election results when Alston would learn the truth.

He ate and drank heavily, his cheeks coloring as intensely as his purple coat. As he washed down the fried eggs with a mouthful of bourbon, she hoped he would refill all day and all night. Let him pass out with the alcohol alive on his breath. She would sleep in her own room that night—every night—alone. Yet this piece of her plan she hadn't fully sorted out.

As candle lighting came upon them, long after the pepper cake was consumed and the Bassetts returned to their home, Theodosia wrung her hands. Her father watched, a pained look on his face. He crossed the room, patting a dozing Alston on the knee as he approached her.

His voice low, he said, "Words cannot express—"

"Don't," she said. "I know what I've done, and we both know why. This is all that is between us now."

"Ah, Miss Priss—"

"Papa, I'm fatigued, out of patience, and on the brink of being out of temper. Let us leave things as they are without dissection or reflection. For once."

He rested a palm across his chest and gave a soft bow. "You honor me, *chére fille*."

As angry as his presence made her, him retiring to his room was the last thing she wanted as it left her alone with Alston. She considered retreating, letting Alston stay on the settee, his head lolling back, this first night an easy escape.

But then Tom came in. "Need help, Ma'am?" Tom corrected himself. "Mrs. Alston?"

Her spine shuddered.

Tom's rich baritone roused Alston, and he lumbered to his feet. He shooed away Tom's attempts to help.

"Night then, Ma'am, I mean, Missus, unless you need something else?" She desperately wanted to have something to ask of him, but instead she thanked him and wished him a good night's rest.

Alston leaned against the doorframe for support. "Apologies, my dearest. The excitement of the day has taken its toll."

She seized upon the excuse. "For me as well. Might we say our goodnights here? Allow us both a rest undisturbed?"

His chest heaved with a snort. "As you require, wife."

She smiled away her revulsion and pressed further. "To that point, if you're agreeable, I would prefer our time together as husband and wife to truly begin when we're . . ." She tipped her head toward her father's bedroom. "In a position to have more privacy?"

He shrugged. "Why not?" Her insides leapt with relief until he added, "We've our whole lives for what is to come, my child."

He ambled down the hall, and Theodosia couldn't even savor the momentary victory. *Imagine an entire life of the same. In South Carolina.* She would call on Mrs. Bassett tomorrow and thank her once again as well as apologize for her new "husband" spitting the woman's cake into the flames of the fire.

One day, and already it felt like a lifetime. But she had to endure it—him—for nine more days, until the eleventh of February when the electoral college results would be officially declared and the vote to break the tie taken in the House. One week. She could persist in any endeavor, even one as abhorrent as this, for a span of a single week.

Unexpectedly, Alston made it easier. He left the next morning with letters of introduction to families all throughout the region. Theodosia didn't bother to hide her delight. She let her father be witness to it, wanted him to know and see and feel how much she despised the man. He deserved the guilt that came with knowing he'd forced her into the match. Relief would come soon enough when he learned the truth. Until then, she spent her days walking through the picturesque streets, her nights reading the papers her father had delivered, and every waking moment enjoying his consternation.

On the evening preceding the House of Representatives' vote, Theodosia was browsing through the evening edition of the *New*

*York Commercial Advertiser*, seeking news and rumor alike of what to expect.

She flipped to the announcements page and stepped off the edge of a cliff.

*Married—At Albany, on the 2nd instant, by the Rev. Mr. Bassett, Joseph Alston, of South Carolina, to Theodosia Burr, only child of Aaron Burr, Esq.*

Her hands shook as she collapsed the paper to scan the front page. It was dated February 7, three days ago. Her father had all the city papers delivered to Albany, which meant they were always delayed.

Which meant Philip might have seen this news—might have been believing for *three days*—that she was married. To Alston. The man she professed to despise. The man she swore would not come between them.

Horror ripped through her body, and she sprang from her seat, the paper still clutched in her hand. Her feet pounded the floor, racing from one room to the next. She had to write to him, go to him, she couldn't let him think—

*All for show.* She'd said that, hadn't she? Among her last words to him the night of the Blackwell ball. He'd remember, surely he'd remember! Would he assume this was exactly the thing she'd been alluding to? That she'd known this was to come? Maybe he would see, he would trust, that she hadn't abandoned him and all she'd promised.

She heard the creak of the front door and the heavy thumping of boots freeing themselves of snow and cried out for her father. She hurled herself into the front hall and froze.

*Alston.*

"A pleasant surprise, I hope?" he said, peeling off his outer coat but not bothering to remove his wet boots. He left a trail of icy puddles as he strode into the sitting room. "Unlike this." He clucked his tongue as he pulled a poker from beside the hearth and jabbed at the slow-burning fire. "This needs another log." He pushed the wood around with such force, the pieces splintered, and the flames dwindled further. "Blast it all," he cursed.

He set the poker down with a clatter and faced Theodosia. "That Tom and that Nancy behave with such idleness because you permit it. When we arrive at Oaks, you cannot—"

"No," she growled, unable to contain her anger. "Don't speak of them in such a manner. They're part of my household, not yours, and I'll do and say and treat them however I wish." She shook her head. "I will treat them with the care they deserve."

He smiled with profound amusement. "They are slaves, my child, and they are mine. What's yours is mine, did you not hear the preacher?"

She gritted her teeth. "If they're anyone's, they're my father's. But they won't be for long."

"Is that so? Educate me, wife, for from where I stand, what's yours, what's your father's, it's all the same, and it's all mine. And if you think your father will stand in the way, you're the one in need of education. Quite the abolitionist he is. An attorney who defended slaves, as you know. Did he also tell you how he defended masters?"

Theodosia's heart lodged in her throat.

Alston then reached for the newspaper, crumpled in her hand. He wrenched it free, tearing it in two. He retrieved the fallen half and joined the pieces. "Here it is! Good that they could fit it in so promptly. Cost me dearly, but if my own wife isn't worth it then—"

"This is because of you?"

"Are you pleased? Your friends won't have to wait for the long journey back to delight in the news."

He did this. He orchestrated this. She spun from him.

"Is something amiss?"

She would not let him intimidate her. She steeled herself and faced him. "Mrs. Bassett is expecting me. So if you will excuse—"

He snatched her by the wrist, his fingers pressing hard into her flesh. "Overseeing a plantation has taught me many things." She winced, and he lightened his touch, stroking the inside of her wrist with a single, revolting finger. "Do you want to know the most important?" Her eyes sought the doorway leading out into the hall, but he forced her to meet his harsh gaze. "They always want to run. So you have to be faster. Wilier. Smarter." He let go her wrist and retraced his steps to the front door of the house. He called Theodosia to him.

She didn't want to go, to accede that power to him, but the trepidation in her bones compelled her forward. Standing in the doorway with flakes of melting snow on his shoulders was Reverend Bassett.

Theodosia felt sick. "Reverend?"

"Miss Bartow." His voice trembled.

Alston raised an eyebrow.

The reverend swallowed. "Pardon me, Mrs. Alston."

With a slap on the reverend's back, Alston added, "Officially, isn't that right, Reverend?"

He lowered his chin to his chest, not looking at Theodosia when he conceded "yes."

She stepped closer to him but addressed Alston. "The register takes a bit of time, Joseph. We shouldn't be bothering Reverend Bassett so soon. I'm sure he has many duties to attend to of greater importance."

Alston laughed. "Greater importance? It seems I've already become dull to my new wife. But we're fortunate, my dear, for before I left, I happened to be passing the Bassett home . . . on Market Street? You're familiar?"

Her chest seized, and she could not inhale more than a whisper of breath.

"I dropped in before my travels and had an informative discussion. The result of which was the good reverend facilitating a speedy register of our nuptials. Certificate, register, record. How fortunate are we?"

Theodosia couldn't believe it. Mrs. Bassett had promised. "Reverend? Wonderful, if it is so, of course." She forced a smile. "But we're well aware that the process takes time. Don't feel you must say untruths to please us."

The man's eyes filled with regret. "I wouldn't, Mrs. Alston. It's accomplished as your husband insisted."

Alston frowned. "As I was promised." He opened the door. "Good day to you, Reverend. Pass our blessings on to your wife."

The door closed, and with it, Theodosia's heart. Her vision went white.

"Now, now, Theo, what's this melancholy? Did you wish to frolic longer in that newlywed state? This doesn't require a change in that, not one bit." His taunt could not hide his anger at her trying to make a fool of him. "Or is it something else? A heart not as deeply entrenched as I was led to believe?"

She couldn't speak.

"So it would seem. How very unfortunate. What's done can't be undone, dear wife."

The agony in her heart released as fury. "Annulments happen every day, dear *husband*."

His laughter was like a knife in her chest.

She clenched her jaw. "Go ahead, but when I explain to my father—"

"Do you think your father doesn't know all? Who else would confirm my suspicions about young Philip? Who else would push me to make this trip to this godforsaken place to end your pathetic stalling?"

That knife plunged all the way to its hilt.

Alston strolled past her. "The morning will bring many changes. Do sleep well, my dear."

Her body grew cold, a harrowing buzz echoed in her ears, and she couldn't bear the weight anymore, even of herself. She collapsed onto the floor, her hands landing in a pool of dirty melted snow.

Her father. *He* had done this. To her. This wasn't a betrayal of trust but a ravaging of them. Father and daughter, teacher and student, confidant and confidant, soul mates.

She felt her chest heave as the hot prick of tears built in her eyes, and she slapped the icy water on her cheeks to chase them away.

The last tears she'd shed were for her mother. She wouldn't allow the next that fell to be for him. He wasn't worthy of them. Or her.

# CHAPTER 33

THEODOSIA SEQUESTERED HERSELF IN HER ROOM, not even opening the door when Nancy knocked with tea. She wouldn't give her father the chance to slip inside and attempt to reconcile what he had done. Excuses, justifications, he'd been making them her whole life, for why she should see this person and not that. Attend a party here and a salon there. Befriend an unknown refugee named Nathalie de Lage de Volude. Say goodbye to a handsome suitor named John Vanderlyn.

She should've known then that her father would lay claim to her life. Yet she was as culpable as he. She'd allowed it. Done as he'd asked. Put his needs above her own.

But no longer.

She ate with him but once during the week that would see their lives changed immeasurably—her married to a man she despised, racked with pain and guilt over the one she actually loved, destroyed by the one who should've protected her. February 11 came and went with the electoral college officially declared a tie and the House of Representatives casting its first vote to break it. Its first of many.

It was several days later, with the vote still deadlocked on its thirty-third ballot, when Theodosia permitted herself to sit at the table across from her father. Alston had yet to rise.

She piled her plate full of the fried eggs, toast, bacon, and jams Nancy, having learned from her mother, had prepared. She spooned more sugar than coffee into her mug. She ate slowly, allowing herself this simple enjoyment—both of the food and of her father watching, unable to chastise her.

"Another tie?" she said.

He nodded. "They've been in recess over the weekend. We expect a new ballot taken today."

That "we" no longer included her.

"We" was now her father and Alston. Joined by schemes. Joined by marriage.

One or the other seemed always at home, as if a mutual pledge had been made to maintain vigilance over Theodosia. She could no more run away than send a letter unnoticed.

She slathered butter atop the still loose yolk of her fried egg. "Difficult to have your fate be in the hands of others."

Her father's eyes flickered to the grease dripping onto her plate, but he said nothing.

His strength, vote after vote, came from the House consisting predominantly of Federalists loath to vote for Jefferson, wishing to humiliate the man. It was assumed that Jefferson would carry the staunch Republican states—eight in total—and her father the six Federalist ones. Those split along party lines, like Maryland and Vermont, would be forced to abstain. With each state having but one vote and a majority of nine required for victory, a winner had yet to emerge. A swing one way or another would be enough. But which way that pendulum would ultimately sway was unknown. Members of the House would remain in session until they elected a president or their terms expired on March 3, whichever occurred first.

Burr reached for his dry toast. "Cooper from New York says all stand firm."

Theodosia cocked her head. "So no end to the deadlock?" She took her last bite of toast, oozing with buttery yoke.

"Not yet."

"Well, I'm sure you are well placed. Let us not forget South Carolina and the considerable influence of your son-in-law."

He nodded, his lips pursed as if there was more to say. His silence put the words in Theodosia's mouth instead.

She lifted her empty plate to carry it into the kitchen as she'd come to do. "I wish you success, Papa."

His eyes were solemn. "Do you?"

She noted the gray in his hair, the darkness under his eyes, the lack of energy in his every movement but felt nothing for him—not even pity. "Without it, all I have given up is for nothing. I only hope you find the results worth it." She then turned and walked out of the dining room, her mind and heart already out of his life.

Amid the flurry of letters sent and received by names with gravitas (Hamilton, Jefferson, Burr, Gallatin) the swirling of rumors (militias arming, civil war on the brink, succession of Virginia, even assassination attempts), and the machinations of all in the new capital of Washington, the thirty-sixth and final ballot for president occurred at noon on Tuesday, February 17, a mere two weeks before the scheduled inauguration.

In the end, no Federalists voted for Jefferson. In a display of party unity, Federalist congressmen from Connecticut, Massachusetts, New Hampshire, and Rhode Island stood by Burr. The rest simply abstained, accepting Jefferson but refusing to actually cast a ballot for him. Jefferson swept the election with ten votes. Of the states casting blank ballots was one of note: South Carolina.

Thomas Jefferson became the third president of the United States and Aaron Burr his vice president.

Alston had betrayed them both.

Tension shrouded the Albany home, words scarcely spoken as bags were packed, the house closed up, and the horses readied for the sleigh that would take them through the most wintery part of their journey to the carriages farther south. Alston had hired his own, which in his first-ever act of chivalry, he offered to Theodosia. She accepted without haste. He was to ride in the second with her father.

A bag with books, parchment, and quill on her arm, Theodosia welcomed Tom's help as she stepped into her sleigh. She settled herself, by now quite accustomed to the quiet and solitude.

Her father paused as he passed on his way to his own transport. Rumors spread that Jefferson had won because he'd conceded to certain Federalist demands at the last moment. Burr would not accept any such deal because he refused to be seen as bending to the will of his greatest rival. Though Alston hadn't lived up to the promise he'd made, the blame in Burr's eyes lit only for his daughter. He claimed now that Theodosia's betrayal—falling in love with Philip Hamilton—had forced him to put pride above strategy.

He leaned in, his voice hoarse. "Attempting to falsify the marriage was childish, Theodosia. You have profoundly disappointed me."

Theodosia learned something in that moment: hate was as strong an emotion as love and could be held for the same person at the same time.

She kept her mother's brooch close, wrapped in linen, where she could shield it from the man her father had become.

Her departure from Albany felt like a dream, like she was living someone else's life. Her father vice president and, she, Theodosia Burr Alston. Her tenure would not last as long as his.

As the mounds of snow diminished, and they switched from separate sleighs to one carriage, every rotation of the wheel bringing them closer to Richmond Hill, Theodosia became more convinced that she and Philip would find their way out of this, together. Her heart ached for him and for Nathalie, who would understand and work with her until they found a solution.

Nathalie might not have been blood, but she was the only family Theodosia had left.

# Chapter 34

WHILE ALWAYS ARROGANT, ALSTON HAD PORTRAYED a certain charm in his letters that had come to vanish in person. In their two weeks of marriage, the new husband and wife had barely spoken, which was more than agreeable to Theodosia. They had not shared a bed, which to her great relief had not required contrivances on her part.

As their long, cold, silent journey finally came to an end, they arrived not at Richmond Hill but at the townhome downtown.

"I'll be continuing on," Theodosia said.

Alston shook his head. "Not yet. We'll visit before we depart, but business requires us to stay in the city. Besides, much country life awaits. You'll have your fill soon enough, Theo." He exited the carriage first. "I sent word ahead for your things to be brought here." He assessed her ankle-length, fur-trimmed pelisse and heavy bonnet. "Though you'll have little use for much akin to that at the Oaks."

The entire time Alston gave orders, her father remained silent. The shift in power was palpable.

She trailed behind, allowing herself to revel in the familiar brick and stone of the city before following them into the first floor of Madame de Senat's schoolhouse. The smell of chalk and sight of small desks and the overflowing bookcase brought the first lightness Theodosia had felt in weeks. She pictured herself here with Philip almost a year ago. How ill-mannered she'd been and how much worse she'd thought of him.

Past the hour of schooling, the townhome appeared to be empty. As Alston returned to the street to oversee the unloading of their things, Theodosia pulled her father aside.

"We're home, and it's over, Papa." She lowered her voice, and the words came out as a hiss. "This isn't a marriage, and I won't let it become one. With the presidency decided, there's no need. We owe Alston nothing. He didn't do as he'd vowed."

Sadness deepened the lines around her father's eyes. "But he did. The first of the funds to cover our debts and secure Richmond Hill are to be transferred this afternoon."

Anger still swirled in her veins, but Theodosia couldn't help a relenting in tone when it came to the home they both loved. "I will miss it with all my heart, but it's not enough. We must let it go."

"But so much goes with it, Miss Priss." He hadn't used his nickname for her in days—longer. "For Richmond Hill is more than you and I. The investment from Joseph keeps not just that home safe but this one too." He spread his hands and gestured to the classroom. "This school with the children who rely upon Madame de Senat. And Madame de Senat herself. Along with Nathalie and Frederick and Alexis and Eleonore and all the servants who have been a part of our home for most of their lives. It's my duty to provide for and ensure the well-being of many, Theodosia."

She pulled her hands out of the warmth of her fur-lined pockets. "We'll find a way with Madame, Nathalie will likely be married soon herself, and Frederick is a grown man." Now was the time for her complicity to end and her father's ideals to become truths. "And everyone else, they've been a part of our home, but, Papa, they deserve to be a part of their own. It wouldn't be the first time you've granted liberty. I remember, especially a woman, a Maria, no, a Mary—"

Her father's lips thinned. "A circumstance of its own. Not akin to this."

He put his back to her to end the conversation as if she were a child, as if—despite everything he'd ever said and the manner in which they'd interacted her entire life—her voice didn't matter.

Bile seared her throat. She grabbed him by his coat and spun him to face her. "You speak ill of the South, you rail against Jefferson, but how are you any better? Our servants are not servants. A slave is a slave, Papa. If you can't see that, then perhaps it's no wonder that you're so close to your new son-in-law."

He broke free of her. "That is enough, Theodosia. You embarrass yourself."

"How? By having firmness of mind? As you instructed?" Fury shook her limbs, a white-hot fire gripping her. "Naive, yes. Guilty, absolutely. Too blinded by your words to see how they were at odds with your actions? Yes to all, and that is my sin. But you are a hypocrite and a fraud. Defending slaves one minute and masters the next!"

Shock widened his eyes, but still he maintained his composure. "I believe in abolition, and when that day comes, I will celebrate. But in this, I have no power."

"That's not true!" Flames licked her chest. "In this, you have all the power. You always have. Your incessant worries about politics and appearances have stopped you from doing what we both know is right. If you do nothing now, it's because you choose not to."

His gaze challenged her back. "There is no choice, Theo. I must forestall a sale of Richmond Hill because such would mean a sale of them. All of them." Theodosia recoiled, but her father continued, "I didn't raise you to be starry-eyed or to shy away from difficult choices. Binding them as collateral gave us more time on our debts."

Theodosia placed a hand on her stomach, which roiled in disbelief and revulsion.

"Hard truths, Miss Priss, but what of the alternative? What fate would lie ahead if creditors came to claim what we cannot pay?"

Hard truths . . .? Equality, abolition, right and wrong, his affection for all in his household . . . his words rendered false through his every action.

She'd failed. Everyone. She'd kept silent for too long, and now . . . any influence she ever had as mistress of Richmond Hill was gone. She'd never felt so impotent. Her father had never before allowed it, raising her to believe she wasn't in the same position as those of her gender. But she was. A woman with no home or wealth of her own, dependent on the whims of a husband. A father.

He left soon after with Alston.

She'd intended to see Nathalie first, to share with her all that had happened and together set about a plan to rid herself of Alston. But she no longer needed a plan. She needed money. Her father could not be beholden to Alston. Because then all of them would be.

She stood before the looking glass in the small bedroom on the top floor of the townhome. She'd changed out of her traveling clothes and into one of the dresses brought from Richmond Hill—the red one with the flowers embroidered by Nathalie. Airy and light, the fabric afforded little in practicality for the winter weather, yet she needed it. When Philip saw her swathed in red, he would have to remember the promises she'd made the last time she'd worn the dress. And believe them. Despite the crude request she must make of him. She pinched her pallid cheeks to bring color to them. Then she affixed her mother's brooch and left to meet Philip.

"Miss Burr!" a deep voice said upon seeing her in the doorway. Alexander Hamilton, his hair powdered white despite it being out of fashion, strode toward her as one of the Hamilton servants closed the door behind her.

"Colonel." She bowed respectfully despite the nerves flitting about in her stomach.

He clasped her hand in his. "My apologies, it's Mrs. Alston, if my wife is to be believed." He leaned in. "Which she always is." He extended his arm to invite her into the parlor.

More spacious than in a home farther downtown, the room had a warmth in temperature and tone. Gold velvet curtains hung from ceiling to floor, dark wood tables for tea and games were spread out with enough seating for more than a dozen. A rosewood piano commanded the far corner and a walnut desk near the entry. Affluence gleamed from every corner, and her heart lifted with hope.

He gestured toward a silk taupe chair by the fire. She'd retained her coat, and the heat from the fire mixed with her internal flush to needle her neck with perspiration.

"Let me offer a hearty congratulations on behalf of my entire family, as Mrs. Hamilton and Angelica have taken the children for tea." He chuckled. "Despite the task to wrangle young John into his seat, as it must be." He fixed his deep blue eyes on hers, and she tried to imagine them filled with the contempt they seemed to hold for her father. They had nothing of the kind in them now. "I will be sure to tell Angelica of your visit. She may have been surprised most of all upon your news."

"Yes." She swallowed. "In truth, it was a bit of a surprise even for me. But circumstances required it."

Those eyes remained intensely focused on her, and a bead of sweat trickled down her back. "Circumstances sometimes do." He lowered his voice. "We may have a similar impromptu nuptials in the family ourselves soon."

Another swallow. "Is that so? I wasn't aware that Angelica—"

"No, no. My Angelica's as picky as her namesake. Unlike my firstborn."

All Theodosia's internal heat turned to ice. "Mr. Hamilton?" She spun her head. "Is he . . . at home?"

The colonel beamed. "Hardly at all anymore. The law office that was mine is now his. He's settled into a new life this past month. Professionally and personally." He gracefully crossed his legs and tilted his head to the side. "I believe an engagement is forthcoming. You're friends with Miss Lucinda Wilson, correct?"

Theodosia's stoic face crumpled. All her years of training to present a calm, level exterior disappeared. She didn't care what her father would think or what her mother would do or the times they'd both been before Alexander Hamilton and the pretenses they must have worked hard to maintain. None of it mattered. Not anymore.

That nettling behind her eyes that she refused to give in to when it came to her father now burned with a vengeance, and this time, she let the tears fall. Streaming down her cheeks like the strongest of tidal currents.

As if proof of how upside down her world had become, Alexander Hamilton—her father's enemy since he was practically her age—rose, alarmed. He laid a warm, soft hand on her shoulder. He kept it there, the pressure gentle but reassuring her that she was not alone. He let her cry until her tears shriveled same as her heart already had.

"My dear," he said with concern. He eased her out of the chair and guided her to a more cushioned sofa. He poured her a brandy and situated himself beside her. "Sip, please."

She did, the burn letting her know she was still here, alive, impossibly.

"Good," he said. "Now if I may, I would like to tell you a story."

She gripped the glass and nodded. There was nowhere she belonged anymore.

"I appreciate your indulgence." He arranged himself facing her, his back straight, his hands resting in his lap. "It is a story of two young men who had nothing to lose and everything to gain. They took risks with their lives and the lives of others. They held ideals and fought for them. They killed for them. They were friends and colleagues but stubborn and ambitious. It turned them into something else. Enemies is not the right word, nor is opponent. Each is the measure of the other. Take one away, and the other ceases to exist. But bring them together, and an explosion like a thousand cannons firing at once will blow them all away." He gave a wistful smile. "Excuse the battle metaphor. But then, life is a battle on so many fronts."

So she had come to learn.

He then began to talk of marriage and wives and children—of what happened to a man when he became a father. The lengths he would go to in order to protect his child. He shifted closer to her. "Like when a son comes to a father with pure terror in his eyes, saying the love of his life is at risk, that another threatens to expose a secret that will ruin her and her family, and he lays himself bare, claiming it's all his fault—all because the son could not keep this entrusted secret to himself."

Theodosia's eyes widened, and she couldn't look at him but also couldn't look away.

He sat with elbow bent on the back of the sofa, hand to his temple. "You see, then a father faces a choice. Because to ease the pain of the son, the father must make a sacrifice. For this secret would bring the downfall of the man, the opponent, the father has tirelessly worked to strip of power. The pursuit of which may prove to end the father's career more than the opponent's. Yet here, in this, there is no choice. The father chooses the child." Those oceanic eyes bore into hers. "Every time. His brightest hope. And so a deal is made. With a home beyond one's means, a gaggle of children to feed, and debts aplenty, it is not in the form of an exchange of funds. But an association for the future."

The colonel's words echoed her father's. And ravaged all hope.

He continued, "The secret is kept. The son is on the verge of engagement. Futures are preserved for all."

Tears streamed down Theodosia's face, and Alexander removed a handkerchief from his pocket. He passed it to her, and she rubbed at her eyes as he added, "Sometimes the roles are reversed, and the child sacrifices for the father. It is a strong and brave thing to do, to put others before ourselves. But we cannot live with the people we become if we do not." He took both of her hands in his—hands that reminded her of Philip's. "His heart is shattered, Theodosia.

When he found out . . . we thought we might lose him, his mother and I. He will not survive another blow. What's done is done. It is for the best."

The foreboding in his words draped over her like a heavy, wet blanket, the reality of all she had done, of all she'd asked of Philip, of what she had come to ask now, of what he was willing to do for her. And his father for him. She was as selfish as her own father, putting her needs first and remaining secure in the notion that she could ask forgiveness and it would be given, no harm befalling anyone. She had been wrong.

She stood and attempted to return the handkerchief engraved with the colonel's initials, but he insisted she keep it. She accepted, entirely sure she would need it again.

The warmth inside the Hamilton home faded before she'd even left. Her long coat not enough to combat the chill seeping into her bones as she walked the streets, the train of her dress like a pool of blood against the light flakes of snow now coating the ground. She wandered without aim; the only place she knew she could not go was home.

Alexander Hamilton had intervened, stopping Lucinda from revealing the truth about Theodosia and the magazine. He had saved her—for Philip. And now Philip was to marry someone he barely liked, let alone loved, because of her. He'd made a promise for her, entirely selfless, standing in contrast to all the deals her father made to further himself.

She had to see him, to make sure he was all right. She would not dishonor him by asking for money he did not have or entreating him to renege on promises he'd made because of her. Honor was woven into the fabric of men in this country, even those who might not claim it so, like Philip. If only she hadn't been so much a Burr—so arrogant and sure she could achieve anything she set her mind to. She'd robbed them of the future they could have had together. A circumstance neither of them could change. That she must accept. And she would, but not without seeing him, not without saying goodbye.

The urgency propelled her forward despite the snow and Hamilton's words stirring doubts in her mind.

*"We thought we might lose him."*

Sweat on her brow, hands clammy in their gloves, she arrived across the street from the brick building that housed his law office. Through the front window, she watched him don his wool outer coat, which hung loose about his shoulders. Her heart plowed against her rib cage, reaching for him, hurting for him. She stepped forward to cross the street but paused when she heard the laughter of children mixing with that of a woman. Two women.

Theodosia slunk into the recessed opening of the building behind her just as Mrs. Hamilton, Angelica, and Philip's other siblings rounded the corner on the opposite side of the street. They met Philip just as he exited the office, the family greeting one another with love and laughter, coats brushing against coats from hugs, Mrs. Hamilton asking if he'd eaten, Angelica fruitlessly attempting to stop John from throwing a snowball at his brother, Philip instead scooping up a handful and initiating a playful fight. He and his family had been through so much to find their way here. Philip had been through so much.

*"He will not survive another blow."*

Her, he would not survive her.

She shouldn't have come. Her heart clawed at her chest, but this, seeing him, saying goodbye, was her need, not his.

*"It is a strong and brave thing to do, to put others before ourselves."*

Theodosia pressed her back against the wall as the Hamiltons made their way down the street. She took a single step forward to watch them go, the family she wished were her own. Philip's gait slowed as he bent to pick up one of his sibling's fallen gloves. As he rose, his head turned. Their eyes met. Theodosia remained still. Then, she smiled with all the love and warmth and regret consuming her. She placed one hand on her heart and bowed her head in a silent apology. He stared as if she were an illusion. And then he set his own hand on his breast, dipped his chin, and turned back to his family. She waited until they were gone. Then, without a word, she was gone too.

# CHAPTER 35

THEODOSIA HATED LYING TO NATHALIE. BUT she couldn't bear to tell her the truth. Nathalie practically floated around Theodosia, almost woozy from her infatuation with Thomas Sumter. A woman so in love would not understand walking away from it.

And so she told Nathalie that Philip had chosen Lucinda, solidifying Theodosia's push to the wealthy Alston and to the preservation of Richmond Hill. Theodosia couldn't feign interest in, let alone love, of the man, and Nathalie had long suspected finances were the sum total of Alston's appeal. And she wasn't the only one.

Hannah Gallatin had written to congratulate Theodosia, but she'd also written to Nathalie, inquiring as to the veracity of claims made by Hannah's sister, one of the Nicholson daughters. In her letter to Nathalie, Hannah had relayed her sister's words in detail:

*"Report does not speak well of Alston: it says that he is rich, but he is a great dasher, dissipated, ill-tempered, vain, and silly. I know that he is ugly and of unprepossessing manners. Can it be that the father has sacrificed a daughter to affluence and influential connections?"*

Even Caty Church had complained that *"Alston has robbed of us our dear Theo!"*

With the strength of such gossip behind her, Nathalie would never accept the full truth quietly; she would implore Theodosia to follow her heart, not understanding that Theodosia already was.

Theodosia tucked a strand of Nathalie's blonde hair behind her ear. It hung free down her shoulders making her look younger than her years, like the waif she'd been when she'd arrived at Richmond

Hill all those years ago. When Theodosia mistook her for an enemy, so unwilling had she been to share her father's love with another. So strong a part of their lives had he always been, and yet now they were each on paths that didn't include him.

Yet, for Theodosia, that didn't leave the hole it once would have. What did was a future without Nathalie. Georgetown was so very far from New York City.

"I will miss you terribly, *mon amie*," Nathalie said, her eyes glassy with tears.

"And I you, sister." Theodosia kissed the back of Nathalie's hand. "Who will prevent my fashion missteps?"

Nathalie forced a weak smile. "Even without me, you will shine brighter than all the southern girls combined."

"You flatter well."

"I learned from the best. I am a Burr, after all."

A lump ballooned in Theodosia's throat. "Yes, you are."

"We are daughters of the vice president, Theo. Good must come of that?" Nathalie searched Theodosia's countenance.

"Time will tell," Theodosia said, and then she hugged her best friend, not knowing when she would again.

The trip south was as miserable as Theodosia knew it would be. Starting with riding beneath the barren limbs of the oaks that lined the road leading out from Richmond Hill to the world beyond. It was unfathomable that springtime would arrive without her to witness the budding of leaves and the sprouting of tulips and the humming of bees feeding on the pollen and nectar of flowers she'd cultivated. But all of that would occur at a home, on an estate, still belonging to the Burrs, if only in name, thanks to the man she traveled beside.

Their departure lagged behind that of her father, who had left the day after they'd returned from Albany. He had an inauguration to prepare for. And she had one to attend. Unlike Theodosia, her father had left Richmond Hill for long stretches many times.

She wondered if this one felt any different for him, if he had yet internalized that upon his next return, she would not be there to greet him.

She and her new husband made stops along the way, in New Jersey and Baltimore, visiting Burr friends and family. Decorum prevented any questioning of this unexpected union, but Theodosia could read their hosts' doubt and concern.

And, sometimes, overhear it, as she did at a gathering with Robert Troup, a close friend of her father's from the war, who'd proclaimed Alston "ordinary" and "pedantic." Even with such little exposure to her new husband, Troup had seen Alston's truth, citing a harsh temper and questioning his true political leanings.

In attendance at a dance in Williamsburg, she listened, concealed, as Nelly Custis, George Washington's step-granddaughter, said to a friend: *"Mrs. Alston is a very sweet, little woman, very engaging and pretty—but her husband is the most intolerable mortal I ever beheld."*

Somehow it made her feel better, justified in her own disgust for her husband.

He was aloof on their travels, often staring out the window of the carriage, idle, while she read or wrote letters. If she knew him at all, she'd have said he was depressed. Perhaps he was sapped of the energy required to achieve this end, of maintaining his own pretense all this time. The only bright spot for him came when they reached the new nation's capital of Washington and witnessed her father being sworn in as vice president. Burr covered his disappointment deftly, no hint of all he'd done to try to steal the office now held by the strikingly tall man beside him: President Thomas Jefferson. The new president's laxity in manner was reflected in his entire persona, from his simple suit to his lack of wig and sword to his calm eyes that seemed to understand everything.

As she and Alston departed, her father, smartly dressed in a black wool coat and breeches, a puff of white lace protruding from the center of his crisp shirt, said but the standard, "Safe travels."

And she in return a detached, "I hope you are soon comfortably settled."

The path they'd traveled together formally diverged; joined were they solely in the preservation of the home they loved and those in it they bore responsibility to keep safe.

Deeper into the heat and the sun she and Alston went, yet the chill in Theodosia's veins could not be warmed. They arrived in South Carolina, their marriage barely a marriage, still unconsummated. Even now, weeks later. A sign that this hadn't turned out as he'd expected either.

The Oaks sat along the eastern edge of Georgetown County on a peninsula of land known as Waccamaw Neck. Bordered by a river on one side and a salt marsh on the other, the Oaks was a flourishing rice planation worked by the one hundred slaves Alston's grandfather had bequeathed to him along with the land when Alston was but five years old. Each day Theodosia was reminded of her complicity and her inability to change anyone's circumstances, including her own.

Though an educated man with considerable wealth, Alston tended to the upkeep of the actual plantation home with as little care as he gave to Theodosia now that he'd succeeded in insinuating himself into the world of the Burrs.

She could barely contain her anger when she recalled how he'd dared to speak ill of Richmond Hill knowing this dilapidated wooden frame house on the foul-smelling Waccamaw River was what he called home. One couldn't even see the river from it, only the piddling Oaks Creek. A third of the size of her home in New York, the front porch faced the road. One and a half stories high, the farmhouse's interior walls were coated with a thick application of yellowish-orange plaster, covered with a thin coat of white, which filled in the cracks left by three different patterns of crude and irregular wooden siding. The fine Chinese porcelain and silver-and-bone handled knives on their dining room table sat at odds with the roughness of the structure and interior of the house. One thing the Oaks did have, however, was a garret, ideal for the storage of madeira, which Theodosia took to enjoying at all hours of the day from the incongruously elegant wineglasses.

As dreadful as the dust-covered windows, invasive ivy, and sagging roof, the lackluster home was a palace compared to the double row of slave quarters that lay to the east, far behind the endless fields of rice. She'd taken a carriage to the cabins of the slaves just once before Alston informed the overseer not to permit it. Alston thought what she couldn't see wouldn't haunt her. Perhaps he could live his life that way, but she could not. So many ghosts, both dead and alive, carved out corners of her mind.

Her naivety as a child and perhaps willful ignorance as an adult had left her accustomed to seeing the servants in her own home and those of others in the city, but nothing had prepared her for the reality of the South.

A sea of dark-skinned faces. Ceaseless hours under the sweltering sun. Mud and dirt and mistresses who spat in pots of leftover food to discourage consumption by the kitchen slaves. Overseers who did much worse. She had a husband who insisted such vile practices were not the way here, unwilling to see the vileness in the institution itself.

She started small. "Leave it to me," she said at the table to Alston one morning after she'd devised a system for the Oaks slaves to be taught to read and write, just as her father had done at Richmond Hill. "If you allow me free rein—"

"And what would my family think then? I won't have you drag us deeper into the muck. Already they talk of the Oaks as if it were a blight on our family name."

A name that impossibly was now her own.

"Such disrespect," he muttered, then barely audible, "and to me, the eldest."

It was the first dent in the armor of arrogance Alston wore. No wonder he and her father had gravitated toward each other, two broken, insecure men in need of perpetual validation. But same as with her father, the manipulative road that had led them here and the choices he continued to make disallowed any sympathy.

Despite his initial rebuff, she'd persisted in trying to persuade him, only to be met with resistance from him and every member of his family, who filled Alston's ear with their disapproval. Alston's four siblings occupied other—nicer—homes along the Waccamaw, which she'd at first frequented. But her desire to educate the slaves was as ill-received as her refusal to attend the hypocrisy of their church on Sunday, and she was made to feel most unwelcome at any but the most necessary of family gatherings.

She refrained from socializing not just with her new family but with the women of the nearby plantations. While her and Alston's infrequent excursions to his three-story brick home on Church Street in Charleston brought some sense of normalcy in the more habitable surroundings, the cooling breeze off the water, and the white porch pillars that reminded her of Richmond Hill's portico, the bustle of the city could not match that of New York, same as its people. She wrote letters to Nathalie daily chronicling her day, as boring and repetitive as it was. She wrote to Philip too—letters that would never be sent and instead were tucked away inside the handkerchief with his father's "A.H." embroidered in the corner. The one person she didn't write to was her father, though before long, his letters came to her. Each one attempting to draw out his old confidant, yet she was not to return.

She had been enduring the stench of the creek for nearly two months when Nathalie sent word that she was finally returning home to France. Theodosia's heart both soared and drowned. Nathalie would be accompanying the man who would become her husband: Thomas Sumter, chosen as part of an American legation to France, serving as secretary to Chancellor Robert Livingston, newly appointed Minster of France by Jefferson.

The position had initially been offered to Alston. It was the first letter her father had sent, entirely predictable. The top half

lamenting their distance, no acknowledgment of what had transpired between them:

*"On your absence, my only solid consolation is the belief that you
will be happy, and the certainty that we will often meet."* Then, out of
the blue, he had asked: *"Would Mr. Alston be willing to go as secretary to Chancellor Livingston? I beg his immediate answer."*

The position would have sent Alston and Theodosia to France.
An olive branch, perhaps? For Theodosia to leave this mosqui-
to-infested swamp of a state for the country she'd been immersed
in since she was a child? Though of course, her father had added
that such a position would permit Alston to make political and
business contacts important to him.

Still, it was France. And Nathalie would surely have accompanied them. The notion had visibly lifted Theodosia's spirits—perhaps too high. For after much contemplation, Alston had decided
a planter's life was the one for him. Though he wrote her father
letters he thought she knew nothing of, seeking advice for his
own career in politics—the House or governorship? Alston over-
estimated his relationship with her father, who, in his letters to
Theodosia, spared no detail in a fruitless attempt to restore their
bond.

The position that Alston declined had then been offered to
Sumter. Though Thomas and Nathalie were not yet officially
betrothed, such a commitment was assured. She planned to sail
with him. Finally, she would once again set foot in the country of
her birth.

Theodosia was determined to return to Richmond Hill, to hold
her sister in her arms when she said her goodbye. As loath as she
was to admit how much of a Burr she actually was, she had it to
thank for ensuring her wish became reality.

As she spread butter atop a biscuit, avoiding yet another serving
of the leathery salted pork served at nearly every meal, Theodosia
swallowed the pride she'd been raised to display and planted the
first seed.

"The heat is already thick," she said, "don't you agree?"

Alston shoved a massive bite of pork into his mouth and said while spitting out flakes of meat, "Not even what we'd call warm. You must learn to adjust your internal temperature."

"Hmm . . ." She looked at her plate instead of the half-chewed piece of pork protruding from between his teeth. "I'm sure I will in time. Yet until then, the North offers a reprieve. The capital and Philadelphia are lovely this time of year."

Alston seemed to consider, his desire to enter political life and connect with those of influence a draw to those particular cities, but then shook his head. "Yet still full of arrogance and conde-scension and wretched cookery." He rose from the table to unlock the box of sugar in the corner of the dining room. He refilled the sugar bowl and spooned a heap of shiny granules into his coffee. "Perhaps another time. I have too much to do here for such a lengthy trip."

She nodded as if this was not exactly the outcome she'd intended. She would say no more. The water to sprout that seed would come from elsewhere. Her father would never permit his daughters to be separated without a proper goodbye. Especially when he remained desperate for forgiveness from his biological one.

The first drops of ink stained her parchment in self-betrayal, but as the lines became letters and the letters words, she assured herself that the end was well worth this means.

When Burr's letters arrived in short succession, first one to her and then to Alston, Theodosia was not at all surprised that the solution he proposed to interest Alston served her father as much as it did her: a bridal tour through the northern states, ending at Niagara Falls. A chance for the young couple to show off for Burr and carry word to some of his acquaintances. On what political dealings this time, she knew naught—and didn't care to learn. She was done with all of that.

Though they wouldn't set sail until June, another three weeks, Theodosia was already packed. Her father had done as she'd asked and devised a way for Alston to believe a trip north would serve him most of all. Out of necessity to plan the tour, her correspondence with her father had resumed, though it remained terse and intermittent—unlike his. Underneath every word in his letters to her was a plea for forgiveness. His desperation showed in his heavy strokes and his too-jovial tone. He needed her love like he needed air to breathe. But she couldn't fulfill his needs anymore.

She would never fulfill Alston's—as much out of her lack of desire as his. While their initial few weeks at the Oaks did see them spending time together—visits with his family, gatherings to receive the congratulations of his friends, meals eaten across the same table more often than not—that had dwindled with the passage of time. Their days were entirely separate. He didn't confide in her his political aspirations, didn't request her input on running the plantation, didn't ask her to entertain or host guests. As the trip north neared, even their meals became ones taken apart, as if they each sought the distance that would soon be impossible once traveling. Throughout, their nights remained as separate as their days—there was much comfort in that.

In June they set sail, and she celebrated her eighteenth birthday aboard the ship. Alston had come to her that night—inexplicably after months of self-imposed abstinence. She'd tricked herself into thinking that their life as brother and sister rather than man and wife wouldn't have cause to change.

Perhaps it was the roll of the ship combating the ocean waves . . . the heat of the claustrophobic cabin . . . the revulsion in her eyes. She'd cringed upon his first touch. Instantly he stood, pitching from side to side, then turned and retreated to his own cabin, where he remained until they docked in the harbor of New York City.

After an overnight at Richmond Hill, their tour would begin. There, in her childhood home, she'd hoped to stay up all night with Nathalie, a brief visit to tide her over until the longer one planned for their return trip. Yet instead of her sister, she found her father.

The reunion between Burr and Alston contained all the warmth that should have existed between father and child.

When her father embraced Theodosia with "the Little Matron," she shrank back.

His shoulders sagged, and his eyes clouded. Her rejection wounded him in a way that should have been comforting, should have made her feel vindicated for what he'd done to her. Yet as she lay that first night in the bed and home she'd hoped to share with Philip, all she felt was confusion over how they'd gotten here.

Her father was weak. And perhaps, so was she.

# CHAPTER 36

"MAGNIFICENT," THEODOSIA SAID, HER VOICE BARELY a whisper. Even the one word strained her lungs, so breathless she'd become at the sight before her, one her mind could scarcely comprehend. A sheet of brilliant white cascading with the strength of a thousand horses beneath a blue jewel-colored sky. The volume of water defying quantification, the raging thunder altogether deafening, the constant mist swirling and dampening even her lashes.

Niagara Falls marked the end of their bridal tour, but she couldn't imagine anything feeling more like a beginning. A cleansing of the soul—a baptism, she supposed, to those more religious than she.

"Wet," Alston said, tossing droplets off his shoulder and onto Theodosia's cape. This bridal tour had been such in name only. Their relationship remained platonic.

"But the edge," she said, vexed at his apparent lack of awe. She grasped for the right words to express the grandeur. Every one that came into her head seemed to lose half its significance as it left her lips. "So unforgiving. Such a height. And yet I find myself wanting to retreat as much as dive in. To feel that power."

At this, Alston spoke up. "I haven't for much of my life. But now . . . well, it seems your father and I make quite the team."

A sentiment formerly true of her. That, like so much in her life, had changed. On this trip north, homes and hosts had welcomed the newlywed Alstons throughout the state of New York until they'd finally arrived at these Niagara Falls. Their tour hadn't been designed to serve its traditional purpose of introducing the young couple to those unable to attend the nuptials.

Instead, this journey had been concocted as a means of seeking support for future financial investments and dealings on behalf of her father and new husband. As such, the two men had arranged an elaborate party of servants and packhorses for the trip. Theodosia's guilt at the extravagance was measured by the fact that the size of the group ensured she was never alone with her husband.

He glanced at his pocket watch. "I'm as drenched as a rat in a swamp." He adjusted his hat and looked at her, his eyes softening, his smile stripped of its usual smug. "You are able to endure much more than me."

She felt a disquiet at his words, nearly complimentary.

He glanced down, uncomfortably, then forced himself to meet her gaze once again. "Our rooms are said to be quite large, big enough for two in each."

Her eyebrows rose, and a laugh burst forth, sure that he was joking. But his flushing cheeks and the abrupt turn of his back let her know that he'd been sincere.

"Remain if you wish," he said gruffly. "I am through. Fortunate it is that I paid to have our rooms ready early."

The tension between them lifted so rarely, each seemingly accustomed to the constant strain. For her, it had become akin to a hair shirt, a punishment for causing all this. She'd never really considered how it made Alston feel, that he might even tire of it.

Her eyes drifted from him to the falls. She could've stayed here all day, a lifetime. If Nathalie were here, she would have taken her hand and led them in a reverent dance before this indescribable natural wonder. Washington Irving would go on to set his stories nowhere but here. John Vanderlyn would have labored to create a masterpiece, coming much closer to conveying the extraordinariness than these sketches she'd purchased as souvenirs. And Philip, Philip would have left with inspiration for a hundred poems that would melt Theodosia's heart.

Shoulders hunched, Alston set off for the hotel. As Theodosia walked behind him, sat across from him at a silent supper, and laid her head on the pillow in the room beside his, she thought of those she loved, those who had left her, and those she had left behind. Comfort came in knowing she'd see some of them soon. This new life of hers had finally taught her the one thing her father could not: patience.

When she and Alston returned to New York City, the humidity of August greeted them. Theodosia said a perfunctory goodbye to her husband, who would continue south to meet with her father in Washington. Meanwhile, Theodosia would enjoy the last of Nathalie's company before her friend set sail for France.

A sense of freedom sweetened the air entering Theodosia's lungs, as she relished being surrounded by the streets and docks and river she knew like the lines carved into her palm. She gave the driver instructions for a circuitous route through the city before heading for Richmond Hill: past the bakery where she would signal the newsboy Georgie, the bookstore where she'd purchased the volume of poetry for Philip, the offices of the ladies' magazine, the secret tavern, and eventually, the Hamilton law office.

The nondescript carriage, not belonging to the Burrs, permitted them to pause right in front. Theodosia inched back the window's curtain. They were all inside: Colonel and Mrs. Hamilton, Angelica, John, and their numerous other siblings, and Philip. A large, iced cake sat atop Philip's desk. They appeared to be celebrating something—a birthday?

Philip must have been so busy—so committed—that the celebration came to him rather than him leave to go to it. Their attention to him, their devotion to him, filled her heart with warmth, and she began to smile when, from inside, a head turned her way: Angelica. Theodosia yanked the curtain closed and called for the driver to depart, but they'd barely rounded the corner before Angelica cried out, running behind them.

Worried all would see and hear—*Philip would see and hear*—Theodosia halted the carriage. She clambered out onto the sidewalk. Angelica, brow damp with sweat, rushed to her.

"I'm sorry," Theodosia said quickly, anticipating a scolding. "I was just passing . . ." She stopped mid lie. "I shouldn't have come."

She aimed to reenter the carriage when Angelica put a hand on her arm. "You're right." Theodosia sucked in a breath. "You should have come sooner."

Angelica's face somber, her eyes a mix of anger and affection, she set aside the ill will she must have been holding toward Theodosia and instead spoke on behalf of the person she loved most in the world. She wiped at the corner of her eyes as she listed the changes in Philip, the distance, the smiles only for their younger siblings, the hours spent in the law office to the exclusion of all else. Their father was proud and fulfilled. "But Philip is not who he was." With a hand still on Theodosia's arm, Angelica pulled her closer. "For him, something will always be missing. He will never be the man he could have been without you in his life." She leaned in and kissed Theodosia's cheek before whispering in her ear, "If you love him, don't let him go. He doesn't believe in impossible, and neither should you."

That night, Theodosia tried to forget Angelica's plea as she and Nathalie talked like the young children they once were but also as the women they were now.

"My heart is full for you," Theodosia said as they sat on Nathalie's bed in the shifts they would wear to sleep, backs against the headboard like they'd done months ago and years ago and might never do again.

"And mine for you, though I fear not in the same way." Nathalie scooped up Theodosia's empty glass and refilled one of Burr's finest French reds to the rim.

Theodosia accepted the wine but said nothing, simply stared at the vase with a single blue aster beside Nathalie's bed, a lone early bloom, as if the plant knew Theodosia was coming. But what it was trying to say, she had no idea.

Nathalie clinked her glass against Theodosia's before taking a sip. "À *ta santé*." She then ran her finger along the stem. "I'm serious, Theo, your sadness makes my own heart ache. You don't have to pretend with me."

Theodosia sighed. "All right."

"All right?"

"You know this was necessary. For us all." Theodosia flicked her wrist to refer to the furniture and the room and the walls and all those within. "It is no different from the fate of many women, like Lottie and Angelica and nearly all in your own lineage to be sure, but it is not a dream brought to life. I won't pretend it is. Not even for a girl such as myself."

Nathalie faced her. "Your whole life has been pretending, in some way. My love for your father will always remain, but he did a disservice to you, trying so hard to take the girl out of you, as if something were wrong with it."

A denial sprang to the tip of Theodosia's tongue. Because that wasn't his aim, nor her mother's. They didn't wish to remove something and replace it with something else but to prove that inherently girls had the same capacity to learn and reason as their male counterparts. Perhaps if the girl was missing from Theodosia, the fault lay within herself. Was that a piece of the puzzle that had led her here? Theodosia drank deeply of her wine. "Is there word of how your family stands?"

"On two feet, I should still hope, despite being stripped of silk sheets and fine china and luscious chocolates."

"It is good you have Thomas, then." So much for being the godchild of a king and queen and the daughter of a founder of a new nation.

Nathalie tamped down the smile that came with being happily betrothed. "But I've left you with the toad. Perhaps once we marry, you can come live with us!"

Theodosia forced herself to return the smile. She wouldn't let her own ensnarement taint Nathalie's hopes of her future any more than she'd relay its true depth and lay a burden that was not hers on Nathalie's heart. One that might divide surrogate father and daughter forever. Something Theodosia couldn't do to either of them.

She let out a long breath and said simply, "I will miss you, sister."

"And I you. But even though we live apart, that doesn't mean we are not together." Theodosia would never know what she had done to deserve this gift of Nathalie in her life. "But I have one demand before I go."

Theodosia let out a soft laugh. "I would expect nothing less from royalty."

Nathalie set down her glass. "Stop pretending. Don't be afraid to be who you are. Because you are someone worthy of love."

*For what else do I live?*

A hollowness filled Theodosia's chest.

Perceptive as always, Nathalie eased the moment by teasing, "Receiving my love, despite how horribly you treated my charming self when I first arrived, proves it."

Theodosia wrapped her arms around her best friend and embraced her with love, gratitude, and parting that felt all too permanent.

Nathalie would leave for France the following day, back to what remained of her family. To her mother, who, after years, had finally felt safe enough to send word. So much time lost. Yet her mother made the sacrifice so her daughter would be spared. The same way Alexander Hamilton had sacrificed for Philip. And Theodosia's father had done the opposite.

She allowed herself to sit in his chair behind his desk. She held his quill, ran her hand along the books and papers left behind, breathed in the air that no longer smelled like him. And then, she searched.

Books and drawers and bundles tied with ribbon until she found what she hoped she would not. But what she knew she would.

That old—opened—letter from John Vanderlyn, the one declaring his love and asking Theodosia to wait for him.

Though she now knew love wasn't what she'd felt for John, this was further proof. It was time to be free of her father.

She said a silent apology to her mother and went to Philip.

# CHAPTER 37

WORDS WERE NOT SPOKEN, NOT AT first. There were too many tears, sad and happy and full of promise and desire and need.

Theodosia had ridden with Nancy tucked tight to her back. The full moon and the horse's instincts had afforded safe passage through the night. Under a blanket of stars glimmering and winking their approval she'd reached the Hamilton home. She'd sent Nancy to the door with a folded note, the single word "Philip" in Theodosia's sure hand.

He appeared in the doorway. Recognition of her handwriting etched lines around his heart-shaped lips as he opened her note.

She'd written a longer one. Of how Alston would never let her go, less out of pride and more for the favor sought from her father. The patronage a vice president as father-in-law offered could only be topped by that of president, and Thomas Jefferson's daughters were already wed. Alston would never agree to an annulment, would fight a divorce petition all the way to trial, besmirching their family names, and even then, the most realistic hope would be a divorce of bed and board, which would prevent her from remarrying until his death. Fleeing would lead to newspaper notices in every state advertising a substantial reward for a runaway wife. A long-distance affair, perhaps they could manage, the sporadic clandestine night on her travels north and his south—the most heart-wrenching of all the options of which she could conceive. But Philip lived in the same world as she. All this, he knew. Otherwise he would have come to her on the street outside his office all those months ago. Instead, the note read:

*A single night to last us a lifetime. Friend of my heart, come.*

That was all she had written. It was enough.

She and Nancy had waited out of sight. He'd appeared aback the same horse he always rode. She had led. He had followed.

Back to Richmond Hill, where, at the house, he lifted his arms and helped Nancy to the ground, the entire time not meeting Theodosia's eyes. When finally they'd dismounted at the rise whose grasses grew from the happiness they'd shared, he had looked at her.

Her cape fell, revealing only her chemise. The thin fabric afforded little modesty. The outline of her body disclosed from shoulder to hip to thigh. The linen shifted as she moved, sliding over her breasts, and he groaned.

Buttons undone, laces untied, boots tugged free, each removal unveiling all she had longed to see. Cloth slipped free to divulge tanned forearms, taut shoulders, and a dark tuft of hair on his chest. Her fingers were drawn to it, gently curling the soft strands, and he shuddered at her touch. Yet he remained otherwise still, ceding control. She skimmed the flat of her palm along his arms and down the concave sides of his torso, all the while bringing her body closer to his. He hardly breathed. She explored each new territory as if mapping him in her mind. All the while ignoring the one place they each longed for her to go. His cheeks reddened as it rose between them, but she shook her head to absolve him, placing the tip of her finger on his bottom lip. His mouth opened a hair, an invitation she couldn't resist.

They kissed like they used to and like they never had before. With love and anger and misery and hope and relief, and the reality of the last few unfathomable months vanished. She slipped out of her shift and guided his hand, asking him to trace her as she did him. When they arrived at the light auburn hair between her thighs, she parted them for him. They sunk to the ground and came together as man and wife without any official ceremony but more real than the past few months had been with her lawful husband.

Her back arched, and he paused in concern, but she urged him on, her whispers of assent the first words spoken between them.

She welcomed the twinge of pain and heat entwined just as they now were. They fit, as simply and as complicated as could be. Tenderness gave way to urgency, and they fell back on the grass, breathless.

Arms, thighs, feet, all touching, they drew in the crispness of the air lifting off the river, the sounds of the slow-moving current a lullaby, but she wouldn't sleep, not miss a moment of this. She pushed the loose strands of hair from her damp forehead, imagining her face as ruddy with satisfaction and embarrassment as his. She rounded her body onto her side and draped her head across his chest. She listened as the thump of his heart receded, willing hers to keep the same rhythm, not just now but always, for a lifetime.

One they both knew they would never have together.

Though her hands were clean, they felt coated with dirt, and she was back in the carriage the day of her mother's funeral, the first time she was overwhelmed by such a profound sense of loss.

"I'm so sorry, Philip," she choked out. Tears pooled and trickled down her cheek onto his bare chest. He soothed her with loving whispers and held her to him until they both felt the tears subside, leaving only a coolness on their skin. "It wasn't supposed to be. And it hasn't. Not . . . like this. Not once."

He lifted her chin, his eyes awash in relief, and she kissed him as if to prove it. He shifted her fully back onto her side, sheltered her from breast to thigh with his shirt, and propped himself on his elbow before her. "It has tormented me, the thought of you with him. I drove myself nearly to the brink." *We almost lost him.* "But here you are like a dream given life, and all I wish is that we never wake."

She drank in his words, savoring the sound of his voice after all this time. She then drew her chemise over him and told him about Alston. Everything. Her father and the election and the false marriage and Bassett and forestalling the sale of Richmond Hill and those tied to it, and he listened intently with flashes of anger and pain and helplessness. And forgiveness. The only piece she left out was her conversation with his father. Such a disclosure would serve but one purpose: engendering hostility between father and son. And in truth, no matter the words of Colonel Hamilton, ultimately it was her decision to go. She did tell him about Angelica, wanting him to know, as if he didn't already, how loyal his sister was to him.

He laughed at her mention of seeing him in the law office, at witnessing his new dedication. "Befittingly, it's what freed me from the clutches of Miss Wilson. She said I'd become too dull and ended our arrangement. To think, my whole life I perceived pranks and devilry as the way to achieve one's end when it turns out being as bland as unbaked bread would have done so even more swiftly."

She hastened a breath. "It's over then?"

"My love, it never began. How could it when my heart was tethered to another. *Is*. Will always be."

Their silence spoke everything their words could not. In her mind, Theodosia saw their life together. Passion and fire that gave way to something as intangible but somehow more solid—trust and reliance and the shared experience of what it meant to be alive. A home filled with children, friends, family, brought together by two people truly in love. The life she would never have with Alston.

"Do you regret it?" she asked. "Asking me to dance at the Clintons' party?"

Philip rested his hand on the curve above her hip, something so foreign yet entirely natural. "Yes," he said with a swiftness that shocked her. "I regret not asking for your hand at Madame de Senat's or the Nicholson salon or on the ice when we were schoolchildren. Any earlier time that would have led to a different outcome."

Such presumed that one was possible. But fate would have never dealt kindly with a Hamilton and Burr.

Theodosia placed her hand on top of his. "I want it, and I shamefully accept it, but I honestly don't know how you can forgive me."

"The same way you forgave me for telling your secret." His brow creased in thought. "It's not the easy choice, to sort through the pain and hurt to find forgiveness. We think it makes us weak. We think by maintaining our anger, we're able to inflict our hurt on the one who wronged us. But that anger eats away at us, not them. We forgive for our own sake more than theirs." He pulled her closer. "Without forgiveness, we would have never had this. The choice to forgive becomes simple when it's the only one your heart, your soul, can make. That's when it's a love that endures. I believe it must have been the same for my parents." Renewed love and respect lit in his eyes. "These past few months I haven't been the most agreeable, and yet they all stood by my side. I am indebted to them."

His family was no longer the prison it had once been. Perhaps there was some kindness to fate after all, the loss of one love being replaced by another.

He glanced at her from beneath those seductively long lashes, then cupped her breast and bent to kiss her nipple, and a tingle alit from crown to toe. He drew her to him, hoisting her body onto his, letting their skin meet, warming each other, but all Theodosia felt was a cold dread. It prickled gooseflesh on her arms that Philip gently rubbed.

Alston and her father and Philip's, Richmond Hill and the White House and politics, rumors and gossip and the insidious nature of this place and its families and the lives they led.

Fate was not to blame.

Philip's fingertips traveled the length of her, a sensation she longed for without having ever felt it. And then his lips were on her neck, his hands on her breasts, his hips rising to join them once again, and the ache in her body, the need for him, pushed her to meet him.

This time was at once more satisfying and less. Because now that she'd lived such pleasures, she could not bear for them to end.

The solution came as clearly as the rising sun. *France*. The ship Nathalie would board in the morning. They must be on it. Starting over without commitments, without the burdens of what they would each leave behind: without the legacies they were to carry on. Just like she should've done the night of the Blackwell ball when Philip had begged her to run away. All this time lost. All this time filled with regret.

Leaving was the only way. She knew it like she knew the way back home. The home that was no longer hers. The thought more than the encroaching dew brought a chill, and they reluctantly untwined and dressed. Theodosia's heart sunk at losing sight of his bare chest, at no longer feeling the heat of his skin against hers.

He lay his coat down as a barrier against the dampening grass, and they sat, their horses hitched behind them, the tidal flux of the Hudson before them, and far off in the distance, the harbor and the ship that would afford them a new life. She pictured herself boarding that ship, Philip by her side, each leaving everything behind. Each being happy.

*"Being happy when she is gone would be an impossible task if not for you, Theo. You . . . you are my everything."*

Her eyes snapped open. *No.* She would not allow it. Her father had trespassed on every part of her life, every choice had been his, she merely his proxy. This choice, finally, was hers.

Her heart fluttered like a hummingbird's wings as she gently threaded her arm through Philip's to prepare him for the gravity of what she must ask. "France," she said, the single word releasing as a whisper but received with a volume that was deafening.

His eyes brightened with all the comprehension and hope that sent her own heart soaring, and she felt as if she were floating, off to the life they both wanted, deserved, and her mind began packing her things and telling Nathalie and then . . . his face crumpled, lines drawing his lips tight, paining his brow, and his "Oh, Theo," came out in a tone as raw as an open wound.

The air left her lungs, hollowing her in body as much as mind. So unexpected was his response, a response that said so much with so little. A response that said it all, the impracticalities of starting over without funds or support, of landing in a country fresh from war where the Hamilton name was one of enemy, of the fate of those for whom he bore responsibility as much as love who'd be left behind. And therein, truly, lay everything.

Philip was his father's brightest hope, finally on the verge of a sound relationship with him, the thing he most desperately wanted even if he could not admit it. He was the bedrock of his family. They needed him, and he needed them.

Philip leaned in and kissed her forehead in a manner so platonic, she nearly cringed. Roles reversed, the fantasy she'd created revealed itself to be just that. Her chest contracted, her own mind a jumble of thoughts and images and futures and pasts all merging into a reality she could not fathom.

But a single truth. Boarding that ship would not just end the Hamilton legacy but her own. Her father's heart would turn to dust. With Theodosia gone, he would cease to entertain any lightness, any sense of the man, the father, he would have, could have, been had her mother lived. Darker than a shadow, with as little substance. His life would subsist solely of the pursuit of power. There would never be enough. He would be broken. As he had broken her.

Her heart seized as if suddenly pumping venom, the image of her father on his knees before her as a child and not long ago as a woman on the verge of marriage crippling her.

*His needs are plenty and insistent.*

Oh, Mama, how they had been!

*He gives a fidelity and devotion many men reserve for God.*

But only in his *own* mind. He reasoned that every choice he made was for them both, but he had been too selfish and consumed with his own needs to place value on her as someone independent from him. This she knew; she could reason through and analyze and speak Latin and French and Italian and do ciphers in her sleep and converse with generals, entertain royalty, because of him. She wouldn't be who she was without him.

The coolness of the dirt beneath her feet spread like gooseflesh through her body and bore deep into her veins until it echoed in her bones and she were one with it. With this place. With the home it was, not for the house or the grounds but for the one who'd provided it and for all those living within whom she could not abandon any more than Philip could leave all whom he held dear.

He encased her hand in his, eyes gleaming with determination. "I told you, I don't believe in never. I believe in possibilities. And this country, my parents, your own, are all proof of the impossible becoming possible. Even if, when it does, I am old and gray with a cane and one tooth, I will come for you."

Lightness would not ease the tension of the moment, but he would not be the man she loved if he did not try. She looked at him, those long lashes, those gentle lips, those deep brown eyes, full of love and faith and . . . parting. She drew in a steadying breath and followed his lead. "And I will welcome you." She fought the ravaging of her heart to offer a pinched smile. "Our love is pure and strong, and if we believe in it . . ."

"It will endure." He swallowed audibly as if stemming a strangled cry. Then she placed her hand on his cheek, a catch basin for the tears that escaped.

She lay with him until his chest rose and fell with the deep, heavy breaths of sleep. She stayed until across the sky the sun painted the red of that dress she'd had sewn and worn just for him. Richmond Hill enveloped her: the chirp of the birds that lived in the rustling leaves of the trees above, that grew from the soil seeped into her skin, dampened by the mist from the river she'd breathed in since before her mother died, and after, after she'd made the promise she as a Burr would not break. Because she now understood it was as much for her as it was him.

This was the world in which they lived, one of contradictions that led a country to fight for independence while denying it to all, a husband to claim eternal love for the one to whom he was wed while bringing another to his bed, a father to invest his every thought and hope into a child except the one the child deserves.

She wouldn't be who she was without her father, but she couldn't be who she hoped to become with him. And yet Philip's words of forgiveness and impossibilities took root like the hardiest sapling, budding into the contradiction that even now she knew would consume her heart and mind forever more: she would never forgive her father, but she would never forgive herself if she didn't try.

Gentle as a hand behind a newborn's head, she extracted herself from Philip's embrace. She hovered over him, using all her strength to resist a brush of her lips against his that would wake him. For with his eyes open and looking into hers, she couldn't do what they both knew they must.

She etched his face into memory as she slipped on her cape. She unfastened her mother's brooch from it and kissed the tortoiseshell whose greens and reds and browns danced in the morning light. She laid it beside his head where he would be sure to see it.

And then, she grabbed hold of the reins of her horse and guided the mare back to Richmond Hill, where she would say goodbye to this life and begin another.

*Georgetown County, South Carolina*

# November 1801

THEODOSIA REACHES FOR THE NEWSPAPER CLIPPING floating on the wood floor. She cannot bear to read it again. But she holds it against her belly as she picks up the letter that had accompanied it. It is signed: A. *Ham*.

Fastened through the parchment is her mother's tortoiseshell brooch.

The colonel writes of the mission Philip had been on these past few months. Unbeknownst to Theodosia, Philip had been petitioning his father to intervene on their behalf, to use his influence to rid Theodosia of Alston. Philip beseeched him with declarations of his love, with the importance of family, with the need to make the two one. Colonel Hamilton's sorrowful words turn to guilt, for his pride, his stubbornness, his refusal to acquiesce.

One evening, at a recent play, Philip verbally attacked Mr. George Eacker, publicly chastising him for unflattering comments Eacker had made about Philip's father on the Fourth of July. Months earlier. For reasons unknown to all but his father, and now Theodosia, Philip chose that moment to defend his father's honor to prove just how much family meant to him. He challenged Eacker to a duel.

He lost.

Theodosia grips the windowsill and forces the glass open, not caring of the mosquitoes and the diseases carried on their wings.

*Philip? Her Philip? In a duel?*

The ache of not being with him had come to live in her skin, meld to her bones, as core to her being as the blood in her veins. Something she was still learning to live with, same as she was learning to live in this place, in this marriage, neither of which would cede easily to the name she was born with and the mind she had cultivated. Such had caused her to once again pick up her quill, penning new stories under her old pseudonym of Miss P. to try to change hearts and minds on the education of young girls, on the rights of those girls as they become women, and on the enslaved both in the South and the North. She sent every published one to her father. She took on the expected role of overseeing the medical welfare of the plantation's slaves, using it to better their lives in the only way she could, at least for now. She knew how the game was played, and so she'd chosen to play it.

But Philip had not been playing a game. He had been fighting their war.

On the grass at Richmond Hill, they had been so sure it was the only way. But as she stands watching the palms sway, her mind reels with a thousand other ways. And yet she cannot take back what is done, no more than she can take back what she carries with her.

She presses the clipping to her belly, hugging the small new life within, Philip's legacy and all she has left. She squashes a mosquito against the newly painted white sill, its blood staining her fingers, doing what she must to protect it.

For this legacy is not just his, it's theirs.

# Author's Note

*L*ove, *Theodosia* is a work of historical fiction, spanning a year
and a half in the life of Theodosia Burr, a time that would end
with her adding "Alston" to her surname. How Theodosia became
Mrs. Joseph Alston blends historical fact and authorial imagination, as the romance between Theodosia and Philip Hamilton is
entirely fictional.

While I am the daughter of a history teacher who has never
met a rabbit hole she wouldn't scramble down, I am a novelist,
not a historian. Yet, personally, I'm always eager to learn the story
behind the story, the real pieces of history woven into the work
of fiction. With that in mind, I offer some of the most interesting
pieces of my research that informed and provided the backbone for
*Love, Theodosia*.

The spark for *Love, Theodosia* came during my first viewing
of Lin-Manuel Miranda's *Hamilton*. In one of the more subdued
moments of *Hamilton*, Founding Fathers Alexander Hamilton and
Aaron Burr sing of their newborn children—one a boy, the other a
girl. They sing of the fathers they wish to be, the world they want
to pass on to them, and the hope they have for the lives these
two will lead. Immediately, a *Romeo & Juliet* story popped into my
mind. What would happen if a romance developed between these
two children, born a year or so apart to two of the most important,
prominent, yet flawed men of their time who had become sworn
enemies?

I had no conception of how much I would learn about—and
from—Theodosia Burr Alston, a young woman who led an extraordinary life full of passion, tragedy, and an intense devotion to her

father, who may not have deserved such admiration. And yet he is the one who pushed Theodosia, or Theo as her friends called her, to be the woman she became: a prodigy regarded as the first truly educated woman in the United States.

Females were not educated in the same manner as males, partially due to a common perception that females lacked the necessary intellectual capacity. In a time when women were to be educated "just enough" to be "companions" to their husbands, when the reading of novels was to be monitored by men, for women were prone to "confusing fiction with fact," and when skill at piano, song, and embroidery were prized far above speaking multiple languages or skill in math, Theo was an anomaly. And, despite the gossip that swirled around her, she relished being one.

Theodosia was also one of the biggest name droppers of her time. Her life intersected with some of the most well-known figures in history: George Washington, Washington Irving, Marie Antoinette, Alexander Hamilton, and his son, Philip. As children, the two attended a French school together. Aristocratic New York City families traveled in the same circles. While the song in *Hamilton* was my inspiration, these facts became the ones I hung my story on.

For this was not to be a story of the fathers, it was to be a story of the children—two people with fascinating, complex, and tragic tales of their own. I committed to developing this forbidden love story in context with the historical timeline and true events and chose to set it in the year of 1800 when one of the most controversial and ultimately landscape-changing presidential elections was held. This was a year that saw Theo in her most important role in facilitating her father's career aspirations.

This story relies on history, with nearly all of the characters being actual people with whom Theodosia interacted, and I have both my journalism degree and my type A personality to thank for helping this come to be. For months, my walls were lined with scrolls of art paper on which I tracked every event and date in the election and every home, business, and travel of the characters. Pieced together from biographies and letters written by the major parties, I developed a timeline of the historical facts of Theodosia's and Philip's lives and wove into that real timeline the events of this imagined romance. One of the most enjoyable parts of creating this story was finding ways to incorporate recorded comments or speech pulled from letters and newspaper accounts, often denoted in italics in the novel.

While we have some correspondence to fill in the pieces of this period of Theodosia's life, the bulk of the letters she wrote and those written to her by those she was closest to, namely her father, were either destroyed or lost at sea. Unfortunately the true motivation behind some of the most peculiar decisions in her life—namely a hasty marriage to South Carolina's Joseph Alston—will never be known. Enter my imagination to fill in the pieces. This is not a story that did happen—as far as we know. But it could have. And it honors a woman who, while not without fault herself, deserves to have her own story told—a story that still resonates today as women fight to achieve the highest positions in our own world of politics, corporation, and invention. She is a role model to us all even now.

As Mr. Miranda says, we have no control over who lives, who dies, or who tells our story, but this—Theo's story—is one I've been honored to fill these pages with. This history is really *herstory*.

# A Detailed Account of the History
## in *Love, Theodosia*

M OST OF THE KEY FIGURES IN the book with whom Theodosia
interacts were true acquaintances, friends, or family, includ-
ing: her father, Aaron Burr; Philip Hamilton; Alexander Hamilton;
Joseph Alston; Nathalie de Lage de Volude (alternate spellings
include Natalie Delage de Volude, Nathalie de Lage de Volunde);
Madame de Senat; Angelica Hamilton; Washington Irving; John
Vanderlyn; Dr. Eustis; Caty Church; Hannah Gallatin; Kitty Few;
Thomas Sumter; Thomas Jefferson; the families of the Nicholsons,
Livingstons, and Clintons; and several of the Richmond Hill
slaves, namely Alexis, Eleonore, Tom, and Nancy.

The true history of Theodosia's relationships with many of these
characters is infused into the novel, for example, Theodosia and
Philip attended the same French school as children; Washington
Irving was a good friend to both Theodosia and her father,
attended school across the street from her when they were young,
and reportedly accompanied Theodosia and Nathalie to many
dances and parties. While it is rumored that Irving was a suitor, no
evidence exists to claim the relationship as a romantic one.

Aaron Burr was a patron of the artist John Vanderlyn and commissioned him to paint portraits of Theodosia, himself, and several
close friends (though there is no evidence of one of those friends
being Commodore Nicholson). Vanderlyn did stay at Richmond
Hill as their artist in residence as depicted in the novel and lived in
Paris, returning there with assistance from Burr, though the manner in which he is sent in the novel is my own speculation, based on
suggestions that despite Vanderlyn having interest in Theodosia,
Burr's eye was on a match that would afford more financial and

political support. Vanderlyn never married and remained a life-long friend to the Burrs, spending considerable time with Aaron Burr when he was in Paris in 1810–1811.

The inclusion of family details for Philip, Aaron Burr, and Theodosia are rooted in historical fact. Philip was the eldest of eight children, attended Columbia College (which became Columbia University) and went on to study law, and suffered a near-fatal illness in 1797, during which his father administered his every dose of medicine.

Aaron Burr suffered the loss of his parents and grandparents all before the age of three. He nearly died as a baby, and his mother's words of him being "given to me from the dead" as well as her belief that his survival made him destined for something special are based on recorded evidence.

Theodosia's mother, Theodosia Bartow Prevost Burr, was previously married to a British officer and during the war was forced to play both sides to keep her home of the Hermitage in New Jersey. She and Aaron Burr, whom she called "friend of my heart," became enamored while she was still married, with differing reports of their level of intimacy before her first husband died. The elder Theodosia had children with her first husband (reports of the number and those who survived differ). It is known that Burr took a liking to her sons, John Bartow Prevost and Frederick Prevost, giving them clerkships in his law office. Theodosia Burr Alston's half-siblings were much older, though evidence exists of prolonged correspondence with them as well as affection. For the purposes of simplicity, the novel solely includes specific mention of Frederick, who was indeed forced to sell his house and farm to cover a bond he signed for his stepfather. The elder Theodosia, who long suffered from illness deemed "an incurable disorder of the uterus" and possibly was cancer, died at Richmond Hill while her husband was in Philadelphia. The elder Theodosia was well aware of how sick she was but retained her humor throughout and insisted her husband not be home to cater to her as she believed in the importance of his political work. Her death was a severe blow to Burr, and he considered her his great love, "the best and finest lady" he had ever known, one not to be matched regardless of his future intimacies.

Burr, a Francophile, took in the refugees Nathalie and Madame de Senat, and the rivalry leading to sisterly love between Theodosia and Nathalie is based in fact, as is Nathalie's ultimate marriage to Thomas Sumter. At the time, the prominent families in New York City, like the Hamiltons and Burrs, would move in the same circles, and there are reports of the Hamiltons attending functions at Richmond Hill before the death of Theodosia's mother. The young Theodosia's specific relationships with Philip and Angelica are born of this fact and my imagination.

Of the few characters who were invented for the facilitation of the plot are Lucinda Wilson and Lottie Jewell, though their circumstances as women of the day are in accordance with the time period.

Theodosia's relationship with her father, Aaron Burr, was one of mutual respect and adoration, maintained through their extensive correspondence, and it is true that Theodosia could never write often enough to please her father. From the time Theodosia could write until her death, the two exchanged detailed and often sarcastic letters about everything from her education to the care of their home to friends, family, politics, and, yes, even his sexual escapades. They delighted in witfully criticizing each other.

Aaron Burr's wife, Theodosia, did not have the formal education they both wanted for their daughter, but the elder Theodosia was reportedly highly intelligent with a mind her husband loved. They both believed in the philosophy of Mary Wollstonecraft, a British writer and advocate of educational and social equality for women, and aimed to ensure their daughter had the same level of education she would have had if she'd been a son, unusual thinking for the time. Burr pushed his daughter to undertake the same diligent study as he had undertaken himself. She was reportedly extremely intelligent, charismatic, and hosted the elite at Richmond Hill from a young age. Theodosia, whom he called Theo, Miss Priss, and then my Little Matron, was her father's personal and political confidant and strategist. Not all believed women should be educated as such, and criticisms from society included in the novel, such as calling Theodosia "wholly masculine" and "blissfully ignorant of domestic matters," are true.

In the novel as in life, Theodosia's immersion in her father's political life comes to shape her future when she marries Joseph Alston. The circumstances that led to these hurried nuptials began with the New York City legislature election of 1800, which is where the novel begins. To the best of my efforts, I have portrayed the true happenings of all the political events of the book, adhering to the historical timeline, places, and travel of the characters (one interesting tidbit being that Burr, Alston, and Philip were all traveling through Boston, Providence, and other parts of New England at the same time; it's hard to imagine the paths of such prominent men didn't cross).

The election of 1800 was a pivotal one in the early formation of America, the first time a peaceful transfer of power occurred, the beginnings of our two-party system, and evidence of political manipulation, half-truths, and total falsehoods being a part of the nation's political past. Details on the legislature election, the bitter partisanship, the insults in the newspapers, and the scheming of all political figures come from fact. The role of South Carolina as a pivotal player in the presidential election is based in truth, as are the details surrounding the tie between Burr and Jefferson, only broken on the thirty-sixth House of Representatives' vote. The quotation from "A Rice Planter" in the *Charleston City Gazette* is true, and speculation is that it was Alston or a member of his family.

While there are suggestions of deals between the Federalists being floated to both Burr and Jefferson, and rumors that Jefferson finally agreed right before Burr, the notion that it was Theodosia's relationship with Philip that prevented her father from giving in is pure creative license. What is not pure creative license is Theodosia's decision to marry Alston. Quotes included in the novel from Theodosia's friends, from Robert Troup, and from Nelly Custis regarding Alston are true. Her father did seek political help in this election, South Carolina was an important player, and Alston had influence as well as wealth. The Burrs were in perpetual debt; they had been selling off possessions and had taken loans they could not repay. It was not a stretch then for those to believe Theodosia married Alston for political or financial reasons. The date of her marriage to Alston in Albany is accurate. While the exact location of the ceremony is unknown, the true conductor of the ceremony was not Reverend John Bassett, though he and his wife, Anna, did reside in Albany at the time. The story of Bassett being passed over for the senior role of minister and his wife's reaction to it are based in fact and occurred around the time of the novel. The Bassetts would eventually leave and move to Long Island.

It is unclear if the flirtation (often what we would deem "snarky") seen in Theodosia's letters to Alston was born of true affection or to facilitate the marriage for political or financial gain. I imagine it was a bit of both. Theodosia was a smart woman who understood, despite her education, her future was limited and only secured by the wealth of the men around her. And she was dedicated to her father. She also loved Richmond Hill.

The history of Richmond Hill does include serving as the headquarters for General George Washington during the American Revolution. That was when Aaron Burr first became familiar with the estate, which he would acquire on a sixty-nine-year lease from Trinity Church in 1797. Vice President John Adams and his wife, Abigail, occupied the mansion, and it is Abigail's description of the estate's home and grounds that I include in the novel. Burr oversaw the transformation of the home with its window-lined gallery and extensive library. It was a place for visitors, foreign travelers, literati, French exiles, and struggling artists. The Burrs, who also had the townhome in the city, loved Richmond Hill, but Burr was forced to sell his lease on the property in 1803 to John Jacob Astor, who divided it into residential lots and added to his considerable wealth. Located in an area now bound by the streets Varick, Charlton, MacDougal, and King in Greenwich Village, the mansion itself was moved on logs about 100 feet, became a theater, then an opera house, then a roadhouse and saloon before it was ultimately demolished in 1849.

Political accusations and insults from Hamilton, Burr, and others, including the satirical poem "Aristocracy," are true; to denote these and other exact quotes, the novel puts them in italics. Nearly all excerpts of letters from Burr to Theodosia, Theodosia to Alston and vice versa, and Alexander Hamilton to Philip, and Jefferson to Burr, also in italics, are true letters.

Among other interesting historical facts included in the novel are: the right of women in New Jersey to vote (though it may have come from a loophole in the state's constitution); the ladies' magazines of the day, for which Theodosia secretly writes (though her writing for one and the riff on Irving's *Rip Van Winkle* are entirely fictional); the French fantasy volumes Burr scoured the bookstores to find for his daughter; and the description of the Alston home in Charleston, which stands to this day (and I stood before it) and of Oaks Plantation, which is no longer in existence. The ruins left of Oaks and its slave quarters can be seen on tours given by the institution that now claims the property in Georgetown County, South Carolina. A botanical and sculptural garden called Brookgreen Gardens now sits on the land that Oaks once did. Interestingly, I have family in the area and had visited Brookgreen years before the spark of this novel came to me.

The Alstons' bridal tour through the North, ending at Niagara Falls is also true, and the Alstons seem to have gained fame for making the Falls a honeymoon destination. Theodosia's thoughts of Niagara Falls come from her actual words: "If you wish to have an idea of real sublimity, visit the Falls of Niagara—they are magnificent; words when applied to express their grandeur appear to lose half their significance—to describe them is impossible; they must be seen."

While the party Burr shifts to was technically referred to as the Democratic Republicans, it was commonly called the Republican party, and as such that is my usage in the novel. I have occasionally taken leniencies within the novel, such as with traditions of the time like dinner and supper as well as with formality in language.

I have attempted to portray Aaron Burr's complicated and hypocritical position on slavery, which receives only passing mention in biographies. Reports differ on slave ownership in the Burr line, but it is certain that there were slaves in the Prevost household, and those would and did transfer to Aaron Burr upon his marriage to his wife. Without doubt, like a substantial portion of homes in New York City at the time, slaves were a part of the Burr household, including Richmond Hill. Alexis, Tom, Sam, Eleonore, and Nancy are all names taken from recorded mention of the Burr slaves (though the tie of mother and daughter between Eleonore and Nancy is my own addition to represent the truth of children born into the institution). My research indicates the following: Burr did support abolition, he did criticize those who thought his servant, Carlos, incapable of playing the violin well due to the color of his skin, and he did ensure his slaves were taught to read and write. He proposed a bill to abolish slavery in New York. As an attorney, he defended slaves. But he also defended masters. As encapsulated by Nancy Isenberg in her *Fallen Founder* biography, Burr seemed to consider slavery "a temporary condition of servitude rather than a status based on racial inferiority." The fact is he, like many prominent men of the time, including Alexander Hamilton, owned slaves while proclaiming to support abolition. This is a clear contradiction and one I have endeavored to portray in the novel. I could find no evidence of his daughter Theodosia's stance on slavery nor her thoughts on her father's views and actions being at odds. Based on her letters, which do criticize the practices in the South and advocate for the education of slaves, I have chosen to have her embody the reality of many women of the time who had beliefs but little power to put them into practice to effect change, in their own homes or more widely.

One Burr slave, a woman by the name of Mary, is mentioned briefly in the novel. This is a reference to Mary Emmons, born in India, and likely brought to North America by way of Haiti by James Marcus Prevost, the first husband of Theodosia Bartow Prevost Burr. Upon Prevost's death and Theodosia's marriage to Aaron, Mary became a part of the Burr household. Reports uncovered now confirm that Aaron Burr fathered two children with Mary, Louisa Charlotte and John Pierre. He kept Mary and this family secret throughout his life, and biographies scarcely mention it, if at all. While some reports suggest Burr's wife, Theodosia, may have been aware of at least one of these children, the evidence is unclear. For the younger Theodosia, little exists to indicate what she knew. As such, and with Mary and her children no longer part of the Burr household during the time period covered in the novel but in Philadelphia, my mention of her is brief and from Theodosia's limited perspective. However, her inclusion was important to paint a more complete picture of Aaron Burr and slavery. For those interested in more on Mary Emmons, I suggest the work of historical fiction, *The Secret Wife of Aaron Burr*, by Susan Holloway Scott.

While the romance between Theodosia and Philip is entirely of my own imagination, I have woven their story amid the true events and exact timeline of history; the child she carries in November of 1801 could have been conceived on her actual trip north that August. Theodosia and Philip lived lives of high expectations thanks to who their fathers were, flawed men who achieved great things, loved their families, but also hurt their families.

Philip's story comes to an end in the novel the same way it did in his life: he died on November 24, 1801, a day after his duel with

George Eacker. Philip did challenge Eacker months after Eacker's July Fourth comments disparaging Philip's father; the reason for his reckoning coming so much later is unknown. His death sent his father into a depression that some say he never recovered from and is thought to have precipitated his sister Angelica's mental breakdown and lifelong mental deterioration.

Theodosia went on to live in South Carolina, a place she never fully embraced, and have her child, a son, named for her father. But Aaron Burr Alston died when he was eleven years old, devasting mother and grandfather. Theodosia's adult life mirrored her mother's, plagued by illness. She stood by her father her entire life, whether it was after the duel in which he killed Alexander Hamilton or in his trial for treason, often using her education to advocate on his behalf. In December 1812, in poor health, Theodosia wished to see her father in New York City. Unable to travel the long distance in a coach, passage was booked on a swift schooner, the *Patriot*. It was to reach New York in less than a week. It set sail on December 31, 1812, but never reached its destination. It was lost at sea off the Carolina coast (as was the abundance of letters, her own and her father's that he'd entrusted to her), likely due to a violent storm, though tales of pirates and of Theodosia secretly surviving and embarking on a new life under a new name have long floated.

These are the facts as I have researched and interpreted them, but in the end, this is a work of historical fiction with all the creative license and human error therein. Historical fiction authors and historians are complementary but different, to paraphrase author Hilary Mantel. No matter the extent of my research, the novel is not presented as fact nor should be read as such.

Readers who would like to engage in their own discussion of fact versus fiction will find book club discussion questions on the author's web site: www.lorigoldsteinbooks.com.

# Acknowledgments

I'D LIKE TO THANK ALL MY readers who enjoy rabbit holes as much as I do. This novel is for you and for all the fans of *Hamilton* who yearned for more. While many eyes and ears have been along for my journey of bringing this novel to life, a few deserve specific mention. My sincerest thanks go to my perpetual cheerleader and advocate, my agent, Katelyn Detweiler, and all at Jill Grinberg Literary Management who make my writing of books the publishing of books. The latter would not be possible without my dedicated editor, Lilly Golden, and the team at Arcade. Thank you for sharing my love of Theodosia and bringing her into the hands of readers. The research and writing of this novel have occupied several years of my life; it's been a project I've worked on in fits and starts within deadlines for other books as well as my teaching and consulting. I owe a huge debt of gratitude to my good friend and fellow author Chandler Baker for initiating our writing sprints. This book would not have been written without them. Though it might have been written faster without our never-ending text chain. Speaking of never-ending text chains, my heartfelt thanks go to my good friend and fellow author Alycia Kelly, whose exclamation points come right when I need them. My thanks also to author and friend Charlotte Huang. And, as always, thank you to my husband, Marc, my first reader, fellow Hamilfan, and the person without whom I would have never started writing in the first place.

# BIBLIOGRAPHY

M<small>Y RESEARCH OWES A DEBT TO</small> the following published works: *Fallen Founder, The Life of Aaron Burr* by Nancy Isenberg (Penguin Books, 2007); *Theodosia Burr Alston: Portrait of a Prodigy* by Richard N. Cote (Corinthian Books, 2003); *The Heartbreak of Aaron Burr* by H. W. Brands (Anchor Books, 2012); *Correspondence of Aaron Burr and his Daughter, Theodosia* (Covici-Friede, 1929); "Thomas Jefferson, Aaron Burr and the Election of 1800," by John Ferling (*Smithsonian Magazine*, 2004); *From Bullets to Ballots: The Election of 1800 and the First Peaceful Transfer of Political Power* by John Zvesper (The Claremont Institute, 2003); "Party Time" by Jill Lepore (*The New Yorker*, September 17, 2007); "The Revolution of 1800: The Presidential Election that Tested the United States" by Edward J. Larson (HistoryNet); "The Election of 1800-1801," Lehrman Institute; "Peter Hess Describes Early 1800s Albany" (New York Almanac); "The Excavation of Joseph and Theodosia Burr Alston's House Site, the Oaks Plantation" by James L. Michie (Coastal Carolina University, 1994); New York Public Library Photo Collections; National Archives, Founders Online.